Terri NIXON

The Secrets of Pencarrack Moor

PIATKUS

PIATKUS

First published in Great Britain in 2023 by Piatkus

1 3 5 7 9 10 8 6 4 2

A CIP catalogue record for this book
is available from the British Library.

ISBN 978-0-349-43167-3

Typeset in Caslon by M Rules
Printed and bound in Great Britain by
Clays Ltd, Elcograf S.p.A.

Papers used by Piatkus are from well-managed forests
and other responsible sources.

Piatkus
An imprint of
Little, Brown Book Group
Carmelite House
50 Victoria Embankment
London EC4Y 0DZ

An Hachette UK Company
www.hachette.co.uk

www.littlebrown.co.uk

Terri Nixon was born in Plymouth, England, in 1965. At the age of nine she moved with her family to a small village on the fringe of Bodmin Moor, where she discovered a love of writing that has stayed with her ever since.

Since publishing in paperback (through independent small press BeWrite) in 2002, Terri has appeared in both print and online fiction collections, and published *Maid of Oaklands Manor* with Piatkus in 2013.

By Terri Nixon

The Fox Bay Saga

A Cornish Inheritance
A Cornish Promise
A Cornish Homecoming

The Penhaligon Saga

Penhaligon's Attic
Penhaligon's Pride
Penhaligon's Gift

The Oaklands Manor Trilogy

Maid of Oaklands Manor
Evie's Choice
Kitty's War

This story is dedicated to two of my very
best-est and 'bikiest' friends, Liz and Jill.

Old times, good times, dangerous times, heady times…
We might have grown up, and settled down a bit,
but no-one can deny we had the BEST of times!

PROLOGUE

Royal Edward Dock, Bristol
1926

The young woman, known only as Smith, looked from her friend to her lover, who faced each other across the yard. She shivered, and it had little to do with her drenched clothing, though the rain had lost its softness now and was plinking off pipes, splashing on stone and corrugated iron, and muffling the familiar night-sounds of the nearby railway. Her attention was all on Jenny and Victor, who did not speak, though their eyes and their stances said it all: brother and sister they might be, but tonight they confronted one another as enemies. And tonight neither one of them would back down.

At twenty-six, Jenny Lyons was the undisputed queen of the North Twenty, women selected for their charm, wit and grace, who had their own specialisms but who had also become skilled pickpockets under newcomer Smith's tutelage. They brazenly went about town on the arms of unknowing victims, in full view of the public they sought to relieve of their valuables; nowhere was a safe place to hide money or trinkets when the Twenties were on the whiz. Not bags, purses, coat pockets or wardrobes; not cars, safes, shops or even banks. Clothing and vehicles were regularly taken too, while their owners were otherwise engaged in witty conversation with a beguiling companion.

Occasionally one of the Twenties would fall foul of the local constables, but the monthly sum each member paid into the syndicate easily paid for solicitors or fines ... and had also greased an influential palm or two. This slippery but successful practice had naturally come to the attention of the newly founded Docklands mob, who'd forced out their rivals, now named the Redcliffe Cavers, and whose alliance with the Twenties worked well for both syndicates; the Dockers lent their muscle, and credible threats, where needed, and the Twenties applied their own particular skills to the Dockers' scams when more subtlety was required.

Several of the Twenties had even found romantic matches among the Docklands mob. Jenny was naturally drawn to Ronnie Jackson, the Dockers' leader, and Smith herself had fallen for Ronnie's right-hand man Victor, who was also Jenny's brother. The four of them shared a house in the fashionable part of town, and the excitement and financial rewards of their activities made for heady – and often hedonistic – times, but Smith had known from experience that times like that never lasted long, and she'd been right. Because now everything had turned on its head, and in the worst way imaginable.

Jenny had called a meeting that afternoon in their headquarters, an otherwise disused barn between Filton Airfield and the railway line. Twelve of the nineteen other members had been able to assemble on short notice, and Jenny sat on the table at the front, swinging her legs and studying each of them in turn. She spent so long just looking that several of the girls began to shift in their seats, and Smith grew tense too, particularly when Jenny dismissed two of the girls with a simple nod towards the door. She seemed to be assessing her gang for their trustworthiness, which meant this was big. They all had the motto embroidered on their handkerchiefs: *fides omnia; loyalty is everything*, but theory and practice are two very different things, and there was no telling what secrets someone was hiding. If anyone knew that, it was Jenny Lyons; she hadn't become their syndicate queen by accident.

'The Dockers have come up good,' she said at length. 'Really good, in fact, but they need our help for this one, and we owe them for that time they broke up the fight down the Barrels.' Her gaze swept over the remaining ten girls once more, and then she pointed at Smith. 'I need you with me tonight. Wait behind after, alright?'

Smith nodded with outward calm. Her place was unquestionably at Jenny's side, but there was something more going on tonight, and she wondered if she'd feel the same when she knew what it was.

'The rest of you,' Jenny went on, 'no questions, but we're going to need plenty of diversions later, especially round the docks. Seven-thirty onwards, you get those Rozzers pulled away from everywhere between King Edward's and the railway, got it?'

The Twenties nodded, and after a few suggestions and some minor chit-chat, during which Smith's curiosity and unease climbed higher, she and Jenny were finally left alone in the musty-smelling barn. Jenny turned her assessing gaze on Smith once more, and evidently made her decision. 'It's guns.'

3

Smith kept her expression neutral and nodded, inwardly conflicted for the first time since she'd joined the Twenties three years ago. Until now it had been easy to convince themselves that they weren't really hurting anyone, just amassing the funds they'd need in their old age if they didn't want the servitude of marriage. But this was different; she couldn't even discount the death penalty if things turned sour. Her sense of foreboding wasn't eased as Jenny went on to explain.

'The Cavers are due to collect eight boxes of .22 Brownings tonight, labelled as privately shipped housewares, and sell them on to Birmingham, Manchester and London.'

No-one ever dared to ask how Jenny found these things out, and Smith didn't question it now. She just listened as Jenny laid out her plan in simple terms, finishing with words that were a chilling reminder that they were moving in new, darker, territory now.

'Those dealers from up the line will be down here sharpish, just as soon as word gets back that the guns have gone missing, so we'd best lay low after this one. Let the boys take the heat, they'll be the ones armed for a fight, after all.' She slid down off the table. 'I've got to talk to Ronnie, so you go straight back home, and don't talk to anyone. Not *anyone*,' she stressed. 'Be ready to leave by six, and,' she winked, 'wear your slinkiest dress.'

So tonight the North Twenty had once again joined forces with the Docklands mob. Smith's and Jenny's combined role was straightforward enough: they would park across the lane that ran alongside a side section of railway track, until the Cavers had collected the stolen guns and were on their way out. When the van inevitably had to stop, they would claim car trouble, and beg prettily for help, while the Dockers moved in and quietly transferred the boxes of guns from the van into one of the disused railway carriages, waiting open nearby.

'Should be here any minute,' Jenny said into the silence, as they sat waiting in the car.

'The Cavers are sure to see them shifting the boxes,' Smith said. 'And then what?'

'That's up to Ronnie and his lot.' Jenny shrugged. 'It's a Dockers' haul, not ours. No doubt they've made their contingency plans, but we're just doing our bit, as agreed.'

Smith had an all-too clear idea of what Ronnie Jackson's *contingency plans* might be, but that was none of her business. 'Why does it need two of us?'

'It's guns this time, they're bound to be more careful. Should only be two blokes though, we can handle that easy.'

Smith fidgeted with her own bag, her fingers twisting nervously at the strap. 'What if they realise what we're up to, before Ronnie and the boys turn up?'

'We won't have to worry about the Cavers.' Jenny pressed the snap fastener on her bag, and opened it so Smith could look inside. Nestling there was an ugly black handgun, incongruous against the pink satin.

'It's an American one, a Colt,' Jenny confided. 'I stole it from Ronnie's collection months ago, and he never even noticed.'

Fear crawled through Smith's veins. 'Would you use it?'

Jenny looked evasive. 'If I had to.'

Smith didn't dare ask if she already had, but she realised she didn't need to; Jenny's calm had always been an asset to the Twenties, but now it just seemed sinister, and hinted that there was much more to this evening's enterprise than she was letting on.

They sat in silence, waiting, and Smith found herself considering something she'd thought had been a good while off yet; that this might be the end of her time with the North Twenty. If it was, she'd have to leave more than the syndicate, she'd have to leave Bristol too; her life wouldn't be worth living if she stayed. In fact, it wouldn't be worth anything at all, especially to Jenny Lyons.

Jenny opened the car door and leaned out to peer back down the path. 'Why do you think they're taking so long?'

'I haven't a clue.'

'Really?' Jenny sounded unconvinced as she got out of the car, and Smith watched her narrowly, her blood running a little cooler as she thought back to where she'd gone after their meeting that afternoon, and who she'd seen. *Go straight home*, Jenny had said. But she hadn't.

'What do *you* think?' she countered. 'That it's not going off after all?'

'Either that or someone's sent us to wait on the wrong path.'

Smith got out too, a light sweat pricking at her skin despite the soft rain that had begun to fall. Her stomach was in knots now. *What had she done?*

'Why would they send us the wrong way,' she ventured, 'when we're doing them the favour?'

'That's what I'd like to know.' Jenny's voice was tight and suspicious, bordering on angry, which Smith found puzzling at first, then a horrible thought struck her.

'It's *not* just a Dockers' haul, is it? Were you thinking of taking some of those guns for yourself?'

'Not for me,' Jenny said, 'for us.' She yanked out her hat pin. 'Look! Even the Cavers have guns, and we have *this!*' She gave it a look of disgust. 'That's why I stole Ronnie's Colt.' She secured her hat once more, and looked back down the path towards the dock. 'Alright, I might as well tell you now: he's supposed to be leaving an extra six Brownings under the front seat of his van.'

'The Caver?'

'Of course the bloody Caver!' Jenny flung her a look. 'How do you think I found out about all this to begin with? We had an ... An understanding.'

'Which was what? You stop him, and collect the guns from his van, so he can claim he was hijacked?'

'He *is* being hijacked! Right now, on the dock. And when he goes back with a light cargo he'll rightly blame all of it on the Dockers. That's when things are going to turn nasty.'

'But why did the Dockers ask us for help tonight, if they've already done the job?'

Jenny didn't answer, but she looked shifty, and Smith breathed out slowly as she realised the truth. 'They didn't ask us at all, did they? They don't even know we're here.'

But she quailed inside, because they did know. They knew because Smith, in the warm afterglow of a tender afternoon with Victor Lyons, and still believing the two gangs were working together, had told him what Jenny wanted her to do. Vic hadn't shown the slightest surprise, but he must have gone straight off and told Ronnie the moment she'd left him.

'I'm pretty sure they heard we'd be here,' Jenny said, uncannily picking up the thread of her thoughts. 'And I'll bet I know who told them, too.' Her eyes slitted as she opened the driver's side door again, and she glared at Smith over the top of the car. 'You'd better watch your back. I haven't even started with you yet.'

She got back into the car, and before Smith could run around to the passenger side, she had turned and was driving back towards the dock. Smith took after her at a run, but by the time she arrived, out of breath and drenched through, Jenny was facing four Dockers across the yard. Her bag was on the wet ground beside her, and the stolen gun was gripped tightly in her two hands and pointed at her brother.

'You've ruined everything, Vic,' she shouted across the divide, raising her voice to compensate for the rain now hammering on the tin roof of the nearby storage shed. 'You betrayed us!'

Smith stared at her in dismay; gone was the fun-loving, diamond-hunting, good-time girl with the charming smile, the one who had somehow made it all seem more like adventure than crime. The woman who stood here now was a terrifying stranger. Ronnie Jackson stood by, clearly stunned by the speed with which his carefully planned heist had gone awry, and the Redcliffe Cavers' driver was standing beside his own open van, bemused and nervous-looking.

'Jenny,' Smith pleaded. 'Just stop and think. This is your *brother* . . .'

Jenny turned to her. 'It *was* you who told him, wasn't it?' For a moment the barrel of the gun wavered away from Victor and onto her. 'Well, he betrayed you too, Smith!'

She swung the Colt back, but in the split second her attention had been distracted, Victor had drawn his own weapon and now he cocked it, the sound loud and horribly final as he levelled it at Jenny's chest.

'Put down the gun, Jen.' His voice was also unsteady, barely recognisable as the man who'd spoken with such affection only that afternoon. 'I swear on all that's holy, I *will* kill you.'

Smith backed away slowly, trying to stay calm, and sensing she would soon need every bit of breath she could draw. She knew Jenny Lyons all too well, and Jenny wouldn't hesitate to pull that trigger; she had a reputation to protect, and if she lost that, her career would be over. Jenny Lyons, Queen of the Twenties, would never allow that to happen.

But Smith knew Victor too, and she knew he would kill to protect himself and his leader – it didn't matter that the threat he was protecting them from was his sister; one of them was going to die tonight, and Smith couldn't stay here a moment longer to find out which of them it would be. She had to get out of Bristol, away from the North Twenty, and far, far away from Jenny and Victor Lyons.

She turned and ran, and as she passed out of the feeble dockside light and into the dark alley beyond, from behind her she heard the flat sound of a gunshot.

CHAPTER ONE

Caernoweth Air Training Base, Cornwall
August 1930

The envelope sat in its pigeonhole in the flying school dormitory building, as innocuous-looking as the letters from home that sat in many of the others. But this wasn't a letter from home, and nor was it in any way innocuous.

Gwenna Rosdew slid it out of the small wooden compartment, but she couldn't bring herself to open it yet, she just stared at her name, printed carelessly on the envelope. There was no address, because this had not come through the postal system, it had been delivered by hand from Flight Lieutenant Graham Bowden's classroom across the yard, and while it remained unopened, all things were possible.

'Good luck,' a passing voice murmured, and Gwenna looked up to see one of her fellow trainees glancing at her with sympathy, as well he might. Everyone else from Gwenna's intake had progressed on to actual training flights, and she had yet to pass her second instruments test with a mark high enough to satisfy her instructor. It was baffling and upsetting.

'I've worked as hard as anyone else,' she'd said to her roommate that morning, 'and harder than some.'

'Harder than me,' Tory had agreed with her usual frank honesty. 'It's really not fair, Gwen.'

'Gwen-*na*. And I've got all the technical knowledge down pat! I know every bit as much as you and Bertie, and look at you two now. I know I can do it, and so does everyone else.'

But Barry Hocking, the most kindly of the flight instructors, had told her quite firmly that she had a long way to go before he would feel confident in taking her up in his Avro again. Coming from him, and even delivered with evident sympathy, it was a sore blow indeed; his gentle, encouraging style made him one of the most popular instructors on the civilian pilots' course, and his students generally did very well. So, twice a week, Gwenna could only watch from the classroom as her two best friends donned their heavy coats, scarves and gloves, and set out across the yard. She even envied Tory, who'd had the rotten luck to be paired with Bowden, their strict and dismissive classroom instructor, for her practical lessons.

Her own first choice had been Jude Singleton, the only female flight instructor on the base, who'd flown incognito during the war heading off Zeppelins over the coast, but that honour had gone to Bertie. Gwenna wouldn't have minded who she'd been assigned after that, even Bowden, if they'd only let her prove what she knew she could do. It would have been easier to bear if she hadn't gone on that initial flight when, although none of them had been allowed to take control of their planes, they had all come back breathless with excitement and babbling at nineteen to the dozen; now that she'd had that taste of the skies, and the freedom to travel them, every step she took on the ground felt like a failure.

Gwenna finally opened the envelope and drew out the paper, but before she unfolded it she allowed herself a glance out of the lobby window, to the pale blue August sky with its light puffs of cloud. Tory and Bertie were up there now, and Tory was due back any minute . . . This time next week she might be doing the same. Her fingers shook as she opened up the single page, and she held her breath and finally made herself look down at the formal, typewritten note.

```
Miss Rosdew.
    You scored 67% on your recent test - an
improvement, but still not an adequate score
I'm afraid.
    I have informed Flt Lt Bowden that you may
re-take this on Friday at 9am, alongside the
current cohort.
                                    B. Hocking.
```

Then, handwritten below:

ps. Don't worry, Gwenna, you'll get there!
                                    Barry.

Somehow the friendly encouragement felt worse, at that moment, than not attaining the 70% pass mark required, and Gwenna blinked hard to clear away the sting of tears before anyone saw them. But no-one was paying any attention now. Even her well-wishing fellow trainee hadn't waited around to find out whether or not his encouragement had been in vain; he had more important things to be thinking about, as did everyone else passing through the hallway. Most of them were going to or from the airfield or the classroom block, all striving for those moments of weightless joy that had now been yanked away from Gwenna yet again.

She shoved the note back into the envelope, and went tiredly through to the dorm. She had a lot of reading to do before tomorrow morning.

She was still deep in diagrams some time later, when Tory's voice cut through her concentration. 'Have you seen her yet?'

'Hmm?' Gwenna looked up from her text book, frowning. It took her a moment to focus on what her room-mate was talking about, then her thoughts caught up. 'The new girl, you mean?'

'Of course I do.' Tory hung up her heavy flying coat and fluffed out her newly styled, short blonde curls. 'She was due an hour ago, I thought she'd be here by now.'

'She's not turned up yet.' Gwenna removed her finger from where she'd placed it in the text, and resumed reading.

'What's her name again?'

'Hmm?' Gwenna repeated, then looked up again. 'Irene.'

'I wonder what she'll be like? I hope she won't be boring, and that we'll find lots to talk about.' Tory seemed unaware that her prattling was disturbing Gwenna's study, but it was hard to be annoyed with her for long, and Gwenna gave up and shut the book.

'How did today's flight go?'

Tory seemed about to launch into details of her lesson, but

stopped, an apologetic expression crossing her face. 'Never mind that, did you get your test result back?'

'Sixty-seven.'

'Oh, Gwenna.' Tory sighed. 'I'm so sorry.'

'Thanks.' Gwenna hurried on before her emotions got the better of her. 'So how *did* it go?'

'It was okay,' Tory said vaguely, and pulled a face at herself in the mirror as she re-curled a flattened lock of hair.

'You can tell me, you know,' Gwenna said. 'It's not your fault I've been pulled back from flying.'

'It's rotten though!' Tory turned back to her. 'Why is your instructor such a pig? He seemed so nice at the start.'

'He *is* nice,' Gwenna defended him, 'he just thinks I need to study the theory a bit more. He's probably right, I mean I *did* fail advanced instruments.'

'He could at least take you up, even if you don't take the controls yet. Seems dead keen to keep your feet on the ground if you ask me. I'll bet your father would give him a thing or two to think about.'

'Don't be silly!'

Both Tory and Bertie were careful not to enthuse too much in front of her, but she only had to look at them to see how much they were changing as a result of their advancement on the course. Their confidence, and the way they chatted easily and knowledgeably to the mechanics when they returned their planes, made Gwenna feel like a silly first-former hanging around the fringes of a sixth-form picnic.

The embarrassment of it almost outweighed the disappointment and frustration, especially given that she'd made such a song and dance about her wartime flying ace father when she'd started. Even her fiancé had stopped asking her about it, as if he were embarrassed on her behalf; Peter was the local bobby in Caernoweth, and being seven years her senior, at thirty, he had a habit of siding with her father over many things, not least Gwenna's progress as a pilot.

'The way things are going,' Gwenna said with forced lightness, 'this Irene person will get up before I do.' It sounded less like a joke when she heard it out loud, and she wished she'd kept quiet.

'Let's hope *she* gets Hocking too then,' Tory said, licking her finger and wiping at a smudge of oil on her cheek. 'You don't suppose it's because of your father, do you?'

It was no secret that the only way Gwenna had been able to afford the training was because Jonas Rosdew was well known locally for his wartime endeavours, and the flying school had awarded their scholarship solely on that basis.

'They can't deny I've progressed on my own merit,' Gwenna pointed out, a little tightly. 'They would have thrown me out after the first month's assessment if not, like they did with that lad from Liskeard.'

'True.' Tory sighed. 'Well, hopefully he'll get bored, and give someone else a rough time for a while.' She straightened her blouse and finally seemed happy with her appearance. 'What time are we meeting Bertie?'

'Six-ish, I think.' Gwenna took up her book again. 'Be a love and shove off for a bit, would you? I need to memorise this page of charts before the morning.'

Tory cheerfully obliged, so Gwenna was alone when, half an hour later, a timid knock at the door announced the arrival of the girl who would take the third of the four dormitory beds.

'Come in,' she called, 'it's not locked.'

The door opened to admit a slender young woman, as tall as Gwenna, who usually felt she towered over her friends. She was dressed conservatively but practically, in trousers and a belted blouse, and carried a small case and a hat, both clutched in the same hand while she kept the other on the door handle. Ready to run away? Gwenna felt a twinge of sympathy; the girl looked terrified.

'Hello,' she said, and stood up with her own hand out. 'I'm Gwenna Rosdew.'

The newcomer finally relinquished her grip on the door and shook hands. 'Irene Lewis.' She looked around the dorm with an expression of wariness. Not dislike, exactly, but she was clearly used to a certain standard of living and had already decided that this new venture was not likely to provide it. Gwenna wondered why she was here at all if she felt like this. Perhaps she was simply being encouraged into it, in which case she'd probably last about a week.

'Tory's out at the moment,' she said. She gestured to the freshly made bed in the corner. 'That's yours. Make yourself at home, and then I'll show you around the base if you like.'

Irene put her suitcase on the bed. 'No rush,' she said, a little dismissively, and Gwenna blinked in surprise; it had been the first thing she and the others had wanted to do, and it was hard to imagine anyone not leaping on the opportunity.

'Where can I hang my things?' Irene asked, attempting to flap the creases out of a rather smart, pale blue cotton dress. Gwenna couldn't place her accent, exactly, but she wasn't local. Midlands, perhaps?

'That wardrobe's empty.' She pointed to the smaller of two

sturdy cupboards, side by side against the wall. 'I moved Tory's things into the other one, with mine.'

'Thanks. Who's in the fourth bed?'

'No-one, yet. We're hoping to persuade our friend Bertie.'

'Who?' Irene looked alarmed, and Gwenna smiled.

'Bertie's a girl. Roberta Fox.'

'Oh!' Irene relaxed. 'Where does she live at the moment then?'

'The flats at the top of town. You know the converted hotel?'

'I've seen it. Why doesn't she move in here, if you're such pals?'

Gwenna hesitated; Bertie had had her reasons at the start, but it wasn't really anyone else's place to explain them. 'Oh, just . . . you know. The way things worked out. Anyway, I'll just carry on with my reading then, if you don't want to look around.'

Irene looked a little deflated, but nodded. 'Of course.'

'Unless you've changed your mind?'

'Well, I'd quite like to see the village. But if you're busy I'm quite happy to go alone.'

Gwenna could think of a hundred better things to do. She was always keen to poke her nose into the hangars on the base, no matter how busy she was, and would have been pleased to have had the excuse, but the village was as dull as you like, and hardly worth wasting precious studying time on. Irene did seem to have something of a pleading look about her though, and she had looked so nervous when she came in, so Gwenna nodded.

'Let me get my outdoor shoes on, and we'll go for a walk. I'm meeting the others at six though, so make sure you've got your own key to get back in.'

Irene jangled the key she'd been given, and tucked it into her handbag. 'This is very kind of you.' She gestured at the text book. 'You do seem busy.'

'I am.' Gwenna saw Irene's faintly embarrassed look, and regretted her bluntness. 'But I could do with some new soap,' she added, 'and if we go now we might get there before the shop shuts. You can only look at a chart for so long, before it all goes blurred and you end up just staring and not learning. You'll find that out soon enough.' She'd hoped for a returned smile, but Irene just nodded solemnly and Gwenna had the feeling she'd only made things worse.

Outside, she reluctantly ignored the hangars, and instead crossed the base to the wire perimeter fence, and emerged onto the road to Pencarrack. Turning left would have taken them down the road to Caernoweth, but, of the choice between town and village, she was glad Irene had asked to see the village instead. Caernoweth was closer, bigger, and very pretty, but also quite steep as it wound its way down the long hill towards the sea. Coming back up would have been a terrible slog in this weather. Pencarrack, on the other hand, was around ten minutes in the other direction, but the walk was along the flat ground, lying as it did on the same high level of moorland as the air training base.

On the exposed road across Pencarrack Moor, the light summer wind lessened the sun's heat, and made the walk less of a chore than it otherwise might have been. Gwenna pointed out the distant white peaks of the china clay pit, standing like small mountains on the horizon, and after a few more minutes Irene stopped to peer across the grassland.

'What's that?' She pointed to an ornate stone structure in the distance. It had the appearance of a castle in miniature, with its walls overgrown with ivy, and gorse bushes around its base. 'Is it really that small?'

Gwenna nodded. 'It's called Tyndall's Folly. It was built by the town's founder, Malcolm Penworthy, back in the sixteenth century to commemorate his sister. She was taken by a pirate called Edmund Tyndall, and this was built as a sort of sop to him, to win his favour so he didn't treat the girl too badly.'

'Gosh. Did it work?'

'Who knows? It's very pretty close up, even if it is absolutely pointless. It makes a nice landmark though, much nicer than the china clay pits. Apparently it's a common place to meet for . . .' A little embarrassed, she left the implication hanging.

'You mean courting couples?'

'I suppose.' Gwenna looked away, and a familiar sound made her squint up at the sky, glad of the excuse to change the subject. The unmistakeable outline of Jude Singleton's plane, and the distinctive stuttering of its engine, filled her with the usual mixture of joy and envy.

'There she is!' She waved, knowing she probably wouldn't be seen from up there, but somehow it felt like the right thing to do anyway. 'It's Bertie.'

Irene glanced briefly upwards, and nodded. 'Very nice.'

'*Nice?*' Gwenna couldn't bite back the incredulous retort. 'That's a Sopwith Camel, it actually flew in the war!' This earned little more than a polite incline of the head. 'You'll be up there soon,' she said, 'just imagine that. Exciting, eh?'

Irene gave her a smile then, and it did make her look a lot nicer. 'Oh, I'm sure that'll be quite some time away yet.' She sounded relieved about that, so Gwenna didn't push any further but it was good to know it was nerves making the newcomer so distant, and not a sense of superiority after all.

'How d'you know that's your friend, anyway?' Irene went on. 'Surely you can't see from this distance?'

Gwenna pushed down another swell of envy. 'Because her instructor's the only one with that kind of plane, it's been specially adapted so she can give lessons in it, and *she* only picks one trainee every couple of intakes. On our lot she picked Bertie.' She hoped she didn't sound too sour, as she went on, 'You might be lucky and get her too, though.'

'A woman trainer?' Irene frowned. 'Not sure I'd feel safe.'

There were too many comments to make to that, so Gwenna sat on them all. Instead she pointed up the road, and the first few houses on the outskirts of Pencarrack. 'We're here now.'

'It's quite a new place, isn't it?'

'Fairly, yes. Tory's the one to ask, since she's originally from town, but I gather the village grew from what was just a row of miners' and quarrymen's cottages called Furzy Row. They were developed by the family who live at Pencarrack House, so everyone just used the name for the village too and they made it official.'

'So most of the people who live there now are just quarry and pit workers?' Irene sounded disappointed, as if she'd expected a more wealthy class of neighbour.

'There are still the families who had houses here before the village grew up around them,' Gwenna said. 'From when the flying school was an RFC military base during the war. My instructor lives in one of the bigger ones on the outskirts, actually.'

Irene picked up her feet. 'Come on then, if you're meeting your friend soon we'd better hoof it. Looks like she's coming in to land.'

The Camel had banked up ahead and was coming back in the direction of the airfield, and Gwenna checked her watch; she probably had half an hour or so to spare, and it wouldn't take that long to show the new arrival the delights of Pencarrack. One or two farms and larger homesteads dotted the distant landscape, but they were of no real interest unless you lived there. She gestured briefly at St Gwinear's Church and the village school as they passed them on the right, and the densely wooded area opposite, and then they rounded the corner of the village itself.

'Right,' she said, as they came onto Fore Street, 'useful places to know . . . Damn, I left my purse on my bed, after all that.' She sighed; no new soap today then. 'There's a cobbler just up on that side, then there's Mrs Donithorn, the seamstress; the post office; the sweet shop, and that's the doctor's house.'

'That's all?'

'Quite a lot really, for a village. There are more shops in the town though.' Gwenna peered more closely at the doctor's residence, noticing all the curtains were closed. She saw a note on the door and stepped up to read it.

Surgery opening Monday 25 August.

'It looks as if he hasn't even arrived yet, so scratch that one too. There's a doctor in Caernoweth if you need one, the number's in the common room. Oh, and there's a church. Anglican, if you're interested.'

'I thought you said there was a village shop?'

'Sort of. They sell some essentials in the post office, including the soap I wanted. But there's a much better one in Caernoweth. My family's, actually.'

'So you're local too?'

Gwenna shrugged. 'Not so's you'd notice. We moved here

after the war, and took over the shop from the Watts family, but I'm sure people still think of us as having only been here a week. There's a nice little pub called the Tin Streamer's Arms,' she added, 'which we call the Tinner's. Oh, and there's a decent book shop in town too. Penhaligon's Attic. If you like reading, you should visit.'

'I'm not much of a reader, but I'd like to look around the town anyway, when there's more time.'

'I'm sure you'll like it. And speaking of time,' Gwenna looked at her watch again, 'I'm going to start back now. Bertie will have almost finished post-flight checks, and we're going to the Cliffside Fort for dinner. I'd invite you along,' she added, feeling she ought to address the subject, 'but it's—'

'Oh gosh, no.' Irene smiled again. 'I understand, you three are pals.'

'It's not that, it's just that it's another friend's birthday and they're not expecting anyone else. It's not really my place.'

'Don't give it a thought.' Irene shoved her hands into her pockets. 'I'll walk back with you, and then just spend the evening settling in.' She pulled a face. 'It's been such a long day, I shall probably be asleep within the hour.'

'We'll try not to disturb you when we come in,' Gwenna promised.

They parted ways at the air base, where Irene let herself back into the dorm, and Gwenna found Tory waiting in her motor in the civilian car parking area outside the perimeter fence. Bertie was, presumably, still finishing things off with her flight trainer, so Gwenna slipped into the back of the 4-seater to wait.

'I've met Irene,' she said. 'We went for a walk up to Pencarrack.'

'What's she like?'

'She seems alright. A bit . . . distant. No, that's not it.' Gwenna frowned. 'Dis*tanced*, maybe.'

'What's the difference?'

'Well, I don't think she's deliberately setting herself apart, it's just that she's not at all excited. As if it hasn't touched her yet.'

'Nervous? Second thoughts?' Tory suggested.

'Seems like it.' Gwenna shrugged. 'Which means she probably won't be around for long.'

'Fair enough.' Tory dismissed the subject. 'Right, tonight's job then.' She twisted in the driver's seat so she could look directly at Gwenna. 'We finally persuade Milady of Fox Bay to move out of those awful flats, and into the dorm on the base. Agreed?'

'Agreed.' Gwenna was about to continue, then she stopped with an irritated click of her tongue. 'I'll be back in a minute, I've left my purse. Again.'

She ran back along the path to the dormitory building, and let herself into the dorm quietly, in case Irene was already sleeping off a long journey. But the new girl was sitting on her bed, bent over a writing pad on her lap. Like Gwenna, she had shunned the short, bobbed hairstyle favoured by Bertie, and more recently Tory, and kept enough length in her mid-brown hair to pin it up. It had come loose from its pins now, and swung down in front of her face as she concentrated, and Gwenna saw a fleeting look of annoyance cross her face as she looked up and pushed it aside.

'Sorry to disturb you,' she said quickly. 'I'll just pick this up and . . . Are you alright?'

'Quite alright, thank you,' Irene said, but Gwenna noticed her hand was spread over the page on which she'd been writing, almost like a school child trying to prevent someone from copying her work. Surely she must have smudged it horribly. The other hand gripped the pen tightly, then relaxed, but it was clear it was a conscious act of will. Irene's face wore that odd smile again now, the one that sat awkwardly and made her look as if she wished she were anywhere but there.

'Letters home?' Gwenna asked, eaten alive by curiosity, but determined not to show it. Perhaps it was a note to a beau, or someone she shouldn't have been seeing. 'Such a difficult thing, I suppose, if you're far away from your loved ones.'

'Yes.'

'And are you?'

'What?'

'Far away from—'

'Oh.' Irene nodded. 'Quite a long way, yes. Wolverhampton. It's very awkward,' she went on, almost babbling now, 'Mother says she wants to know absolutely all, but you just know, don't you, that she'd rather not? I mean, ignorance is bliss, isn't it, in some ways?'

'Well.' Gwenna didn't quite know what to say to that, her own parents being determined to squeeze every last detail out of her whenever she went home at weekends. 'I'm sure she'll be glad to hear from you, whatever you have to say.'

'I thought you were meeting your friends?' Irene went on, looking pointedly at the clock. 'It's gone six.'

'Bertie's running a bit late, and I forgot this.' Gwenna held up her purse and slipped it into her pocket. 'We'll have a proper chat later, perhaps, when Tory's here.'

'That'll be nice.' Irene still had one hand protectively over her paper, but seemed to realise it looked a little silly since Gwenna wouldn't be able to read it anyway, and removed it. But she didn't continue writing, and didn't speak again until Gwenna said goodbye in the doorway. Then she smiled again, and her face lost all its awkwardness and became friendly once more.

Gwenna pulled the door closed behind her, her own smile turning into a frown. Letters home be damned . . . That girl would bear watching.

CHAPTER TWO

Cliffside Fort Hotel

Tory waited for a chance to begin nudging the conversation onto the right track, but Tommy Ash, the aircraft engineer whose twenty-fifth birthday it was, had engaged Bertie Fox in a string of anecdotes about a mutual friend who'd died earlier that year. Despite the sorrow they both felt, his stories were funny, irreverent and affectionate, and the usually reserved Bertie's shocked laughter frequently rang out, as she learned more about what her much-missed friend had got up to during his time on the training base.

Tory turned, instead, to Gwenna, who had been oddly reflective since she'd re-joined her in the car. 'This Irene, then; what did you mean when you came back with your purse and said she was a bit shifty?'

'Exactly that.' Gwenna speared a piece of carrot. 'It's how she looked at me, and she was definitely hiding the letter she was writing.'

'To a bloke, you think?'

'That was my first thought,' Gwenna admitted, 'but if it *was* a man, it was someone she shouldn't have been writing to.'

'She's probably got a crush on someone's husband or something. Is she pretty?'

'What's that got to do with it?'

'If she is, there's more of a chance he'll write back.' Tory winked. 'So, is she?'

'Fairly, I suppose. About my height, and with lovely hair. Bit cold though.'

'Give her a chance,' Tory protested. 'She's *just* arrived! Must be terrified.'

'Say what you like, I'm going to keep a close eye on her.' Gwenna looked across at Bertie and Tommy. 'You couldn't get a tissue paper between those two, could you?'

'Just as it should be.'

Tory was delighted at the way her two friends were getting along; Bertie had had things unimaginably tough for the past year, since the motorcycle accident that had resulted in the loss of the lower part of her right leg. Tommy, who was lively and popular, and a friend to Bertie from the start, was one of the few people able to pull her out of a serious mood. He was clearly smitten too; Bertie had come straight from training tonight, and, thanks to her flying helmet, her usually glossy dark hair was tangled in places and sticking up in others. On top of that she still wore her dun-coloured trousers and boots, but Tommy's eyes were drinking her in as if she were a Hollywood star dressed in sequins.

Tory waited for a lull in their conversation then jumped in. 'So, when are you moving into the dorm then, Bertie?'

Bertie blinked. 'Where did *that* come from?'

'Gwenna and I were talking about it again today. It's so silly you living in town, when there's a perfectly good bed right there on the base.'

'You know why I—'

'Yes,' Tory said patiently, 'we know why you didn't do it at the start, but now we *know* you have a metal leg, and so does everyone else, so there's no need to be shy about it anymore.'

'Tory!' Bertie glanced around them, but no-one was paying any attention. 'It wasn't a question of being shy about my leg, it was more that I wanted to fit in and not just be the centre of gossip.'

'Well, you did, and you're not, so now there's no reason not to join us.'

'She's right,' Gwenna put in. 'There's no need to hide away in those awful little square flats now.'

'No,' Tommy said with a grin. 'You can move into the awful little square dormitory instead.'

Tory rolled her eyes. 'You're not helping. Oh, come on, Bertie! There aren't any stairs in the dorms, for a start, and the lift in those flats is always breaking, you said so.'

'And I've seen your flat too,' Gwenna added. 'The space you'd get in the dorm is actually bigger.'

Bertie's face relaxed into a reluctant smile. Tory had the feeling that, deep down, she'd been wanting to make the move, and all she needed was a push; she caught Tommy's attention, and gave him a tiny, encouraging nod.

'They're right, Bertie,' he said obediently. 'Closer to training, closer to your friends, makes perfect sense to me. And it's my birthday,' he reminded her, 'you have to do what—'

'Alright!' Bertie held up a hand. 'You've convinced me.'

She turned back to Tory. 'Will you help carry my things from the flat?'

'We can use my car. Plenty of room in the back.'

Bertie nodded. 'Alright. I'll move in at the weekend then.'

'Wonderful.' Tory raised her glass. 'Here's to a fourth person to do the laundry!' She grinned. 'Sorry, I mean: here's to our new room-mate!'

Gwenna echoed the toast, and Tommy chimed in with, 'To no more excuses for being late for training,' which earned him a dig in the ribs from Bertie, and Tory smiled into her glass; those two were definitely moving into even more comfortable territory.

'Will you be pitching in as well?' she asked Gwenna, who shook her head.

'Afraid not, I'm needed at home this weekend.'

'You're making it sound like a full-scale house move,' Bertie protested. 'It's only a few bags and some books.'

'I half envy you, actually,' Tory said. 'There's nothing like a change of living space to give your life a bit of a kick.'

'Well, you're welcome to move into my flat instead,' Bertie suggested with an innocent look. Tory pointedly ignored her, and Bertie laughed. 'Your place in London can't have been much bigger.'

'Not as big as the apartment in France, either,' Tory agreed.

'I still can't understand why you'd choose Cornwall over France,' Gwenna said, with a wistful little sigh. 'You must be barmy.'

'Neither of them had as much space to mess about in as Hawthorn Cottage. That's the one down the hill, that we rented from the Battens when I was little, but we lost that place when Charles Batten died.' Tory pushed aside the sour memory those

30

words gave her. She was well practised at that. 'I don't know who lives there now, but my grandparents used to have Priddy Farm just across the way, so Mum and us four kids went to live there.'

'Four?' Gwenna asked, but Tommy spoke over her.

'Bobby Gale lives at Hawthorn now. You know him, don't you?'

'Knew him, rather. Bobby was the leader of our gang when we were kids. A right tearaway he was.'

'Still is,' Gwenna said. 'Never out of trouble of one kind or another, according to Peter.'

'He's alright,' Tommy protested. 'We get along fine – he's just a bit of a one, that's all. Once he knows you're not on his back over anything he's a decent enough bloke.'

'How do you know him, anyway?' Tory asked, but a moment later she caught sight of a woman being shown to a table, and she lowered her fork so fast it clattered against her plate and silenced Tommy's explanation. Hot on the heels of her memories of Hawthorn Cottage, this was too much.

'What's the matter?' Bertie twisted in her seat to follow Tory's shocked gaze. 'Who is it?'

'Believe it or not, it's my mother,' Tory managed, past a sudden tightness in her throat. It was as if she'd conjured her simply by mentioning her childhood. 'I haven't seen her for . . .' Her words trailed away as she worked it out; it was around sixteen years. 'Since the start of the war.'

Tommy and Gwenna immediately strained to see the table, where a much younger woman, a girl really, with reddish-blonde hair, was rising to greet the newcomer with a warm smile and a kiss on the cheek. Tory didn't recognise the girl, but was relieved to see that at least it wasn't a man her mother was meeting.

'What happened?' Bertie asked. 'You must have only been little.'

Tory shook her head. 'Look, this isn't a story for a birthday party.' She let out a slow, controlled breath, and turned back to Tommy. 'Sorry, you were going to tell me how you and Bobby Gale crossed paths.'

'Don't be silly.' Bertie frowned. 'You look as white as a sheet. Never mind birthday parties, if you want to tell us, we want to listen.'

'Maybe later.' But she knew she would find a way to deflect then, too. It wouldn't be difficult; she'd been ducking questions about her mother for years.

She watched with a kind of reluctant fascination, as her mother settled into her seat and smiled up at the suddenly attentive waiter. She was dressed much as Tory always pictured her: neat, but plain, although her clothes were no longer patched. Her blonde hair had paled to grey at the roots, but was still thick and luxuriant, twisted this evening into a neat chignon and fastened with basic pins. She had never needed anything in the way of decoration, and still didn't; any attempt to look fancy would just be redundant on that face and form.

Tory had been hearing comments about her mother's beauty all her life. Straight-backed and clear-skinned, with bewitching, light blue eyes and a surprisingly low but pleasing voice, the widow Gilbert had been praised by many for the way she'd coped with long hours of manual labour on the farm, and bringing up her four beautifully behaved children alone. What had been less openly lauded was the reputation she had later gained for herself in town—

'Look, this has been a shock for you,' Bertie said gently,

breaking into her thoughts just in time. 'Why don't we finish up here and go back to my flat, where it's more private?'

'It's Tommy's birthday,' Tory protested. 'You can't just end the meal because of me.'

'Not because of you at all,' Tommy said. 'I've got an early start in the morning anyway, and I was wondering how I could politely tell you all to ... um, to go away and leave me alone.'

'You're such a gentleman,' Bertie said drily, but she looked grateful nevertheless.

Gwenna looked over her shoulder at Nancy. 'Are you going to speak to her?'

'Not yet. I want to know if anyone else has seen her first.'

'Your brothers, you mean?'

Tory nodded. 'Gerald was nineteen, and always seemed to be angry, but he still missed her. And Matty was only seven. I want to know if she's been to see him at least, to explain, before I'll know how to speak to her.'

'How could she have left you to care for Matty like that?' Bertie looked appalled. 'And a girl needs her mother when she's growing up.'

'I had my Granny Ruth at least. And she had help from some of the women in town. Anna Penhaligon was very kind, and so was her stepdaughter.' Tory stood up, suddenly needing to be out in the fresh air. 'You stay and finish, I'll be outside. Tommy, I'm sorry, and thank you. I hope you've enjoyed your birthday meal, at least.'

The clatter of her chair turned a few heads her way, and one of them was her mother's, but she turned back to her companion again and Tory's eyes flooded. She'd imagined this moment for so many years, and didn't know what she'd expected, or secretly hoped for: a meeting of the eyes, a realisation, a display of deep emotion ... Surely something about her own daughter would draw her, instinctively, to some flicker of recognition?

Outside, she walked a short way, then lit a cigarette and leaned against the wall while she waited for the others to finish their meal and join her. There should have been much to look at out here; the hotel's architect had purposely left the broken-down castle defences, and the external walls too, while they'd modernised and converted the inside, and it all added to the unspoilt charm of the landscape. All along the coastline, and the rugged headlands in the distance, the summer evening sky was beginning to paint everything with a faint orange-pink glow, and the familiar booming of the incoming tide far below gave everything another layer of texture; it was a beautiful evening, and a glorious place to be, but all Tory could think about was that brief glance, and then ... nothing.

'There she is. Tory!'

She looked up to see Bertie and Gwenna emerging from the hotel. Bertie was leaning on her stick after a long day, and Gwenna carried Tory's bag. Tory stubbed out her cigarette on the wall and went over to join them by the entrance.

'We couldn't stay in there,' Bertie said, 'not after what you said. Come back to my flat.'

'Thanks,' Tory said, taking her bag from Gwenna, 'but I'm just going to go back to the dorm actually, if you don't mind?'

'Don't you want to talk?'

'Not tonight, I'd rather just think. And anyway I need to write to Matty and Gerald.'

'That reminds me,' Gwenna put in. 'Earlier you said there were four of you?'

'There were. Joseph was between Gerald and me.' Tory swallowed hard. 'He got called up in 1918 and never came home.'

'You've never said.' Bertie's face was pale. 'All this time we've known you.'

'I've never found the right time really,' Tory said. 'Joseph was ... well, I know it's wrong to have favourites, but still.'

'I'm so sorry.' Gwenna murmured. 'So close to the end of the war, too.'

'Do you think your mother ever knew what happened to him?' Bertie glanced back towards the hotel as they walked to Tory's car. 'She would still have been his next of kin, wouldn't she?'

'He listed Granny Ruth, so I've no idea if Mum found out somehow. Nothing she's done so far tells me she cared enough to find out though, and I doubt very much if she knows he's named on the Pencarrack memorial either.'

Tory was aware she was causing a black cloud over the little gathering, and as a silence fell over them she wished she could bring her usual breeziness back, but her own mood had been coloured by tonight's not-quite encounter; she needed to speak to her mother, to put everything into its proper place so she could concentrate on her own life again.

'Who's that, do you think?' Gwenna asked, perhaps seeking to distract her by pointing at one of the final training flights of the day returning to the airfield. 'Whoever it is isn't concentrating very hard. Even I could make a better job of that approach, and I've only been up once.'

'I think it's Hocking's plane, isn't it?' Tory said, frowning at the serial number painted on the underside of the wing. 'Yes, it is. Whoever's flying it is making a right pig's ear out of it.'

She followed the Avro's wavering progress, wondering if she would ever feel the same thrill as Bertie, or the same passion as Gwenna, when she flew; she couldn't help feeling guilty, whenever Gwenna received another knockback, that she herself just didn't seem to feel the privilege as deeply as she ought to. She enjoyed it well enough, but whenever Bertie returned from her flying sessions she had a glow about her that Tory had quickly come to realise she lacked, though thank goodness she seemed to have let go of that eager but lunatic notion of taking up combat flying.

Gwenna decided that she too should get an early night, since she was re-taking her test tomorrow, so in the end Tory just dropped Bertie back at her lonely little flat in the holiday block at the top of town.

'Do you mind if we explain to this new girl about why you've left it so long to move into the dorm?' Gwenna asked, as Bertie climbed out. 'I felt a bit strange earlier, just brushing it off.'

'No, that's alright,' Bertie said, on a yawn. 'I don't mind any-more, honestly.'

'Is the lift working?' Tory pulled a face as she looked through the open door at the grey box near the entrance. She couldn't imagine being cooped up in such a horrid little space, it made her skin shrink on her bones just to imagine it; what if it broke down, or the door jammed?

'The lift's fine.' Bertie gave them each a hug. 'Now push off, you two. I'll see you tomorrow, bright and early.'

'Do you think she and Tommy are secretly an item?' Tory asked, waving as she drove away.

'Not yet. But I'm sure it won't be long.'

'She's over that farmer boy of hers, then?'

'I'd say so. He seemed nice enough, but he wants children, and she definitely doesn't, so they made the right choice. Tommy's perfect for her.'

'As long as he doesn't want children either,' Tory pointed out, and they exchanged a quick glance; the odds were slim, they both knew that, and Bertie had made her decision quite clear. Still, there was a chance she might change her mind, once she'd got this flying bug out of her system, and that it would no longer be an issue. They parked by the wire gates of the compound, and started up the path to the dorm block.

'What about you?' Gwenna asked, as they drew near the door.

'What about me?'

'You've never even been engaged, and you're older than either of us.'

Tory laughed. 'Not everyone wants to be engaged, Gwen. Or married off, with a brood.'

'Gwen-*na!* And anyway, didn't you have a bit of a fancy for that lad who works at Bertie's family's hotel?'

Tory smiled. They'd recently attended Bertie's birthday celebrations at Fox Bay, and she and Martin Berry, the Foxes' loyal receptionist, had enjoyed a minor fling. 'He's sweet enough,' she allowed, 'probably *too* sweet, so not for the long haul. Not for me.'

'That's a shame.'

'Not really. It was nice while it lasted, but he deserves someone with lots of time to look after him, and it'd be such a slog from here to Trethkellis every time we wanted to see each other. No, Martin's best forgotten.'

They stopped outside the dorm block, which had been locked

at eight o'clock as usual, and as Tory fished in her bag for her keys, Gwenna spoke in a low, hesitant voice. 'Are you *sure* you don't want to talk about why your mother has suddenly turned up in town?'

'She'll have her reasons,' Tory said shortly. 'I just hope they're temporary.' She changed the subject quickly. 'I'll be able to meet Irene hopefully, since we're home early.'

But when they went in, and despite Gwenna's insistence that Irene had planned an early night, their dorm was empty.

'She must have changed her mind,' Gwenna said. 'Maybe she went for a stroll into Caernoweth after all, since it's a nice evening.'

'She's certainly been familiarising herself with the area,' Tory mused, picking up a small pile of local maps from Irene's bedside table. 'Look at these. Where did you say she was from?'

'Somewhere in the Midlands, I can't remember exactly.'

'She must have quite an interest in Cornwall then, to have come down here to train instead of using one of the bigger schools up there.' Tory flipped through the maps. 'Caernoweth and Pencarrack, Truro, St Austell, Bodmin ... All the way up as far as Lynher Mill, and around Liskeard and Launceston.'

'She'll be seeing it all from that same angle too, before long,' Gwenna said, more than a little enviously as she looked at the aerial drawings.

'So will you,' Tory soothed, replacing the maps. 'Don't worry, you'll sail through tomorrow. You must have been reading for hours this afternoon, and that's on top of all the studying you did for the first two tests.'

'Which made no difference whatsoever,' Gwenna pointed out. 'Right, I'm going to have a bath and go to bed.' She took her washbag down the hall to the communal bathroom, leaving Tory alone with her memories of the morning her mother had left, and everything had changed forever.

She remembered waking at her usual early hour; July was always a busy time on any farm, and, as a healthy twelve-year-old girl she'd had a lot of chores to get through before school. She'd splashed herself with water from the ewer on the stand, and dressed quickly, but arriving in the kitchen she'd been surprised to find it empty except for Matty, who was solemnly eating a hunk of bread he'd torn from the loaf on the table.

'Where's Ma?' He shrugged and continued eating, and Tory clicked her tongue. 'Well, where's Gran then?'

'Fetchin' eggs.'

Tory looked out of the window to see their grandmother emerging backwards from the henhouses, and she went to the door to repeat her query. Gran looked uncomfortable, and glanced past her to where Matty was sitting. Then she sighed.

'She's gone, love.'

'Gone where? Up to Pencarrack already?' The farm cart took fresh produce daily up to the big manor at the top of town, but it wouldn't be ready for hours yet.

'No, not there.'

'Oh. Well, will she be back soon?'

'She's not coming back, maid. I'm that sorry.'

It had taken Tory a moment to digest this. She remembered the scruffy little note that Gran had pulled from her apron pocket and handed to her; how she had squinted at the sparse but laboured scrawl printed on it.

ma
plees look after them
i will rite soon.
Sory.

And then the only word written with evident confidence:

Nancy.

Sitting on her bed now, Tory knew she'd never forget the dizzy feeling that had swept over her; as if she'd been standing on solid ground one minute, only to have it open beneath her feet the next. Falling into nothing, and with no-one to catch her.

And *had* her mother written? Not once in the five more years Tory had remained at Priddy Farm, though who knew if she had done so after that? War had broken into their safe little world only a couple of weeks later; a lot of men from town, of all ages, had gone off to fight, and still there was nothing from Nancy, not even to ask whether her eldest son had gone with them. When Gerald *had* joined up, a few months later, the rest of the family had gone to Bodmin to wave him off at the station and Tory had looked around, expecting to see Ma at the last minute, come to say goodbye. But she hadn't, and Gerald, still only a boy underneath his soldier's façade, had tried unsuccessfully to hide devastated tears from his younger siblings. From that moment Tory had buried their mother in the very back of her mind, in all but her deepest dreams.

She looked up as Gwenna returned, changed ready for bed and already yawning in anticipation, but knew she herself wouldn't sleep for a while yet. The heat had gone from the day, so she picked up her coat. 'I'm going for a walk.'

'Now?'

'Just a circuit of the base to work off this headache. I'll try not to wake you when I come in.'

She wandered slowly alongside the perimeter fence in the almost-dark, turning over in her mind all the possible reasons her mother might have returned now. Illness? A new relationship, or the simple wish, at the demise of an old one, to be somewhere familiar? It was so hard to understand, without knowing why she'd left in the first place; she had been gone before the gossip ever took hold, so—

'Here!'

She jumped at the sound of the low voice, and looked over to where someone was standing on the far side of one of the mechanics' vans. She couldn't see who it was, but they weren't calling to her in any case; someone else had come through the gate and was hurrying up the road. Just a hunched shape of a man who met the caller at the van, exchanged a few murmured words, and then climbed in behind the wheel, yet something familiar about the way he moved told her it was her old childhood friend Bobby Gale, of whom Gwenna's fiancé still apparently disapproved. Seemingly with good reason. Civilians weren't allowed to borrow airfield vehicles, so whoever had agreed to this loan would be in enormous trouble too, if the bigwigs found out. Losing their job would be the least of it, which meant they were probably making enough money off it to justify the danger of discovery. She hoped for Bertie's sake it wasn't Tommy Ash.

Tory stood very still until the van had driven off the base and she was sure she hadn't been seen, and then continued on her way. For a few minutes she idly pondered why Bobby might be

41

using airfield property at all, since he had his own transport, but before too long thoughts of her own family intruded once again, and she began to mentally compose letters to her two brothers. How would they feel, knowing their mother was back and hadn't contacted them? Or perhaps she had, and it was only Tory who'd been left in the dark? She wasn't sure which would be worse.

By the time she had walked twice more around the compound, she was as exhausted by the twists her mind was taking, as by the long day she'd had, and was looking forward to a creamy hot chocolate and some clean, starched sheets. She reached the dorm building in time to see a dark-haired girl she didn't recognise hurrying up to the door.

'Hello,' she called out cheerfully. 'Are you Irene?'

The girl stopped and turned, and the light falling across her face from the doorway emphasised startled eyes. 'Yes? Oh, you must be Tory.'

'Pleased to meet you.' Tory held out her hand and the girl shook it. She gestured for Irene to precede her into the hall. 'I was going to make hot chocolate, will you join me?'

Irene hesitated, but only for a moment. 'I was going to try and sleep,' she said, 'but when I started to think about beginning lessons tomorrow I got a bit nervous. How silly to begin on a Friday.'

'We thought that, but you'll be studying in the hangars on Saturday too, and it's a great way to break you in gently.'

'Perhaps. Anyway, yes please, hot chocolate might just do the trick.'

They found the communal kitchen deserted, and Tory set to work boiling milk and rinsing cups. She kept up an amiable chatter, with one eye on the new girl, who had removed her coat and now sat idly playing with the salt cruet while her eyes scanned the empty room. Irene was smartly dressed, and wore her hair tied neatly back off her face; her features were small and quite dainty, and she reminded Tory a little of Gwenna in her manner; a little stiff and formal, but she was probably just shy. A chat would be just the thing to settle her in.

Tory carried two steaming mugs over to the table, and sat down with a little sigh of relief.

'Why don't you tell me a bit about yourself?' she offered. 'You don't sound as if you're from around here, so what made you choose Cornwall?'

'I, I just ... did.' Irene, seemed taken aback slightly, by the directness of the question, and Tory gave her an apologetic smile.

'Sorry,' she said, 'I'm always being told off for demanding answers. Why don't I tell you about us, instead. Would that be better?'

Irene relaxed. 'Much, thank you. I've met Gwenna, she seems very nice.'

'She is. But,' Tory went on solemnly, 'and this is a very serious warning, don't ever call her Gwen.'

'Why, what will she do?' Irene looked mildly alarmed.

Tory grinned. 'She'll *almost* roll her eyes, and she'll correct you very politely, but my word you'll feel as if you've just dug up her prize-winning rose bush.'

Irene laughed aloud at that. 'Noted. What about this Bertie person I've heard about?'

'I was a little bit scared of her at first,' Tory confessed. 'She came into our first lesson late, and we already knew she'd refused her place in the dorm, so we didn't know anything about her.

We thought she might be the most awful snob, and only taking lessons to impress her society friends.'

'Society friends?'

'Her family owns Fox Bay Hotel, have you heard of it?'

Irene put down her chocolate and stared at her. 'The place where that movie star nearly died?'

'That's the place. Daisy Conrad and Freddie Wishart were both staying there at the time, they get lots of Hollywood types now.'

'And Bertie's family *owns* it?'

Tory nodded. 'But you needn't worry, she's not at all superior. Bright as they come, and *very* keen flyer. Not at all snobbish.'

'Why doesn't she want to stay in the dorm? Gwenna was awfully vague about that.'

'She didn't feel it was her place to tell you, but about a year ago, Bertie was riding her motorcycle home, from a race that *should* have started her off with a fantastic career. It was what she was desperate to do, you see, and she'd been spotted by another racer, who was putting a touring team together.'

'What happened?'

'A dog ran out in front of her, and she crashed trying to avoid it. She broke her leg and was out all night in the rain, and the leg got infected so she had to have it taken off just below the knee.'

Irene paled. 'How awful.'

'She was devastated, of course. Now, though, she has a metal prosthetic, and has been so determined to make the best of things, you'd hardly know it. Unless she's really tired, then she uses a stick.'

'But she didn't want you and Gwenna to know about it?'

'Not at first. She wanted to be seen as just the same as everyone else, so she kept it all under her hat and took a room at the flats at the top of town. But tonight we persuaded her to move in after all, so she's joining us on Saturday. You'll meet her at teatime tomorrow.'

'She sounds like quite the character. And what about you? Where are you from?'

'I was born here, moved away after the war and spent some time in London, and now I'm back.' Tory shrugged. 'Nothing more to tell really. My grandparents used to own the farm down the hill.'

'What about family? Brothers and sisters?'

'Just two brothers now, one was killed in action.'

'Oh.' Irene looked momentarily unsure what to say. 'I'm really sorry.'

'Thanks.' It was always hard to say those words, *killed in action*, as if Joseph – with his wide grin, his left-handed awkwardness, and his love of swimming – had never been more than a foot-note in the town's records. 'Now it's your turn,' she added, with determined brightness.

Irene pursed her lips. 'Okay, I'm from Wolverhampton, I have one sister, no brothers, and, to answer your question properly, I came to Cornwall because I love the countryside. Horses, in particular.'

'Horses!' Tory brightened. 'Me too! I used to be allowed to ride a horse who was stabled on our farm, but his owner moved away recently.'

'I learned to ride when I was little,' Irene said, 'but it's years since I had the chance. I was hoping there might be a riding school somewhere nearby, so I could refresh my lessons.'

Tory gave her an apologetic shrug. 'Not that I know of, sorry. Most people in the country tend to learn from a very young age, and on local farms, but so many horses were taken for the army anyway. Bill was too old by then, thank goodness, so Tristan was able to keep him, and he let me and his sister ride him.'

'Are you very good, then?'

'Good enough.' Tory frowned into her nearly-empty mug. 'Well, Gwenna's gone to bed early to prepare for her re-test tomorrow, so—'

'Re-test?'

'Re-re-test really. She failed her advanced instruments twice, poor thing. Always seems to just miss the mark, somehow, even though she's brighter than just about everyone.'

Irene frowned. 'That's rotten.'

'We all feel desperately sorry for her,' Tory agreed. 'She's keener than everyone too, except Bertie of course, but her instructor just won't give her a chance to get up where she wants to be.'

'Top of the class?'

Tory blinked in surprise. 'The sky.'

'Ah. Who's her instructor?'

'Bloke called Barry Hocking. Nice as pie, but absolutely dead set on following the rules, and refuses to even take Gwenna up on a flight, never mind let her take over.'

Before Tory could say anything further the door opened to admit two instructors, and she grinned at Irene and blew an exaggerated sigh of relief that neither of them was Hocking, then swirled the last of her chocolate around her mug and drank it down.

'I'm off to see if I can get some sleep. Are you ready to turn in?'

'In a little while, I still have half my drink left. Leave your mug, I'll wash it.'

'Thanks. Goodnight then, I'll see you bright and breezy in the morning.'

She left Irene to finish her drink, and as she collected her washbag from the dorm and headed towards the bathroom she couldn't help wondering whether the new girl hoped to catch the eye of a friendly instructor, and thus avoid Gwenna's fate. She'd be in for a rude awakening if so.

CHAPTER THREE

Bertie chanted to herself the way she always did, as the mechanics lifted the aircraft's tail around so it faced into the light summer wind ready for taxiing: *Don't look at the controls, look at the horizon.* The Sopwith Camel rumbled across the grass, and Bertie eased the stick forward and felt the tail lift slightly, putting her in position for what she hoped would be a perfect take-off. With her gaze fixed on the distant outline of the Cliffside Fort Hotel, she imagined her instructor's voice as clearly as if Jude had already spoken: *Right rudder, Bertie; she's not like the Avro . . .*

Bertie felt the tail lift, and she eased back slowly on the stick until the bumping beneath the wheels stopped; they were climbing now, and there was that sense of weightless freedom again, the one for which she found herself living during every in-between moment, when everyday life took over.

A pat on her shoulder from Jude told her the take-off was everything it should have been, and although she hadn't needed the confirmation, she acknowledged it with a smile of pride. But now came the real test; Joey, the Camel, was a dream to taxi and get airborne, but had a tendency to climb too fast if she was allowed to. Bertie held the stick steady, keeping her in check until they levelled out at around three thousand feet, and then banked right and settled into their usual flight pattern, heading up the coast.

For a while she enjoyed the opportunity to simply sit there and soak up the feeling of being utterly disconnected from everything humdrum and routine that was still going on far below her. Who had the time, or capacity, to care about whether there were trousers pressed for tomorrow, or whether the bath had been left clean? But before long Jude began giving her instructions through her headset; climbing turns, which came naturally enough now, and Jude had no need to comment, but then came time for the most recent lesson: vertical turns.

Bertie's concentration was complete then, all pleasure was pushed to the back of her mind as she worked right and left rudder, and made minute adjustments to the control stick. Her shortened right leg had become attuned to feeling the pressure in a different way than her left foot, and now she barely noticed it as the plane dipped and turned under her command, then climbed and banked again. The blood pumped fast and hot through her veins, heavily laced with adrenalin as she prayed the engine wouldn't stutter and stall, potentially sending them into a spin.

Jude barked instructions throughout, in her familiar Leeds accent. 'Change to left rudder now. Smoothly! Stick back ... laterally central ... Good! Don't let the nose drop. Three-quarter left.'

When they had gone through the manoeuvres several times, Jude told her to check the fuel and turn back. Bertie gently banked Joey and they levelled out to begin their return to the airfield. They were chuntering over Pencarrack Moor, and Bertie was once more allowing herself to simply enjoy the sensation of flying, when her attention was arrested by something glinting in the bracken near Tyndall's Folly. She squinted down as they flew over, and saw the sunlight had hit the glass of one of the airfield's vans which was parked near the folly with its back open.

'Pull up!' Jude bellowed, out of nowhere. 'Climb to the left!'

Bertie gasped and instinctively put pressure on the rudder, pulling back on the stick at the same time. The Camel went into a steep climb, rolling to the left, and Bertie had a moment's panic as she wondered if she'd allowed her concentration lapse to the point that she'd come close to hitting the church steeple. She brought Joey level again, and dabbed a heavy drop of sweat off her eyebrow with her glove, before looking down. She was nowhere near the church.

'Was that a test?' she demanded, her heartbeat still thudding in her ears.

Jude's voice was bland through her headset. 'Take us down.'

Bertie chided herself under her breath, certain now that Jude had guessed her attention had been wandering. She hoped it wouldn't result in the same restrictions poor Gwenna was under; she didn't fancy re-sitting tests just for the sake of it. She took particular care over her landing, just in case, and made an extra circuit to ensure she was at around sixty miles per hour before she glided in and cut the engine, sitting the Camel down in a passable three-point-landing with only a tiny bump. She pushed the stick forward and pulled it back, breathing a sigh of relief as the bounce evened out and they came to a stop in almost the right place.

Jude patted her shoulder again and climbed out, and Bertie

joined her. 'I wasn't wool-gathering,' she began as she removed her headset, but Jude raised her hand.

'I know you weren't, you never do. Not to the extent where you'd be a danger anyway.' She looked around them, as she took her helmet off and stuffed her gloves into it. 'You did alright today. Bit heavy on the left rudder, and a bit more finesse wanted on the approach, but that'll come.'

'Thank you. I'll put more work into it.'

'How do you feel about the new manoeuvres?'

Bertie considered blurting out what she thought Jude wanted to hear, but just stopped herself; her instructor wouldn't be fooled by over-enthusiasm, she was far too sharp. 'They'll take a bit of getting used to,' she said instead. 'The risk of stalling is a lot higher.'

'And the thought of silence up there still makes you feel a little bit sick, I reckon?'

Bertie's insides rolled at the words. 'Very.'

'Good. That means you'll be more careful.' Jude unwrapped her scarf. 'Are you busy tomorrow?'

'I'm moving into the dorm on the base.'

'Do that tonight.' Jude strode into the office, beckoning Bertie to follow. 'I want you to meet me tomorrow instead, I have something to discuss with you.'

'But Tory's going to drive me—'

'Can't she do it tonight?' Jude looked at her, and, as always, Bertie found it hard to argue with that stare.

She shrugged. 'I can ask.'

'Good. Now then.' Jude searched the desk until she found a scrap of paper, and took up a stub of a thick pencil to scribble on it. 'We'll be spending some time here.'

Bertie took the paper, and frowned. 'This is just co-ordinates.'

'Call it a part of the lesson.' Jude looked at her again, unblinking. 'Well, go on then, I've got a set of plugs to clean.'

'I don't have a car,' Bertie said. 'How do I get there?'

'How do you know it's not five minutes' walk away?'

Bertie goldfished for a moment, then shook her head. 'Is it?'

'No, it's a fair way out, on Bodmin Moor, and that's all I'm telling you. Wait outside the gates here at nine. Off you go!' Jude made a shooing gesture. 'Unless you want to clean the plugs for me?'

Bertie shook her head again. 'It turns out I have some moving to do,' she pointed out, and Jude's face at last broke into a grin.

'Good girl.'

Tory proved more than happy to bring the Tourer down to the holiday flats and help load Bertie's things into it. It was gratifying how keen the girls were for Bertie to move in, and Bertie herself was starting to look forward to it too, although, like her new manoeuvres, it would take a little adjustment; apart from a few days last Christmas, when Tory had come to stay at Fox Bay, she hadn't shared sleeping arrangements since she'd been in hospital. But Tory's enthusiasm helped dispel the nervousness, and together they made short work of packing Bertie's things into a few boxes borrowed from the air base kitchens.

'Have you worked out where Jude's taking you tomorrow?' Tory asked, as she followed Bertie out with the last box.

'No, just somewhere on the moors. It looks as if it's part of orientation, so she'll probably want me to navigate. I'd better make sure I check the details before she picks me up in the morning.'

'Make sure you tell me all,' Tory said with a faintly worried look. 'Bowden will probably be doing the same with me, at some point.'

'Well, if he does he's not likely to be taking you to the same place, not when he knows we all talk to each other.'

'Bit rough doing it on a Saturday though,' Tory grumbled, putting the box on the back seat of her car. 'We're supposed to have Saturdays off now.'

'Unlike Irene. I do feel sorry for her, so much to take in, and that classroom will have been like an oven today. I remember how dozy we were on our first afternoon, and that was in the spring.'

'It'll be unbearable, poor things.' Tory surveyed the array of bags and boxes in the car. 'Are you sure that's it?'

'All of it. I told you, I don't have that much.'

'Right, let's get you settled in. Then we can all go to the pub and have a nice drink.'

Bertie was exhausted, and opened her mouth to decline, but she didn't like the thought of everyone else bonding, and leaving her on the outside; it would be just like her early days in Caernoweth all over again. So instead she smiled brightly. 'Perfect! Let's get on with it then.'

She was relieved, therefore, when the new girl, as polite and pleasant as she seemed, shook her head. 'I'm too tired to be much company,' she said, 'today has really taken it out of me. And I have to do it all again tomorrow, unlike you lucky things.'

'Not so lucky for Bertie,' Tory said with a laugh. 'She's got to do orientation training out on the moors tomorrow.'

'Which means a drink isn't really a good idea for me either,' Bertie said, with a decent show of regret. 'I'll go to the training room and look at the maps, instead.'

'Oh, Irene has some of those,' Tory blurted, then flushed when the new girl turned to her. 'I'm sorry, I saw them yesterday, they were just lying on your table.' She added this last as if it excused her peeking, and Irene smiled and shrugged, but Bertie thought she still looked a bit put out.

'The perils of communal living, I'm afraid,' she said, to try and take the edge off the atmosphere. 'I'll have to get used to it, as well.'

'I don't mind,' Irene said. 'You're welcome to borrow my maps if you like.'

'Thank you. I'll use the classroom ones though,' Bertie said. 'They're military ones, so they've got a lot of other information on them that I might need.'

'It's just about dinner time,' Gwenna ventured, into the silence that followed. 'Shall we go in?'

'Oh!' Bertie remembered. 'How was the test?'

Gwenna pulled a face. 'I feel as if I did alright, but then I always do until the results come back, and there I am. Close, but not close enough.' She sighed. 'I'll just have to wait until tomorrow to see if I've finally scored enough. I've asked Lieutenant Bowden to let me see the actual paper, and not just tell me the mark, but he says it wouldn't be fair to give me the chance to revise one particular aspect.'

'That's rotten,' Irene sympathised as they made their way to the canteen.

'Barry is saving them for me though, so I can see them all once I've passed.'

'That's decent of him.' Bertie saw a troubled look playing about Irene's face, and felt bad. 'Don't let this worry you,' she said quickly. 'There's plenty of time before your first tests.'

'Do you know yet who your instructor will be?' Tory asked.

Irene shook her head. 'Not until the end of the first full week.'

'Well, hopefully you'll get someone other than Bowden,' Tory said, and Bertie gave her a warning look. 'I just mean he's a bit strict,' Tory added quickly, 'not that he's mean or anything. None of them are *mean*. Exactly. Oh, except for Jude, making you do orientation in the middle of nowhere, on a Saturday.' She grinned at Bertie. 'I'll think of you while I'm enjoying the beach tomorrow.' She linked her arm through Irene's, clearly startling the new girl. 'Come on, we might still get a seat by the window.'

The following morning, armed with copies of maps from the classroom, Bertie waited for Jude by the perimeter gate. She and her former fiancé, Jowan Nancarrow, had ridden their motorcycles all over the place when they'd been younger, exploring and enjoying their freedom, but she had gleaned, from the coordinates and the maps, that she was going somewhere new. She was wearing her stoutest boots, and at the last minute had decided to bring her stick too; Bodmin Moor was filled with hidden and half-hidden dangers, ready to trap the unwary or over-confident, especially those unfamiliar with the area.

There was no sign of Jude yet. Bertie peered down the road towards Pencarrack, where her instructor lived, but there were no vehicles moving along it. Behind her she heard a low, phutting sound that made her stomach lurch as it always did these days: a motorcycle was approaching slowly, from the Caernoweth road. She flexed her fingers to stop them from tightening into fists, and made herself turn and look.

It was stupid to feel like this, she knew it; she'd been riding from the age of thirteen, and on the day of the accident she'd just ridden the fastest race of her life. But one low-speed slide to avoid an excited dog, and she had lost her leg, and very nearly her life. Countless near-misses, just one serious fall, and still the sound of a bike made her feel sick. Stupid.

As the bike, a BSA, came closer, she recognised its rider and waved. 'Tommy!'

He pulled to a stop beside her and unclipped a spare helmet. 'Hop on.'

Bertie's smile dropped away and she took a step back. 'I, I can't,' she said, glad she had an excuse. 'Jude's picking me up any minute for orienteering practice.'

'No she isn't. I'm taking you to her.'

Bertie's mouth dried. 'What?' she managed, and it came out as little more than a whisper.

'She asked me to take you.' He climbed off and came over to her, the spare helmet still in his hands. 'She knows,' he said gently. 'We both do.'

'Knows what?'

'How this will make you feel.'

'Do you?' She shook her head. 'I don't think so.'

Tommy touched her arm. 'You live for flying, don't you? You haven't let what happened to Xander put you off.'

Bertie gave him a betrayed look; Xander Nicholls had been a good friend to them both, albeit separately, and his death during a training flight had hit her with a force of grief she hadn't felt since losing her father ten years before. 'Don't,' she said. 'Perhaps you don't really understand what he meant to me, but—'

'Of course I understand. You know I do. He loved and respected you, valued your friendship, and never stopped talking about the way you rode, even though he only saw you do it once.'

'Then don't use him like that. It's cruel.'

He looked chastened. 'I don't mean it to be. I just meant to remind you that your accident, as dreadful as the consequences were, shouldn't blot out the memory of what came before it. The love of it.'

Bertie chewed at the inside of her cheek, looking at the BSA and trying to fight down the panic that kept rising. For months after the accident she hadn't even been able to look at her formerly cherished Scott Flying Squirrel without feeling queasy; now she was expected to simply climb back on – and on the pillion seat, moreover, where she had absolutely no control whatsoever – and put all that horror behind her.

'Well?' Tommy said quietly, proffering the spare helmet once again.

'How long will it take to get there, by road?'

'Not long.'

'That doesn't tell me much.' Bertie thought about Jude's belief in her, and Tommy's, and then she thought about Xander. He'd been such a joyous soul; throwing himself into everything with gusto; laughing his way through social gaffes, and making everyone else laugh with him. He and his sister Lynette had together pulled Bertie through the most horrific time of her life, and she thought about what he'd say now if he saw her dithering about a few miles with an experienced rider. *Get on with it, Bertram, you idiot! You've only got to sit there!*

Before she had time to change her mind she reached out and took the spare helmet from Tommy's hand. 'Come on then.'

She waited for Tommy to settle into the slightly lower front saddle, and then climbed on behind him, putting her stick upright between them to keep it clear of the wheel. She settled her false foot onto the peg with her hand, and felt her stomach disappear as Tommy raised his knee in preparation for kick-starting the machine, but the moment the engine spluttered to life under his boot she felt her muscles relax. The rattly single-cylinder engine was totally different to the smoother sound of the Squirrel, and when they pulled away she could feel the difference in the handling even though she wasn't riding. As the road melted away beneath the wheels she realised she was leaning into the bends without thinking about it.

After a few minutes, she stopped watching the hedgerows for emerging dogs or sheep, and began to look around her, her hands resting on her thighs instead of gripping the bar either side of the small rear saddle. With Tommy bending low over the tank, and his lower position leaving her exposed, the wind buffeted her in her seat, but leaning into it made her feel a little more as she had in the riding seat of her own bike; more in touch with every movement, and almost as if she had some control after all.

They covered the distance between Caernoweth and the place on Bodmin Moor, where Jude waited, in a little over half an hour by Bertie's reckoning. When they turned off the road and onto the grassland she was reminded of those long moorland rides with Jowan; the bumps and tuffets felt familiar beneath the wheels, and she found her movements compensating, again without conscious thought. Her relief had soon melted into the simple joy of remembering what she had loved so much about riding, and how she had made it through countless spills and scrapes during her learning weeks without even thinking of giving up. The accident had cloaked those happy memories with new fear, and although she knew it was understandable, she welcomed their return with a much-lightened spirit.

It didn't take long to see why Jude had arranged to meet her out here. They had passed a village a mile or so back, and now came out onto the nearest thing she'd seen to a flat plain; a rare sight out here, and in the distance was the familiar outline of Joey the Camel. This must be one of the few places Jude could land out here, but it didn't explain why she'd had to come by air; if they were going to fly today they could have taken off from Caernoweth as usual.

Tommy pulled up beside the Camel, and Jude, who'd been waiting in the cockpit, jumped down. Her gaze went from Tommy to Bertie, questioning, and Bertie grinned.

'I'm fine. Better than fine, actually. I took a little persuading, but I'm glad you fixed this up for me. Thank you.'

Jude visibly relaxed. 'Good. Now, we have something important to talk about. Thanks, Tommy, you can buzz off now, and don't come back until dinner time.'

Tommy saluted and kicked the BSA into life again, and as he rode away Bertie frowned.

'What's he going to do until dinner time? Surely he's not going all the way back to the base?'

'He'll go and see his family, they live nearby. That's why I knew he'd be happy to bring you out here.'

'Oh, that village we passed? The one with the burned-down mill?'

'That's the one.' Jude seemed to be sizing Bertie up, and there seemed to be some doubt, suddenly, that she was doing the right thing. 'I meant it when I said it was important,' she said at length. 'It's also absolutely between the two of us. And Tommy of course. Whether you agree with my proposal or not, this *must* stay secret. Understand?'

Bertie's curiosity grew. 'Of course.'

'Don't just say *of course*, and then go running back to your friends and tell them,' Jude cautioned, and Bertie bristled.

'If you think I'm that sort of person, perhaps you shouldn't be talking to me at all.'

Jude looked at her steadily for a moment. 'Right, how do you feel your lessons have been going?'

'Apart from the bumpy landing yesterday, I think they're going well.' Bertie spoke cautiously despite the confident words; she had the sinking feeling that she was about to be told she needed extra lessons.

But Jude waved a dismissive hand. 'You pulled out of that, and set her down square. You did well. So well, in fact, that I think it's time.'

'Time for what?'

'To learn some ... different manoeuvres. More challenging ones.'

Bertie caught her breath. 'You mean *combat* flying?'

'That's exactly what I mean.'

'Already?'

Jude shrugged. 'You've got the instinct. I knew you had that, even before you arrived.'

'Xander again, I suppose?'

'Instructors have a lot of time to talk to their pupils in this job. He was one of my best students, and you were one of his favourite subjects.' Jude's expression flickered into melancholy for a moment, then she shook it away. 'You yourself said it was what you wanted, isn't that still the case?'

Earlier in the year she had hinted that there was more to flying fighter planes than transporting them around the country, and

Bertie had learned that she'd flown incognito during the war and had protected parts of the coast against Zeppelin raids. She herself had indicated that she wanted to learn everything too, in time, but had been under the impression that would be months away, even years. She was too stunned to speak, and could only stare at the ground, trying to work out whether she was more excited at the thought, or terrified.

'Well?' Jude took out her cigarette case and lighter. 'What do you think?'

'How would we get it past Flight Lieutenant Bowden? Only the men are supposed to be doing military training.'

'And them not for a good while yet,' Jude said, with an unmistakeably mischievous glint in her eyes as she flicked her lighter. 'How'd you like to be the first, even if you can't tell anyone?'

She turned her back to the breeze and sheltered the flame, and Bertie used the time to consider her response. After the triumph of overcoming her terror of motorcycles, her blood was still running fast through her veins, and the blue August sky just seemed to invite further adventure. She tried to imagine being up there and performing evasive rolls and dives, and imaginary target practice, and, much the same way as she had grabbed the spare helmet from Tommy, she now heard herself saying, 'Yes.'

Jude turned back, drawing on her cigarette, and nodded as she blew out the smoke. 'Good.'

'We're not …' Bertie hesitated. 'We're not going to start today, are we?'

'You're not, no. But you're coming up with me while I show you how it's done.'

*

Later, a somewhat dizzy Bertie slid down from the wing and back onto solid ground. She felt terrified, and elated, and if her heart had been pounding as she'd climbed onto the back of Tommy's BSA, it now felt as if she should have heard it even over Joey's engine.

Jude had ensured she was well strapped in, and then taken them up to a height of nearly four thousand feet before going into a breath-stealing series of rolls, spins, loops, and vertical dives . . . This last had Bertie clutching at her harness, determined to keep her eyes open, but feeling the almost overwhelming urge to close them until it was all over. The fact that Jude shut the engine off to perform some of these manoeuvres, only bringing it back midway through a roll or spin, made the whole thing seem surreal, and Bertie wondered how she'd ever find the confidence to do such a thing.

But above everything else, as she looked back at Joey now sitting silent on the grass as if nothing had happened, there was exhilaration. Part of her desperately wanted to try something today, while the memory was bright in her mind, but Jude needed her remaining fuel to get safely back to the base. Besides, Bertie had a lot of studying to do before she'd be able to try any of it; Jude had barely explained anything as she flew, she'd just let the sensation take over.

'Well?' Jude asked, over the sound of Tommy's timely return. 'What do you think? Are you still interested?'

'I hope all that wasn't a way of trying to frighten me out of it.'

Jude laughed. 'Just as if! It was to show you what's possible, and that you don't need to be a man to be able to do it. Because when you and your friends see your male classmates begin their combat training, that's going to be what you're told.'

'I'm more than interested.' Bertie looked over to where the BSA was phutting noisily to a stop. 'How much does Tommy know about this?'

'All of it.' Jude tucked her scarf in, in readiness for flying back to the coast. 'Young Tommy Ash and I go back quite a while, I trust him. You'll have to think of a good excuse to tell your friends though.' She handed Bertie her stick and walked back to the Camel. 'I mean it,' she called back over her shoulder, 'you must keep this between us or I'll lose my job, and you'll lose your place on the course.'

'I will.'

Bertie made her careful way over to meet Tommy, who grinned at her. 'I saw what she was doing up there,' he said. 'Surprised you're not being sick into a mine shaft somewhere. I would be.'

Bertie laughed. 'I was completely terrified, but I can't wait to start.' She wrapped her scarf over her mouth and tucked it back inside her coat.

Tommy kicked the bike into life and lifted his voice over the engine. 'Are you up to a little detour before we go back?'

'Where?'

Tommy pointed in the direction of the distant village. 'Lynher Mill. It's where I grew up, and I'd love to show you around.' He sounded a little hesitant now, as if shy of her reply, but Bertie nodded and took her seat behind him.

'Show me everything,' she said. 'After all, you know everything about me now.'

'Not quite.' He turned in the saddle, and searched her face soberly for a moment. 'But I'd like to.'

Bertie felt a slow smile start inside her, and although her mouth was covered by her scarf, she knew it was showing in her eyes, simply by the way it was reflected in his. Her heart expanded a little bit, allowing the affection of friendship a little more room to grow, and this time when the bike began to move across the grass, she ignored the rail and wrapped her arms around his waist instead.

CHAPTER FOUR

Gwenna pushed open the back door of her home, bracing herself to tell her father that, once again, she had failed her second instruments test. Her mother was tying her apron, ready to take over in the shop, and she took one look at Gwenna's face before letting out a heavy sigh.

'Oh, love. How soon can you re-take it?'

'I actually did it yesterday,' Gwenna hung her bag on the back of a kitchen chair, 'but I won't get the result until Monday.'

'Do you think you've done it this time?'

'I thought I'd done it *last* time,' Gwenna pointed out. 'I still don't know where I went wrong.'

Her father came through from the shop and gave Gwenna a tired smile, having evidently guessed by her gloomy expression that she was not following in his illustrious footsteps; the fact that he didn't look the slightest bit surprised was even more upsetting.

'She's already re-taken it,' her mother said quickly, before he could say anything.

'Good.' Jonas merely nodded; the questions would come later. 'Here to help with the stocktake, then?'

'If you need it,' Gwenna returned dutifully. He didn't like to be reminded that he wasn't as physically strong as he'd been as a young man. The Distinguished Flying Cross had afforded him local acclaim, and a place in military history, but it didn't make up for the injuries he'd sustained in the earning of it. His back and neck still pained him badly, and more than once Gwenna had seen him stiffen and turn pale, before throwing a big smile her way and making some comment to distract her.

'She'll be in d'rectly, Jonas,' Rachel said, 'you go back in the shop for a bit. Gwenna, let's get you a cuppa before you and your dad start in the storeroom.'

Over a cup of tea in her parents' bright kitchen, Gwenna studied her mother carefully. Rachel Rosdew had always been youthful in her outlook, and that was reflected in her manner and her appearance, but today she looked tired, tight around the eyes, and her speech had an unfamiliar jerkiness about it, as if she had to keep pulling her train of thought back onto the right track before she spoke.

'Is the shop doing alright?' Gwenna asked.

'It's fine.'

'Then what's the matter? You look as if you haven't slept in days.'

Rachel rubbed her eyes with her free hand. 'It's so hot at night. And the light comes in at the window before five o'clock this time of year, there's no sleeping after that.'

Gwenna subsided, but she wasn't convinced. Her parents had been using that same bedroom since they'd moved here; nothing had altered, not even the curtains. She changed the subject. 'There's a new girl in our dorm. Irene, she's called. Seems very nice, but a bit secretive.'

'Give her a chance,' Rachel said, sounding uncharacteristically irritated as she unknowingly echoed Tory's reaction. 'Not every-one wants to share their life the moment they meet someone.'

Gwenna fell silent, chastened, and sipped at her tea. After an awkward silence, conversation started up again but was so stilted she was actually glad when her father came back out from the shop.

'Are you ready yet?'

'Coming.' Gwenna stood up, and noticed how her mother avoided looking at her father; at first she thought they must have had a row about something, but Jonas looked equally at sea, as he picked up his ledger and waited for Gwenna to rinse her cup.

'Shop, love,' he reminded his wife gently.

She finally looked up. 'I'll hear if someone comes in! You two go on and get started.'

Gwenna followed her father to the storeroom down the hall, and took the ledger he passed back to her as he unlocked the door to the large stockroom. She chewed the end of her pen, waiting for the questions that would inevitably come from the former air ace. They did.

Did you calculate using indicated *airspeed, and specify IAS on the paper? Are you* sure *you calculated correctly for wind resistance and the difference it could make? What else did they ask?*

She answered in as much detail as she could remember, and he nodded and sighed. 'I'm sure you'll be fine this time.'

'It's so hard seeing Bertie and Tory going up,' she said. 'And today Bertie's even going out on the moors, for orienteering with Jude Singleton.'

'She's still around then, is she?'

'Bertie?'

'Singleton!' Jonas shook his head. 'She was quite the legend up north during the war, I can't believe we've not met since she came down here. Doesn't even come into the shop. She must have heard of me, has she never even asked?'

Gwenna shook her head, feeling a stab of guilt for the look of disappointment on her father's face, but it was hardly her fault. 'I don't see her much,' she said, almost by way of an apology. 'She comes in for the lessons, and to do maintenance on her Camel, but she doesn't spend much time on the base apart from that. None of them do, except Bowden, and that's only because he takes classroom instruction as well.'

'Haven't *you* told her who I am?'

'I've never even spoken to her!' Gwenna was growing irritated now, a rare thing when she was talking to her father. 'Besides, it would sound too much like I'm trying to use your name to get along. At the moment that's the worst thing I could do.'

Jonas pursed his lips, then shrugged. 'I suppose.' He reverted to his former brisk tone. 'Right, let's get this done then. Picked up the stock yesterday, so we've plenty to check through.'

Gwenna was kept busy for a while counting tins of stew and corned beef, though her mind kept wandering and she kept having to re-count and amend her totals. Eventually, an exasperated Jonas took the ledger off her and gave her his notebook instead.

'You're neither use nor ornament today, girl. Go up and check the shelf stock instead, will you?'

Gwenna gave him an apologetic smile, and went back up the passageway to the shop. She paused with one hand on the latch, hearing the familiar Irish accent of her mother's best friend on the other side of the door, but pitched low as if they were engaged in a private discussion. She was about to leave them to it, when Anna Penhaligon spoke again.

'You can tell me though, love. What's wrong?'

Gwenna stepped towards the door again, and leaned close.

'I think ...' Her mother gave an audible sigh. 'No, I'm sure, actually. Jonas has a lover.'

Gwenna's skin seemed to shrink onto her bones, and she looked quickly down the passageway, but the storeroom door remained closed.

'What makes you think that?' Anna's voice was curious but nothing more, and Gwenna frowned. Why wasn't she surprised?

'Just his manner,' Rachel said. 'He's being ... evasive about where he goes. He's distracted, he's short-tempered sometimes, too. As if I irritate him.'

That didn't sound conclusive at all though, and it seemed Anna felt the same. 'But you've not *seen* him with anyone?'

'No. And I can't think who it might be, either. It's not likely to be anyone in town, that's too risky.'

'Have you talked to him about it?'

'Of course not! You're the first person I've ... What have you just thought of?'

'Nothing. Why?'

'Come on, Anna! We've been friends for over ten years now, I know when you're hiding something. Do *you* know who might have caught his eye?'

There was a long pause, and Gwenna heard her oblivious father moving about in the storeroom. It was an unthinkable accusation to level at him, and she felt the bite of anger towards her mother and Anna, both of whom should surely know better.

'You're not to take this as gospel,' Anna said slowly, her voice dropping even further, so that now Gwenna had to press her ear to the door, 'and you're certainly not to go charging off and confronting anyone.'

'I won't.' Rachel sounded uneasy. 'Out with it, then.'

'There's this woman who used to live down the hill, at Hawthorn Cottage: Nancy Gilbert, she's called. She was a widow when I knew her, with four children, but she up and left the poor mites with her parents at Priddy Farm, just before the war.'

Gwenna's heart began to beat uncomfortably fast, and she wiped a suddenly sweating hand on her overall.

'And where is she now?' Rachel wanted to know.

'Well . . . I heard someone say they thought they'd seen her last week, up at Pencarrack.'

Rachel's voice had thickened. 'What makes you think Jonas would be interested in a widow with four children?'

Gwenna felt like shouting, *He wouldn't!*

'They're grown up and out on their own,' Anna pointed out, 'not that it matters. And sadly there are only three now; the middle boy didn't make it back from France. But to be honest, it might be more that *she's* interested in *him,* given her past.'

That sounded more palatable to the listening Gwenna, who couldn't bring herself to believe her father would prove unfaithful to his vows. He loved his wife, any fool could see that.

'What about her past?' Rachel wanted to know.

'She carried on with my cousin Keir for a while, and she did have a bit of a fancy for Matthew, too, at one time. He lived at Hawthorn Cottage before her, and she would keep on at him to come and sort things out for her. Rattling roof tiles, broken gates, that sort of thing.'

'Matthew and Jonas don't look a bit alike though,' Rachel pointed out. 'They're as different as two men can be, not just in height, but in colouring too. Though Jonas isn't so dark as he once was.'

'They're both nice-looking,' Anna said, 'and both popular, which was always a draw for Nancy. Keir was new in town, so he was a novelty, and besides everything else your Jonas is famous.'

'He's just a grocer now,' Rachel said bluntly, and Gwenna flinched, glad her father couldn't hear.

'So she likes to be seen with popular men then?'

'The thing is,' Anna began, then stopped. 'I don't think it's my place to be spreading tales, though.'

'This isn't spreading tales, Anna! If—'

The shop door's bell jingled, and the women's conversation switched abruptly onto the upcoming Penworthy Festival, a discussion eagerly joined by the newcomer. Gwenna was about to go in, since it was obvious she'd hear no more hushed conversation today about Tory's mother, but she waited for a minute or two so it wasn't obvious she'd been eavesdropping.

Alice Donithorn had been affectionately known as 'Big Alice' for years, simply to differentiate between herself and the tiny, but extremely vocal, Alice Packem, who had run the Widows Guild until 1913. Formerly a bal maiden at the now closed Wheal Furzy mine, Big Alice had taken up work as a seamstress in Pencarrack, and was apparently being kept busy mending and altering clothes ready for the dance. This conversation provided a lively backdrop to the atmosphere as Gwenna eventually pushed open the door and went in.

'I've come to do the shelves,' she explained, trying

not to scrutinise her mother too closely. 'Hello, Mrs Donithorn, Anna.'

Alice nodded back, while Anna, a handsome woman in her early fifties, with a kind smile, greeted Gwenna warmly and asked about her training. Gwenna brushed over her latest failure by saying, in a confident voice, that she was almost ready to take to the skies again.

'Oh, that reminds me.' Alice turned to Anna. 'How's *your* boy doing up at the flying school?'

Robert Penhaligon, four years younger than Gwenna, had joined the flying school at the same time, having saved up for almost two years to pay the six months' fees. Gwenna knew he was regretting it already, but not whether he'd admitted that to his parents yet.

Anna sighed. 'After all that fuss he made when the school opened, I actually think he'd rather be doing what Matthew does.'

'The fishing, or the writing?'

Anna pulled a face, which made Gwenna smile. 'Give him a pen, and he'll carve it into a hook and throw it in the water.'

Rachel took a pencil from behind her ear as Alice handed her her shopping list. 'So you don't think he'll carry on after the initial training is over, then?'

'I'm fully expecting him to tell Matthew he wants to go back out on the boat with him, now the six months is nearly up. What a waste of money!'

'But will Matthew be pleased?'

Anna's face softened, as it always did when she talked about her husband. 'I'll say. He'll just nod, and maybe ruffle the lad's hair, but he'd hire a brass band to march up and down the street if he could.'

Alice nodded at Gwenna. 'And when are you and that lovely constable getting wed then, Miss Rosdew? Soon be *Mrs Bolitho*, eh?' Before Gwenna could reply, she went on, 'Nice to see him helpin' your pa so much, now you're not here.'

'I am here,' Gwenna pointed out politely, and tapped the notebook with her pen. 'Working, see?'

'Gwenna,' Rachel murmured, and Alice looked embarrassed.

'I din't mean you weren't a help, maid. Just that you've got your new interests now.'

'And Peter's got his own job to do.' Gwenna turned back to the shelf she was checking, but she couldn't help wondering what it was that Peter had been doing; she would have to ask him later. 'If my father needs anyone else to help out full-time, I'm sure he'll be advertising on the board at the civic hall, like everyone else.'

'Perhaps he'll ask Nancy Gilbert,' Rachel said, her voice sounding faraway, even a little dreamlike.

Alice visibly started, and her face clouded. 'There's a name I've not heard in a year or two.'

Anna drew a quick breath, and her fair skin coloured. 'I'm so sorry, Alice. I didn't think.'

'Think what?' Rachel asked. 'She doesn't seem to have been right popular, this Nancy.'

'No, well—'

'She would keep trying to get her hooks into the men,' Alice said, and her face tightened with suppressed grief. 'My Ellen would tell you the same.'

Ellen Garvey, nee Donithorn, had been a cheerful, hard-working soul, and was much missed by everyone in town since her death last Christmas. Those she'd left behind were still raw from her loss, and Alice's own light had noticeably dimmed at the mention of Nancy Gilbert.

'Ellen were happily wed to your cousin,' she said to Anna, her voice harsh now, 'you know that so well as anyone, but she never trusted the widow Gilbert, not one inch. She would have lit the clifftop beacons when that woman left town, if she could.'

'So Nancy's one of that type, is she?' Rachel finished ticking off Alice's purchases, and Gwenna thought the pencil marks looked deeper and blacker the further down the list she went . . . or the longer into the conversation, depending how you looked at it.

'Are you talking about Tory's mother?' she put in casually, and part of her enjoyed the sudden flash of guilt on Anna's face. She didn't mention that she'd seen Nancy with her own eyes, in case she was asked, and forced to admit, how beautiful the woman still was. 'Tory said she'd left her and her brothers when they were just little,' she added.

'Evidently she's back,' Rachel said shortly. 'Anyway, Alice, that'll be eight shillings all in. Shall I put it on your note for Monday?'

'Please,' Alice said. 'I'll come by first thing, as usual.'

Rachel made a note on the list and pinned it to the little stack on the side of the counter. She was clearly now wishing she hadn't brought up the subject of Nancy, and Alice was equally keen to let it drop, so when another customer came in and Anna made her farewells, talk turned once more to the festival.

Gwenna returned to work, and to watching her mother covertly while she did so; there were smiles, passing conversations, and nothing outwardly untoward, but she could still see the tightness around the eyes, and hear it in the voice she knew so well. But her mother was mistaken in her belief, Gwenna was sure of that. Whatever gossip was going around, and no matter how attractive Nancy Gilbert might be, Jonas Rosdew would never stoop to something as sordid as an affair. He was true-hearted and solid, certainly not weak-willed enough to have his head turned by a pretty face and a beckoning finger.

All the same, she couldn't block out the phrase *no smoke without fire*, that kept intruding on her thoughts as she worked in angry silence; something had wafted the smoke in Rachel's direction, whether Jonas was blameless or not, and Gwenna made up her mind to find out what it was.

On Sunday she attended chapel with Peter, and afterwards they walked down to the beach together, as they usually did. They passed Priddy Farm on their way, and Gwenna took her chance to bring the subject up.

'Tory saw her mum the other night,' she said, pausing to lean on the gate. 'Up at the Cliffside Fort. Did you know she was back?'

Peter fidgeted and crossed his arms, one hand tugging at his blond sideburns. 'Yes,' he admitted at length. 'I've seen her.'

'At the shop?'

'What?' He blinked. 'No, why?'

She shrugged. 'Just wondered where you'd seen her.'

'I do a lot of patrolling on foot,' he pointed out, 'and that includes Pencarrack.'

'House, moor, or village?'

75

'Is this an interrogation?' he asked, sounding only half-amused. 'Village, if you must know. Why?'

'Well, Tory was pretty upset, considering Nancy hasn't so much as written to her since she left. I think it'd be only fair if she knew why she's come back after all this time and *still* hasn't come to find her.'

Peter looked sideways at her. He wasn't a tall man, and their faces were on a level thanks to Gwenna's own height, and she noticed how his gaze slipped away again immediately she met it. She frowned. 'When did you see her?'

'Are you actually trying to ask me how long she's been back?'

'I suppose.' Gwenna moved away from the gate and continued down the hill. 'So?'

'I saw her yesterday morning, looking in at the window of the new doctor's house. I told her he hadn't yet moved in, and directed her to Bartholomew instead.'

'Was she ill?'

'She didn't seem to be. Perhaps she was looking for work as his housekeeper.' Peter was clearly bored by the subject, or perhaps just as keen to move away from it as Alice had been yesterday. 'We ought to talk about the wedding,' he said. 'People are always asking me when we're planning to marry.'

'And me.'

'Well?'

'Well what?'

He sighed. 'Shouldn't we at least have a date in mind?'

'Do you have one?' She knew she was being irritating, but she had absolutely no desire to talk about weddings today. She relented, however, for the sake of avoiding another row. 'I'd like a spring wedding, I think. Perhaps next April.'

It was his turn to stop walking. 'April? That's ...' He did a quick count on his fingers. 'Eight months away!'

'Plenty of time for making arrangements,' she said reasonably. 'We don't want to rush things.'

'*You* don't, no. It seems I have no choice in the matter.'

'Why the hurry?' Gwenna was hunting among the brambles for juicy blackberries, and shook a spindly-legged spider off her hand with a little shudder.

'We've been courting a long time now,' Peter said. 'What will your dad say if we keep putting it off?'

Gwenna turned to him in surprise. 'My *dad*? He won't mind in the least.'

'Well, I mean, he's not going to take me seriously as a member of your family if you can't bring yourself to even name the day.'

She couldn't help but laugh. 'Are you marrying me or my dad?'

'Don't be silly.' He changed the subject. 'Tell me how the training's going, then. Did you pass your instruments?'

'I'm still waiting for the result of my re-test,' she said carefully, avoiding mentioning that this was actually her second one. She felt despondency creep over her as she saw the disappointment on his face, and blurted out her secret fear. 'I honestly don't know if I can carry on if I don't pass this time.'

'Of course you must! Even if you don't pass,' he added. 'You've got to stick at it, Gwenna.' Her spirits lifted a little; it seemed she'd misjudged him after all. Then he added, 'Think how your dad would feel if you gave it up now.'

Gwenna blew out a breath. 'That again! Why *are* you so obsessed with what my dad thinks?' He didn't answer, and she added, 'Alice Donithorn says you've been helping him out a lot too, while I'm training.'

He shrugged. 'A bit.'

'Why you though?'

'Because he knows he can count on me.' He frowned, as if he'd had no control over the words. 'I didn't mean that the way it sounded.'

Gwenna looked at the flawless sky. 'Perhaps it's time we went back,' she said, and gave him a pointed look. 'It looks like rain.'

'There's no need to be snippy.'

'I'm sure there are some jobs you could do for Dad on your day off. He'd be *ever* so grateful.'

'Gwenna—'

'Look!' She rounded on him. 'I don't mind at all that you admire him, but I'm starting to question why you're marrying me at all. Is it just so that you can say you belong to the same family as a war hero?'

'And *I'm* starting to wonder why you've got such a thing against him,' Peter countered. He gave her a sidelong look and ignored her suggestion to turn back, so they continued walking down the hill. 'Ever since yesterday evening you've been behaving as if he's knocked an old lady off her bicycle. What on earth's the matter?'

She fought against telling him, then gave in. 'I've heard something, and maybe he's ... just not the man either of us thinks he is.'

'What does that mean?' Peter's voice sharpened.

'Well, you're the policeman; has he been acting strangely that you've noticed?'

'Not in the slightest.'

'That was a very quick answer,' Gwenna said, then sighed. 'Please, Peter, think. Has he been sloping off anywhere when you've gone around to help? Taken advantage of you being there, to . . . perhaps go out and pick up supplies that didn't seem necessary?'

'No!' Peter began tugging goose-grass from the hedgerow, and when Gwenna looked at him she saw his face set in a scowl, but an uneasy one.

'Do you think you might possibly keep a closer eye then?' she persisted.

'For what?' Peter yanked the length of sticky weed free, but instead of sticking it to her jumper, as he might have done a little while ago, to make her laugh, he flung it back into the hedge. 'You're asking me to spy on a man who's done nothing wrong. I do have a full-time job, it's not like I hang around your bloody shop every spare minute! Anyway, how on earth am I supposed to question him if he *does* go out?'

'When do you help him?'

'I just step in now and again after my shift, if he needs a hand shifting stock around. You know how heavy those boxes full of tins are.'

'Well . . . On those times when you've "stepped in", has it ever been because he needed to go somewhere?'

'Like where?' Peter managed to make those two words sound crosser than ever, but Gwenna pushed on.

'Anywhere! I mean, he's not going to be telling you, is he?'

'Telling me what?' Now there was exasperation and a definite lack of patience in his voice. 'This is ridiculous. Your father's a hard-working man, who—'

'Mum thinks he might be seeing another woman.'

For a minute, only the sound of the sea rolling in over shingle punctuated the silence between them, then Peter let out his pent-up breath.

'An affair? *Jonas?*'

'It's not a trivial matter,' Gwenna said coldly, noting the little smile that touched the corners of his mouth. 'You might think it's nothing, but then you're a man too.'

'With Mrs Gilbert?' He gave a short laugh at her surprised look. 'Like you said, I'm a policeman. It's not an enormous leap, from the way you were asking about her.'

'Alright then, yes. That's what An . . . what my mother thinks.'

'What someone's put into her head, more like.' He looked at her shrewdly, no doubt guessing which name she had been about to say. 'Honestly, this town has more gossip than gull droppings! Look, I've never seen Nancy Gilbert at the shop, and I've certainly never been called upon to stand in for your father while he goes off on a jaunt. Now, are we going to enjoy this walk, or shall I take you home?'

'Will you tell me though, if you think he's acting oddly?' For a moment she thought he was going to argue again, but in the end he just shrugged.

'If it'll make you happy, and if it'll keep your father beyond your petty reproaches, then yes, alright, I'll tell you. Not that there'll be anything to tell,' he added. He just couldn't seem to help himself.

Gwenna nodded her thanks. 'I think I'd like to go home anyway. Mum's not herself, and I want to help her as much as I can, before I go back in tomorrow and find out if I've failed that stupid test again.'

'What will you do if you have? You won't really give up, will you?'

'I mustn't upset my father, must I?' she said, with an edge of bitterness to her voice. But she knew that, while Jonas had been the one to push her into the training, it wasn't for his sake that she stayed; she would do everything in her power to get back up into the sky again, even if it meant sitting the test another twenty times. She just didn't think her nerves would stand another disappointment in her pigeonhole tomorrow morning.

CHAPTER FIVE

Late on Sunday evening, as the sun was starting to dip towards the sea, Tory pushed open the gate of Priddy Farm for the first time in twelve years. She felt an odd mixture of nostalgia and bitterness at the sight of the familiar house across the yard, and had to force herself not to turn her back on it and return to a cleaner kind of familiarity. This felt tainted now.

The farmer, Keir Garvey, was kicking the bottom of the barn door to test what looked like a half-rotten plank, and he turned as she approached. A tall, powerfully built man with a shock of black hair, he had the kind of features that weren't generally considered handsome, certainly not in the way Matthew Penhaligon and Jonas Rosdew were, but striking nevertheless, and appealing in their strength. The broad scar that twisted along his jaw gave him a dangerous air that immediately melted away when he smiled. He was smiling now.

'Well well. I heard you were back.' His accent had lost all trace of his years in New Zealand, but still retained those of his Irish ancestry, thanks to living near his cousin Anna.

Tory smiled back, glad she had come after all. 'You recognise me?'

'It's been a while,' he admitted, 'and you've done something different to your hair, but I could never forget that quiet little kid with the solemn face and the impeccable manners.' His smile softened. 'It's nice to see you, Tory.'

'And you.'

'What can I do for you? Come to have a look at the old place?'

'Partly. I wanted to ask a favour of you though.'

'A favour? I'm not sure what I could possibly help you with, but I'll try. Come in.'

Tory followed him into the kitchen. 'I was that sorry to hear about Ellen.'

He turned away, ostensibly to fill the kettle from the tap, but she watched his shoulders come up as he composed himself. 'We're getting by. But never mind us, I hear you've joined the flying school.'

'The Caernoweth clarions are at it again, I see.' Tory smiled, and took a seat at the table as he put cups out. 'Yes, I've joined that mad group of people who can't seem to keep their feet on the ground.'

'Good for you. Those planes saved us more times than I care to remember, over in . . .' He caught himself, and his face lost all expression for a moment. 'I'm sorry, love. I was forgetting about young Joe for a moment.'

'No need to be sorry. It's . . . would have been, his birthday in a week or so. It's nice to remember him.' Tory smiled, then looked around her, to break the moment of stillness.

The kitchen was clean enough, and certainly tidy, but it lacked a homely touch; it was as if the bare minimum had been done in order to make the room liveable. Granted, it was summer, and the hours were long on the farm, but her own memories of this place were peppered with photos in frames; letters stacked in the holder on the mantle; piles of laundry folded on the stool in the corner ... This room looked like the place where people went to change their shoes, and to put food into their bodies simply as fuel. No heart. Ellen Garvey had taken that with her.

'What's this favour then?' Keir asked, putting a jug of milk on the table.

'Actually, there was something else I wanted to ask first.' Tory's resolve faltered; Keir was just beginning to find his way past the devastation of losing his wife, so was now really the best time to bring up his former lover? She took a deep breath and pushed on. 'Do you know why my mother's back?'

Keir's smile turned puzzled, as if he hadn't grasped the question, then it vanished altogether. 'What?'

'She's back,' Tory clarified. 'I saw her the other night, dining with a girl I've never seen before, at the Cliffside Fort.' She saw the scowl begin to pull his eyebrows down, and gave him a faint smile. 'That answers my question. She's not back for you then.'

'Good thing too,' he said shortly, then held up a hand. 'I'm sorry. I shouldn't have said that, she's still your mother.'

'A mother who abandoned four children,' Tory said. 'Don't apologise on my account.' She accepted a cup of tea, and splashed milk into it while she watched him stir sugar into his own. 'Anna knows she's back, I'm surprised she hasn't told you.'

'Probably for the best, after ... You know.' He took a sip, and his manner relaxed again. 'We actually got along fine you know, your ma and me. Even at the end.'

'Why'd you break up then?' From his expression Tory realised it was presumptuous of her to ask, bordering on rude, even, but she felt she had the right to know. 'We all liked you,' she said. 'When you came around to Hawthorne Cottage you never made us feel like we were in the way. And Mum was always happier when she'd seen you. So why did it end?'

'All things do,' he said, his bright blue eyes taking on a faraway look. 'Good, bad, dull, thrilling. All of them.'

'Tell me why you and Mum did, then,' Tory said quietly.

'I heard something about her that wasn't . . . That seemed . . .' He sighed. 'I didn't judge her for it, but I didn't like what it reminded me of about myself, either. It made me think, and I didn't want to think. So I broke it off.' He took another, bigger gulp of tea, and Tory was surprised to see a smile of reminiscence touch his lips as he replaced his cup. 'I'll not forget what she said to me though.' It was almost as if he were speaking to himself now. 'We were out there,' he nodded towards the window, 'in the barn. She listened to my rambling rubbish about why we were over, then she grabbed the front of my shirt, kissed me, and said, *"This isn't the end of us. You only think it is."* Just like that.'

Tory could hear those words, spoken in her mother's low voice, and imagine her laughing eyes while she said it, but she knew the laughter would have been hiding something deeper. Keir had been a big part of the Gilbert family's life for a while, and it was as if a light had gone out in Nancy's life when he'd ended things.

'She was wrong though,' she said, probing. 'It *was* the end. Wasn't it?'

Keir nodded. 'Back then I didn't even know Ellen was the one for me. We argued all the time, although I respected her like mad. She could be a real handful.' He smiled again, and she could see the pain behind it. 'A lot like your mother, in fact.'

'So what was it that you heard? About Mum?'

Keir shook his head. 'It doesn't matter. It's all in the past.'

'Please?'

'It's not my place to repeat gossip, Tory. If your mum wants you to know she'll tell you.'

'Fat chance,' Tory said bitterly. 'She stared right through me when she saw me at the hotel.'

Keir gave her a sympathetic look. 'It's been a long time, and you've done a lot of growing up in those years. You're a young woman now.'

'*You* recognised me,' she pointed out.

'That's different, you know it is,' he reproached gently. 'I already knew you were in town. She's probably heard you moved away, and in a crowded place like that you'd have been the last person she expected to see.'

Tory conceded the point. 'It doesn't matter why you broke up really, I just want to know why she moved away and never got in touch.' She grimaced. 'I'm going to have to go and see her at the hotel, aren't I?'

'What about Gerald and Matty, have they heard anything?'

'I've written to them both.'

'Then yes, if you don't want to wait until you hear back from them, I'd say a face-to-face visit's your best bet.' He hesitated. 'I'm sorry, love. I'm as much in the dark as you are about it all.'

'I know. Thanks though.'

'Was that the favour you wanted to ask? To know about your ma?'

Tory brought herself back into the present. 'No, there was something else. One of the other girls at the base, a new girl, told me she'd like to keep up her horse riding while she's here. I wondered if you had a working horse she could exercise for you now and again. Tristan and Freya took Bill when they moved up to Scotland, didn't they?'

'They did,' Keir nodded regretfully. 'But I've got a couple she can choose from. Or you could both ride them, if you're still interested in that sort of thing yourself.'

Tory brightened. 'I am. Very much so.'

'Come tomorrow then, if you're free, and bring your friend. We can talk about it.'

'I'll drive us down in our lunch break if you'll be around?'

'I'll make sure I'm working nearby.' Keir finished his tea. 'And you can let me know if you've heard anything about Nancy by then.'

'Thank you, I will.' Tory replaced her cup on its saucer and looked out at the yard, which was growing dark now. 'I'll have to start back if I want to get there before they close the kitchen.'

She walked slowly back up the hill though, despite her concerns about supper; her mind was on the seemingly subtle shift in the direction of Keir's reminiscences, from the reason for their break up on to the way Nancy had reacted to it. What could possibly have been so awful that it had made Keir throw his happiness aside like that?

*

There was nothing in Gwenna's pigeonhole on Monday. She'd approached it with a mixture of trepidation and excitement; this time, surely, she had done enough? Discussion with Bertie and Tory last night seemed to indicate she'd provided the same answers as they had done, as far as they remembered. And she knew her stuff, she'd worked through the problems with pinpoint concentration, and checked her answers twice before handing in the paper. She had noted on the paper that she'd calculated the calibrated airspeed correctly . . . There was nothing more she could have done. Yet here she was, her fingers meeting only rough wood when she reached into her pigeonhole for the results. Her spirits plummeted.

'That doesn't mean you've failed,' Tory said sensibly. 'Go and see him before his classes start.'

'I suppose he never promised I'd hear first thing,' Gwenna admitted. She might have prepared herself for disappointment, but deep down she'd been *so* sure that this time would be different. 'I can't go chasing after him, looking all impatient.'

'But if you don't go he might think you don't care anymore, and stop trying to help you.'

Gwenna frowned. It was a fine line, for certain. She turned to Bertie, who was readying herself for her mechanics class. 'Have you still got those maps you took from the classroom?'

Bertie pulled a face. 'Damn. I meant to take them back yesterday. I'll be late now.'

'I'll do it,' Gwenna said quickly, and started back towards the dorm. 'Then I can talk to Bowden, he's sure to know how I did, at least. He might even have the marked paper there ready for delivery.'

'Good idea. The maps are in my dressing table drawer.'

Irene was still in the dorm when Gwenna went back in, reading a letter and still in her indoor clothes. 'Bowden's very hot on punctuality,' Gwenna warned, crossing to Bertie's dresser. 'If you're late he singles you out and makes you feel really stupid. I'll walk with you, if you like,' she added. She opened the desk drawer and took out a slim folder with the classroom number stencilled in ink on its cover. 'I've got to take these back anyway.'

'I can take those for you.'

'No, it's fine. I wanted to speak to someone.'

Irene put away her letter, and hunted about for her shoes. 'You go on,' she said after a moment, looking up and evidently noting Gwenna's growing impatience. 'I'll be a while yet.'

Gwenna shrugged and left her, wondering how she expected to get on, with that attitude. It rankled, somewhat, when she herself was doing everything possible to stay on the good side of the instructors, and to prove how keen she was. Well, if the girl didn't shift herself into gear pretty quickly she'd find herself floundering and she'd have no-one to blame but herself; there were only so many times you could pull someone back from the fire.

Walking in to Flight Lieutenant Bowden's classroom, she was relieved to see both Bowden and Barry Hocking talking quietly together in the otherwise empty room. They both turned to her, naturally surprised to see her come marching in without knocking, and Bowden's heavy eyebrows and military bearing seemed to shout at her without him uttering a word.

'Excuse me,' she said, trying to muster a confident tone while remaining polite, 'I was expecting the result of my test this morning, but there's nothing in my pigeonhole. I wondered if I might pick it up from here, instead.'

'The re-take of the second instruments test,' Hocking reminded Bowden, who was looking blank. 'Friday, alongside those taking it for the first time.'

'Ah yes, I remember. Miss Rosdew.' Bowden turned a frown on her. 'No-one's more surprised than I that you keep failing, but you'll be given the mark when it's available to you, which will be at the same time as the other candidates receive theirs.'

'And when will that be?' Gwenna blurted, all her pent-up tension leaving her in a rush of frustration. 'I honestly don't think I can bear waiting much longer!'

'Your manners do you no credit, Miss Rosdew.' Bowden's voice was hard. 'And impatience is no quality for a pilot, either. Perhaps it's as well you can't grasp the finer points of instrument reading.'

Gwenna's temper flared. 'I understand it perfectly well, and you know it!'

Hocking's eyes widened, but Bowden's narrowed. 'Leave this classroom immediately, Miss Rosdew,' he said coldly. 'I won't have displays of this—'

'Come with me, Gwenna.' Hocking gestured to the door. 'We'll have a little chat outside and let Lieutenant Bowden get ready for his class.'

Gwenna preceded him outside, her spirits sinking again; she could see herself following Robert Penhaligon's example and leaving at the end of the training. Hocking drew her around the side of the classroom block and offered her a cigarette, which she refused. Her nerves were in knots now, wondering what he was going to say, and she was hard-pressed to keep another outburst in check as he faced away from her, lit his own cigarette with maddening calm, and put his lighter away.

Eventually he turned back. 'I've marked your paper already, I just haven't sent it back to Lieutenant Bowden yet.' His smile surfaced at last. 'You've passed, Gwenna. Well done.'

Gwenna stared at him for a moment, not sure she'd heard correctly. 'Passed?' she managed at length. It was on the tip of her tongue to ask why he hadn't said so at the start, before she'd made an ass of herself in front of Bowden, but the sudden thrill of success took over. 'I've *passed!*'

His smile broadened. 'You have,' he confirmed. 'Eighty-three per cent. *Very* well done.'

Gwenna had to stop herself from flinging her arms around him in gratitude. 'Thank you!'

'Don't thank me, you were the one who put the work in. I simply acknowledged it.'

Gwenna's own smile was so wide she felt her face beginning to ache with it. She couldn't wait to tell Tory and Bertie. She looked up at the sky, squinting against the late August sun, and feeling her heart expand with joy at the thought that she'd soon be up there again.

'When can I go up?'

Hocking's smile faded a little. 'Ah.'

'What?' Her excitement subsided. 'You said that when—'

'Other concerns have come to light as a result of our little setback.' Hocking took another drag on his cigarette and, for all his kindly encouragement over the past months, Gwenna wanted to rip it from his fingers and stamp on it, but she folded her arms instead, and waited. After a moment he cocked an eyebrow and sighed.

'You have been displaying an unfortunate temperament at times lately. Fiery. Which is perfectly wonderful in almost any other walk of life, of course, but you need to learn to be part of a team here, Gwenna. It's been noted that you haven't coped well with being behind in your studies. That you appear to believe you should be out in front of everything you do. As if,' he hesitated, 'as if you feel you're somehow better. Perhaps because of your father?'

'I don't think that,' Gwenna countered quickly. 'I was just a little on edge today, that's all. And that's only because of all the times I thought I'd passed this test. Now that I have, I won't have any need to be short-tempered.'

'Until the next time something doesn't go your way.' Hocking's appraising gaze crawled over her until she felt herself shrinking beneath it. He had lost his twinkly-eyed geniality, and now spoke in a low, almost conspiratorial voice. 'I think you're going to need to prove your willingness to pitch in. Work hard on the ground. Do a little … extra.'

Gwenna tensed, and when he laid a hand on her arm she had to fight not to pull it away. 'Like what?'

He didn't answer for a moment, but to Gwenna's relief he did at least remove his hand. He glanced along the side of the building towards the door where the new trainees were filing through to the classrooms, and evidently came to a decision. 'You drive, of course?'

'I can,' she said carefully, 'though I don't have my own motor.'

'That's alright. You can do a little job for me. I need some spare parts picking up from the railway depot, and my regular driver's not available.' He paused, concerned again. 'It's a night-time drive though, are you happy to do that?'

'Of course.' Gwenna almost melted in relief.

'Good.' He nodded, and relaxed. 'You should take someone with you though. A man. For protection, you know.'

'I can ask my fiancé, he's a policeman.'

'Good idea.' Hocking's smile was back in full force now. 'Excellent! Well, come and see me at ten o'clock tonight, and be prepared not to get back to your bed until the early hours.'

'After I've done it, you'll consider taking me up in the Avro again?' She hated sounding so needy, but after the all-too brief moment of joy, she needed something definite to hold on to.

Hocking patted her shoulder. 'Let's see how well you do on

this first job, shall we? Driving at night isn't for everyone, and we don't want any dents in the van.'

'But if it goes well?'

He relented. 'Alright. Mind you don't go blurting it around, it might give the wrong impression.'

'What impression?'

'Well, that you're sucking up.'

'Can't I tell my friends at least? They won't think that.'

'Of course you may tell them. But I suggest you wait until you're back from the first trip, just in case something happens and it all falls flat again. You won't want to have to admit to another failure, will you?' Hocking turned to leave, but he gave her a final, warm smile to take the edge off his words. 'You've worked hard, Gwenna. You've earned this even more than your friends have, so you have every right to be proud of yourself.'

'Thank you. I am, at last.'

'Good. I'll see you and your fiancé tonight, then.'

Gwenna watched him go, then checked her watch; she had a little over an hour before she was due to join her own class for mechanical maintenance training, which gave her enough time to run into town and find Peter.

She went straight to the police house, and peeked through window; to her relief he was there, talking to his sergeant and drinking tea. He turned as she knocked on the window, and came outside, the remnants of their difficult walk still lurking in his wary expression.

She grasped his arm and kissed his cheek, excitement bubbling up again. 'I've passed!'

The cloud vanished and he beamed. 'Thank goodness! You must be thrilled, have you told your fa ... your friends?'

He'd clearly switched that word at the last minute, but she didn't want to fight again, not now. 'No, I have to do something for Barry first. Mr Hocking I mean, and I need you to help me.'

He automatically checked the time. 'I'm due at the courthouse in Bodmin this afternoon, we have to leave soon.'

'It's tonight, actually.' Gwenna told him what Barry had said, and as she talked, she was dismayed to see his expression close down. 'What's wrong?'

'I don't much like that he's asked you, to be honest. Do you have to do it?'

'Well, no, I suppose not. But it would show willing, wouldn't it? Like Barry said, I've been noted as not being very reliable as part of a team, and this would prove I can be trusted with important tasks.'

Peter's mouth tightened. 'You're determined then?'

'Yes! And if you won't help me, I'll find someone else. Tommy Ash, perhaps. He's sure to pitch in.'

'No.' He caught her arm as she turned away, and she bit down on a triumphant smile; he had always been jealous of Tommy's easy-going nature, and the way it won him friends without trying. He drew her back to face him. 'I'll do it. But I won't come onto the base.'

'Why not?'

'Because ...' He flicked a glance over his shoulder, where Sergeant Couch was watching them with a broad, knowing grin on his face. He looked back at Gwenna. 'It's the job. Anyone sees a policeman, especially in his own clothes, marching around the training camp, and word will come straight back that I'm doing private jobs of some kind.'

'But it's only—'

'Lazybones Couch is retiring soon,' he went on. 'If I want to take over as sergeant I can't afford the accusation, even if it's found to be perfectly innocent.' He shook his head. 'I'll come with you, but ... well. I really don't think you should do it at all, if I'm honest.'

'I don't much care whether you do or not.' Gwenna's own temper was perilously close to cracking now; he was supposed to understand how much this meant to her. 'Barry says it'll help me win over the other instructors, and if I'm to stand any chance at all of learning to fly fighter aircraft I *have* to be seen in a good light. Taken seriously.'

He shook his head. 'Why are you so set on that, anyway? You'll never fly in combat, you're a woman.' He followed her gaze to where his hand was still locked around her arm, and let go. 'You can never do what he did,' he said quietly, and she didn't need to ask who he meant.

'That's not the point,' she said, keeping her voice cool, with an effort. 'If I want to do anything useful in the industry I'm going to need as many skills as possible. I'm not doing this for the fun of it, Peter, I thought you knew that.'

'I thought it was just a challenge for you,' he confessed, 'an expensive one, too, and you'd never have been able to do it if it weren't for your father's reputation. But what on earth do you plan to do when you've qualified? You can't be part of the military, there's no Women's Air Force anymore. And if you think you'll get a job somewhere like Imperial—'

'Stop it!' Gwenna's throat was tight with frustration and disappointment. 'Look, Bertie imagines she's going to be able to actually train as a fighter pilot, but we all know she's dreaming, even she knows that. Still, it makes her happy to dream, so we let her. But the truth is, if we can learn to at least maintain and fly combat aircraft, we can do it as civilians. Work on them, and even transport them from the manufacturers to the bases. Think about it, I'd be flying *for a living!*'

'But the war's been over for twelve years,' Peter argued. 'There's no call for them now.'

'Then why is the training available to men?' She saw his trapped expression, and pressed on. 'They don't put this much money into resources they don't think they'll need someday. And if I never have to fly one, then so be it. But if the need comes up, and Bertie and I are qualified, we'll have an advantage over anyone who isn't, won't we?'

'And for that remote chance, you're going to risk your neck driving around in the dark delivering spare parts. For no pay.'

'Barry says it'll help me, and he'd know. And if he wants me to do any other trips I'll do those too. Now are you going to help me, or shall I ask Tommy?'

He seemed to be struggling with his response, then nodded with evident reluctance. 'Yes, I'll help you.'

'Thank you. Now, I've got to be back in time for maintenance training. We're looking at adjusting tail fins today ...' One look at his face told her he was less than interested, and she didn't elaborate. 'See you at ten,' she said instead.

'Ten,' he repeated, in a stiff voice. 'Now run along, you don't want to be late, do you, and undo all that good work you did?'

Her spirits deflating more by the minute, she started back up the path, but stopped as he called out, 'I meant it though, well done on passing the test.'

The row had clearly affected him, and for a moment she wanted to go back and patch things up, just to avoid bad feeling plaguing her all afternoon, but her class awaited. She nodded, and turned back towards the base, and as she walked she pushed the sour atmosphere to the back of her mind and allowed the glorious reality to flood back: she would finally be allowed to fly again.

CHAPTER SIX

When the afternoon's classes were over, Bertie washed the oil off her hands and face, and changed out of her overalls. 'Want to come for a walk?' she asked Tory, who was finger-curling her hair. 'I'm going down to collect my post from the flats.'

'I can't, I've got to do something.' Tory gave herself another critical look in the mirror, and turned to face Bertie. 'Do I look calm?'

'*Calm?*' Bertie laughed. 'That wasn't the question I was expecting. You look very pretty, and perfectly neat. Calm though?'

'I'm going to see if I can speak to my mother. I want her to see me as grown-up, respectable, decent, and . . . yes, calm. Unruffled. Like she hasn't got under my skin, see?'

'Ah. Then yes, you look all those things. Are you going to the hotel?'

Tory nodded. 'Do you want to ride with me as far as the flats?'

The old Bertie would have immediately tensed, suspecting a hint that she wasn't capable of walking that far. But things had changed now; she was no longer touchy about it, or overly sensitive, and besides, she knew Tory well enough to understand it was a casual, unthinking offer that she would have made to anyone.

'No thanks, it's nice out. And not far.' Bertie reached for her lightweight summer jacket. 'Is Gwenna still in class?'

'I think so, I haven't seen her since breakfast.'

'I wonder if she passed this time?'

Tory frowned. 'I hope she's not keeping her distance because she's had bad news again. We'll find out at dinner though, I suppose.' She tugged her skirt straight, and sighed. 'Wish me luck, I think I'm going to need it.'

The walk was becoming easier every time, and Bertie arrived at the flats in just a few minutes, having waved at Tory as she'd roared past in the Tourer. She did wish her friend well, but hoped she wasn't making a mistake by pursuing something that might upset her. It took courage though, and Bertie mentally tipped her hat in Tory's direction.

She collected the weekend's post from the reception desk at the flats, and left her forwarding address, then wandered outside into the sunshine again, flicking through the few envelopes. There was a letter from her younger sister Fiona, who was training to be a nurse, and a reply from her very best friend Lynette, who lived in Brighton, both of which she looked forward to reading later. But the one that caught her eye was postmarked from Edinburgh, and was heavier than the others, with something small sliding about inside.

She was due to meet Jude in twenty minutes so she hurried back to the base and, rather than go back to the dorm, she leaned against the hangar where Jude was working. She opened the heavier envelope and a small box fell into her hand; a flat square of around two inches. Inside was an ornately carved brooch in brownish red; a mixture of curved lines and sharp edges; inter-locking whorls and twists … intriguing and unusual.

She looked at the letter, it was from Leah, her mother's out-going – and often outrageous – best friend, and honorary aunt to the Fox Cubs, as she'd always called Bertie and her siblings.

Dearest Bertie,

I'm writing with news that I'm now a respectable married woman! Adam and I tied the knot a week ago while we were visiting his family here in Leith. It wasn't planned, or we would certainly have made a big splash and invited everyone, but we do plan to hold a big party when we return to Cornwall. I missed having you and Fiona as my bridesmaids, but it really was a very quick and boringly official little ceremony, and nothing to feel you've missed.

I have sent you something I found in a little shop on our way up here. It's a dara knot, the Celtic symbol for strength, and when I saw it was in the image of a fox I knew who had to have it: the strongest Fox Cub of them all! My plan is to come and visit you as soon as Adam and I return from Scotland, in around a week.

I have several people to write to with the news, so please do excuse my signing off quickly now, but with love, and with great pride in my new name,

Leah Coleridge.

Bertie looked at the brooch again, and turned it around in the palm of her hand to see that Leah was right; two of the point-edged curves stuck up in the form of ears, and the other three formed the pointed, cunning face of a fox. The colour gave it extra life.

A broad smile crossed Bertie's face as she skimmed the letter again; Leah, and Adam Coleridge, another close family friend, hadn't had the easiest of courtships, but they'd become engaged earlier that year so it wasn't a total surprise that they'd decided on the spur of the moment to make it official. Bertie couldn't have been more thrilled if her mother had announced her own remarriage.

'Ah, Fox. There you are.'

She looked up to see Tommy crossing the grass, and for the first time she felt an unexpected jolt at the sight of him. It so surprised her that she fumbled with the letter she was trying to put back in the envelope, and dropped everything. She stooped to pick it up, wondering what on earth had just happened; perhaps it was because Leah's marriage was on her mind, and her thoughts had been unusually romantic ... Then Tommy was beside her, crouching to help as Leah's letter fluttered a few feet away in the late afternoon breeze.

Bertie had always felt general warmth towards him; he'd been so kind to her from the moment they'd met, when she'd come down here with Xander to see if it might be something she wanted to do. When she'd begun training he'd been the same; he made her laugh, and never minded when she couldn't suppress the sharper side of her nature. A brotherly presence. A friend. Then, out on the moors on Saturday there had been a deepening of that warmth, and she had begun to imagine they might perhaps have dinner one night, or even go dancing and naturally succumb to the low lights and soft music ... She certainly hadn't expected it to hit her in broad daylight like this, and so hard.

His dark hair stirred in the breeze as he looked up and handed her the letter, and the thick lashes filtered the sunlight onto his familiar hazel eyes so they suddenly seemed mysterious and shadowed. He tilted his head, and there was a faintly quizzical look on his face now, that made her wonder if he'd felt this disturbingly pleasant shift, too. She couldn't seem to tear her gaze away from his mouth as his lips parted to ask her if she was alright, and it was only when he took her hand to place Leah's letter in it that she dragged herself back to the moment.

'You're away with the fairies,' he said, concerned, as he stood up again. 'I hope that's not bad news.' He nodded at the letter, and she fixed her eyes on that instead. It helped focus her mind.

'No, quite the opposite,' she said, and smiled up at him. 'My aunt, well, my mother's friend, has got married.'

'That's nice. Are you close?'

'Haven't I mentioned Leah to you before? The woman who used to stay at Fox Bay, and pretend to be a hundred different characters just to while away the time?'

'Oh, the confidence trickster?'

'I think she prefers *grifter*,' Bertie said, with another smile as she recalled how Leah's trickery had brought her to Adam Coleridge's attention in the first place. 'But yes, that's her. She hopes to visit soon.'

'You'll have to introduce me.'

There seemed to be a weight behind Tommy's words, and Bertie looked more closely at him. Introduce him as what, a friend? Something more? Her earlier suspicion that he'd felt something change too, grew stronger. He was looking at her intently, and the usual laughter and light-heartedness that characterised their conversations was absent. She found her eyes drifting over his face, and lingering on the open neck of his shirt, where the sun and wind-kissed skin looked particularly inviting to the touch … She curled her fingers around the letters in her hand to remind herself she mustn't.

'You'll like her,' she said, instead.

'I'm sure. Anyway, I came over to ask you to come with me to Lynher Mill tomorrow evening. It's my brother's birthday.'

'Oh, I can't intrude on a family—'

'I knew you'd say that.' He shook his head. 'It's not a party or anything, we're just going to have a nice dinner, and it'll be a belated birthday meal for me as well, since Nate doesn't drive so he couldn't come down for mine. My sister and her husband will be there, too. It'll be a good chance for you to meet everyone.'

'And why would I need a chance to do that?' Bertie raised her eyes to his again, meeting them boldly. It was a challenge, and he accepted it, his voice low.

'Because I think it's only right and proper that they should get to know the girl I never stop talking about.' Seeing her sceptical look, he smiled. 'That's no exaggeration, I think they feel they know you already.'

Bertie couldn't help laughing at that. 'What on earth do you find to say?'

'Stop fishing for compliments!' Tommy's grin faded, and he reached for her hand. 'I think you know as well as I do that we have … That we're … That our relationship is moving faster than we are,' he finished, a little helplessly. 'We're lagging behind it, all tangled up in politeness and friendship.'

'You're saying it's time we caught up?'

'Are *you* saying you don't agree?' Tommy cast a quick look around them, then stepped closer, blocking the sunlight. The press of his lips on her brow felt natural, and she welcomed it, but when he touched her chin, and lifted it so his mouth found hers, she felt a rush of heat that she'd never known before. Not even with Jowan. Tommy's lips moved gently, coaxing, and his fingers slipped around the back of her head, holding her closer. Bertie's hands stole around his waist, still clutching the crushed letters, and she felt him move closer still.

From somewhere in the distance she heard a voice, but she shut it out and gave herself entirely to the sensations spreading through her; a slow, delicious awareness of every part of herself, reacting to each breath that passed between them. When the kiss broke he moved back just far enough so he could look into her eyes, and she hoped they told him everything she was feeling. They felt as heavy-lidded as his, and she could feel her skin was flushed with longing. If only they were alone . . .

'Have we caught up now?' he asked, as if the only way to make sense of what had happened was to lighten it, to bring them out of the startlingly intense, private world into which they had just fallen.

Bertie didn't trust herself to speak, so she just nodded, and took a steadying breath. Tommy touched her cheek once more, then stepped back, and that was when Bertie realised the voice she'd heard, and that they'd both completely ignored, was Jude's. She felt a flicker of horror crawl through her; to have been seen in such a moment, here of all places, and by an instructor to whom she was trying to prove she wasn't just another giddy female . . . It was unthinkable.

Jude merely nodded as Tommy left, and then turned her grim, unsmiling attention on Bertie. 'Tomorrow suit you then?'

'Pardon?' For a moment Bertie thought she'd been there long enough to have heard Tommy's invitation, and was relieved when Jude clarified.

'After lunch, for your first training session. We're due a lesson anyway, so Joey will be booked out to you. We'll just take her back out onto the moors instead, that's all.'

Bertie felt a sweep of relief. 'Yes. Of course.' She shook herself free of the mental fog that still enveloped her. 'Look, what you just saw, it wasn't something we—'

'I don't want to know. All that concerns me is that you won't be distracted during your lesson.' Jude eyed her seriously. 'The last thing you want to be doing is mooning about some young man, when your life and mine are on the line.'

'I won't,' Bertie assured her, her heart still racing, and still not sure the past five minutes had been anything but a silly, romantic dream. 'I promise you, I'll be absolutely focused.'

'Well, good.' Jude turned to leave, and muttered, 'Bloody young 'uns.' But Bertie could have sworn she saw the woman's shoulders shaking, and knew she was right when she heard a low, throaty chuckle drift back to her across the grass. 'Tommy can pick you up after, and take you to that dinner. Say happy birthday to his brother from me.'

*

It was almost quarter to ten, and in the busy students' common room a nervous Gwenna looked around at each of her room-mates. She'd told them she hadn't yet heard about her test result, and had received enough sympathy and encouragement to make her feel guilty for lying to them, but it couldn't be helped. She'd tell them tomorrow morning.

In the meantime they were all busy: Tory was frowning over a letter she was writing – presumably another one to her broth-ers; she'd gone looking for her mother at the Cliffside Fort this evening, but returned with the news that Nancy had checked out, and now there was no way of finding her beyond prowling the streets.

Bertie, who'd been in a complete cloud all evening and kept staring into space with a dippy look on her face, was reading a letter of her own, and smiling; and Irene was in conversation with one of her classmates. It would probably raise more questions than it might answer if Gwenna told them she was going out, so she slipped quietly from the common room and left a note on her bed in the dorm instead.

Mum not feeling well, have gone to help out. Might stay overnight. Gwenna.

Then she picked up her heaviest coat, the one she'd have used for flying if only she were allowed, and went out into the night, her heart beating faster than usual.

Barry Hocking was waiting in his classroom, and when Gwenna poked her head around the door he looked up from his desk with visible relief, as if he hadn't been sure of her. He didn't greet her, beyond a brisk nod, just led her around the back of the classroom block to where the van waited.

'We've got four crates coming up from Falmouth Docks, so you'll be picking them up at the Truro rail depot. It's pistons and belt drives, so they'll obviously be quite heavy. I hope you've got your fiancé to help.'

'He'll be waiting outside the gate,' Gwenna assured him. 'Although I'm sure I could manage, I help my father in the shop all the time, unloading things.'

'And you're a fine help to him I'm sure, but we don't want you straining your wrists or your back, do we? Not now you're ready

106

to go up again.' He smiled and handed her the key to the van. 'A pilot needs to be in tip-top physical condition, you know that, so let your policeman do all the lifting. I want you personally to get the paperwork signed, though. Make sure you go and see the depot manager as soon as you get there.'

Gwenna nodded and climbed into the driver's seat, but before she started the engine she took a moment to familiarise herself with the controls; they looked a little different to her father's grocery van, but it all looked straightforward enough. She wished it were still daylight, but there was no arguing with the train schedule, and Hocking had pointed out how the mechanics would need some of these parts before they could start work first thing tomorrow.

'Remember,' he cautioned now, 'keep an eye on the hedges, they can creep into the road a bit in the summer, when the going gets narrow, and I don't want any marks at all on this van, understand? Can you imagine what they'd say about a pilot who can't even navigate a Morris van down a Cornish lane?'

She could, and only too well, but he gave her another of his friendliest smiles to relax her. 'This is your chance to show some real skill, and grit, Gwenna, so don't waste it. Put those doubters to shame, my dear.' He checked his pocket watch. 'Off you go then, or it'll be breakfast time before you get back.'

Gwenna stopped outside the gate to let Peter in. He still seemed stiff and resentful, and she expected him to offer to take over the driving, but he didn't. A good thing too; she was concentrating on the road and couldn't afford to be distracted by another argument. To her relief, the atmosphere between them gradually mellowed as they rumbled through the darkness of the country roads beyond Pencarrack.

'So it's Truro we're going to, is it?' Peter asked, peering out into the night as they took a sharp left turn.

Gwenna nodded, keen to build on this opening to a conversation. 'These parts have come in by sea,' she said, 'so they'll have unloaded the freight from the Falmouth branch line. Barry said we've had some old rotary engines donated, but they need ... Never mind.' Once again his lack of interest was painfully obvious.

'Let's talk about something nice,' Peter said, when the silence grew uncomfortable again. 'Like our wedding.'

Gwenna could once again think of a dozen conversations she'd rather have, but she dutifully chatted about bridesmaids and flowers for a while, and after what felt like a painfully long time they arrived at the station. She followed the signs to the yard at the back, and parked near a large storage shed, but as she prepared to get out of the van Peter stopped her with a hand on her arm.

'Leave it to me,' he said. 'You stay here.'

'But I've got paperwork.'

'I'll take it. I'm sure I can find the right person to talk to.'

'Barry told me to—'

'Barry's not here! And I don't mind, honestly.'

Before she could protest again, he had taken the paperwork and now went in search of the manager. She supposed she could have followed him, but it would almost certainly achieve little except a dismissive nod and a feeling she was in the way. She slumped back against the seat again and waited, eager now to just get it done and get back to the dorm.

It hadn't been more than perhaps five minutes before she felt the van rock, and realised someone was pulling open the doors at the back; she twisted in her seat to see Peter, who had a strangely hard expression on his face as he spoke in a low voice to his companion, but he seemed perfectly comfortable with what he was doing so she didn't interfere. Presently the van tipped again, with the weight of heavy boxes sliding into the back, and this time she got out, feeling bad for making Peter do all the work. She might as well not even be here.

She rounded the back of the van and was surprised to see four men: two coming towards the van from the depot doorway, with a large crate slung between them, and Peter and a man who looked as if he could be the depot manager waiting to take it from them. They evidently all had defined roles, and those boxes really did look heavy, so it was probably a good thing she'd left Peter to it, after all. All four looked at her as she made her appearance, and then questioningly at Peter.

Gwenna straightened her shoulders and gave them a confident smile. 'I'll take the paperwork, shall I?' she offered. 'Save it getting crushed. Is it signed yet?'

'Who's this?' the manager asked, quite rudely, she thought, since he'd ignored her and spoken directly to Peter. She was about to introduce herself but Peter replied first.

'Just my driver. Local girl.'

Gwenna had heard of people gaping at one another, but this was the first time she'd consciously caught herself doing it, and now Peter was looking at her with a kind of desperation. 'Hop back in the van, there's a good girl,' he said. 'You don't want to get in the way.'

She felt her indignation fade into unease, and quietly climbed back behind the wheel. Something else was happening in the back, movement of the crates, rustling of papers, and a smell she couldn't quite identify at first, but associated with school. Paste, that was it. But she stared fixedly ahead until the van doors closed, a few raised voices cut across the yard, and then Peter got back in and shut the door.

'Off we go,' he said, with infuriating cheeriness. 'Should be back in good time after all.'

'What was all that about?' she asked, not making a move to start the van.

'All what?'

'Peter!' She turned to him, angry now. '*You* clearly didn't want me to be seen, but Barry didn't mind. He never told me to stay in the van and out of sight, in fact . . .' She frowned. '*He* told me to be sure I took the paperwork personally. So why did it matter so much to you?'

'Let's just start back, love.'

'Stop talking to me as if I'm mad! I want to know why—'

'We don't want to cause a disturbance, do we?' His tone was calm, but in the light from the depot she could see he was staring straight ahead, and his hands were clutching at the material of his trousers. 'Come on. We can talk on the way.'

Gwenna shoved the van into gear too hard, which made a grating crunch, and drove out of the yard crosser than ever. She negotiated the narrow lanes in tight-lipped silence, until she reached the more familiar road to Caernoweth.

'Right,' she said, feeling calmer herself now, but still annoyed. 'Out with it.'

'Can we just get back to the base first?'

'You said we could talk on the way back. Why didn't you want me to be seen back there?'

'I don't know why you think that. I just didn't want you to get—'

'In the way,' she finished for him, feeling her jaw tighten

110

again. She waited a moment, then said, 'You've done this before, haven't you?'

'No.'

'Oh, of course you have! Why on earth would you lie about it though?' Gwenna spared a glance away from the road, and saw that his face now wore the sullen expression of someone caught out, with no excuses. 'Barry didn't sound the faintest bit surprised when I said you were the one I'd asked to come with me, he even seemed to expect it, but I don't understand why picking up spare parts should be such an issue. Do you go down there with his usual driver then? And who *is* his usual driver?'

He didn't respond, beyond letting out a sigh she could hear even over the engine. It sounded irritated rather than resigned, which made her even pricklier. 'Peter!'

'Let it alone!'

'I don't know why I was even asked to do this,' Gwenna said, her hands gripping the steering wheel so tightly now that her knuckles ached. 'Why didn't he just get you to do it? You can drive as well as anyone.'

'It's safer on the road with two.'

He didn't expand on that, and Gwenna fell into her own thoughts; on one hand it was naturally safer for any driver to have a companion, in case of accidents, but on the other she had to wonder if the threat was more particular than general. Might someone have tried to pull her over and take the spare engine parts, perhaps for selling on at a profit? She would certainly have been in a lot of trouble if that had happened, and it would have spelled the end of her chances of getting back up in the sky.

After several miles in tense silence they approached the gates

111

at the air base, and Gwenna pulled up. When Peter didn't move, she looked across at him. 'Don't you want me to drop you here?'

He frowned. 'Why would you? I'll be unloading the boxes.'

'Well, you didn't want to come onto the base earlier,' she reminded him. 'You told me it was because of your job.'

'Which is the same reason I didn't want *you* to know I occasionally run errands for Hocking.' Peter put a hand on her arm as she prepared to drive onto the base. 'Look, I told you I wasn't right pleased that you were doing this.'

'You needn't have worried, I'm quite capable. And I didn't dent the van either.'

'No. But ... Just tell Barry no-one saw you, alright?'

'I *knew* it!' Gwenna sat back and stared at him. 'You were keeping me out of sight, and he wanted the opposite. Why?'

'Because he wants you locked in!' he blurted, and Gwenna recoiled in surprise.

'Locked into what?'

'Into his scheme.' Peter sighed and lowered his voice again. 'He's lost his regular driver, and he needed a replacement who wouldn't raise any kind of suspicion. You're that person, Gwenna; respectable, innocent, and from a good local family. Why do you think he made you so desperate to fly that you'd do *anything* for the chance?'

'You mean ...' Gwenna stared in dismay as she realised. 'The tests?'

'Yes, the tests! And he wanted to make sure they saw you down at the depot, so you're implicated and he can use you whenever he wants. And he will, believe me. This was certainly not the last time, not by a long way.'

Gwenna sat still for a moment, absorbing his words. 'What's

in the boxes?' she said at length, her voice even, but her pulse racing. She felt ill.

'It doesn't matter.' He sounded defeated now. 'Just drive me around to the store, and I'll get them unloaded. Anyone using that place will be gone by now, I won't be seen.'

'I want to know what Barry has got me into.'

Peter looked at her, his expression pleading. 'The less you know, the better.'

'It's too late now.' Gwenna's trembling hand shifted the van into gear, and she eased the van forward onto the base and towards the hangar now used for storage. 'Is there someone waiting to help you unload?' He nodded. 'Who?'

'Never mind.'

She let out a steadying breath, giving up on that part. 'Right. Then you can tell me everything afterwards. I'll be waiting outside the gates.'

'It's gone midnight,' he argued. 'You'll need some sleep if you've got lessons in the morning.'

'Do you suppose I'll sleep a wink now?' she fired back, rattled again. She pulled up outside the hangar with a jerk, and slammed the van door before striding away towards the dormitory block. When she was out of the sight of anyone who might be watching, she changed direction and went to wait outside the gate for Peter. She kept thinking about the times she'd supposedly failed that final test, and how puzzled everyone had been – including Flight Lieutenant Bowden, who had taught her for almost six months and knew how capable she was. How stupid she'd been!

Now she had her ticket into the sky, but when she was eventually up there she would be with a man who owned her, and who could make her do anything on pain of dismissal, or worse. What would her father think, if he heard how she'd finally earned her wings? Gwenna groaned softly, the sound cutting through the night. Why hadn't she simply requested another instructor?

But she knew why: Barry Hocking was the most popular instructor on the base, so who in their right mind would have asked to swap just because they were continually failing? Hocking would say he had simply been making sure she was ready, confident in her ability to calculate, and react to, the readings that might one day save her life. His kindly grandfather act had been just that, and everyone fell for it, including her ...

'Gwenna.' Peter's voice spoke at her shoulder, and she jumped and turned to face the shadowy outline at the gate.

She walked further down the fence in case anyone was listening nearby, and she was aware of him following, but he said nothing, and after a minute she found her own voice. 'I sold my soul for something I'd already earned,' she said, her voice cracking under the strain of holding back furious tears. 'And I can't even tell anyone, because I'll lose my place, and my father will be devastated.'

'I tried to—'

'Don't you dare tell me you tried to warn me!' Gwenna wrenched herself away from his grasping hand. 'You could have told me outright! You were just too busy trying to protect your own stupid job.'

'It's hardly a stupid job,' he bit back. 'Look, I did what I could to protect you, but you wouldn't listen.'

She couldn't even argue with that. She folded her arms and tried once more to pick him out in the darkness. 'And what was it that pulled *you* in? What price *your* soul, Peter?'

His feet shuffled in the grass. 'I'm in, and that's that.'

'Your precious job, no doubt. I wonder what he'd have done if I'd asked Tommy Ash, or someone else?'

'Probably made me arrest them.'

Gwenna was about to let him have it for being flippant, when she abruptly realised what he meant, and that he was deadly serious. 'Bobby Gale's his usual driver, isn't he? And you've arrested *him*.'

'Hocking wanted to bring you in, instead,' Peter said, 'so he needed Bobby out of the way. There was plenty we could get him on, after all.'

'Wait a moment.' Gwenna's stomach turned over. 'Is *that* why you blathered on and on about me staying in training? You knew Hocking was doing this to me?'

'No!' Peter took her hand again. 'I knew he was recruiting someone, and he told me he'd have to push things along a bit, though he didn't say why. I think now that maybe Bobby was starting to question what Hocking was doing, but I promise you, darling Gwenna, I didn't—'

'*Darling?*' Gwenna once more yanked herself out of his grip. 'I never want to speak to you again. The engagement's off.'

He spoke reasonably. 'You don't know what you're saying. You're just angry.'

'Off,' Gwenna repeated, her voice as cold as her heart felt. 'I'd not marry you now if you were the only bachelor in all of Cornwall.'

As she spoke she was feeling her way back along the wire fence, and now she came to the gateway again and slipped through it. For a second she felt stronger, lighter; she was valued here, she had ambition, and a goal, and she had friends ... Then she was hit again by the realisation that she couldn't unburden to either

115

Bertie or Tory; she might be on the inside of the fence, but she was truly outside the warm circle of friendship she treasured above everything else.

'Gwenna!' Peter's voice came closer, and she realised he'd followed her up the path. 'What do I tell people?'

'Tell them whatever you like. But just make sure they know it was my decision, not yours. We can blame it on the age difference, if you like, there are plenty who said you were too old and dull for me.' It felt cruel to say it, but it was true, and she didn't feel like holding back tonight.

'And you always said they were wrong,' Peter said, clearly stung.

'Well, I won't tell my father the truth, if you won't.'

'There really is no arguing with you, is there?' Peter said, his voice tight, and Gwenna smiled, though it was a grim little smile and there was no pleasure in it.

'That's about *all* there is, if we're honest. We've not been right together for a while, have we?' She didn't wait for a response, but followed the path to the dorm block, keeping her eyes on the pinprick of light from the lamp over the door until she was standing beneath it. Only then did she look back, not sure herself whether she hoped he was still watching her, but he'd already gone. Gwenna crept into the dorm, seeing the light from the hallway spill onto the three oblivious and slumbering shapes in the other beds, before closing the door and draping them all in darkness once again.

CHAPTER SEVEN

At midday on Tuesday, Tory and Irene kept their appointment at Priddy Farm, taking Tory's motor to save time, since they only had an hour, and nudging it into the gateway as far as it would go.

'Strange to think of you living here as a little girl,' Irene said, eyeing the sprawling farmhouse with frank appreciation. She seemed a good deal more relaxed today than Tory had yet seen her; either she was relieved to be away from lessons, or they were already going very well and she'd stopped worrying. It made for a much easier companionship.

'Even when we lived up the road we spent a lot of time here.' Tory hung her satchel across her back and pushed open the gate, feeling another pang of regret that she'd been so far away when her grandparents had died, within a year of each other. 'The stable's over there.'

Both girls were wearing trousers and boots, but thankfully there was little mud at this time of year to get them dirty as they crossed the yard to the stable, where three horses poked inquisitive noses over their half-doors to see who was visiting.

'Where's Mr Garvey?' Irene asked, approaching the first in

line; a dark bay with a snip of white at the bottom of his nose. She reached out a hand, but drew it back as the horse tossed his head and whickered.

'He'll be working, but he knows we're coming, and he should have heard the car.' Tory heard the gate creak, and turned to look. 'Here he is.'

Keir wiped his hand on his work trousers before holding it out to Irene. 'Glad to meet you, Miss Lewis. Done much riding then?'

'I used to do a bit, but there's not much opportunity where I live.'

'Oh? Where's that?'

'Birmingham.' Irene looked around her rather briskly, clearly keen to get to the subject at hand. 'This is a lovely stable.'

Keir obediently turned his attention to the horses. 'That one you're looking at is one of our younger horses, he'd be particularly glad of the extra exercise.'

'What's his name?' Irene rubbed the white snip between the horse's nostrils, and this time the horse stood still.

'We call him Mack.' He nudged Tory. 'He was sired by Tristan MacKenzie's horse.'

'Who was his dam?' Tory asked, pleased to know there was still something of Bill around on the farm.

'The one you're stood next to,' Keir said, moving to stroke the calm-looking mare, who was eyeing her colt across the tops of their doors. 'This is Bonnie, she was Ellen's favourite.'

'I don't remember Ellen riding,' Tory said, surprised, and Keir smiled, clearly amused by the thought.

'God, no. But she was always out here talking to Bonnie, and she spent all night with her when Mack there was born.'

'Why don't we just let Bonnie and Mack get to know us for a

bit for now, and then perhaps we can come back on Sunday for a ride, when we're both free?'

Keir nodded. 'Sunday suits me. It's the festival on Saturday, anyway, so that wouldn't be any good. The horses will be working a lot at the moment, but it'll be nice for them to get out on the moor and stretch their legs now and again.'

Keir left the girls to their introductions, and Tory reached into her satchel and withdrew a couple of apples. 'Right, let's go in and let them have a good old sniff of us. You seem to have taken a shine to young Mack there, so this'll get you off to a good start with him.'

Irene took an apple, and Tory led the way into the stable, where the bright sun dappled the hay and the woodwork at the front, but left plenty of shade at the back. She heard Irene start to talk in a low voice to Mack, and Bonnie issued a snort of maternal warning before accepting her own treat.

'Easy,' Tory murmured, running her hand over Bonnie's bay coat. She guessed the horse's height at around fourteen hands, while her son stood a couple of hands taller; both were powerfully built, as Bill had been, and firmly muscled through hard farm work. She moved around slowly, smoothing Bonnie and letting her get to know the stranger in her stall, but after only a couple of minutes the peace was shattered by a shuffle and a short yelp from the stall next door. Tory raised herself on tiptoe to look over, and was dismayed to see Irene limping away into the back of the stable, making tiny whimpering sounds. Mack was shifting and stamping, and Tory leaned over as far as she could and patted his neck until he settled. Then she joined Irene, who was sitting on a bale of hay.

'What happened?'

'It's nothing, just a knock.'

119

'Did he kick you?'

Irene rubbed at her shin. 'I was probably crowding him.'

'Probably,' Tory agreed. 'I doubt he's used to having people in his stall. How is it?'

'Fine.'

'Best go back in and make it up with him,' Tory said. 'He's calm again now.'

'Isn't it time we went back?'

Tory looked at her watch, and uttered an oath. 'That went fast! We'll have to hurry too, if you don't want to get shut out of Bowden's classroom for the afternoon.' She turned to leave, but looked back as Irene gave another hiss when she tried to put weight on her left leg. 'Are you sure you're alright?'

'Perfectly,' Irene snapped, and looked ashamed at Tory's surprise. 'Sorry. I just feel a bit silly. I'm not as used to strange horses as you seem to be, I only rode ones I knew, before.'

'Perhaps it'd be best if you took Bonnie out on Sunday, rather than Mack.' Tory lent Irene her arm to lean on. 'He seems a little excitable.'

They waved at Keir as they passed through the yard. He was bringing water up from the well to mix with the pigs' feed, and nodded to them. 'Sunday then? Just come down, I'll leave the tack ready.'

'Thank you!' Tory called back.

'Don't let him see me limping,' Irene muttered, and let go of Tory's arm, but Keir had already turned back to his task, and Tory helped Irene into the car without drawing his attention again. As they pulled into the parking area outside the base a few minutes later she noticed Irene was looking a little green, and kept rubbing at her leg.

'Let me look at it,' she offered. 'I'll explain to Bowden if you're late. It's like Bertie always says; we're paying for this training. He just likes to act important.'

She went around to the passenger side and crouched by the open door, while Irene rolled the leg of her trousers back. The skin wasn't broken, but it looked as if a nasty bruise would soon be making an appearance.

'What does it look like?'

Tory glanced up to see that Irene had half-closed her eyes and was looking away. She tried not to laugh. 'Your bone isn't *quite* poking out,' she began, and regretted it when Irene gave a sharp cry and yanked her leg away. 'It's alright! I think it'll bruise nicely, but it's probably more painful than damaged.'

'I wonder if I ought to see the doctor,' Irene fretted, still not looking.

Tory lifted the trouser cuff again; there was quite a lump rising on Irene's shin. 'Well, it couldn't hurt to have it checked over,' she conceded.

Irene nodded. 'I saw the sign on the doctor's house in Pencarrack the other day, that said the new bloke should have moved in over the weekend.'

'I'll drive you. Swing back in, then.' Tory patted Irene's knee and went back around to the driver's side. As she was closing the door she spotted Flight Lieutenant Bowden crossing to the classroom, jingling his key in his hand. 'Just a moment,' she said, and ran over to him to explain. Bowden seemed in quite a chirpy mood for once, and waved across at where Irene sat waiting.

'Tell her not to hurry back,' he said. 'She's showing a lot of promise already, I'm sure she can afford a few hours, in an emergency. By the way, this afternoon's flight will have to wait; I've got to get the Avro looked at. Sorry.' He stopped short of patting Tory's arm, but she was still a bit stunned as she re-joined Irene and passed on his message.

'I've never seen him so cheerful,' she said, starting the car again. 'And apparently you've already done well, after just a couple of days.'

'He must just be in a good mood,' Irene said, rather gloomily, 'because he certainly hasn't given *me* that impression.'

'Well, whatever the reason, now we can take our time with the doctor and not worry.'

Tory drove carefully up to the village, and noticed Irene peering back as they drove past where Tyndall's Folly stood, small but distinct against the skyline; it certainly looked very pretty today in the sunshine, with the bell heather blooming all around it. She drew up outside the doctor's house, and was relieved to see that it was indeed now occupied; the door stood invitingly ajar, and the curtains at the windows were tied back. She helped Irene from the car, and lent an arm once again.

Inside, in the cool, they found themselves in a large room, bare except for a polished desk in the corner and several straight-backed chairs lining two of the walls; only one other person was waiting: an elderly man with his hand wrapped in a bandage. There were two doors leading off this waiting room, one closed – obviously the doctor's consultation room – and another that led deeper into the house and that stood half-open.

The girl at the desk, whose head had been down as she wrote in a large ledger, looked up brightly and smiled. She looked familiar, but Tory couldn't quite place her.

'Good afternoon, ladies,' she said, and her American-accented voice was clear and sharp. 'Please take a seat, I'll be with you in just a minute.'

They did so, and after a moment she looked over at them again, her pen poised. 'Okay. Can I take your names?'

Irene gave hers, but Tory, having been distracted by the receptionist's accent, now remembered with a start where she'd seen her before; at the Cliffside Fort Hotel, dining with Nancy. Her hair was done differently today, it was much more formal, and it made a difference to her whole face. Even as the recognition clicked into place, Nancy herself came in from the street, carrying a heavy-looking basket of groceries. Not sparing anyone else a glance, she crossed to speak worriedly to the girl at the desk.

'Is he back yet?'

'He came back around twenty minutes ago. He's telephoning the hospital right now though, so Mr Peacock can go get his hand looked at.'

'Thank you.' Nancy hurried through the second door and pulled it closed behind her, and Tory sat very still, in a state of bemused excitement; if Nancy was working for the doctor, it was likely she'd come back here to stay . . . Tory might finally find out what had driven her away all those years ago, and worse, had kept her away. She was about to lean forward and engage the girl's attention when the doctor's door opened and a pleasant-looking man in his mid-forties came out, his sleeves rolled up and his tie crooked, but with an air of unmistakeable importance about him nevertheless. He nodded briefly around at the three people waiting, then spoke to the girl.

'Honey?'

'Hi, Daddy. Nancy's out back. She was worried she was late, I think.'

'She's fine.' He waved a hand. 'Could you call that place in Bude, and have them make dinner reservations for Mr Fry and me at eight? He has some ideas he'd like to discuss for the Bude surgery, so we'll be checking that out after we close here.'

She made a note. 'Sure.'

The doctor turned to the other patient. 'Mr Peacock, they're expecting you at the infirmary this afternoon, if you can make it. Tell them Doctor Stuart sent you, and they'll fix you right up.'

Mr Peacock nodded his thanks and left, and the girl smiled at Irene and Tory as the doctor vanished back into his office. 'Just another couple minutes.'

Tory felt as if she were taking part in a play where she had no idea of the plot. Her mother was evidently nervous of being late and upsetting the doctor, but she just as clearly knew him and his daughter well enough to have taken dinner with the girl on Thursday evening. It was more likely she and this Doctor Stuart were more than employer and housekeeper after all.

A bell sounded behind the reception desk. 'Doctor Stuart's ready now,' the girl said, looking up and catching Tory's eyes on her, 'you can take your friend through. Unless you'd rather wait out here?'

'I'll wait,' Tory began, thinking it might be her best chance to speak to Nancy, but she relented as Irene sent her a pleading look. 'Alright, I'll come in.'

Irene smiled her thanks. 'Can I lean on you again? This leg's stiffening up a bit now.'

The doctor's room was empty, but it too had a second door leading into the house; this door was ajar and they could hear low-voiced discussions coming from the hallway beyond. Tory recognised her mother's voice but couldn't pick out any words, and settled for helping Irene onto the couch and folding her trouser leg back neatly so it wouldn't unroll. The bruise was coming out already, and the skin looked stretched and rather shiny as the lump swelled.

'I don't think anything's broken,' she said, 'or you'd not be able to walk on it at all I shouldn't think.'

The second door opened properly, but instead of the doctor, Nancy came in carrying a small pile of towels. She smiled at Irene, and began to greet them both, but as she turned to Tory she fell silent. Tory simply looked at her and watched all the same emotions she'd felt on Thursday parade across her mother's face.

'Tory?' Nancy managed at last, and her voice shook a little.

'You can't be that surprised to see me,' Tory said bluntly, though her heart was hammering. 'I'm not the one who walked out, after all.'

'But your granny and grandad said you'd left! I didn't know . . . I hadn't—'

'This leg's very sore,' Irene put in politely, but she was looking from one to the other with wide eyes, and would probably have been content to watch this unfold if she hadn't been in pain.

'Yes,' Tory said, turning more business-like. 'Irene was kicked by a horse, and needs to have her leg looked at. So if you wouldn't mind . . . ?' she added, as Nancy remained motionless. They could hear the doctor in the next room, opening and closing drawers as he prepared himself for seeing his new patient.

Nancy visibly pulled herself together. 'Of course, I'm sorry. This was very unprofessional of me. I'll just . . . ' She gestured at the door, and slipped back out of it.

Tory looked at Irene, and raised her eyes to the ceiling. 'Families,' she said, adopting a weary tone, but trying hard to control the tightness in her throat. Seeing Nancy again at the Cliffside Fort had been one thing, at a distance and knowing she hadn't been recognised, but this was different. This time they'd been a few feet apart, and the light blue eyes that had once gazed at her with love had rested on hers once again; this time with something that looked almost like fear. As if she expected recriminations and accusations, but wasn't yet ready with her armour.

The door opened, and Tory and Irene looked around ready to greet the doctor, but it was Nancy again, this time wearing a white coat. She wordlessly washed her hands at the sink and then, ignoring Tory's astonished gaze, she took a towel off the stack she'd just brought in, and turned to Irene.

'Miss Lewis, I'm Doctor Stuart. You'd better tell me exactly what happened.'

*

Jude gestured to the pilot's seat in the front of the adapted two-seater, and Bertie walked around to climb onto the wing, feeling the flutter of the nerves she thought she'd shaken off for good. She'd been careful to breakfast well, knowing she'd have a long day ahead, but when she remembered the death-defying plunge into a vertical dive that had ended Jude's demonstration, she wondered if that had perhaps been a bad idea after all. Sliding into the now-familiar seat, she tried to tell herself it was just another lesson, only with a couple of new manoeuvres thrown in, but she knew it was actually the beginning of something that might change her life forever.

The excitement was one thing, but the danger of discovery was another; Jude's assertion that she would lose her job if anyone found out what she was doing, still troubled Bertie's thoughts. They could not stop Jude from continuing her lessons privately, since Joey was her own aircraft, but she would be denied access to the hangar, the mechanics, and the fuel, not to mention the income from teaching. It would be the end of everything for her. Bertie touched the brooch she now wore beneath her flying jacket, remembering Leah's words: *the strongest Fox Cub of all.* Now was the time to believe it.

'Right,' Jude said, leaning forward to speak directly into her ear before settling back into her own seat, 'a couple of things to remember before we start.'

Bertie nodded. 'Listening.'

'One of the things that makes this bird such a good fighter is her fast right turn. Good for close-quarters scrapping. You'll need to know her inside out though, to get the best out of her, and that's what we're going to be learning before we try anything like those moves I showed you before.'

Bertie felt some of the tension melt away. 'Like what?'

'The difference between the climbing turn, and the turning climb, to begin with. Then diving – not vertical, don't worry – and I thought we might try a loop too. That'll do to begin with, I think, don't you?'

Bertie heard the grin in her voice, and pictured the blue eyes glinting behind the mask. 'I should think so,' she returned, feigning confidence by sketching a salute against her helmet.

'You'll be doing a roll without power,' Jude added, 'so be ready for that.'

Bertie swallowed; she had always hated that silence, even when it was just for a second, and to deliberately cut the engine would go against every instinct she possessed. She didn't want to ask, but she had to. 'How fast will we be going?'

'At the right altitude we can do up to two hundred without any issues, but make sure you're listening to me carefully when you're coming out of it, because you'll have to let the stick back very slowly. And when you re-start the engine, do it throttled-down and open up gradually.' She slapped Bertie on the upper arm. 'Right. Take her up, then. Switching to radio communication.' Her presence disappeared from Bertie's shoulder, and Bertie checked her harness and braced herself for what might very well prove to be the most terrifying experience of her life.

Once up, and at a safe altitude, she began to relax again. They flew out towards the place on the moors near Lynher Mill, where Jude had demonstrated last week, and Jude took her through some of the usual basic manoeuvres. Then, with a mind no doubt on the fuel usage, she began to coach on the fine rudder techniques needed to perfect the roll.

'Take her back to 75 IAS,' the tinny voice in Bertie's ear cautioned. 'Remember what I told you.'

Bertie gripped the stick and waited for Jude's harsh, *go!* Then she pulled the stick back and to the right, and applied the right rudder as Jude had instructed. She shut the engine off at the same time, feeling a sick fear as the only sound that remained was the rattling of the wind in the propellor. Then they were upside down, her shoulders pulling at the harness as she fell away from her seat by a few inches. Before she had time to think about what could happen if the engine never started again, they were almost over and it was time to centralise the controls and bring the engine back again.

The dive flattened out, and Bertie heard a loud, triumphant yell that was almost lost in the splutter of the engine – she assumed it was Jude until she recognised her own voice, and started to laugh. Her blood was fizzing through her veins like champagne, and the urge to repeat the manoeuvre was almost overwhelming; the feeling was indescribable, and she wanted it again. Now.

Jude's warm praise came over the headpiece, adding to that urge, but the instructor made her go back to spins for a while, something that Bertie now knew how to do so well she almost found it boring. It was as if someone had shown her how to swim in the wildest part of the sea, and was now making her paddle in the shallows again.

As their lesson time drew to an end, Jude spoke again. 'Now. About that loop.'

Bertie's heartbeat picked up again. 'Yes?'

'Do you want to try it today, or wait until you've had more spin practice?'

'Today!' Bertie said at once. She felt invincible; the queen of the skies. Joey was an extension of her own hand now, as tame as a kitten, and Bertie's concentration had been so sharpened that anything less than learning something new would be a waste. 'If you think I'm ready,' she added, a little worried at Jude's silence.

'Alright. Listen carefully.' Jude fell silent again, and Bertie began to feel the trepidation eating away at her confidence. But she couldn't change her mind now.

'I'm listening,' she prompted, hoping her voice didn't sound as shaky over Jude's headpiece as it did to her.

Jude began her instruction, and Bertie concentrated hard, ticking off the main points with a finger against her leg. Then, at Jude's command she checked their speed, and when the needle showed 110 miles per hour she eased back on the stick, working the rudder pedal with her left foot at the same time. Joey's nose obligingly looked up, and, remembering Jude's warning not to give in to the temptation to bring the stick back further, Bertie held their position steady. Her heart was slamming against her ribs so hard, as the plane began to tilt beyond the vertical, that the sound of it in her ears almost drowned out the engine until, to her horror, she realised there was no engine noise to drown out.

The courage it had taken the cut the engine during the earlier roll was one thing, and her exhilaration had been its reward. This unplanned and unexpected silence, as the Camel sat on her back at the top of this loop, was the most terrifying thing Bertie had ever experienced. Panic crawled through her, and she felt herself drawing a breath to scream, but that breath was snatched away as the plane fell abruptly into a spin. Not like the ones she had been practising; those had usually pushed her down into her seat, this was pulling her out of it. An outward, inverted spin that made her feel as if she were being thrown forcibly out of the plane, her weight straining at the shoulder straps of her harness. The ground, which had seemed so comfortably far away, now rushed at her with horrifying inevitability; mocking the contempt she'd shown it—

'Right rudder!' Jude's boot connected with the back of Bertie's seat in a fierce, flat-footed kick. '*Bertie, listen!* Stick back, and—'

'Yes!' Bertie cried, but her hand was shaking too hard, at first, to grip the stick properly. Then her fingers closed tight and she pulled back and to the right, and applied the rudder. After an eternity, the plane went into an ordinary right-spin, which Bertie was able to flatten out in under half a turn as the engine came back. She finally understood Jude's insistence on spending all that time on 'boring' spins.

'Alright, take her down,' Jude said, her voice calm but a little tighter than usual. 'That's enough for today.'

Bertie checked the fuel gauge, and found her voice. 'Once more.'

'Bertie—'

'*Please!* If she stalls again I'll be ready.' When Jude didn't reply, she went on, 'I can't leave it like that. If I do, I'll never want to try it again. Do you trust me?'

'Of course.'

'Then once more.'

A pause. 'Alright.'

Bertie settled herself firmly, double-checked her harness, and checked the speed. At 110 mph she eased the stick back, and held steady as the Camel began to climb, and climb, and then to hit the vertical for that breathless moment before looping back. This time the engine stayed strong, and at the end of the loop Bertie brought the stick back a touch more, bringing them safely out and back onto a level flying course. It was as if the earlier terror had been a dream, wiped out by the burst of sunshine in sleepy, confused eyes; the calm that fell over her as she brought the Camel back down, to an admittedly bumpy landing, banished all but the most clinical memory of the fear she'd felt.

As she removed her headset and climbed out onto solid ground again, she caught sight of Tommy's bike, propped against a rock, and then of Tommy himself, his arms wrapped across his chest as if holding his heart in place. The moment Bertie stepped clear of the wing he was pulling her into his arms.

'Oh my god, Bertie,' he muttered against her hair. 'I thought that was ... you were ... ' He shook his head, and she could feel the shallow tightness of his breathing as he let it out in a controlled rush. 'You're going to be the death of me.'

'You saw the spin, then?'

'I was just pulling up.' He put a hand to the back of her neck and pressed his lips to her forehead. 'I nearly dropped the bike. I think I might actually have screamed, I'm not sure.'

'Thankfully no-one was around to hear you then,' Bertie said, deeply touched despite her teasing words. She saw a wry smile lift his expression at last, and leaned willingly against him until they realised they were becoming lost in the moment again, and that Jude was waiting patiently beside Joey. They broke apart, and Bertie went back over to Jude, raising her voice over the engine.

'Thank you for letting me try again.'

'I didn't really have a great deal of choice, did I?' Jude's face broke into a grin. 'You did well. Even if you did give me palpitations for a minute.'

'Thanks for the kick,' Bertie said, rubbing the base of her spine. 'It was just what I needed.'

'Oh, I'm happy to kick you anytime.' Jude looked over at Tommy. 'Give you a bit of a fright too, did she?'

'I'm never watching her again,' he confirmed, but he was smiling properly now. 'You're sure it's alright if I just take her off?'

'Don't make a habit of it, but it's alright for today.' Jude reached into the cockpit and handed Bertie her stick. 'Next lesson's on Friday, but it'll be a normal one.'

Bertie tried not to look too disappointed. 'When can we do this again?'

'Well, flights are logged, and the fuel has to be accounted for, but leave it with me. I'll work something out like I have for today.' She pressed Bertie's arm. 'I meant it, you did well. I'd like to keep up the momentum, but we have to be careful.' She swung into the cockpit and fastened her headset over her helmet, and a moment later Joey was moving away across the grass.

Bertie climbed onto the back of Tommy's bike and put her stick between them, reflecting that, as terrifying as she'd found it on Saturday, now it felt as safe as sitting in a car. What *was* almost as frightening as hurtling towards the ground, in excess of 200 miles per hour, was the thought that she must now go and face Tommy's entire family and be introduced as his girlfriend. She wrapped her arms about his waist and closed her eyes; there was no right-rudder quick fix for this one.

CHAPTER EIGHT

Gwenna watched the last practice flight of the day lumbering across the field, knowing full well she could have matched that landing, probably surpassed it, even after only observing how it was done. The Avro came to a stop and, after a few minutes' discussion with his student, Barry Hocking climbed down, lifting off his helmet as he strode back towards the hangar. Gwenna waited a little longer, biding her time, but tapping her fingers irritably against her folded arms as she forced herself to watch Hocking's student carry out checks on the aircraft after the session.

Eventually Hocking reappeared, having filed his report and fuel usage, and no doubt now looking forward to a relaxing evening at home with his family. Gwenna's blood heated again as she watched him chatting amiably with Jude, who'd returned a little earlier, just as if he really were the genial instructor everyone wanted as their own. He laughed at something Jude said, and the hatred crackled along Gwenna's veins; how dare he? He'd upended her life and destroyed everything she'd thought she was, and could be, and he stood there laughing ... She closed her eyes and counted very slowly to five, then looked up to see him resuming his walk across the grass and past the study block, towards the storage shed. This was probably the first opportunity he'd had to check the boxes she'd brought back last night.

Glancing around her she noted plenty of people about their business, but no-one was paying any particular attention to either herself or to Hocking, so she hurried after him and called out before he could slide the small side door shut behind him. He turned in surprise, but smiled when he saw her. It was the wide, sincere smile she was used to, and it set her back on her heels for a moment, until she remembered he didn't know yet that she had any suspicions.

'Gwenna, dear. I gather it all went well last night. Well done.'

'It went very well, thank you. No dents in the van, either.'

He looked around the hangar, which appeared unoccupied. 'Good. Now we must have a little chat about it, but perhaps tomorrow would be a better time. I've still got work to do.'

'No, let's chat now.'

He must have heard the edge in her voice, because he frowned and looked around again. There was no movement from anywhere among the boxes and crates of aircraft parts, laundry, provisions and other goods stacked high around them, but someone might still be working quietly somewhere with a clipboard and pen.

He gave a little cough. 'Very well. Perhaps outside in the sunshine?'

'Here's just as good.'

His eyes narrowed, and he walked away, peering among the crates to satisfy himself that they were in fact alone. Gwenna could see the newest boxes; they were still nailed shut. She gestured to them.

'What's in those?'

'I told you,' he said smoothly. 'Pistons and belt drives.'

'Can I see them?'

'Why would you want to see them?' His voice was losing its forced conviviality now.

Gwenna took a deep breath, seeing the end of everything looming now the pretence was over. 'Because I don't believe you're telling me the truth. And where are the engines you said had been donated?'

He didn't say anything, but neither did he appear guilty. He just looked at her, no doubt taking in the way she stood with her fingers clenched into fists, and noting the high colour she could feel as heat in her face.

'What's really in those boxes?' She hoped her voice wasn't shaking as badly as it sounded to her.

'That, young lady, is none of your concern,' he said softly. 'I have another job for you though.'

'I won't do it.'

He studied her with pursed lips, then shrugged. 'That's alright, don't worry. I can find someone else.' Gwenna almost expressed relief, but bit down on the words when it became clear he hadn't finished. 'I was just going to say,' he went on, with a great show of mock regret, 'that it's a pity you'd have to leave the course.'

'I've passed the exam,' she pointed out. 'You'd never be allowed to dismiss me without an—'

'I'm quite within my rights to mark that paper again if there's any reasonable suspicion of cheating. Especially since you're the only one who knows you've finally passed.'

'I didn't fail at all.' Gwenna took a step forward, driven by anger and frustration. 'Those old test papers will prove it.'

'Don't be silly,' Hocking said calmly. 'I don't keep old, completed tests lying around. We don't want newer recruits finding them and having the advantage, do we? No,' he went on, shoving his hands into his pockets, 'I'm sorry if you feel I misled you, but those are destroyed immediately the test is re-taken. If you elect to take the test again the slate's wiped clean.'

Throughout this complacent little speech Gwenna had felt herself growing more and more tense, and the fiery temper she'd tried so hard to keep in check was bursting to get free. But the knowing smile on the face she had trusted so completely told her she'd only be making things worse.

'This other job then,' Hocking said, evidently realising that the hoped-for outburst wasn't forthcoming after all. 'I'll expect you to be available on Saturday evening, just as you were last night.'

'But it's the festival dance,' Gwenna protested, and he gave her a withering look.

'Worried you're going to miss the fun?'

'No,' she said coldly, 'wondering how I'll explain my absence.'

'I'm sure your policeman will give you an alibi.' Hocking grinned at his little joke, but it quickly faded as she told him she and Peter were no longer engaged. He withdrew his hands from his pockets and folded them in front of him, as if trying to control the urge to throttle her. 'And why is this?'

Gwenna was about to explain, but she realised it might put Peter in danger if Hocking knew he'd spoken out of turn. 'We argued on the drive back,' she said instead. 'I realised we don't have anything in common.'

'And you didn't mention your suspicions to him?'

'Of course not! I'd only be showing myself up on the wrong

side of the law, wouldn't I? I'd never be able to prove I had no idea what I was doing.'

'Well done. So as far as he's aware, you were merely picking up engine parts, as we said.'

Gwenna nodded. 'Won't you at least tell me now, what's in the boxes?'

'Will you agree to this job?'

'Will it be the last one?'

Hocking laughed, and it was disturbingly sympathetic. 'Not by a long way, I'm afraid. The thing is though, it's within my gift to make the rest of your training go as smoothly and as well as you like, or,' he shrugged, 'to ensure your illustrious father gets to find out you've been cheating from the very start.'

Gwenna drew a quick, painful breath. 'He'd never believe it.'

'And,' Hocking went on as if she hadn't spoken, 'if it ever got out that there was anything at all stored on this base that shouldn't be, he'd certainly discover that you were the one bringing it in. What would that do to *his* reputation? To have a criminal for a daughter?'

'But I'd tell him the truth! And Peter, too. You know he's a policeman, so they'll—'

'And I'd advise *them* to check with the staff down at the Truro freight depot. They'll certainly remember a strapping girl like you turning up, giving them all something to gawp at in the middle of the night. Of course, they don't know what's in the boxes either, they've only got the paperwork. Which, I assume, you gave them?'

Once again she almost blurted that Peter had advised her to stay in the van, against Hocking's explicit instructions, but instead she just nodded miserably. Hocking seemed bizarrely chummy now, as if by becoming co-conspirators they should somehow be friends.

'After this run on Saturday we can discuss more exciting prospects for you that will occasionally crop up.'

'A flight?' She hated to hear the eagerness in her voice.

He waved a hand. 'In good time. No, these are a different matter entirely, and I need someone I can trust.'

'Why can't you trust your other driver?' She wanted to hear him admit he'd made Peter arrest Bobby Gale, but he held up a hand.

'Ask me no questions, dear girl,' that infuriatingly playful tone was back in his voice, 'and I'll tell you no lies.'

'You've done nothing *but* lie,' Gwenna said, her throat tight with the injustice of it all.

'Don't dwell on it,' he advised. 'This way you get your wish, and I get mine. As for Saturday, I wouldn't worry about missing the dance, you'll be able to get away for an hour without raising any questions, I'm sure.'

'I can't do it in an hour!'

'Hush! You're not doing the station run.' He looked around, although they both knew they were the only ones in earshot. 'There's more to this business than collecting the goods, as I'm sure you understand.'

'What goods though?' she persisted. 'Why don't you at least tell me that?'

He looked at her with exasperation, and then thew his hands up. 'Alright! If it'll stop you nagging me I'll tell you. But if I discover anyone else knows ...' He didn't finish the threat, but it was easy to interpret the warning look on his face.

'I won't tell anyone,' she promised, 'but I have the right to know, if anyone does.'

'Alright then. We import large quantities of tobacco products and alcohol to sell on to various hospitality establishments. They buy cheap from us, though not as cheaply as we buy it, of course, and sell it on for whatever extortionate price they choose. And I'm assured they get a *very* good price for it.'

Gwenna knew enough, from hearing her father's complaints, to recognise tax evasion, and she felt deeply uneasy about it. Then she frowned. 'Tobacco's pretty light,' she pointed out. 'Those crates looked too heavy for that, even if there were bottles of booze in there as well.'

'Of course they did!' Hocking shot her a look of irritation at this further questioning. 'Each has a layer of engine components on the top, in case Customs and Excise decide to open one on the ship, or at the rail depot. Or even in here. Now will you just listen?'

'Go on then.'

'We have a few regular buyers who distribute as they see fit, I neither know nor care how. One of them will be coming on Saturday night to collect it.'

'Here?'

He gave her a look that questioned her intelligence. 'Tyndall's Folly,' he said with forced patience. 'You know it, of course?'

She nodded. 'So that's where you do your trading?'

'It makes a good meeting place. It's off the main road, but not away in the middle of nowhere. Easy to find, and its walls might not be huge, but they conceal quite a lot from the road.' Hocking raised an eyebrow. 'Happy now?'

'So we'll load the boxes and drive out to Tyndall's Folly. Then what?'

'Then my customer will transfer them into his own vehicle,

complete with whatever fresh labels he chooses to apply, and pay me rather a lot of money for them.'

So that was what the smell of paste had been; Peter had been re-labelling the crates right there in the freight yard. Risky, but doubtless he wasn't the first, or the last, and many a blind eye would have been turned through the years.

'Why do I need to drive you to the folly?' she asked. 'Why can't the two of you manage it between yourselves? Unless it's just so you can incriminate me further.'

'There is that, it's true.' Hocking's expression grew serious again. 'But it's mainly because I'm going to need you for protection, in case my customer decides he'd prefer not to pay up once the crates are in his van.'

Gwenna stared at him, baffled. 'What on earth can *I* do?'

'You'll cover him with this.' Hocking lifted the bottom of his coat, to reveal a small hand gun tucked into a leather clasp at his belt. 'And you'll be prepared to use it.'

*

Tuesday evening saw Tory eating dinner alone, just when she had most need of her friends. Her mother's startling revelation that afternoon had left her reeling, and she'd simply walked from the surgery in a daze, sensing Nancy and Irene watching her, but not looking back. She couldn't make sense of this; a widowed mother of four disappears overnight, nothing's seen or heard of her until she turns up again sixteen years later, without notice or fanfare. And a doctor, to boot. There were too many questions to focus on just one, so Tory had simply paced up and down Fore Street, the village's main thoroughfare, until she saw Irene come out of the surgery. She was limping, but putting enough weight on her leg to indicate there were no bones cracked or broken, and she waved as Tory came closer.

'What on earth happened there?' she wanted to know. 'Was that really your mother?'

'Apparently.'

'What does that mean?

Tory shook her head. 'You'd better get back before you miss too much of your class. It doesn't matter how good a mood Bowden's in, it's a devil to catch up sometimes.'

So she'd taken Irene back to the base, but she hadn't attended her own class that afternoon, instead she'd taken herself away to the clifftop near the old fort, and stared out over the white caps in the distance while her mind went over and over what could possibly have brought Nancy back here, and under such astonishing circumstances. She'd hoped to chat to Bertie and Gwenna about it at dinner, but Gwenna was nowhere to be found, and Bertie must still be with Tommy and his family.

Tory had seldom felt so lonely. She'd saved every spare penny since her mother's disappearance, and when the war was over, and the men lucky enough to come home wanted their jobs back, she was happy to give up her role on the farm, take her savings, and go. She'd told herself and others that she was searching for her mother, but deep down she knew she'd given up on Nancy Gilbert; she was simply looking for adventure, and life beyond the small town.

She had found it. In London, to begin with, then moving around various cities as and when the opportunities to travel arose. Most recently she had found work rehabilitating and re-training horses which had returned, skittish and often terrified, from the battlefields of Europe, and the job took her to places she'd otherwise never have seen; some of them darker and more dangerous than she'd expected. But something about Cornwall had never quite left her alone, and now she was back home.

And so was Nancy. Doctor Stuart, she reminded herself now, with renewed incredulity, as she ate her solitary meal at the table which usually buzzed and leaped with criss-crossing conversations. So who else had recognised her? She'd been back for nearly a week, but no-one had said anything to Tory. Why not? Was she deliberately keeping a low profile until someone needed her skills?

It was a relief to break out of the endless cycle of questions when a tray appeared on the table in front of her, and she raised her eyes to see Irene preparing to sit down.

'Thank God,' she said. 'Talk to me.'

'What about?' Irene sat down, easing her sore leg straight beneath the table.

'Anything! I'm going a bit mad thinking about my bloody mother!' Tory put down her fork and rubbed her eyes. 'How's the leg? Was Bowden still in a decent mood?'

'My leg's fine, just bruised. I'll be able to come riding on Sunday, but I think you're right, Bonnie would probably be better for me. And Flight Lieutenant Bowden was weirdly cheerful all afternoon. Word's going about that he's going to be leaving for a better job.'

'Well, if *that* word's going about, it's about time someone told me,' Tory retorted. 'He's my flight trainer as well as the main classroom instructor.'

Irene shrugged. 'Well, it might not be true. Would it bother you, having to find another trainer?'

Tory thought it over, then sighed. 'I'm not even sure I want to continue, to be quite honest. I've done what I set out to do.'

'Which was what?' Irene began tucking into her dinner.

'Prove to myself I could do it, I suppose. Perhaps I'm ready for something else now.'

'Oh.' Irene looked gratifyingly disappointed. 'Here? Or would you move away again?'

'I don't know. I feel strangely happy to be back, considering how keen I was to get away, but . . . ' Tory pushed her water glass around idly, then said what had been lurking at the back of her mind. 'I just don't know that I can live so close to Nancy, after what she's done. She's poisoned Caernoweth for me now.'

'Then I think you should talk to her, and find out what's behind it all. Not just try to hijack her in her place of work,' Irene added, seeing Tory about to speak, 'but sit down somewhere you can be alone to talk properly.'

'How could anything excuse leaving your children and not even writing to them?' Tory remembered the poorly written note Nancy had left. 'She wasn't well educated, but she could make herself understood. There's no reason that I can think of that would make me forgive that.'

Irene shook her head. 'I'd be the last person to say family is everything, but you wanted to know, didn't you? So you can stop driving yourself mad wondering? At least give yourself that.'

Tory wanted to ask Irene what had prompted that comment about family, but the girl had been so secretive since she'd arrived that she didn't invite questions. Instead, Tory picked up her water glass and drained it. 'Perhaps,' she conceded. 'Speaking of family, I hope Gwenna's mum's feeling better, I don't think Gwenna came back last night.'

'She did,' Irene said. 'I heard her come in at around quarter past one. She was very quiet,' she added, when Tory looked surprised, 'and I'm a light sleeper.'

'Strange time to come back though,' Tory said, frowning. 'Can't think why she didn't just stay the night once it got that late.'

'And *I* wonder if she's got her result yet,' Irene said. 'She must be beside herself having to wait an extra day.'

'I suppose since there were students from the June cohort taking it at the same time, they'd all have to wait until all the papers are marked.'

'Do you think many people who do this training go on to become pilots?' Irene mused, tearing some bread to wipe her soup plate. 'There would be an awful lot of them, if so.'

'Well, we've already established that I'm probably not,' Tory pointed out. 'The Rowe boys are failing every test going, and Robert Penhaligon's going back to work on his dad's boat, so Gwenna says. That's four of us out of our intake alone who won't be looking for work as pilots, plus the ones who got sent home after the first exams.'

'Hmm.'

'Why are *you* doing it?'

Irene looked blank for a moment, and filled the silence by tearing more bread. 'My aunt suggested it,' she said at length. 'She'd read a lot of stuff about that American woman, Amelia Earhart, and now there's that Amy someone—'

'Johnson? The girl from Yorkshire?'

'Yes, her, if she's the one who flew to Australia. My aunt thought it sounded just the thing to keep me out of trouble, so she put up the money for three months of lessons to begin with.'

'Out of trouble?' Tory raised an eyebrow. 'You'll pardon my presumption, I hope, but you don't look as if you've been a trouble a day in your life. You look like ... like a ...'

'A prefect?' It was Irene's turn to look askance. 'That's what everyone says. Gwenna must get that a lot, too.'

'She does. Whereas I look an absolute horror, but was the most well-behaved child I know.' Tory laughed. 'It's true, you know. Ask anyone who remembers me from around here.' She paused, then, driven on by this new friendliness between them, she seized the bull by the horns. 'On your first day, Gwenna saw you writing a letter and she thought you looked a bit, well, a bit shifty about it.'

'Did she now?' Irene's mouth tightened. 'Does she often go spreading that sort of gossip?'

'It wasn't gossip,' Tory protested. 'She just happened to walk into the room at the time, and you seemed to wish she hadn't.' She thought it best not to bring up the maps again, or question Irene's reaction to the fact they'd been noted. 'I'm not asking you to explain yourself,' she went on quickly, 'but since you seemed put out that we've misunderstood you, I thought perhaps that might explain something of why we might have.' She made herself stop talking before she burrowed any deeper. 'Anyway, we can put that right. Why don't you tell me a bit about yourself? Do you have a boyfriend?'

'No.' The answer came very quickly. 'I did, once, but he ... But now I don't.' Irene swilled the last of her water around her glass and finished it. 'I have to study,' she said, standing up. 'Bowden's testing us tomorrow on fuel mixtures.'

'At least he's given you advance warning.' Tory laughed, to hide her irritation at herself for driving Irene away. 'He used to drop these things on us in the middle of the morning, just to catch us out.'

Irene returned the smile as she stacked her plate, but she

looked a bit distracted and Tory accepted that she'd lost her chance to draw her out this evening. When she was alone again she cleared her own crockery, and went outside to consider the advice Irene had given her. Perhaps she should drop a note in at the surgery, inviting Nancy to meet somewhere to chat? The thought made her feel queasy with nerves, after all this time, and she had the feeling she might blurt out something she regretted if anger got the better of her, but she'd never be able to switch off these nagging questions otherwise.

She started back to the dorm to fetch her writing case, and as she passed through the hall she saw a group of the young men from the new intake playing with yo-yos, cheering one another on with raucous shouts and good-natured jeers when the wooden disc fell motionless at the end of the string. She stopped to watch for a while, but when one of them offered to let her try she shook her head and laughed.

'I'd kill it stone dead,' she said. 'And shouldn't you be studying, anyway?' She'd meant it only as a parting joke, but stopped when they looked at one another in surprise.

'Studying for what?'

'Well, for your fuel test tomorrow.'

'There's a test?' More puzzled looks passed between them. 'First I've heard of it. Bowden never lets on, so I've heard.'

'Do you know something we don't?' another asked.

Tory chewed her lip thoughtfully, and then glanced over towards her dormitory door. 'Certainly seems like it,' she murmured. 'Best get those books out, boys.'

She turned away from the dorm, not trusting herself to speak to Irene just yet, and instead went to the common room, where she found Bertie just sinking into a chair with a little sigh of relief.

'You look shattered,' she said, sitting opposite. 'I'm so glad to see you though, I have quite a lot to tell you.' She peered closer. 'You really *do* look tired, you must have had quite a day.'

'Tommy's family are a handful,' Bertie agreed. 'Very nice, but ridiculously lively. His father's a stone mason, you know. How was your flight lesson?'

'Postponed. Bowden's got plane trouble. What about yours?'

'Fine.' Bertie waved a dismissive hand. 'It was lovely meeting Tommy's brother and sister, too. He's a farrier, so I expect you'd get on like a house of fire. And Lynher Mill is the prettiest little village, there's a stone circle and everything.'

It was so unlike Bertie to pass over the chance to describe every moment of a training flight that Tory felt she was beginning to lose her grip on the day. She let Bertie prattle on about the Ash family for a few minutes more, then, during a brief pause, she jumped in.

'I've met the new doctor.'

'Oh.' Bertie immediately looked concerned. 'Are you alright?'

'I'm fine. She's my mother.'

Into the stunned silence that followed, Tory explained what had happened at the farm, and what had followed, and as she watched the expressions cross Bertie's face, she felt a unexpectedly strong wave of relief. Thank God for friends.

'So what do you make of that?' she finished.

Bertie repeated Irene's advice. 'Write the note,' she urged. 'Do it tonight, or you'll talk yourself out of it.'

'I was on my way to get paper and a pen a few minutes ago, actually' Tory said, 'but I think there's something going on with our new room-mate, and I don't know whether I ought to mention it higher up. Then again I wouldn't know who to mention it to.'

'Something like what?'

'She told me she has a test in class tomorrow.'

'Poor thing, she'll need to ... Hold on.' Bertie frowned. 'She *knows* about it?'

'Exactly. D'you see what I mean?'

'And she's never worried about being late, either,' Bertie mused. 'Or about missing classes. Do you think she's receiving preferential treatment?'

Tory shrugged. 'I have no idea. She's pretty secretive, was a bit snappy when I asked about lovers, and you remember how she was with those maps?'

'Gwenna saw her writing to someone we thought was a secret lover too,' Bertie added. 'She's definitely hiding something. Not that it's any of our business, I suppose.'

'It is if she's getting preferential treatment in her classes.' Tory pulled a face. 'It wouldn't be Bowden she's running around with, would it? I mean, he's married.'

'Good grief!' Bertie's eyes shot wide. 'I shouldn't think so, he's old enough to be her father!'

'No, you're right. Silly notion. Something's up, though.'

The sounds of a busy common room rose and fell around them as they sat quietly in thought. Irene seemed nice enough, and Tory had started to feel something of a bond with her, especially after this afternoon. But she was becoming more wrapped up in mystery as time went on, rather than less, which was unsettling.

'What can we do to get her to be a bit more forthcoming?' Bertie asked, loosening the laces on her boots. She seemed to be settling in for a long chat, as opposed to becoming bored, and Tory relaxed even more.

'We could just start up a casual conversation when we're all together, about our families or something. Then I'm sure she'll feel she has to chip in with something, at least.'

Bertie nodded. 'Maybe we can start by discussing the festival dance, and who we know that might be coming along.'

'Good idea. Perhaps at dinner tomorrow, if we're all here.'

'Speaking of which, I haven't seen Gwenna since this morning. Have you heard anything about her test?'

Tory shook her head. 'Irene said she heard her come back in the early hours, but I've no idea how she—'

'She passed!'

They twisted in their seats to see Gwenna smiling at them. 'I found out this afternoon. Wonderful, isn't it?' She accepted their delighted exclamations and hugs of congratulations, then dragged a nearby chair over and sat down. 'So what are we talking about, with you both looking so serious?'

Tory caught Bertie's eye and it seemed the same thought passed between them: better not to bring up the possibility of Irene getting an unfair hand up the ladder, it would only spoil this long-awaited moment of triumph for Gwenna. Instead, Tory explained about her mother, and assured them both that she *would* put a note through the surgery letterbox, first thing in the morning.

'Good.' Gwenna's smile was wide, but Tory began to think it seemed forced. She belatedly realised why.

'I'm so sorry,' she said, 'I didn't think to ask, how's your own mum?'

'She's much better, thanks. She's not been sleeping, so she needed a little help. The thing is, and I'm only saying this because of what you've just told me, but she's got it into her head that my father is having an affair.' She shot a nervous glance at Tory, then sighed. 'With your mother.'

150

'*What?*'

'You know Anna Penhaligon, from the bookshop?'

'I know her very well.'

'Oh, of course. Well, when my mother told her she suspected Dad of seeing someone else, Anna said more or less straight away that she'd seen Nancy was back, and that she had—in the past, I mean—been attracted to married men. Particularly the popular ones in town.'

'Like who?'

'Anna's husband Matthew, for one. She didn't say who else, but she knows more. Dad's popular, and considered quite good-looking, so now Mum's convinced Anna's got the right of it. That's why she's not been sleeping.'

'I definitely need to talk to my mother then,' Tory muttered, her heart sinking. 'If it's true, Gwenna, I'm that sorry—'

'Don't be silly. It wouldn't be your fault. Anyway, we don't know if they're both jumping at shadows, so let's wait until we learn a bit more about Nancy, shall we?'

'If her and the male doctor you mentioned are both Doctor Stuart,' Bertie mused, 'then presumably she's married to him. That makes it a hundred times worse, if Anna's right.'

'I suspect she *is* right,' Tory said. A childhood memory had surfaced, now cursed with an adult's understanding. She caught the looks from the other two and swallowed, with difficulty. 'If anyone's going to know how low she'd stoop, it'll be me.'

'What happened?' Bertie asked gently. 'What have you remembered?'

'That after our father died, we sometimes had a visitor. We always had to sit quietly at the table while she ... entertained him upstairs. Always the same man,' Tory went on quickly, keen not to create the wrong impression when the right one was bad enough. 'We had to be absolutely quiet. She would take him upstairs, we would sit and eat, and then he would go and we'd have her back again.'

Tory's voice caught as she remembered the mixed atmosphere that had always pervaded the house when the man had gone: the returning lightness, the smiles, her mother picking her or Matty up and swinging them around, while Gerald simply left the room, or the house, depending on the time of year. He'd been angry, even the eight-year-old Tory had sensed that, and she'd thought him silly to have deliberately missed out on the happier times. Now she knew why, of course, and she wondered what his letter would say when he replied.

'You don't know who this man was?' Gwenna asked.

'No.'

'And will you ask her?'

Tory nodded. 'I suppose so. If it seems important.' She fell silent again as the memories piled in. 'He gave her things,' she said after a moment. 'A pretty scarf once, I remember. That caused a big row with her and Keir Garvey, since they were together at the time.'

The urge to go up to Pencarrack right now, and confront her mother, was growing, but she contented herself with the thought that she could do it properly tomorrow, with a clear head and a calmer heart.

'Well, it's been a long day,' Bertie said, looking at them in turn. 'I think we all ought to get some sleep, there's been a lot going on for all of us, it seems.' She brightened, as they all rose to go back to the dorm. 'So, Gwenna, when will you go up again?'

'I'm not sure. But soon, I hope.'

'I'll bet Hocking's pleased,' Bertie put in. 'He's been championing you for ages to pass this test, he must be so proud.'

'Oh, he's delighted.' Gwenna uttered a short laugh, but Bertie and Tory exchanged troubled glances as they closed the door on the lively common room; it hadn't sounded like a happy laugh at all.

CHAPTER NINE

Wednesday afternoons were for maintenance, on Bertie's rota, and today, for the first time, she was bored. Jude had warned her she might feel like this after the dizzy excitement of her first combat lesson, and it might have helped take her mind off it if she'd had her friends to chatter to as they worked, but Tory had fallen into the worrying habit of skipping some of her sessions; today she had gone to write her note to her mother, before her postponed flight lesson later today. Gwenna was still catching up with some delayed cockpit training, prior to her going out with Barry Hocking later in the week, so she too was in another part of the training camp.

Bertie wished she were at least working on the Camel, she was sure she'd concentrate more, but instead she and Robert Penhaligon were paired together on one of the Avros, fixing a fuel problem manufactured by their instructor. Bertie was finding it hard not to keep seeking out Tommy, who was working across the hangar from them, and Robert grinned.

'Let him alone, that's Bowden's plane he's trying to sort out. Tory won't thank you for stopping him, not if she wants to get up this evening.'

Bertie flushed and pulled a face at him, but he just grinned more widely until, seeing their instructor's attention on them, he pointed into the cockpit. 'That's where the problem is,' he said loudly. 'The block tube's jamming where it connects to the carburettor. The fuel to air mixture's buggered.'

'Hmm.' Bertie's glance drifted back to Tommy, who seemed to feel it. He looked up, his hair falling across his eyes, and sent Bertie a heart-stopping smile as he brushed it back with an oily hand. *Get on with your work,* he mouthed, and she turned away, biting the inside of her cheek to stop herself laughing. 'The mixture, you say?' she mused, as loudly and slowly as Robert had done. 'Can we compensate using the fine adjustment tap, do you think?'

Robert tilted his head and stroked an imaginary beard. 'We could, in flight, but I think we need to address the main issue, since we're on the ground.'

The instructor rolled his eyes at this pantomime and moved on, and Bertie turned again to see Tommy watching her across the fuselage of Bowden's Avro. This time he wasn't smiling, and Bertie's insides did a quick somersault at the intensity of his gaze.

He shifted his gaze to the door, and back to her. *Come out with me, after?* She nodded, and he pointed at the clock and held up his hand, fingers and thumb splayed. *By the gate.*

The afternoon dragged. Bertie studiously avoided looking at Tommy again, and at five o'clock she stripped off her overalls and seized her coat, along with the flying helmet that had replaced Tommy's spare when she went on the bike with him.

Tommy was waiting by the gate with the BSA, and Bertie accepted his hand to climb onto the seat behind him, leaning in close as he started up the road. She'd expected him to continue out towards Lynher Mill, but to her surprise he veered off the road before they'd even reached Pencarrack, following a faint path onto the moor out towards Tyndall's Folly. The mud and grass were dry at this time of the year, so it was hard to tell whether the path was often travelled, but she herself had never been out here, and nerves took hold she remembered what people said about this being a spot for lovers. She wasn't sure whether she hoped they'd be alone here or not, but this balmy, late summer evening had an air of irrevocable steps and breathless plunges. Of caution thrown to four indifferent winds.

The bike rolled to a stop, and when Tommy didn't move from his position gripping the handlebars, Bertie tossed away her stick and leaned closer, resting her cheek on his back. Her hands, which had been gripping the sides of his coat, now eased around his waist, and she remained just as still as Tommy, while the ticking of the cooling engine began to fade. Her meaning couldn't be clearer, it was just a question of whether she'd misinterpreted Tommy's intentions.

After a moment Tommy's bowed head came up, and he twisted to look at her. She slipped from the saddle and waited for him to steady the bike against one of the granite boulders that lay in the grass at the side of the folly, then led him wordlessly towards the small arched doorway into the folly. She glanced into the gloomy interior of the miniature castle tower, in case they weren't alone after all, but it was empty, and when she turned to search Tommy's face the question hanging in the fragrant air was as loud as a thunderclap.

Bertie faltered, needing to be sure they weren't making a horrible mistake. The same thing had happened with her former fiancé, Jowan Nancarrow, and they had never recovered their easy, teasing closeness, no matter how much both had tried to believe it; something pure had withered between them as their relationship changed, and it had never flourished again. She couldn't bring herself to think about losing Tommy in the same way, and that alone told her the answer, and that it had to come from her.

She placed both hands on his chest, and felt the catch of his breath; she wanted to feel the beat of his heart too, but his coat was too thick so she grasped his lapels and pulled them open. She buried her face into the angle beneath his jaw, and breathed in the warmth of him as his pulse beat against her lips, and after a moment of stillness he eased away and kissed her.

They lay quietly, side-by-side between the patches of glorious purple bell heather, clothing discarded, and naked skin scratched by the grass, heightening awareness of every sensation. Lips both gave pleasure, and greedily took it; fingers brushed, entwined, loosened, and trailed paths of heat along breasts, ribs and hips. Bertie could barely identify anything Tommy was doing; it all melted into a single sensation of pulsing delight, and she could tell from his quickened breathing, and the small gasps he gave, that he was equally lost.

He'd pulled his discarded coat up over their heads to shelter Bertie's eyes from the dazzling late afternoon sun, when he'd realised she wasn't going to close her eyes against it; how could she, when he was looking down at her with such desire and wonder? She didn't want to miss a moment of him. The shadows flickered across his face as he moved inside her, and the heat flared again, spreading from her belly, down her thighs and up into her chest ... she could feel it in her blood, and as his movements became more rhythmic, and faster, she held back the urge to give herself over to the inevitable rush towards the end.

She became aware of him chanting her name softly as he moved, and her hands, which had been braced against his chest, now slipped around to his back. She made herself concentrate on the contrast of smooth skin beneath her fingers, and the rough material of his coat that pressed against the backs of her hands . . . Anything to prolong this exquisite moment. But as he built towards his own climax he slowed down, and drew out almost completely, and she uttered a low, frustrated cry and pushed her own hips upwards. He drove in once more, and she tightened her hold, both of them rocking together until he was spent, and still Bertie felt fiery threads shooting up into her belly with each fading spasm.

Gradually she came back to the reality of dry grass against her skin, a sheen of sweat covering her body, and a heartbeat that pounded in her ears, drowning out any other sounds. The coat that had covered them was now lying on the ground; Tommy had flung it off at some point, she hadn't noticed when. He was lying beside her now, breathing as hard as she was, one hand over his eyes to blot out the sun, the other patting the ground beside him, looking for her hand. She gave it to him, and they lay in silence until the distant hum of a car passing along the main road between town and village made Bertie sit up and scrabble for her clothes.

As she did so she caught sight of her prosthetic, fastened to her thigh with its ugly leather harness. She shot a look at Tommy. Knowing about it, and seeing it, were two very different things, and she felt a shifting fear inside as she realised there was no way she could dress now without drawing attention to it. Would

158

remembering how different she was make him regret what had happened? She didn't really think so, but it might make him think twice about what he wanted to do next.

She found her trousers and drew them towards her, with half her attention on Tommy who still had one hand across his eyes.

'What's the rush?' he murmured, sounding drowsy and content. 'Lie down again, darling. Talk to me.'

'Someone might come.' Bertie changed position so her back was to him, and pulled on her underwear. She felt him move, and then he was kneeling behind her and gently lifting her short hair away from the back of her neck. His lips felt cool against her hot skin, and for a moment she let herself enjoy it, then she wriggled away to get a better grip on her trousers.

'What's wrong?' He touched her shoulder. 'Why won't you ...' He fell silent, and when she twisted to see why, he was looking over her shoulder at her leg, and at the harness attached to her thigh.

'Let me get dressed,' she said quietly. 'Please?'

'You're not embarrassed, surely?' Tommy moved away to fetch his own clothes, standing in the folly's doorway to pull on his trousers.

'Not embarrassed, no.' Bertie lifted her leg with her hands and slid her trousers over it. 'I'm just wondering if it makes a difference to you. To what you expect from us.'

'Are you trying to tell me you're *not* going to play centre forward for Plymouth Argyle? Why, then I'm afraid we're not at all compatible, Miss Fox.'

Bertie wanted to smile at his attempt to deflect the seriousness of her worries, but she couldn't. 'You know what I mean,' she said. She stood up to tuck in her shirt, and started to look for her jumper. 'When I was with Jowan we always assumed I'd work with him on the farm, and that we'd go bike riding together, walking, and dancing . . . You know, the usual things.'

'And now you're doing something else.' Tommy shrugged. He dragged his own shirt on, at least making an effort in case walkers should come upon them, but he remained bootless and unbuttoned as he faced her. 'I know you think more of me than to assume that *that*,' he pointed to her leg, 'could turn me off you. Now I just need you to believe me when I say that, if anything, it makes me love you more.'

'What?'

'Well, you've come through a lot,' he went on, oblivious to her stunned look. 'So much more than most people I've met, and I've known you long enough to see how determined you are, and that you can be ambitious, and passionate, but still make me laugh, and—'

'Great, yes. Thank you.' Bertie waved a hand. 'I meant . . . What? You *love* me?'

Tommy's laugh echoed through the folly's ancient walls. 'You'll do for me, you idiot.' He smiled as he took her hands in his. 'You didn't know? What did you think all this was about?' He nodded around them to indicate what had just happened. 'Some sleazy little engineer-student playtime?'

Bertie stepped closer, pulling her hands from his and rested them over his heart. Now she could feel it, without the barrier of clothing; skin to skin, beat to beat, as her own pulse picked it up. 'I love you too, Thomas Richard Ash. Madly.' She kissed him, and he linked his hands in the small of her back and drew her closer.

'I suppose I ought to finish dressing,' she said at length, and with real disappointment. 'I feel bad; I'd arranged to have dinner with the others but I've probably missed it. Tory said she's going to hurry back from her flight, too.'

'I wouldn't worry about Tory. We couldn't sort Bowden's Avro, so he'll have had to postpone all his lessons again.' Tommy looked at his watch. 'We can still get back in time, if we leave now.' He began buttoning his shirt, and Bertie made a show of great disappointment to see his lean body hidden behind the material, which made him laugh again. 'You're one to watch, Miss Fox.'

'Have you seen my jumper? Ah.' She spotted the sleeve lying across the doorway. 'How on earth did it get over there?'

'Things were ... flung,' Tommy said. He was lacing his boots now, and grinned up at her. 'I can't possibly say who by, or why.'

Bertie drew the jumper over her head, smiling as she listened to him humming under his breath while he brushed down his trousers. He not only made her absurdly happy whenever he talked to her, it seemed he could now turn lights on in every part of her body just by looking at her in a certain way. She'd definitely been hit hard, she acknowledged, but it didn't scare her at all. Not this time.

She picked up her coat, but as she drew one sleeve up her arm she stopped and looked again at the front of her jumper; something was missing. She felt a stirring of dismay. 'My brooch!'

Tommy levered himself off the wall, where he'd been leaning and watching her with an appreciative smile that now faded. 'It's fallen off?' He glanced around them at the ground. 'What colour am I looking for?'

'Reddish brown. It's a Celtic knot in the shape of a fox.'

Tommy immediately dropped to his knees and began crawling around where they'd lain, parting clumps of grass. 'Is it valuable?'

'I don't think so. Leah sent it to me though, and it means a lot.'

'That's your mum's friend, isn't it? The one who wrote to you?'

Bertie nodded, poking around the base of a gorse bush. 'I said I'd tell you about her, but all you need to know for the moment is that she put up with all my horrid tantrums when I lost my leg. I made her life miserable, but she never gave up on me. Mind you, she could be pretty harsh with it.'

'She sounds like a good friend to you, as well as to your mum.'

'She is. She's a partner in a private investigation firm now.' Bertie gave a short laugh. 'Ironically *she* could probably find the brooch in two minutes flat.'

'Your jumper was in here, wasn't it?' Tommy ducked into the folly, and muttered a curse. 'It's not big in here, but it's really dark after being outside.'

Bertie went in after him. He was right; the contrast with the bright sun made the room seem even darker, and she crouched in the doorway to pat around the stone floor. Tommy was prodding into the corners with his booted foot, but found nothing.

'Fetch your bike over,' Bertie suggested. 'You can shine the light in.'

'Good idea.' He wheeled the motorcycle around and switched on the headlamp, and Bertie blinked at the brightness, then gave a shout of relief. 'Got it!' She picked up the brooch to pin it to her jumper, and didn't register, until she'd checked the fastening was secure, that Tommy had not shut off the headlamp.

'What's the matter?' She followed his gaze as he peered past her into one corner of the folly. 'What have you seen?' She moved to stand next to Tommy, who was pointing to the rear wall.

'What do you reckon to that?'

Bertie looked more closely. 'Nothing. Why?'

Tommy stepped closer and bent for a closer look. 'The stone's different here.' He reached out to brush a hand over a chunk of the granite. 'This hasn't got nearly as much quartz and mica in it as the rest of the place. I'd never have noticed if the light hadn't fallen like that, but you can see the glitter in the rest of it. There's next to nothing here, look.'

'Repaired, perhaps, with stone from a different quarry?'

'Hmm. I don't know, but my dad would.' Tommy straightened again and went back outside. 'I don't want to flatten the battery,' he called back, 'or we'll have to bump-start the bike.'

The motorcycle's light went off, but Tommy didn't come back in, and when Bertie went to find him he was around the back of the folly, frowning at the wall. Then he paced down the side of the building, counting under his breath. 'How thick would you say these walls are?'

'About a foot, I should think. Not much more. Why the fascination?'

Tommy went back inside and paced the interior, still counting. When he came back out he was looking intrigued. 'I thought so. That's definitely a false wall. Well alright, a real one,' he amended, before Bertie could chip in, 'but built a good couple of feet further in.'

'Not a big enough difference for there to be an actual room,' Bertie said, 'but maybe a secret hiding place. It must be from when the folly was built. Edmund Tyndall *was* a pirate, after all,' she added over her shoulder as she went back into the folly, and he laughed.

'You're expecting to find a treasure chest hidden in there?'

'You're the one who spotted there was something odd about it,' she pointed out, but his interest was infectious. 'Anything would be exciting though, wouldn't it? Even an old flask, or maybe just a leather purse or something.'

She let her eyes adjust again, as well as they could, then studied the wall. Her father had owned several of Carolyn Wells's mystery books, and she remembered him sitting at the dinner table in their big house in Bristol, trying to engage his children in how ingenious some of the secret passageway mechanisms had been. With that in mind she pressed several of the irregularly shaped lumps of granite, listening for clicks, or whirring sounds from within. Nothing happened.

Tommy appeared at her shoulder. 'I thought you wanted to start back.'

'Not until I've found out what Tyndall was hiding here.'

'We might never find a way in.' He leaned on a few random stones, as she had, and then went to the archway to study the stones that formed it, but shook his head. 'Why don't you have your dinner with the others? We can come up here again, and have a good look around when we've got more time.'

Bertie sighed. She knew he was right, and she and Tory had agreed to try and draw Irene out over dinner tonight as well. Outside, she bent to pick up her stick from where she'd thrown it when they'd stopped, and paused; something niggled her about the grass, but she couldn't quite place what it was. It was just as long there as everywhere else, but ... Then she saw what was bothering her: behind the boulder that Tommy had leaned his bike against, at the rear of the folly, there was a patch of bare ground where the absence of bell heather was just a little bit too neat. Elsewhere the grassy interludes were few and far between; strips and curves, a clump of bracken here and there, and the odd yellow flowering gorse. It all grew right up to the folly wall except in that one place, all but hidden in the boulder's shadow.

Bertie straightened, and turned to Tommy. He was already

164

astride the BSA and tightening the strap on his helmet, but he climbed off again and came over when she gestured.

'What've you found now, Miss Holmes?'

'What if the entrance isn't inside, after all, but out here? People will poke around in there, or shelter if they're caught in rain, but who cares about exploring around out here?' Her excitement grew. 'This odd patch of grass corresponds to where they've built that extra wall inside. It's like the heather can't grow here anymore.'

'It's a nice idea but you'd still have to get through the granite somehow, and it looks pretty solid to me.' He ran a practised finger down the stone. 'That's all original wall.'

Bertie subsided, as she looked more closely and had to agree; these stones were weathered, and as embedded with minerals as the rest of the external stonework. 'You have to admit it looks strange though,' she persisted. 'Think of it this way: if it turns out I'm barking up the wrong tree, you can tell me I'm an idiot. Again.'

'I can't resist that.' Tommy removed his helmet. 'Come on then, let's have a closer look.'

Together they squatted and examined the grass, and the wall behind it. Bertie winced as the unusual position cause the harness on her thigh to pinch the skin, and as she shifted to release the stinging pressure she toppled forward and put out a hand to steady herself. The ground flexed slightly beneath her weight, and she gave a short cry and snatched her hand away, but Tommy had seen it and looked up at her, his eyes widening.

'Bloody hell! You were right.' He leaned over to look more closely. 'It's so well hidden, but when you know where to look you can see where the grass looks just a tiny bit less lush, along this line here.'

Bertie patted around the grass where he indicated, and then came back to look at the opposite side again. A barely noticeable channel had opened where she'd inadvertently shoved at the ground and pushed it away, and when she explored it, her fingers found a hard edge beneath the waxy blades of grass and the thick moss. Her heart thumped in excitement as she worked her fingertips down as far as they would go, and gripped. 'Come round and help me!'

After a few minutes of grappling to find the right handholds, they were able to easily lift the edge of a square of grass-covered wood, measuring roughly three feet, and they slid it aside to lie on the grass next to them. They both stared down into the blackness, feeling the unexpected chill of subterranean air on their skin.

'Where's that coming from?' Bertie muttered. 'A tunnel?'

'If it is, it must come all the way from the inlet under the old fort.'

Bertie nodded. 'Perfect for smuggling then. Tory says Tyndall didn't actually build this place himself, it was built by the same landowner who founded Caernoweth.'

'Malcolm Penworthy, yeah.' Tommy tapped the wooden trapdoor with the toe of his boot. 'But *this* hasn't been here for hundreds of years.' It was well made, and a perfect fit for minimum chance of accidental discovery. 'This looks a few years old at the most. No more than five, I'd say.'

'So someone found the tunnel more recently, and put it to use for themselves.' Bertie peered down to where a set of solid-looking wooden steps led away into the darkness. 'Tyndall and Penworthy must have used the tunnel to get stuff away from the coast once they'd got their hands on it, and now someone else is doing the same.' She started, as she remembered. 'I saw someone out here!'

'Hmm?' Tommy was still frowning at the hole in the ground.

'Last week, on my lesson. I was flying back to the airfield, and I got distracted by a flash. When I looked down, I saw a van here with the door open, and the flash must have been the sun hitting the moving window.' She gave him an uncomfortable look. 'It was one of the base's vans, but I couldn't see who was there.'

'You think someone is hiding stuff down here? Or even bringing things in from the shore and collecting them from here?'

'I don't know.' She was glad he didn't immediately try to tell her she'd been wrong, just to protect his fellow engineers. 'I wish we had a torch,' she said, staring down the flight of steps. She could see the foundations of the original back wall of the folly, extending down several feet on the left side of the staircase, and ahead was the space between the walls which accommodated the wide, shallow steps. It all looked designed to present as little danger or difficulty as possible when carrying something, and it would be interesting know who'd been driving that van.

Tommy started down. 'I'm going for a look.'

'Be quick then!' Bertie looked anxiously around them; they'd been alone out here for a long time now, and a balmy summer evening like this would be sure to bring people out soon, walking off their evening meal. It felt as if they'd pushed their luck far enough now.

Tommy went quite quickly down the first two or three steps, which were clearly outlined in the light that reached the top of the stairway, then he slowed down and put his hands out either side of him as he felt the way ahead with his foot. Bertie would have given almost anything to have been able to just leap into action like that, but steps were a difficulty at the best of times, even shallow ones like this. It would have been foolish to try, but that didn't mean the adventuress in her didn't ache to be exploring down there instead of waiting up here. As Tommy passed the level of the foundations, and vanished into the darkness, she shivered and sat down.

Wooden steps should surely have rotted quickly in the dampness of the soil, but she touched the wood and noted it was smooth, weather-treated, and well seasoned; someone was evidently very serious about what they were doing, and willing to spend good money to protect it. And it must have taken a great deal of work and secret organisation to dig out the staircase and then to bring in more granite and create the false wall to hide it as well; this was certainly not a temporary arrangement.

'There *is* a tunnel . . . and a door!' Tommy's excited voice floated back up the steps, then he sighed. 'It's either locked, or just stuck from disuse.'

'Come back up,' Bertie said, growing nervous as she stood up again.

'Is someone coming?'

'Not yet, but I'm scared they will soon. If the door's locked there's nothing else you can do. Come on, we still have to put the cover back and make it look as good as before.' Privately she wasn't convinced that would be possible; the grasses and the heather around the hole had been crushed in several places where they'd knelt, and a sharp eye, on a lookout for such things, might well realise their secret had been discovered.

To her relief Tommy's face appeared again, and a moment later he was helping her to drag the heavy wooden cover back across to conceal the stairway. They slid it into place and spent a few minutes straightening the grass they'd flattened, and when they stepped away Bertie was glad to see they'd done a decent job, despite her fears.

'You'd never know, would you?' Tommy said, echoing her relief. He grinned at her. '*Now* are you ready to eat?'

Bertie looked at her watch. 'I doubt we'll be in time for the main meal now,' she said, 'but I've certainly worked up an appetite.'

'Dinner for two in the kitchen it is, then.' He looked behind them once more as they walked towards the motorcycle. 'Quite a day for discoveries,' he said, taking her hand. His smile softened as he pulled her towards him and linked his hands behind her. 'And you, Miss Roberta Fox, are my favourite discovery of all.'

FILTON AIRFIELD, BRISTOL

Jenny Lyons: Queen of the Twenties. Unafraid of anything or anyone ... Except that wasn't true anymore, was it? She had been genuinely fearless once, made so by circumstance, but now everything was falling apart, and her reputation was the least of it.

The North Twenty had grown in number since that day four years ago, when the traitor had left her to fight alone on the docks. The day Smith, or whatever her name might be, had shown her true, cowardly colours. Ronnie had warned Jenny about her the moment Smith had set her eyes on Jenny's brother: Watch that one, Jen, she'll blind you. She's all shine on the surface, nothing is real.

Jenny wondered now if it hadn't been jealousy that had led Ronnie to mistrust the new arrival, right from the off, because it was true: Smith did *shine. Her skills – for which she'd earned her 'Fingersmith' reputation and nickname long before she'd even joined the Twenties – far outweighed any Ronnie and his boys claimed; she was the best whiz artist there was, and happy to share her expertise. She and Jenny had become the best of friends, and the Twenties and the Dockers an unbeatable co-operative ... Until the night Smith and Victor had betrayed her.*

Four years later the rage still crackled like fire. Jenny had been weakened by trust, and that was poor leadership, but in the end it was Smith's fault she'd had to shoot Victor, her fault he had lain screaming on the rainswept docks, until a shocked and sobbing Ronnie had finished the job.

That night, all goodwill and cordiality between the Twenties and the Dockers had ceased; both syndicates worked their separate patches with sullen, grudging co-operation, but no longer calling upon one another to share their particular skills. Now it had come to a head, and it was Jenny who must step in and fix it.

Two of her newer girls, boosted by liquor and a misplaced sense of invincibility, had made the fatal mistake of trying to rip off a Frenchman in the Barrels. It had since emerged that this Alain was one of Ronnie's lot, so of course now Ronnie was out for revenge. He had a point to make, and a reputation to sustain, and Jenny could hardly even blame him. She'd be exactly the same. But seeing his point wasn't the issue, not now that the Dockers' threats had come back to her; there was only one way to protect those girls now, one way to protect the Twenties' future.

She opened her dresser drawer, withdrew the Colt that had mortally wounded her brother, and placed it into her brightly beaded evening bag. She faced herself in the chipped and smudged mirror; her mouth was tight, the lines of tension either side making her look much older, but there was a thin smile there too. She clipped her bag shut, her eyes glittering in the glass. She was scared, yes, but she was ready for Ronnie Jackson, and this time she wouldn't turn away like a coward.

And if she ever ran into Smith again, she'd be ready for her too.

CHAPTER TEN

'Contact!'

Tory watched the prop swinger carefully, with one hand on the fine adjustment lever, but it took three attempts to catch the engine as the large propeller spun. She hissed in annoyance; she'd already lost half the day waiting and preparing for this twice-delayed lesson, and missed most of the Penworthy Festival. Everyone else had dressed up and gone off with their pockets and purses jingling, and Tory could hear the music coming all the way up from Pencarrack House. Until the Avro started, of course, then all she could hear was the deafening rattle of the Le Rhône rotary engine, and Graham Bowden burbling in her ear about revs per minute and checking the fuel tank pressure gauge.

Once the RPM settled, Tory blipped the engine to allow the ground crew to remove the chocks safely, and in another minute they were up. She tried to draw the same joy from the flight that she'd so often seen in Bertie, but to her the lumbering engine was soulless and unwieldy. Unlike the horses she'd worked with, there was no sense of accomplishment in getting this machine to do her bidding; it would either work, or it would fail. And if it failed it would only be because it was designed to behave a certain way under certain conditions.

If the fuel line became blocked, the fuel would not get through unless it was fixed – no kind words or gentle encouragement would change that. If Tory removed her hands and feet from the controls and didn't replace them, the Avro would go into a spin and they would crash. A soothing word, or inspired idea would make no difference to this hunk of metal, wood and engineered components; it had no free will. No heart. There was satisfaction, and an aesthetic pleasure in seeing the ground from so far up, but as Tory carried out Bowden's instructions she realised, once and for all, that she didn't care about flying anymore.

It was a relief when Bowden cut the lesson short, explaining he had to allow others to catch up too. Even before he'd finished his apologies, she had positioned the Avro into the wind and cut the fuel supply, gliding down to a three-point landing she'd have been excited and happy about just a few short weeks ago. As they carried out their post-flight checks she remembered what Irene had told her about Bowden, and broached the subject.

'Is it true you're leaving?'

His head snapped up. 'What? Who told you that?'

'I just heard it somewhere,' Tory said, rather lamely. 'Sorry, I didn't realise it was confidential.'

'Heard it where?'

'Just . . . in the common room, I think. I can't remember who was saying it, and I might have heard wrong, anyway.'

Bowden muttered something under his breath, then nodded. 'I've secured a civilian post within the military. Based in London. You're not to allow this to go any further, mind,' he added, shooting her a warning glare. 'I don't want the rest of the trainees thinking they can get away with murder in the classroom.'

'I don't think it'll spread,' Tory assured him, realising it was likely that only Irene, Bertie and herself knew about it anyway. And whoever had told Irene, of course. 'How do you suppose it got out then?'

'I have no idea. I've certainly not been making it known. I only found out myself on Tuesday.' The day he'd been surprisingly chipper, so that would explain why Irene hadn't been in trouble for being late.

'Well . . . I wish you lots of luck,' she said. 'It must be exciting for you.' There was that envy again; someone else starting on a new adventure.

Bowden nodded and checked his watch. 'Right, you'd best get away to the festival, since it's already two, and it's supposed to be your day off.'

'When do you leave?'

'Never you mind!' He picked up his clipboard and made a mark. 'You did well today. Next flight's on Wednesday.'

Tory nodded, but she already knew she wouldn't be doing it. It wasn't fair on the ones who really wanted this life, for her to take up flight time that was already at a premium. She set off to find the others, an odd lightness in her step now the decision was made, but along with the niggling and all-too familiar question: *what next?*

Next today, though, was simple enough. Since Wednesday morning, when she'd posted the letter to her mother, Tory had existed in two worlds: the world of aircraft, chatter, and curiosity about their new room-mate; and another where she had retreated into a corner of her mind, and questioned the wisdom of approaching Nancy directly.

She had written the note, as promised, carefully addressing it to Doctor N. Stuart – having ascertained that the male doctor's name was Frank – and kept it very short:

Penworthy Festival, 4pm. By the stables at Pencarrack House. I need to know why.

Victoria Gilbert.

She'd looked at the way she signed it, wondering at the instinctive formality of it, then shrugged; her friends and her family called her Tory, and Nancy was neither. Not anymore.

She hadn't been able to bring herself to go up to the village and put the note through the door herself, in case she'd bumped into Nancy; instead, she'd posted it from the little box halfway down the hill in Caernoweth, and as it dropped from her hand she changed her mind and her fingers tightened momentarily – but they tightened on air. It was too late. There was always the option of just not turning up, but she couldn't do that; it would make her little better than her mother.

Tory knew she'd go quietly mad if she just sat and waited for the time to come, so she hurried back to the dorm to wash and change into a summer dress and cardigan. A rare sight, she mused, as she checked her hair and re-curled it where it had been flattened by her flying helmet, and not something she felt comfortable in, but at least she wouldn't feel drab amongst all that colour.

Half an hour later she was walking through the gates of the

large manor house at the top of town, from which the nearby village had taken its name, and seeking out her friends among the throng. The sights, sounds and smells did a lot to suppress the tension that had been building in her since she'd posted that note, and she absorbed, with some relief, the familiarity of things she hadn't even realised she'd missed during her years away from Caernoweth.

Every year the Batten family opened the grounds of Pencarrack House for the Penworthy Festival. There were stalls and games; local businesses provided food and drinks, and in the centre of the field was a tea tent, which would later give way to hosting tonight's dance. Children in fancy dress were flitting in and out, clutching balloons, while their parents enjoyed a rare opportunity to sit and chat with friends and neighbours without worrying about the safety of their excitable offspring.

Tory stepped in between family groups seated on the grass, smiling at the sight of a baby quietly chewing her mother's folded parasol as she lay on the grass, unheeded by all except her big brother, who was grinning and encouraging her. Boy scouts were lining up at the far side of the tea tent, being drilled by their scout leader who was trying to make his voice heard over an adjacent country dancing display; music for which was provided by three accordions and a rather too-enthusiastic tambourine. The audience was clapping along and whooping, and the dancers bowed and turned, skipped and spun, creating intricate loops that Tory was always surprised didn't result in more trips, collisions, and twisted ankles.

She wandered around the edge of the grounds for a while, trying home-made toffee and cider, and seeing who she recognised from her childhood, and after a while she spotted a quoits tournament. She'd always had a good eye, and was lining up to pay for some hoops when she heard a shout.

'Tory!'

She turned to see Bertie and Irene, sitting in their own little patch of sunlit grass, and went over to join them. 'Where's Gwenna?'

'Helping at her parents' stall,' Bertie said. 'I've hardly seen her for days. Do you know when she'll get to go up?'

Tory shook her head. 'We've all been a bit busy these past few days, I feel like we've barely had time to speak to one another.'

'How was the lesson? We waved, of course.'

'Next time I'll loop the loop in reply,' Tory said drily as she sat down. 'What are we talking about?'

'I was just telling Irene a bit about the festival,' Bertie said. She kept sneaking glances around her and it wasn't hard to guess why; since she'd got back from her outing with Tommy Ash the other night she'd been almost girlishly giddy. It was wonderful to see her relaxing like this.

Tory turned to Irene. 'What's she told you?'

'Just that it's to honour the squire whose memorial is at the bottom of town. The one who built the place.'

'True. Malcolm Penworthy owned all the land up here, including what we're sitting on,' Tory added, patting the grass at her side, 'and ended up granting ownership to a lot of his tenants when their families were snatched by pirates.'

'As was his own sister,' Bertie added.

'Which is why he built the folly, and named it for the biggest, baddest pirate of all.'

'I keep meaning to visit the folly,' Irene said, squinting in that direction although it was impossible to see from the garden at Pencarrack House. 'What's it like, close up?'

'No idea,' Bertie said, rather too quickly, and Tory raised an eyebrow, but Bertie turned to Irene before she could say anything. 'How's the leg?'

'It's fine, I went to get it checked again this morning. Speaking of which, Tory, did you write that note to your mother?'

Tory's heart slipped a little and she took a quick, calming breath to settle her nerves again. 'I'm meeting her at four, by the stables.'

'Good!' Bertie pressed her hand. 'It's right the two of you should talk things through. You never know, she might have had a genuine reason for not being able to write to you.'

'She could write well enough when she left, to let someone know where she was going,' Tory said flatly. 'And she's *obviously* learned since.'

'No, I mean—'

'I know what you mean.' Tory sighed. 'But yes, it'll be interesting to find out what stopped her.'

'Did you say four o'clock?' Irene looked at her watch. 'It's five to, now.'

'Oh hell!' Tory scrambled to her feet; she'd spent longer than she'd realised meandering around the field, looking for her friends and getting distracted. She tugged her dress straight and brushed dry grass from the backs of her legs. 'How do I look?'

'Every inch the modern woman, not to be trifled with,' Bertie assured her. 'Good luck.'

Tory flashed her a grateful smile and set off to the stables. Although partially destroyed by fire, and rebuilt, it looked no different to the way it had when she and the rest of her gang had played here, including Harry, the boy who'd lived in the big house. That helped a little, and she felt less like a stranger, more as if she belonged.

She rounded the stables, her eyes scanning the people milling about, searching for a slender, grey-blonde woman with a straight back and unsettling light blue eyes. Her resolve was set; she wouldn't allow gushing words and sorrowful pleas to distract her from her quest for the truth, she would listen, and make her own judgement. It was the only way to remain objective in the face of what was sure to be an emotional moment.

Tory scuffed the ground with her shoe in growing impatience, then made herself stop in case Nancy was watching from a distance before approaching. She was bound to be nervous too, Tory told herself, drawing some comfort from the realisation. She tried to put herself in her mother's shoes, but she couldn't do it; nothing would have kept her away from those who needed her, not for *sixteen years* ... She breathed through a resurgence of anger, and forced herself to relax again and try to keep her mind open.

A girl wandered slowly past, with a young man perhaps a couple of years older. Their likeness indicated they were brother and sister, and Tory once again recognised the receptionist from the surgery. Would she be Nancy's stepdaughter then? Tory's stepsister? It gave her a jolt to think about it, and she stood up straighter, thinking Nancy might not be far behind, but she was nowhere in sight.

After another ten minutes, when her watch told her it was almost half past four, she finally accepted that Nancy was not coming. She felt her eyes prickle with the tears of suddenly released tension, and shook her head and swallowed her disappointment. She had to be sensible about this, she'd sent the note with no return address, so no means of reply; perhaps, being a doctor, Nancy was on duty this afternoon and couldn't break away from the surgery.

It had actually been pretty self-centred to assume a doctor could simply drop everything at her command, and although she herself was burning to find out the answers to her questions, she had to remind herself that Nancy was living in Pencarrack now, and there would be plenty of time. Provided Tory herself stayed, of course.

She spent a few minutes more making a fuss of the Pencarrack horses, then left the stables and went back to the main grounds. She wanted to corner Bertie, to ask her more about that odd reaction to Irene's question about the folly, but Bertie and Irene were nowhere to be seen so instead she exchanged a word or two with Gwenna, who was still minding her parents' stall. Gwenna was distant and distracted, not to mention busy, so Tory soon gave up thoughts of a conversation, and left her to it. So much for a fun day out with her friends; she tried not to feel too grumpy about it, but she was starting to wonder what there was at the festival worth hanging around for. An early night would be no more dull than staying here alone, and with far less expectation.

As she took one final look around, just in case, she noticed the receptionist and her brother standing in the line at the quoits game she had nearly joined earlier. She really must stop thinking of them like that, she told herself; they were her family now, whether or not they liked it. Or even knew it.

She took a deep breath and went over. 'Lovely afternoon,' she said, nodding at them both. 'We met the other day, I don't expect you to remember though,' she added hurriedly, as she saw a flicker of embarrassment cross the girl's face. 'I'm not a patient, I brought my friend over. She'd been kicked by a horse.'

'Oh, yes!' The girl beamed and held out her hand. 'Of course, I remember now. Great to see you again. My name's Rebecca. How is your friend?'

'She's doing very well.' Tory turned an expectant look on the young man, and the girl remembered her manners. 'This is my brother, Aaron. Aaron, this is, oh!' She laughed and touched Tory's arm. 'I'm *so* sorry, I remember your friend's name, Irene, but I never took yours.'

'Tory.' She shook Aaron's hand. 'Nice to meet you, and welcome to Caernoweth.'

'Unusual name,' Aaron said. He had a polite, professionally distant smile, a little odd on a man only in his early twenties, and Tory wondered if he was in the family business too.

'It's short for Victoria,' she said. 'Victoria Gilbert.' She looked back at Rebecca, whose own smile suddenly looked strained.

'Nancy's daughter?'

Tory nodded, heartened by the fact that Nancy had at least acknowledged her existence. 'I wanted to ask you, actually, if you knew whether she planned on coming to the festival at all. Or the dance, later?'

'No.' Rebecca shuffled the quoit she'd bought, from hand to hand, and turned to see how far down the queue they'd moved. 'I mean no, she won't be coming.'

'Oh.' Tory coughed and looked around. She should have expected the change in demeanour, she supposed, but it was still embarrassing. 'She's working, I assume. She must be very busy.'

'No, she's not working, Daddy is on duty today. She's gone shopping in Truro.'

Shopping? Tory could feel her own expression had frozen, but she couldn't tell if it had been in a smile or a look of disbelief. She shifted her gaze to the head of the queue and took a deep breath. 'Good luck with the game,' she managed, turning away and forcing herself to walk several paces before she looked back. Rebecca and Aaron had their backs to her now, which was partly a relief. But it also felt like something of a slap in the face, and knowing her mother had chosen to go shopping, rather than attempt some kind of rapprochement with her daughter, was even more so.

Tory looked around again hopefully, for a friendly face, but none of her friends were in sight apart from Gwenna, who was helping to pack up the stall and whose expression didn't invite interruption. She let out a shaky sigh and made her way over to the tea tent, where the tables were also being cleared ready for packing away. She might as well stay at the festival a little longer after all, the ale and wine would soon be flowing, and might just dull the pain of rejection enough for her to sleep tonight.

The band had arrived and were unpacking their equipment, and Tory found an unexpected smile touching her lips as she saw that it was Billy Lang and the Pure Blues, the same, much-in-demand seven-piece swing band that often played at Bertie's hotel. But the smile faded as she also remembered the last time she'd heard them play; seeing Bertie enveloped in the love of her very close-knit family, the laughter and the teasing that went with it, and the knowledge that Bertie had a warm and safe home if she ever needed one. As did Gwenna, despite the temporary frostiness between her parents.

What did Tory have? A single bed in a dormitory she'd soon be obliged to leave, two brothers who hadn't even bothered to reply to her letters, and a mother who would rather spend money than build bridges. Even the farm down the road no longer had any connection to the Gilbert family; all that remained there for Tory were sour memories. She lifted her chin and briefly closed her eyes while she accepted the truth: leaving Caernoweth had been the right thing to do before, and, with the decision finally made about her future as a pilot, she knew it was the right thing to do now.

*

The dance was well under way when Gwenna stepped out of the tent and turned her face towards the air base. She left the circle of light thrown out by the lights strung around the Pencarrack House grounds, and wandered back up the road casually, as if she'd simply had enough fun for the day and was going back to sleep it off. She was ready with her reasons, if needed, but no-one noticed her go; Irene was nowhere to be seen, and the last time she'd seen Bertie she was sitting at the back of the tent, closely huddled with Tommy Ash, their hands linked on the table between them.

As for Tory, she'd seemed in high but brittle good humour; she'd told them about Nancy choosing between family and a shopping trip, and then gone off and become alarmingly drunk in a very short time. Gwenna saw her outside the tent as she left, surrounded by a group from the new trainee intake, who were teaching her how to use a yo-yo. Her laughter drifted across the grass to Gwenna, who winced at the exaggerated hilarity, and hurried away before she could be dragged into the party.

Back on the base, she let herself into the dorm and changed out of her dress into overalls and flat shoes, trying to battle the rising fear of what she must do now; it had all still felt comfortably distant, as long as she was still in her party wear. She pulled the door closed quietly behind her, feeling like a sneak thief already, although she'd done nothing wrong here tonight. Yet.

Barry Hocking was already seated in the passenger seat of the van parked outside the hangar, and when he looked up and saw her approaching he gestured for her to hurry. 'I've loaded what we're taking, so get a move on.'

'Why aren't you driving?' she asked as she slid behind the wheel.

'Because I'm going to be too busy keeping an eye out.' Hocking patted his pocket, and Gwenna shivered. She'd told herself, when the fear set in during the dark, lonely hours, that showing her the gun had just been a reminder that she was in this booze smuggling ring too deeply to wriggle out. But it seemed he was serious.

She sneaked a sideways look at him as she drove slowly to the gate, and wondered how she could ever have thought he looked grandfatherly and mild. The lights from the base cast moving shadows that played tricks with his set expression, pulling it through a series of grimaces, and she was relieved when they turned onto the main road and darkness fell across them.

She took the turning that led them across the flattened moorland to the folly, and remembered telling Irene that the landmark was pretty, close up, though pointless. But tonight it didn't seem small, or sweet, instead it loomed ahead of her like some gothic castle, and the beauty of the flowering bell heather was lost in the darkness, making it look more like a sinister swamp.

'Stop here,' Hocking said, before they'd reached the folly. Gwenna did so, and now her rapid heartbeat was sounding in her ears.

'Where's the person you're meeting?' she asked, her voice small.

'People,' Hocking muttered as he stared out of his window. 'They won't come alone, any more than I would.'

'Why didn't you get Bobby Gale to do it? Peter says he's out now.'

'He's out, alright.' Hocking turned his glare on her. 'So if he's got any sense he'll also stay out of my way. You can tell him that, if you see him. *If* he's been stupid enough to stay in Caernoweth, that is, which I doubt. But if he has, I'll find him.' He returned to his scrutiny of their surroundings, and he sounded almost offhand. 'Him or his family, I'm not bothered either way.'

Gwenna subsided into the driving seat, feeling sick. If Bobby had put his family at risk by extricating himself from this racket, it stood to reason her own would be put in the same danger. She cursed her own ambition, that it had led to this impossible situation, but had no time to plead with Hocking as she heard the approach of another vehicle.

The van that came towards them over the rutted moorland track was much older and shabbier than the one belonging to the air base, and its yellow lights much dimmer. As it passed them, to park alongside the folly, Gwenna noticed that the back was closed off only by a half-rolled-down canvas.

'Why did you want us to stop here?'

'Because I want to have open space all around us,' Hocking said grimly. 'He can come back here if he doesn't want to carry the boxes that far.' He withdrew his hand from his pocket, and passed the gun to Gwenna. It felt heavy and unwieldy, and she immediately let it drop into her lap.

Hocking snatched it up again and pushed it into her hand. 'You're my protection,' he reminded her through tight lips. 'You keep that trained on whoever gets out of that van, understand?'

Gwenna nodded, swallowing a knot of fear as she climbed out of the van. She tried to look calm as she joined Hocking in the middle of the space between them and the folly, and to match his relaxed stance, but she could feel all her muscles locking up ready to run. If she did though, she could only guess at what might happen; at the very best, Hocking would be sure to tell her father what she was involved with. At worst ... It didn't bear thinking about. And there were countless places to hide a dead body out here, not least down any one of the many disused mine shafts in the area. She renewed her grip on the heavy pistol, and kept it levelled at the van by the folly.

The two men who emerged, one from the driver's seat and one from the back, were nothing more than shadows until they stepped into the circle of light thrown by the vehicles' headlamps. Until that moment, Gwenna had convinced herself she'd actually be able to pull the trigger if it looked as if they were in danger; men and boys had, from necessity, learned to protect themselves and their fellow soldiers during the war. But as soon as she saw features and limbs, and heard voices, she knew she'd never be able to do it. She didn't know either of the men; they weren't particularly pleasant to look at, and both looked capable of breaking an arm or a neck without blinking, but they were flesh and bone, breath and life. She felt nauseous at the very thought of squeezing the trigger around which both her forefingers were curled, but she had to act as if it would be second nature. This was the real test.

'Hocking,' the first of the men said, his voice friendly enough. 'Nice to see you've improved the company you keep.' He nodded at Gwenna, who kept her expression as still as she could.

'I'd bring your van over if I were you,' Hocking said. 'I'm

not coming closer to the folly than this, and these are heavy boxes.'

'I want to talk first.' The newcomer came closer, beckoning to the man behind him who stood at least a head taller, and a foot wider. 'This here's Devereux. He needs . . .' He paused, then shrugged. 'He needs to disappear. Tonight.'

Hocking didn't seem surprised. 'Should I ask why?'

'No.'

Hocking shifted his attention to Devereux. 'Have you got what you need?'

Devereux nodded and indicated a canvas satchel at his shoulder. 'All but food.' His French accent, even in those few words, contrasted with the strong Bristolian of his companion. 'Where can I stay?'

'I'll show you when your friend there's gone.' Hocking gestured to the back of his van. 'Get shifting, then. Since you've got help, you won't be needing me.' He stepped away and, to Gwenna's melting relief, he took the pistol from her. 'Come on then, I haven't got all night.'

The two men made short work of transferring the boxes between the two vans and re-labelling them. Gwenna couldn't see what the new labels said, and didn't much care; she just wanted to get back to Caernoweth and climb into bed, so she could block all this out. Even if her dreams took her to wild and dark places, at least she would awake from them; the effort of keeping reality at bay was suffocating, she could barely bring herself to think about how quickly everything had turned on its head, and how deeply she was buried now.

When the money had changed hands and the other van was gone, Hocking rummaged in the footwell of his own van for a torch, and looked at Devereux. 'Right, come with me. And you,' he called to Gwenna over his shoulder, already striding away towards the folly.

But rather than lead the Frenchman into the ancient building, where Gwenna had imagined the fugitive would curl up awaiting transport out of Cornwall, he went down the side of it to where a collection of granite boulders lay near the rear wall. He gestured Devereux over, and indicated the ground, then looked at Gwenna.

'You'd better get familiar with this, too, since you'll need to bring food up here first thing every morning until I've fixed things up. Someone will meet you with the key.'

'Peter and I aren't—'

'I know, you said. I had someone else in mind.'

'Who, Bobby Gale?'

'I told you about him.' Hocking's eyes gleamed in the torch-light. 'You'll know by morning.'

Before she could respond, he dropped into a crouch and indicated a place where Devereux was to wriggle his fingers among the tufts of grass. The ground first moved, then slid aside, and Gwenna wondered numbly how much further this racket of Hocking's went.

Devereux disappeared without hesitation into the ground, and Hocking tossed the discarded canvas satchel after him and followed. When he emerged again three minutes later he was alone.

'He can't get out, can't risk him letting on where he's been staying. So you'd better not forget to bring him food and water.'

'I won't.' At least the gun was out of sight now, which was a huge relief, but she wasn't relishing the thought of coming up here and facing that slab-muscled Frenchman tomorrow. She wondered who Hocking would send with her, and having ruled out both Peter and Bobby, she could only hope it would be someone with enough strength and presence to subdue Devereux if he should suddenly decide he didn't enjoy being cooped up after all.

CHAPTER ELEVEN

The festival was nearing its end for another year; the dance was still going, but very few people remained now, after a long and active day. Bertie waited until Tommy and his friends had made their way across the garden to the gate and vanished from sight, then went to find the others. She found Tory first, almost hidden in a group of new young trainees; it was only her distinctive bellow of a laugh that identified her, and Bertie caught her attention.

'Have you seen Gwenna?'

'Oh, Tommy's put you down at last, has he?' Tory grinned as she elbowed her way out of the noisy group. 'No, I've not seen her since this afternoon.'

'Are you drunk?'

'Possibly. A little bit. No,' Tory sighed, and her smile dropped away, 'quite a big bit. It seemed the sensible thing to do.'

Bertie put an arm around her friend's shoulders. 'Don't think about her, she's not worth it. Come for a walk and get some air, or you'll feel horrible when you go to bed.'

They left the noisy, smoky dance tent behind, and it soon became apparent to Bertie that Tory's instinct was leading them towards the stables. Once there, Tory leaned her head against the neck of one of the horses, which had whickered in response to their approach and stretched its head towards her. She absently scratched the glossy cheek.

'I'm leaving.'

'Maybe best, you look as if you're going to fall over. A good sleep will—'

'No, I mean *leaving*. At the end of the initial training. I won't be moving on to the next stage, in other words.'

'Leaving Caernoweth altogether, or just leaving the base?'

Tory concentrated on petting the horse. 'Yes. I mean, altogether.'

'Because of your mum?' Bertie tried not to let her disappointment show too much; this was clearly already a difficult choice for Tory to have made.

'Not entirely.' Tory pondered, and Bertie didn't press her. 'I've discovered I don't get the same joy from flying as you and Gwenna do,' Tory said at length, 'and if I don't love it, I won't learn properly. And that would make me dangerous.'

Bertie had to agree, on that point at least. 'But you could still stay in town,' she said hopefully.

'There's nothing here for me. Nowhere to live, for a start, that I could afford anyway. No work, and ...' She didn't have to complete the sentence; *no family*. Bertie heard it in the suddenly bleak tone.

'Don't decide anything yet,' she urged. 'You've had a bit to drink tonight.'

'I decided before that.'

'But even so. We'll all talk properly tomorrow, since it's Sunday we'll have plenty of time. Gwenna will be back by teatime, too.'

Tory rubbed the horse's nose, and returned its gentle huffing sound. 'I won't make any hasty decisions,' she promised, turning back to Bertie. 'I've got a couple of weeks left, yet.'

'Good. Speaking of Gwenna, I wonder where she is?'

'Maybe she got bored and went to bed.'

'Maybe, or maybe she and Peter have had another row.' Bertie didn't feel as comfortable as Tory with horses, so she kept her distance and let her gaze wander around the impressive yard of Pencarrack House. 'I'm glad she broke it off with him though, he never seemed right for her.'

'No, far too pompous.' Tory gave her a speculative look. 'What was all that about earlier, anyhow?'

'All what?'

'That *I have no idea what the folly looks like close up,* thing earlier, when Irene asked about it. And then changing the subject so quickly. Anyone would think she was accusing you of something.'

Bertie could feel the flush starting, and was glad the sun had gone down. 'It wasn't about anything.'

'You and Tommy went there, didn't you?' Tory said, and Bertie could hear the grin in her voice.

'Yes, we did,' she admitted.

'Why the big secret?'

'Come on! You know what people say about that place. I mightn't have minded telling you or Gwenna, I suppose, but I don't know Irene nearly well enough.'

'Did you ... you know?' Tory asked, straightening up and letting go of the horse. 'Well?' she prompted, when Bertie didn't answer. 'Did you?'

'I'm not a child,' Bertie said, a little frostily. 'I've been engaged before you know.'

'I know! But on the moors? Where anyone might have seen you?'

Bertie felt herself growing tense, and could hear the defensive words building behind her lips, but Tory had been her first friend here, and was still her staunchest. She took her by the shoulders and stared directly at her. 'Tory, what can I say? It was bloody wonderful.'

Tory's huge laugh broke free again, startling the horses. 'Good! I'm glad. It's about time you two took that step. Pretty reckless though, or was that half the fun?'

'That'd be telling.' Bertie grinned at last. 'The thing is, we found something.' She looked around, then grabbed Tory's sleeve and pulled her to the path down the side of the manor house. When they were out of earshot of the milling festival-goers she stopped hurrying, but they kept moving until they emerged onto a patch of grass by the lip of the valley behind the house.

'What did you find?' Tory said, impatient when Bertie didn't elaborate.

Bertie sat down, glad to take the weight off her leg after a long day, and began to talk. The ground was a little dewy now, and her drop-waisted party dress was quite thin, but she didn't mind; it was a relief to let out all she'd been keeping secret since Wednesday. Tory sat beside her and listened without interruption, and when Bertie had finished, she nodded.

'I knew about the room, but the door was never locked before, as far as I knew.'

'Oh.' Bertie felt a bit deflated. 'You *knew* there was a false wall inside the folly?'

'No, not that. Nor the trapdoor, though that makes sense, and there definitely weren't steps. We just knew about the room underneath.'

Bertie shook her head. 'How could you know about the room, but not how to get in there?'

'You have to remember I grew up here,' Tory said with a little smile. 'The mine at the top of town, Wheal Furzy, closed just before the war, and after that it was easy to get into the tunnels. They run from the sea, through the adit.'

'The what?'

'At the bottom of the cliffs, just under the Cliffside Fort Hotel, there's a little cove. Have you ever seen it?'

Bertie nodded, but she'd never been there herself because of the difficulty of the cliff walk. 'Tommy said the air we could feel probably came from there.'

'That's because there's a drainage tunnel from Furzy that used to take flood water out to that inlet. That's the adit. It was a way of getting into the mine, too, but it's a little way up the cliff and the tide would have to be out or it'd be too dangerous, with the rocks.'

Bertie pondered a moment, imagining it. 'So ... the adit goes from the cove to the mine, and then someone's taken one of the other tunnels all the way out here, and dug out that room under the folly?'

'I'd say the room was there from when the folly was first built, and so was the hole outside that led down to it. But the tunnel's more recent, and the steps are new. I reckon they're the reason that internal wall you mentioned was put up. You need a bit of room for steps, but you don't need as much for a straight-drop hole in the ground.'

'It's a long way to dig out,' Bertie said doubtfully, picturing the Wheal Furzy engine house. It wasn't that far from her old flat, and the folly was much closer to Pencarrack village.

'Oh, there's tunnels going all over,' Tory said, thumping the ground beneath her by way of illustration. 'Big ones, tiny ones, half-finished ones ... Some you can stand up in and climb up the walls, others you can barely crawl through. It's a maze down there, believe me. And it's not really that far anyway, as the crow flies,' she added. 'Or rather, as the lode runs.'

'Presumably you and your little gang did a lot of exploring then?' Bertie heard the echo of envy in her voice as she thought about it. To have had that kind of childhood companionship was something she'd always longed for.

'All over, once the mine closed down,' Tory said. 'Furzy was opened a good couple of hundred years after Penworthy built the folly, but someone would have spotted the potential for stashing stuff away there. Wouldn't have taken much to divert the tunnel, especially if they'd spotted a likely source of ore in the rock anyway. Or at least claimed they had.'

Bertie tried to imagine what it would have been like down there day after day, hacking away at the solid rock that she'd seen littering the moors. Little wonder there was so much of it on the surface. 'It must have been wonderful to be able to play down there.'

'It was, once.' Tory's voice quietened. 'Right up until me and Harry Batten got lost one time. It was horrible, Bertie. I really thought we were going to die.'

'What happened?'

'Bobby Gale and some of the others took one of the big tunnels, and I found a little one that'd been abandoned when the lode ran out. But there was a ladder going down a shaft that met up with the main one ... Or I thought it did, at any rate.' She cleared her throat, and carried on in a more matter-of-fact voice. 'Harry followed me like he always did. I think, being three years older than me, and brought up in a good family, he felt like he ought to look out for me. It seems the shaft joined up with a different tunnel though, and by the time we realised, we'd taken a few wrong turns. Harry had his dad's torch, and we could still hear the others, all laughing and that, so we weren't too bothered. Then the torch went out, and we realised we couldn't find our way back to them after all.'

Bertie winced in sympathy. 'That must have been terrifying.'

'It was. We were down there long after Bobby and the rest decided we'd gone, and went home themselves. Then Harry found the ladder again. My ma . . . ' She stopped, and Bertie knew she'd caught herself slipping into the language of childhood again. 'My *mum* just about hit the roof, and I had bad dreams for months. Since then I've not really liked being in enclosed spaces.'

'I'm not surprised.' Bertie squeezed her arm. 'Well, I wouldn't be able to manage those steps anyway, so I'm not likely to ask you to give me a guided tour.'

'So, let's talk about these steps then,' Tory said. She seemed to have completely sobered up now, and no longer looked or sounded sleepy or sad. 'What do you suppose is in that room now?'

'I don't know, but I saw a van out there the other day, when I was flying over.'

Bertie told her about the mechanics' van, and how it had been standing at the folly with its door open. 'But I couldn't see who was there,' she finished, 'not from that high up.'

'I bet I know.'

Once again Bertie felt that little stab of envy that she wasn't the first with exciting news after all. 'Who? And how?'

'Bobby Gale. The night I saw my mother, I went for a short walk around the perimeter, to think about it all, and I saw Bobby talking to one of the mechanics. I couldn't see who. Then he just drove the van off the base, as bold as you like!'

'And he'd know about the room, just like you did,' Bertie murmured. 'Didn't Gwenna say he's still a right rogue?'

'She said Peter's always complaining about him,' Tory said. 'Thing is, he's never been a real bad lad. Not like some. He must have changed a lot if he's involved in actual smuggling.'

'He must have. I wonder what he's hiding there?' Bertie felt her excitement lifting again. 'Tommy didn't say what kind of lock was on the door, but imagine if we were able to get in!'

'Well, you couldn't, with that leg, and I'm not going down into a dark little space like that ever again. It'll have to be Gwenna who goes down.'

'How do you cope in the cockpit?' Bertie asked, curious. 'Strapped in, and no quick way out?'

'I can see out, at least,' Tory said. 'The sky, the ground ... I can see it all, so I know it's all still there, if you see what I mean.' She gave Bertie a sheepish look. 'I know it sounds a bit daft, but when Harry and I were lost in those tunnels, it was like it was the rest of the world that had disappeared, and *we* were all that was left. When I'm flying it's more like looking out of a window, just to reassure myself.'

'Is that why you travelled as soon as you could?' Bertie was starting to get a much clearer picture of Tory now; although they'd been friends since March, Tory had always been so good at drawing people out about their lives that she'd never got around to answering questions about her own.

'It's part of it, I suppose.' Tory gave a soft laugh. 'I never really thought of it like that, I just knew I wanted excitement. This seemed like the ultimate thrilling experience, and everything, including that first flight, seemed to be what I was looking for, but I don't feel any emotion for it anymore. I've discovered that inanimate objects just don't offer me what I want.'

'But horses do.'

'They always have done. Probably comes from growing up on the farm.' Tory shrugged. 'Perhaps that's what I need to go back to, after all, there are still a lot of animals that need help.' She spoke slowly, as if it was just occurring to her. 'Perhaps I should train to be a vet.'

'Can you do that and stay here?'

Tory shrugged. 'I doubt it. But I could always come back.'

'You'd better.' Bertie sighed. 'You're my best friend here, Tory, I'll miss you.'

'I'll visit,' Tory promised, hugging Bertie's arm. She broke into a yawn. 'It's getting late.'

'Let's go back then. Tomorrow we can pull Gwenna aside, tell her what we know, and get her to go down and look at that door.'

'You don't want to involve Irene, then?' Tory didn't sound surprised, so Bertie didn't bother to hide her own reservations.

'We don't know her, do we? And there's all that special treatment she seems to be getting. I don't quite trust her yet.'

'She has so many maps of the area,' Tory mused. 'And she does keep asking about the folly, it's a bit like she's testing us to see how interested in it we are.' She frowned. 'What if she and Bobby are in it together, and that's why she's staying here?' She twisted to look Bertie full in the face. 'She was properly cagey when I asked her if she had a boyfriend, too.'

Bertie drew a breath. 'What if she was writing a note to Bobby that night, to tell her she'd arrived?'

'The more I think about this girl, the more I wonder.' Tory stood up. 'We're going riding tomorrow morning, and it's hard to do that without striking up conversations about all kinds of things.' She nodded, her expression turning distant. 'Leave her to me.'

*

Tory and Bertie returned to the dorm where they found, as expected, Gwenna slumbering peacefully in her bed. Irene was sitting up reading, and she pointed wordlessly to the little table by the door, where she'd put the post she'd collected. Bertie had a quick look, passed Tory a letter, and took her washbag off to the bathroom.

Tory looked at the postmark and realised the letter was from Gerald, and the last traces of alcohol haze disappeared as she sat on her bed to read it. She drew the unfolded sheet of paper from the envelope, and her heart sank; it wasn't a reply at all, just the letter she'd sent to him, returned. Her own brief explanation of her return to Caernoweth ended with:

> *Mum is back in town. She didn't recognise me. Do you know why she came back? Does Matty? I have written to him also, and will write again if I find anything out. I don't know if you ever found out why she left, but I would be glad to learn the reason, if you did.*

Tory was about to shove the note back into the envelope in disappointment, when she glimpsed a scrappy bit of handwriting on the other side and turned it over.

> *No, we never learned anything. Nor do we want to. Glad you're back safe.*
>
> *Gerald and Matty.*

Tory was taken aback by the bluntness of the words. She could well understand her brothers' sense of betrayal, and Gerald had never been one for long-winded explanations, but the anger came through the letter as if his voice had wafted off the paper itself, and there was no way of knowing whether it extended to her as well as their mother. She tucked the note away, and, giving Irene's questioning look a bland smile, she whispered a reminder that they had to be up early to take the horses out, then she took her own washbag to wait outside the women's bathroom for her turn.

When Bertie emerged, changed for bed, Tory stopped her. 'I was thinking,' she said in a low voice. 'If Irene won't give up anything about herself, and we still think she might be up to something, we could write to your friend Leah.'

'And say what?'

'Just that we think Irene might be up to something, and can Leah find out anything about her that'll change our minds.'

Bertie looked astonished at the notion. 'That seems very intrusive, no matter what we think. What right do we have to set a private investigator on the poor girl, just because she's a little bit mysterious? Besides,' she added, pulling her house coat tighter around herself, 'Leah doesn't work for free, and *I* can't afford to pay her, can you?'

'No. You're right,' Tory sighed, feeling rightly chastened. 'I was getting carried away, and it was just a thought. I'll see what I can find out during our ride tomorrow, and it'll probably all make perfect sense after all.'

The following morning found her in the yard at Priddy Farm, having saddled both Bonnie and Mack, and still prickling with annoyance at finding the blasé little note in the dorm after her deliberately early breakfast.

Sorry, need to run to the village. Meet you at the farm. Will try not to be too late.

Irene.

The horses had been difficult to tack up too; as soon as they'd realised they were going out, after a long time of plodding through the fields, they'd both become over-excited and it had taken all of Tory's expertise to calm them long enough to check them over before she could begin. Mack stamped and began pawing at the ground, and Tory sighed and swung up into the saddle. She rode slowly around the yard, leading Bonnie, until finally she heard footsteps by the gate and Irene appeared, flushed with running, and still limping a little. She was tying her long brown hair back as she crossed the yard, and turned an anxious face up to Tory.

'I'm so sorry, I'd forgotten I had to run that errand first thing.'

Tory nodded at Irene's ankle. 'Are you sure you're okay to ride?'

'I'm fine, it's just running that's put it out a bit.' Irene finished tying her hair, and held out her hand for Bonnie's rein.

'What was it, anyway, that was so urgent?' Tory tried not to sound bossy; this was supposed to be a pleasant outing after all, not a lesson or an interrogation. Not yet, anyway.

'I remembered I'd promised to return the dress I'd hired for the dance, before Alice Donithorn left for chapel.'

'Well, you're here now. They're both a bit skittish from waiting though.' Tory turned Mack's head and rode towards the gate, then looked back to see Irene fumbling to get her foot into the stirrup. Bonnie was shifting, itching to get going, which didn't help.

'Just try and do it quickly,' Tory said. 'No fuss, you'll soon get back in the swing of it.'

Irene held the stirrup steady and pushed her boot into it, then, with a grunt, pulled herself up into the saddle and gave Tory a look of triumph. 'Ready!'

The ride itself was enjoyable once they moved off the road. They went up past the town through the fields alongside it, and emerged onto flatter moorland not far from the old quarry at Polworra. There they were able to relax more, and amble along in the mid-morning sunshine, and Tory noticed Irene settling more easily into the saddle, and into the rhythm of Bonnie's stride. For herself she was aware that Mack was holding back a great deal of power, and she had to fight the urge to kick him into a canter and let him go with it, but it wouldn't have been fair on Irene. Besides, she'd promised to try and draw Irene out a little on this ride, and this was the perfect time.

The conversation was stilted at first, as Tory asked about Irene's earlier riding experiences, but soon the new girl was expanding on the so-called trouble her aunt had tried to keep her out of, by sending her off into flying lessons.

'It was all pretty silly, really,' she said, as she allowed Bonnie to pick her own way down into a wide ditch. 'You asked about a boyfriend too, and it was all connected. She just thought I was getting into the wrong relationship.'

'Quite an expensive way of getting you out of it,' Tory remarked. 'Still, you seem to be getting on very well, so I expect she's pleased. You're doing very well with this too, by the way.' She nodded at Bonnie, and at the way Irene had instinctively adjusted her seat as they came back up the far side of the ditch. 'Looking very relaxed. All coming back now, eh?'

'Feels like it.'

Tory employed her famous drawing-out skills as they rode, revising her opinion of Irene with every new revelation of mildly rebellious schooldays, and illicit kisses in the dark with first crushes. In turn she told Irene about her time in France with the horses, and in London, and finally about the way Nancy had snubbed her last night. Irene had been appalled, and then furious on Tory's behalf.

'She doesn't deserve you, that's all,' she said, a scowl darkening her expression, and Tory was able to laugh at that.

'No, you're right. She doesn't. Well,' she said regretfully, as she squinted at the sun, 'we'd better turn back soon if we're going to meet the others for lunch. It'll take a while to get these two settled again. Want a quick burst, before we do?'

'Burst?'

Tory gestured up ahead, to the smooth, grassy pathway that led from the quarry pool back towards the top of town. 'I used to give Bill his head along here, and so did his owner. I know it well and there are no nasty surprises, so what do you say?'

Irene looked suddenly unsure, and Tory was about to withdraw the suggestion, until a smile flashed on the other girl's face and a reckless gleam came into her eyes.

'Let's!'

Tory gave a whoop, and turned Mack's face back up the path before kicking him into a canter. As she felt the ground fly beneath her, and absorbed the thunder of hooves on grass, she felt such an unexpected surge of joy that in that moment she couldn't imagine living or being anywhere else. A glance over her shoulder showed her Irene coming up fast, Bonnie's mane flowing and matching Irene's hair, which had pulled loose from its hastily applied band. Irene was laughing, and although the glance was necessarily fleeting, Tory noticed how lightly Irene was riding, how low over Bonnie's neck, and how she barely moved in the saddle. Her lost skills were definitely coming back to her, and Tory couldn't see any reason she'd need a riding school after all.

When they slowed again and turned back down towards the farm, Irene was glowing and looking delighted. 'I don't think I've ever ridden so fast. Bonnie was determined to keep up with her offspring.'

'You rode really well!' Tory said, still breathless and delighted with the way Mack went, once he was given the chance.

'I barely clung on,' Irene protested. 'But it was a lot of fun. Let's do it again sometime.'

They rubbed the horses down, and put them back in their stable to be turned out after lunch, and Tory was glad Bertie had put her foot down so quickly on the idea to investigate the girl more deeply. She was right, they had no right to do such a thing, Tory had just let herself get carried away by all that talk of rooms under the folly, and Bobby Gale getting up to who knew what with the engineers' van.

They made their way companionably back up the hill to the base, talking about more pleasant things as they went; Tory pointed out the Tin Streamer's Arms, the tiny pub that was nevertheless the heart of the town; the bookshop where her friend Freya MacKenzie had lived and worked, and the holiday flats at the top of town where Bertie had lived, which had been the grandest hotel for miles before Norman Pagett's company took it over.

Irene began telling her about some of the new buildings in her own home town, and something which had been niggling Tory for a few days raised its head again.

'So you *do* come from Wolverhampton?'

Irene blinked. 'Yes, why?'

'You told Keir Garvey you were from Birmingham.'

'Yes, well ...' Irene shrugged and smiled. 'I didn't mean to be patronising, but I just chose the nearest place he might have recognised. I mean, I doubt he's travelled a lot. And Birmingham is right on the doorstep after all.'

No it isn't, Tory nearly said. *It's at least ten miles as the crow flies.* But she didn't speak it aloud, because she'd just been served a sharp reminder that, no matter how friendly and easy-going Irene could be when she wanted to be, she lied. A lot.

CHAPTER TWELVE

Somehow, Gwenna held herself together through chapel, nodded at various members of the congregation, spoke to the minister afterwards, and even laughed at something Alice Donithorn said. She eschewed her usual walk to the beach though, in case Peter was walking down at the same time, and instead went home with her parents for the afternoon. She'd managed it all as if she were an actor, playing the part of someone who didn't have the weight of too many secrets on her shoulders, but this morning she had reached saturation point.

She had waited at the folly as instructed, just as the sun had crept over the horizon. In her knapsack, collected from Barry Hocking while it was still pitch dark outside, she understood there to be bread, cheese, ham, and a dewar flask of cold milk; some fruit and various leftovers from the festival bulked out the remainder of the pack, and she let it fall to the ground with a sigh of relief, and massaged her shoulder. At least she wouldn't have to carry it back full.

But there was the question of who was going to be there to unlock the door and stand guard, while she unpacked it all for M. Devereux, and whether whoever it was would be armed. She'd asked Hocking for the gun, but he'd simply looked at her with mild surprise that she should even consider it.

'I don't think so, my dear, do you? Don't worry though, you'll be fine. Now off you go, you'll be met at the folly.'

So she waited, her eyes on the end of the moorland path where it met the Pencarrack road. Someone was coming, but it was too far away to distinguish whether it was someone she'd seen around the base, or in town. She suspected it might be Peter, and was already preparing a frosty reception, but as the figure stepped off the road and onto the grassy track, Gwenna recognised Irene, and she groaned. She remembered the maps, and the interest the girl had shown in this place, and tried to believe Irene was here exploring on her day off, but deep down she knew better. They'd all been played for absolute fools.

'Gwenna?' Irene's voice was low, but carried clearly in the still morning air, and Gwenna stepped around the side of the folly, on her guard in case she was wrong.

'What brings you up here this early?'

'Don't bother,' Irene said, lifting a hand. 'We both know why we're here, so let's just get it done.'

'I'm not sure what—'

'Yes you are.' Irene peered into the dark interior of the folly. 'I've got the key, so where's the way in?'

Gwenna gave in and gestured to the patch of heatherless grass. 'There.'

'Come on, then.' Irene dropped into a crouch and examined

the ground, then worked her fingers under the edge of the board. 'Don't just stand there!' she snapped. 'I'm supposed to be meeting Tory this morning.'

Gwenna lent her strength to the task, and the board slid aside to reveal the hole. She shivered. 'Why are you here?' she asked quietly. 'How much do you know?'

'Not much.' Irene took a torch from her pocket and flashed it down the hole. 'Oh good, decent steps. Have you got the food then?'

Gwenna picked up the knapsack. 'You'd better go first, since you have the key.'

She followed Irene down the steps, taking one last quick look around before she vanished below the level of the ground, but the moorland around them was still deserted. The glow of the rising autumn sun cast a pink light over the ground and the heather, and spread streaks across the lightening sky, but she couldn't appreciate the beauty of it today, not when there was such dark work to do.

At the bottom of the steps, where cool but musty air brushed their skin, Irene had pulled a chain from her pocket and was fitting a key to the padlock securing a heavy-looking wooden door. There was the sound of movement from the other side, where Devereux would have been aware of them from the moment the trapdoor slid away from the hole. Possibly sooner; if there were holes in the hidden room to let in air from the tunnel, they would also let in sound.

Gwenna's heart thumped uncomfortably fast, and she leaned in close to Irene's ear. 'What if he rushes us?' she whispered.

'Why would he? We're doing him a favour.'

'A favour he's paying for, and he might decide to take his own chances from here. Why would Hocking send two of us, if he doesn't think that might happen?'

Irene gave her a pitying look. 'Don't be dense, Gwenna, we're each other's insurance. We know we're both in this now, so we can't rat on one another.'

Gwenna felt foolish, as well as dismayed; had she learned nothing? It also explained why Hocking hadn't told her last night who her opposite number would be, and given her time to back out. 'Did you know I was the one you were meeting?'

'Not now. We'll talk later.' Irene twisted the key and pushed open the door. 'M'sieu? *Nous avons votre* ... food,' she finished, with a shrug.

'He speaks English.' Gwenna shone her torch into the room, and saw the burly Frenchman lift a hand to cover his eyes. 'Sorry.' She lowered the torch, sweeping it around the inside of the room instead.

It seemed even smaller down here than she'd imagined from the size of the folly above it, and it was so dark it was a wonder Devereux hadn't been driven mad overnight; the combined light from the two torches barely crept over the threshold, and she could hear things of indeterminate size scuttling away from the beams, no doubt ready to creep out once darkness reigned again. She shuddered and reflexively scratched her arm.

Devereux seized the knapsack, and emptied it on the pile of blankets that he was using as a bed, picking through what was there with little grunts of either approval or disapproval.

'Go,' he said over his shoulder, 'before someone sees the open stairway.'

'Give us back the bag then,' Irene said, and the words were hardly out before he'd thrown it at her. She fumbled to catch it

209

and dropped her torch, leaving them with only the thin light from Gwenna's. She bent to retrieve it, and rose, shining it directly on Devereux's face. He peered through the light, squinting.

'Is it you?' he said, surprising them both into stopping before Irene could shut the door.

'Is what me?'

'Smith! Is one of you Smith?'

Gwenna looked at Irene. 'I don't know who he's talking about. Do you?'

'No.' Irene pulled the door shut and fastened the padlock again. 'Come on, he's right, anyone could come out here on a day like this.' She pushed at Gwenna, who stumbled up the steps, beyond relieved to be out in the fresh air again.

They manhandled the false ground back into position, and Gwenna still itched to get away, to present herself at home without arousing comment from her parents. But she had to know more about Irene.

'So, *did* you know it would be me?'

'Not until this morning when I collected the key.'

'I'm not doing this through choice,' Gwenna said, quickly.

'Of course you're not. I told you, we're each other's insurance. If either of us was doing this because we wanted to, we wouldn't need that, would we?'

'You seem very matter-of-fact. As if you've done this before.'

'Well, I haven't. And I didn't know anyone else would be with me. I thought I was alone.' Her voice shook a little, emotion surfacing for the first time.

'But you knew about the folly before you arrived.'

'Yes, I knew about it.' Irene stamped down on the corner of the hatchway, but Gwenna couldn't tell if it had been sticking up, or if Irene was just cross. 'I didn't know about the underground room, though, not until last night.'

'Last night?' Gwenna stared at her as she began to walk away, then hurried to catch up. 'You were here? Watching?'

'Of course I was. Un ... Hocking told me to be here by ten, so I left the dance early.'

'Un?'

'What?'

Gwenna grabbed her arm and pulled her to a stop. 'You were going to say "Uncle" then, weren't you? Is Barry Hocking your uncle?'

'Why else would I be here?' Irene yanked her arm away. 'I don't want to learn to fly, any more than Tory does, but I've got no choice.'

'Why?'

'It doesn't matter, does it?' She sounded tired now. 'I'm in it, you're in it, we have to work together, that's it. I don't care about your reasons, you shouldn't care about mine.'

The bravado of that comment sat at odds with her evident relief that she had someone by her side now, but Gwenna didn't press her on it. 'So what happens next?'

'We go back. We do as we're told. You'll go to chapel, I'll go riding with Tory, and we tell no-one at all that we're working together.' Irene began walking again. 'I came to the village this morning to drop off my dress with Mrs Donithorn. I couldn't care less what you tell the others, but we didn't see one another.'

'Who's Smith?'

'How should I know?'

Gwenna frowned. She was sure Irene knew what Devereux

had been talking about, and it felt important, but she didn't know why. 'Is your name really Irene Lewis?'

'Yes! I wouldn't be able to train here if I tried using a false name, they'd sniff me out in two seconds flat. Probably accuse me of being a spy or something.'

Gwenna wasn't so sure, with Barry Hocking for an uncle, but there was clearly no sense in pursuing it now. She had let Irene get a decent head start, then wandered slowly back past the base and into town to meet her parents for chapel.

Now she was watching the two of them eating their Sunday lunch as if they couldn't wait to get away from the table. Most of the anger seemed to be coming from her mother, and Gwenna wondered if things had come to a head last night, when they'd brought everything home from the festival. Neither of them had returned to attend the dance, which was unusual; even if her father was in too much pain to dance he usually enjoyed the chance to take a drink with his friends. And Anna had been there, so it was a surprise that Rachel hadn't wanted to join in the fun too, although her absence had made it much easier for Gwenna to slip away.

The scraping of cutlery on the Sunday best china was beginning to stretch Gwenna's nerves, and she abandoned her own meal long before her plate was empty. 'I'm going outside for a few minutes,' she said, pushing back her chair. 'And then I think I'll go back to the base.'

'Why?' Rachel patted her mouth with her napkin and looked up at her in surprise. 'You always stay for the afternoon, otherwise we never see you.'

'Because I don't think I can sit here and watch the two of you barely saying two words to one another.' Gwenna had tried not to let her emotions show, but it was impossible. 'I don't know what's happened since yesterday, but I really don't—'

'Nothing's happened,' Jonas said, his voice calm. 'Sit down, love. Come on. Your mother's gone to a lot of trouble.'

Rachel's eyes widened a fraction in surprise, but she didn't acknowledge his words. 'At least finish your meal,' she urged. 'Probably the best one you'll get all week.'

'The food at the base is fine.' Gwenna looked at them both in turn. Jonas was steadily making his way through the cabbage and potato mixture that was all he had left, and by contrast Rachel looked as if she couldn't face another mouthful. She herself couldn't taste the meal; all she could think about was Devereux chewing his way through a hunk of bread in the pitch darkness while goodness knows what scurried over the rest of the food. She didn't feel the least bit sorry for him, she knew he was unlikely to be a particularly nice man, but even so it was horrible to think about.

'I'm going for a walk while the weather's still nice.'

'September now,' Rachel said, and sighed. 'Another summer gone by.'

The attempt at small talk was met with silence from both Gwenna and her father, and Rachel picked up her fork and began pushing food around her plate. Gwenna tried to catch her father's eye, but he stared steadfastly downwards, making sure he had every last curl of cabbage on his fork. Something must have happened, she was sure of it, and suddenly she'd had enough.

'What's the matter with the two of you?'

They both looked up, then at each other, then quickly away. 'Nothing,' Rachel said quietly. 'Nothing that need concern you, anyway.'

'Is it that stupid rumour about Dad and Nancy Gilbert?'

'Who?' Jonas looked so convincingly blank that Gwenna felt like crying with relief.

'Gwenna!' Rachel tried to urge her with her eyes to take back the comment, but she pretended not to understand.

'I knew it was rubbish.' She sat down again. 'Gossip. This town is full of it.'

'What gossip?' Jonas wanted to know. He looked at his wife. 'Rachel?'

Rachel looked deeply uncomfortable. 'It's just something Anna said.'

'Only because you said it first!' Gwenna heard the words come out, and knew it was a mistake to plunge on with this, but the combination of two huge secrets was too hard to bear. At least she could talk about this one. 'If you hadn't told Anna what you thought about Dad, she wouldn't have suggested Tory's mother had anything to do with it.'

'Tory's mother?' Jonas looked more baffled than ever now. 'What are you talking about? Rachel, did you tell Anna you thought I was seeing someone behind your back?'

'Were you listening at the door?' Rachel fired at Gwenna, flushing a deep red. 'How dare you?'

'So you *did* tell her!'

They were both shouting now, and Gwenna slammed her hand on the table. 'Stop it!'

They did, more out of surprise than anything else, and Rachel took a gulp of water. 'You shouldn't go eavesdropping, Gwenna, you don't understand what you're saying.'

'I understand you accusing Dad of having an affair! How could you?'

'I'm not seeing anyone,' Jonas said, and Gwenna could tell he'd become tense, because he arched his back slightly and winced.

'Oh there you go,' Rachel said. 'All of a sudden your back's hurting.'

'All of a sudden?' Jonas's eyes narrowed. 'You're telling me you don't believe me?'

There was a heated pause, then Rachel spoke more quietly. 'Of course not, I shouldn't have said that. I'm sorry.'

'And where did you get the idea I'm having an affair? What have I done to make you think that?'

Rachel seemed amazed he'd asked. 'It's all your comings and goings! You *must* see how that looks, when you never say why you're going, or when you'll be back.'

'I tell you where I'm going, I never just disappear.'

'But it's all so vague! You just say you're going to Bodmin, but never who you're meeting there. Or that you won't be home at teatime, and I'm not to wait up for you, but never why. What am I supposed to think?'

'What does it matter? You'll just make it up anyway!'

Their voices were rising again, but this time Gwenna might as well not have been there, and she watched and listened in dismay as these two people she loved most in the world flung accusations and counter-accusations across the table, ignoring congealing meals that had taken time and precious money to prepare. She saw, perhaps for the first time, the long history and separate lives her mother and father had known before she had come along to complete the family. The words they hurled at one another didn't matter, and by and large they didn't even mean anything now, but Jonas's face was becoming paler as his frame tensed, and he frequently lifted a hand to massage the back of his neck; Rachel's knuckles were white where they gripped her cutlery, and her eyes glittered with angry tears.

Gwenna could see both sides, the betrayal on her mother's side, the hurt rebuttal on her father's, but there was no proof he'd done anything wrong, only a feeling; the vague suspicion of someone looking for an explanation, endorsed and bolstered by a careless piece of gossip from a nosy shopkeeper.

'Leave him alone!' she blurted, as she saw her mother's mouth open again to deliver another barb. 'He says he's not seeing anyone else, and I believe him! He wouldn't do that to you.' *To us*, she'd wanted to say, but that new understanding of the many Gwenna-less years in her parents' relationship was still clear in her mind. 'Just stop it!'

'Gwenna, love,' Rachel began, but Gwenna shook her head.

'I'm going back to the dorm. I can't sit and listen to your accusations anymore.'

She rose again, and went to her room to pick up the overnight bag, not yet unpacked, from her bed. She could hear her parents' raised voices again, following her, but this time they were arguing about which of them had driven their daughter away from the family home on the one day of the week they could spend together.

'She cares more about flying than about us,' Rachel was shouting, 'and there's only one person to blame for that!'

'She can't listen to another minute of her mother turning into a harpy, more like,' Jonas returned, his own voice lower, but equally hard.

Gwenna slipped out through the closed shop, instead of having to pass through the kitchen again to use the back door; she couldn't bear the thought of facing her parents again, and the fact that she had deliberately provoked the row from which she now sought to escape niggled at her. But it had brought things to a head, and even a bitter row like this was better than poisoned silence and forced smiles. Perhaps by the time she saw them again they might have mended things. Or even just patched over them, that would be a start.

It felt as if she'd been put through the wringer along with the laundry. She could sleep for a week, and, arriving back at the dorm, she flung her bag on her bed and sat down, grateful to be alone. Bertie would be in the common room writing letters to her family this afternoon, and Tory had said something about going for a walk, so there would be no better time to confront Barry Hocking without arousing curiosity.

Only the maintenance hangars were open and occupied on a Sunday, to allow the mechanics to work on planes that were needed during the week. One of the boys might know which of the big houses Hocking lived in, and, knowing how friendly she and her instructor were, they might be willing to tell her. As she walked across to talk to them, her face hot from the sun and the agitation, she thought through what she would tell Hocking when she saw him.

I can't do this anymore. I won't do it.

You've got Irene, you don't need me.

Don't punish my father for my mistakes, he doesn't deserve to know what I did.

And if it fell to pleading, begging, she would do that too. *I swear I won't tell a soul . . .*

Would he listen? She doubted it, but she also knew she would never forgive herself if she didn't at least try.

The main hangar's doors stood open, and from inside she

could hear the cheerful voices of engineers and mechanics working together; the engineers developing new ways of making the machines more efficient, and safer; the mechanics making rapid repairs to over-taxed training planes. She poked her head around the door, hoping Tommy would be among them, and was gratified to see him walking out of the office at the far end of the hangar. She was about to call him when she saw who had emerged behind him: Bobby Gale. As they parted company, and Tommy returned to his work, he clapped Bobby on the shoulder and made some parting comment that made Bobby laugh aloud.

Gwenna remembered Tommy defending him at his birthday dinner, and had thought then that Tommy should have known better than to be drawn in by Bobby's charm act. Perhaps it was aspirational; Tommy was even now just twenty-five, and very much the innocent, hard-working type, while Bobby was in his early thirties and had become a man over in the trenches. Nowadays he had his fingers in that many pies it was a wonder he had time to pass the time of day with a clean-living aircraft engineer, but he always seemed to find time to drink with his wide circle of friends, and no-one seemed keen to give him up when one of his schemes came unstuck. Gwenna hoped Tommy wasn't taking his example to heart, especially not now that he and Bertie were getting along so well.

She waited outside the hangar, glad the airfield was deserted, and that only the occasional passer-by crossed anywhere near the hangar as they moved between leisure block and dormitory. Bobby emerged, still chuckling, and gave Gwenna a vague nod of recognition as he started down the path to the gate. He must be confident Hocking was nowhere near, to be seen loitering so brazenly around the base.

'Wait a minute, would you?' Gwenna trotted a couple of steps to catch up, and Bobby stopped and sighed.

'Whatever he says I've done, I haven't.'

'What? Who?'

'Your husband-to-be, who else?' Bobby rubbed his face. 'I'm that sick of it, to be honest.'

Gwenna couldn't help the short laugh. '*Honest?* I'm surprised you know the meaning of the word. Anyway, I'm not engaged to Peter Bolitho anymore,' she went on, to forestall the defensive retort she could see coming. She lowered her voice. 'I just wanted to . . . to warn you.' She looked around, but there was no-one near them. 'I know what you've been doing for Barry Hocking. And that you've recently stopped doing it.'

Bobby went very still. 'Do you now?' he asked carefully. 'And what might that be?'

'You've been driving the van down to the rail depots, and picking up . . .' She didn't want to continue, but Bobby didn't make it easy for her, and simply arched a heavy black eyebrow. 'Picking up boxes of things you shouldn't,' she finished.

'And what things are those, then?'

'You know!'

He nodded gravely. 'But do you?'

'Yes I do. Mr Hocking told me.'

Bobby passed an appraising look over her, then shrugged. 'I should have realised you were the one they were talking about.'

'Who?'

'The lads down at the depot. Tall, they said. Long hair. Pretty face, but reminded them of their teachers.'

Gwenna flushed, but she wasn't about to admit it, and incriminate herself. 'Could be anyone.'

'Most likely to be you, considering who else is involved.'

'I told you, Peter and I aren't together anymore.' But they had been at the time, she couldn't deny that, and it didn't take a great deal of intelligence to connect the two of them. Bobby, for all his faults, was blessed with a shrewd mind, and had probably known right from the start that Peter had only arrested him to give her a chance at making the run. Settling her well and truly on the hook. Or perhaps it was a show of power on Hocking's behalf; a reminder that he had the local constabulary poised at the end of a crooked finger.

She still didn't understand what had made Bobby drop everything; she'd have thought it suited him very well; relatively little effort for what was more than likely a very good reward.

He was still looking at her, speculatively now. 'So what was it you was wanting to warn me about?'

'He's gunning for you, now you've left.'

'Of course he is.' Bobby rubbed his face again, and Gwenna saw darkened circles beneath his eyes. She noticed, for the first time, how deep the lines around his mouth were, and at the corners of his eyes. Those eyes had probably seen enough during the war to put thirty years on him, and up close, today, he seemed to be wearing all those extra years despite his jaunty exchange with Tommy.

'I thought you'd want to know that, so you could keep out of his way,' Gwenna said pointedly, looking around them. 'As in, not hanging around his place of work.'

'Nice of you.'

'Why *did* you stop doing it, anyway?'

'Your boyfriend arrested me,' he reminded her.

'You were only out for a couple of days though. Why give up altogether?'

Bobby shoved his hands into his pockets and tilted his head slightly. He was squinting against the sun, but she could still see the way his eyes were clouded. 'Do you really know what's in those boxes, Gwenna?'

His use of her name startled her slightly. 'Tobacco, and alcohol. Whisky, I assume, rather than wine.'

'Alright. Good luck with it.' He turned and started to walk away, but Gwenna caught him up again.

'What is it then?'

'You tell yourself what you want,' he said, lengthening his stride.

'Bobby!'

'It's *guns!*' He swung around as he hissed the word, and Gwenna shrank back in alarm at the look on his face. 'It's guns, maid,' he said again, but this time with a visible effort to calm himself. 'Pistols, rifles, machine guns.' He checked no-one was near, and grasped her shoulders. 'This isn't some harmless way of avoiding tax, or a way to profit off hotels and bars by helping them do the same.' He sounded hollow now. 'Get out, love. You're too young to be getting mired in this.'

Gwenna's heart hammered. 'But I'm already mired in it,' she managed, barely above a whisper. 'How *can* I get out?'

'Just tell him. And then stay out of his way, like I'm doing.'

It was on Gwenna's lips to say that her father must never find out, but something stopped her; Bobby would either laugh or, more likely knowing him, use it against her if he found out how desperate she was not to taint her father's image of her. A moment later she felt ashamed of that thought, as she watched him scratch hard at his face and saw a bead of blood appear beneath his ragged fingernails.

'I don't want no part of this,' he said in a low voice, and the looked he turned on her was suddenly haunted. 'I've seen what they can do to a man.' He gave a short bark of a laugh. 'I don't even poach, nowadays. Not that anyone'll believe that.'

'I believe it,' Gwenna said, equally quietly, surprised to find that it was the truth. 'But I don't know what to do, Bobby. I don't want be involved any more than you do.'

'I'm sorry, maid. I can't help you.' Bobby's smile was faint, and sad. 'Just look after yourself, alright? And remember, those blokes down the yard don't know what they're shifting neither, and if they did, they'd more'n likely be under the next train. So do them a favour too, and keep it to yourself.'

Gwenna shivered at the cold certainty in his voice. 'Hocking knows though. He's not just acting as a go-between.'

'Oh, he knows alright. He set it up with some of them gangs up in Birmingham and Bristol and the like. He don't care who buys it. Gets a good dollop of cash for helping them blow each other to kingdom come, but I'll bet you've not seen any of that money, have you?'

'I wouldn't want any,' Gwenna said at once, and told him, as briefly as she could, how she'd become involved. She didn't mention Irene, but explained how she'd realised Peter had been part of it all along. 'My guess is that Hocking's got a similar hold over him that he has over me,' she said, 'probably something to do with his job. I'm pretty sure Peter doesn't know what's in the boxes though.'

'Maybe not. But he should've stopped you even going down there, while there was still time to back out.'

'He did try. But I was ... well, always have been a bit pig-headed. I thought I knew best.' She looked at him curiously. 'How

222

did you find out it was guns?' Even the word landed like a lead weight, and she had to swallow after she said it, struggling to understand how she'd come to be having a conversation like this.

'One of the crates slipped, getting it into the van. A corner splintered, and I pretended I hadn't noticed, but I've unloaded enough weapons from supply lorries to recognise a barrel sight when I see one.'

'So you just carried on.'

'What else was there to do?' He rubbed at his hair, then began to dig at his face again, clearly agitated.

'Do you know it's not just the boxes?' Gwenna asked him, after another quick look around.

'What do you mean?'

Gwenna wondered at the wisdom of pressing on with this, but unburdening was addictive. Perhaps it was also selfish, but talking to Bobby was a lot easier than talking to cool, matter-of-fact Irene. He was showing a rarely seen side of himself, and it gave her the hope that he might even be able to offer some advice. 'It's people, too.'

Bobby stopped scratching. '*People?*'

'There's a man down there now, under the folly. A Frenchman.' Gwenna's voice dropped again as she heard voices, and two engineers came out of the hangar on their way to the canteen. 'He's waiting to be flown out,' she added, when they'd passed by.

Bobby looked as though his mind was working fast, and Gwenna wished she hadn't said anything. 'Flown where?'

'I have no idea,' she said truthfully. 'But I'm betting he's not the first. He's a member of a gang from Bristol, that's all I know.'

'Must have got himself into something big,' Bobby mused. 'And he must trust Hocking, to let him lock him in like that.'

223

'I got the impression they'd never met. So he must trust whoever sent him here instead.' Gwenna paused. 'Do you know someone around here called Smith?'

'A few.'

'Anyone who might be part of what Hocking's doing?'

'Definitely not. Why?'

'Something the Frenchman said. Someone he's heard of.' Gwenna's mind went back to Irene's short reply when he'd asked them, and the way she'd slammed the door shut. She was Hocking's niece; it was entirely possible Devereux had been told to make contact with her, and that the short exchange had established that contact. Maybe asking about Smith was a form of password ... She realised Bobby was talking, and dragged herself back.

'Sorry? What did you say?'

'I just said not to worry about me, but I'll be careful not to poke him. And you should do the same'

'That's not enough, Bobby. He's threatening your family too.'

Bobby's face tightened. 'Threatening them how?'

'He just said that he didn't much care whether it was you or your family he got hold of. You have to leave.'

'He's all bluster,' Bobby said, but his voice sounded strained. 'I'll talk to Sally though, it might be a good idea to pack her off to our ma's for a bit, until I've convinced Hocking I won't say anything.'

Gwenna had her doubts that it would be enough, but her mind was too full. She watched Bobby out of sight through the gate, and realised she'd forgotten to ask him if he knew where Hocking lived. She wished desperately that she could speak to her friends about Irene, and whether her name might really be Smith, but that avenue was closed off to her for the same reason Bobby would be staying quiet: she couldn't risk bringing them into it. There was nothing to do now but accept that she had, however inadvertently it had begun, chosen to become a criminal.

CHAPTER THIRTEEN

With Gwenna at her parents' home, and Bertie nowhere to be seen either, Tory had a quick lunch and took her thoughts out on the road to Pencarrack. She walked steadily, not really seeing anything of her surroundings, and only realised she had taken the lane that led to the church when she was halfway along it. She immediately knew why her instinct had led her here, however, and, letting out a small sigh of inevitability, she continued.

The church itself was old, but had been absorbed into the new village growing around it, much like several of the other old houses on the outskirts. The grounds were filled with tilting, moss-covered stones, some with barely readable inscriptions, many much newer, and in the corner stood one just ten years old, erected by the parish in memory of the men and boys from the area who'd been lost to the war in Europe.

Tory hadn't visited it since she'd returned, but her feet automatically began carrying her in that direction, her mind returning to the slip-up Irene had made when telling Keir where she came from, and on all the other, seemingly insignificant, things that didn't seem to add up. She stumbled on a clump of grass, which brought her out of her thoughts again and re-focused her on the memorial and the fact that, standing beside it with her back to the path, was her mother.

Nancy had one hand outstretched, the delicate fingers stroking the stone, and the other was pressed either to her eyes or her mouth, it was impossible to say which. But the slim shoulders were shaking, and there was no sound, so Tory had to believe Nancy was stifling sobs. She felt her throat tighten in response, and remained still, blinking away her own tears before they could spill. After a moment Nancy lifted her head and took a deep breath, then pressed the flat of her hand to the stone cross before turning away. She stopped dead as her gaze met Tory's, and the two women stared at one another across the few graves that lay between them. Tory opened her mouth to speak, but Nancy shook her head and resumed walking.

'Not here,' she said in a low voice, as she passed by and re-joined the main path. 'This isn't the place.'

'Then where is?' Tory started after her, her anger rising again. 'Nowhere, if you had your way.'

'What?' Nancy turned, her pale eyes widening in surprise. '*You* were the one who walked out of the surgery!'

'And you were the one who decided shopping was more important than clearing the air between us!'

Nancy blinked, and her lips were parted to speak, but she looked as if she couldn't think of a thing to say, and she resumed walking instead. Tory followed her out of the churchyard back out into the lane where one or two people were meandering down, taking advantage of the last of the summer weather and a Sunday afternoon, but no-one took any notice of Tory or her mother.

'Come down here.' Nancy started down a narrow cut-through, not bothering to wait and see if Tory was following. Which was typical of her, Tory thought with sudden savagery, and she wondered whether she ought to just turn on her heel and go back the way she'd come. But the curiosity was still too strong, so she reluctantly followed.

The offshoot lane was deserted, and a few feet in, there was a gap in the hedge. Nancy ducked through it, moving with the familiarity and assurance of a child taking a favourite short cut, and they emerged into a field that backed onto the far side of a steep-sided valley. Across the way Tory could see the back of Pencarrack House, where she and Bertie had sat just last night listening to the music drifting out from the dance tent, punctuated by the gentle whickering of horses from the stable. It seemed like a different world today. Nancy checked the ground for sheep droppings, and sat down. She looked up at Tory, who wordlessly joined her, and they sat in tense silence for a minute. Then Nancy took another deep breath.

'What did you mean about me going shopping?'

'That's where you went yesterday, isn't it? Instead of coming to the festival?'

'Well yes, I went to Truro. But only because I had no intention of running into the likes of Alice Donithorn or that snooty Anna Penhaligon. Anyway, everyone knows Penworthy now for the violent crook he was, so I don't know why everyone still celebrates him.'

'It's been going on for hundreds of years,' Tory pointed out. 'No-one celebrates *him* anymore, just the town. Anyway,' she plucked irritably at the grass, 'that's not what I meant. You could have at least come to the stables to meet me.'

'I would have, if I'd known you'd be there. Unfortunately I don't read minds as well as I used to.' Nancy gave her a sideways look, as if she thought she might have lightened the moment, but Tory was not to be softened.

'I told you I'd be there, in the letter. I told you what time, and I waited longer than I should have had to. But when you didn't come, I convinced myself you were working. That I shouldn't have been so quick to dismiss you.'

'Letter?' Nancy was looking puzzled again. 'I don't know what you're talking about, I didn't see a letter.'

'I posted it to you in plenty of time.'

'I'm telling you, I didn't get it.' Nancy looked at her earnestly. 'I would have come, Tory, Alice or no Alice. I was devastated when you ran out of the surgery, but I had to stay, to see to your friend. I had no way of finding you afterwards, and just kept hoping to bump into you in town.'

'So you didn't know I'm living at the air base and taking flying lessons?'

'No! How could I?'

Tory faltered; it was extremely hard to disbelieve someone who could look simultaneously horrified and unbearably proud. 'You really didn't receive it then?' she said at last.

'I promise you, I'd have been there.' Nancy's expression faded into one of thoughtful suspicion. 'What did it say, exactly?'

'Just that I needed to know why you left.'

'Becky,' Nancy said on a sigh. 'She's the one who brings the post, but she always opens it first because people don't always know which Doctor Stuart they're writing to.'

'But ... why would she keep it from you?'

Nancy didn't answer for a moment, then she reached out and

clasped Tory's hand before she could think to pull it away. To her own surprise, Tory didn't want to.

'I'm going to tell you everything,' Nancy said, holding Tory's gaze with her own. 'Afterwards you can decide whether you think I've done badly by you, or just behaved stupidly. I'm not a fool, I know it's one or the other, and none of it was anyone's fault but mine. I won't trouble your life if you don't want me to, and none of this is an excuse, it's just ... the way life went.'

'Go on then.' Now Tory did remove her hand from Nancy's, but only because she sensed this might take a while, and she almost unconsciously shifted position so she was sitting cross-legged like a child. The way she had any other time her mother had settled down to tell her a story.

'Alright. You remember the man who used to come to the house?'

Tory nodded. 'We had to stay quiet until he left.'

'It was Charles Batten, our landlord.'

'Harry's grandad,' Tory muttered. She looked across again at Pencarrack House, the home of the Battens.

'Yes. That was ... well, it was how I paid the rent. Which is why, when he died in the Pencarrack House fire, we lost Hawthorn Cottage and had to move back to Priddy Farm with your own gran and grandad.'

'But no-one knew about it, did they?'

'One or two did. Ellen Garvey—Donithorn, that was—would have heard it from Anna Penhaligon.'

'And where did Anna hear it?'

'From her cousin Keir. You know he and I were close at one time, but he found out about Charles, and ... that was it.'

Tory frowned. 'This isn't telling me why you just left out of the blue like that.'

'Alice Donithorn thought I was after Keir again, and knowing Ellen would have told her all about how I'd paid the rent, and bought food and such, I was sure she was going to spread it all around the town. Thinking back now, I doubt she would have,' Nancy added, 'she's not really like that. But at the time I couldn't bear the thought of it.'

'But you were a widow, and Mr Batten a widower. What business was it of Alice Donithorn's?'

Nancy gave her a faint smile. 'Times have changed, Tory. Back then there'd have been no question of Charles having anything to do with the likes of me, and I didn't want him to. I was his grubby little secret, and he was mine. We didn't care for one another one bit, but he took a fancy to me, and I needed to keep his temper sweet so I could keep the house.'

'That's horrible.'

'It wasn't so awful at the time,' Nancy said. 'At least, it didn't seem it.' She gave Tory a quizzical look. 'Come on, love. You must have done things that you look back on and wonder about. We all have.'

Tory shifted on the ground, frowning. 'So you let Alice Donithorn and her gossipy friends break up our family?'

'It didn't *feel* like that.' Nancy shook her head. 'It never does though, does it? If I'd known . . . I just wanted to find somewhere else for us to live, where you and the boys wouldn't be punished for the decisions I'd made. But I couldn't take you all with me, could I? And I knew you'd be well looked after until I found us somewhere.'

'We were,' Tory said. 'But you never came back.'

'I couldn't.'

'Because of the *gossip?* That's—'

'No, my love. Not because of that. I'd never have let something so stupid stop me.' Nancy fiddled with the strap on her shoe while she considered how to continue, and Tory waited, her curiosity building.

'I found work on the east coast,' Nancy said at length. 'St Peter's Plain, in Great Yarmouth. Just housekeeping work, you know, but it was a live-in position, so my expenses were small, and I was saving some money. I was starting to think it would be a good place to bring you; on the coast and all, like here.' Nancy's voice started to crack then. 'The war was happening a long way away—'

'Not for us,' Tory put in, her own voice hardening. 'Gerald joined up almost right away.'

Nancy flinched 'I wrote a letter when I first got my job,' she went on. 'It was in September, and it had a special card in it for . . .' she snatched a quick breath, 'for Joey's birthday. Knowing that my own children, even Matty, could write better than I could, it was difficult and horrible, but I tried. And I promise you, Tory, I posted it! But when I didn't hear back I thought you were all still angry.'

'Maybe Granny Ruth was, and that's why she didn't pass it on.'

'Maybe. She probably thought she was doing what was best for you.'

'Seems we've both been on the receiving end of that little game,' Tory muttered.

Nancy nodded, and a flush touched her cheeks. 'I wondered if maybe she was just waiting until I had something good to tell you all. Like I'd found somewhere we could *all* live. So I didn't write again until I had.'

'So you didn't know about Gerald?'

'No, not until later. A lot later.' Nancy's eyes glittered and she dashed at them impatiently, as if she didn't feel she had the right to cry now. 'After Christmas I started to write again, but before I could finish and post it the town was hit.'

'Hit? You mean—'

'A Zeppelin went over at about nine that night, while I was on my way back from visiting a friend. It was the strangest sight, we didn't really know what was happening. It'd never happened before, and one of our neighbours, Samuel, was just standing in the street watching it—'

'Oh no ...'

'He must have stood there, watching the bomb fall, not understanding what it really meant. He died instantly, they said. I was hit by something, likely a flying brick, and when I woke up in hospital everything was gone from my head. My name, all of you, Granny and Grandad, everything. The letter was still in the house where I worked, and that was destroyed.'

Tory didn't speak, her imagination was rendering words useless and trivial. If her mother hadn't gone out visiting that night ...

'Someone told me a little boy was killed in King's Lynn on that same night,' Nancy went on. 'Fourteen, he was, just three years older than Joseph. God, his poor ma!' The tears came again but this time Nancy let them. Tory leaned forward and drew her mother into an embrace, feeling very much the stronger one now. She let her mother sob until she was spent, knowing there had to be more to come.

At length Nancy drew back and wiped her eyes. She seemed determined to press on now that she had begun. 'Since I didn't have a home or a job when I came out of hospital, I took up work with this nice Canadian doctor who'd cared for me.'

'Doctor Stuart,' Tory guessed, and Nancy nodded.

'He was a couple of years widowed, but there was nothing between us, not at first. Although I knew he wanted there to be. I recovered well, all but my memory, and I had no-one, so I took up the offer to care for his children. Then, when he joined up and went to France as a medic, I stayed with them. We grew close, and they even taught me to read and write properly. They were still learning, themselves, bless their hearts, and would come home from school to pass on what they'd learned that day. I still didn't know who I was though, so we chose a new name for me.' She managed a smile, and touched Tory's face. 'I chose Victoria. I didn't know why, I just knew I felt the name strongly in my heart.'

Tory's chest constricted. The field around them had shrunk to the patch where they were sitting, and she was wholly immersed in her mother's new world; a world that contained only Nancy, Rebecca and Aaron Stuart, and the letters they had received from the Front. The Cornish family had been nowhere now, except in Nancy's sleeping memories, but her choice of name proved she had still felt them, deep down.

'Frank was invalided out of the army in 1917 with a piece of shrapnel in his hip, and he needed basic help in the surgery, so I stepped in. I discovered I was actually quite good at it. I learned fast, and quite soon I was putting in stitches, helping at births, and even diagnosing some illnesses.' Nancy gave Tory a wry smile. 'Quite a long way from collecting eggs and worming sheep, but it felt right.'

'And all this time you were still without your memories?'

Nancy nodded. 'I was told that it would come in time, that trying to force things would likely only send them deeper, so

234

I stopped trying and just waited. And in the meantime I was building a new life. Frank encouraged me to train properly, and he even got a nanny for the children, so I began studying at the London School of Medicine for Women. Of course that meant living away from Frank, and I came to miss him, which is when I realised I did feel something for him, after all. We married the day after I graduated.'

'When did you get your memories back?'

Nancy lowered her eyes. 'Around two years ago.'

Tory tensed. 'And it's taken you this long to come back?'

'I wrote to my parents straight away, at the farm, but the letters were returned. It took a while to find out that they'd been sent on to their new home in Bodmin, but that they'd both died.' Nancy blinked back more tears. 'Aaron tried his hardest to find out what had happened to you all, and the first thing he found was that Joseph had been killed right at the end of the war.'

She cleared her throat, evidently determined not to break down again, but in the harsh sunlight Tory could see the strain around her eyes and mouth. 'He couldn't find anything about Gerald or Matty, and the last thing he found about you, from Anna Penhaligon of all people, was that you'd left Caernoweth in 1919 and just ... disappeared.'

'Anna was very good to us after you left.' But Tory chewed at her lip, feeling her own surge of guilt that she hadn't kept in better touch with her family and friends. She'd written to her two surviving brothers, but rarely had a reliable return address to leave, so even if Aaron Stuart had found them it was unlikely they could have reached her to tell her their mother was searching for her too.

'And why did you come back to Cornwall?' she asked quietly.

'Frank knew I wanted to. I talked about the place all the time, apparently, without even realising I was doing it.' She gave a soft laugh. 'He saw that Doctor Bartholomew had left, and the vacant practice was advertised, and it took him a long time to talk me into it but he convinced me in the end. I thought everything would have been forgotten by now. I certainly didn't expect to see you,' she added, reaching for Tory's hand again. 'I thought you'd left for good, since there was nothing left for you here once Granny Ruth and Grandad were gone.'

'I hadn't planned to come back,' Tory confessed. 'I heard about the flying school though, and I couldn't resist.'

'Flying.' Nancy gave a brief shake of her head, and her smile was a little tremulous, but she seemed relieved to have had the chance to tell her story. 'You always were an adventurous little scrap.'

'And what about when people find out what kind of woman their new doctor is?'

'Was,' Nancy insisted. 'There are only three people alive who know, apart from you and me, and I don't see why any one of them would want to drag that up again now. To what purpose?'

Tory was about to agree that it was unlikely, but her mother's words sparked a sudden suspicion. 'Ellen Garvey died last Christmas.'

'I heard that. There was no love lost between us, but it's still a terrible shame, and I feel badly for Keir.'

'That's not what finally persuaded you to come back, is it? That you found out, and you think you might have a future with Keir after all?'

'Absolutely not!' Nancy looked genuinely appalled, and Tory relaxed a little. Bad feeling like that could make life in town very uncomfortable for the new doctor and her family. The thought of that family prompted her to ask something else.

'Why *did* Rebecca hide the letter?'

Nancy flushed. 'Like I told you, we all grew very close during the war, and have been ever since. She was only three when her father left, so for a long time I was the one she turned to for everything. Aaron was five. I was their whole world for what would have seemed a very long time in their little lives.'

'So she's jealous.'

'Not jealous,' Nancy said gently, 'protective. Please, don't think badly of her.'

'She could have spoiled everything,' Tory said withdrawing into anger again. 'And *you* shouldn't have given up after you didn't hear back from your first letter. Everything might have been so different, if only you'd cared enough to have written again.'

'I did care!' Nancy wrapped her arms around her drawn-up knees, and lowered her head. 'But I was so wrapped up in getting everything sorted out for you all, and the days just flew by—'

'So now you're back, do you expect everything to be perfect, and everyone to be friends?'

'No, I don't expect that,' Nancy said, sounding weary now. 'I just hope for it to happen one day. I want your forgiveness, Tory. Are you ready to give me that, at least?'

'It's not up to me to forgive or not,' Tory said, and a thread of bitterness wound through her again; she'd let her guard down, but the reality was returning. She rose to her feet, simply to break the cosy sense of mother and daughter story time. 'You started a lot of ugliness when you chose to sleep with Charles Batten. We could have moved back into Priddy Farm at any time, but *you* wanted Hawthorn Cottage, and to be seen as independent and strong.

So you became a ...' She stopped herself, appalled at what she had almost said, but Nancy had heard it anyway. She lowered her knees and stood up.

'I can't excuse any of that. But I'll try to prove how much you mean to me,' she said, looking Tory unflinchingly in the eyes. 'I understand it'll take time, but I'm not going to run away again, no matter what comes out now. You mean more than my stupid reputation, Tory, I love you all, no matter what the people around here say. You, Gerald, Matty, and my sweet, lost Joe, are the best parts of me and always have been.'

She walked past Tory and back towards the gap in the hedge, and Tory wanted to call out and stop her, but she couldn't. There was a certain relief in at last knowing what had driven Nancy away, but it was such an awful truth, and she could only pray it would spread no further than those who already knew, otherwise Nancy Stuart's days in Pencarrack were liable to be unpleasant, and few.

The evening was starting to draw in as she picked her way across the beach beneath the Cliffside Fort Hotel, around half an hour later. She had walked straight across Pencarrack Moor, from the village, and the brisk walk had done her good and helped clear her mind of all the unimportant details, while she focused on the heart of what her mother had told her.

The tide was on the rise again now, and the sea hissed its way in and curled back again, dragging the sand and small stones with it. The sound was soothing and familiar, and Tory blew out a long sigh and tilted her face to the evening sun, enjoying the warmth combined with the slightly cooler breeze coming off the water. September was her favourite month for many reasons, but it was always a little bitter-sweet now that Joseph was no longer there to celebrate his birthday. It would be coming around again in a few days, and she would spend some time at the memorial then; it would make up for the fact that she hadn't stayed there today after all.

'Tory!'

She looked around at the sound of the voice cutting through the last of the families packing up for the day, and saw Gwenna sitting on a rock and waving. She crossed the small cove and brushed wet sand off the rock before sitting down. 'What brings you all the way out here?'

Gwenna pulled a face. 'I walked away from a massive argument at home, and came back early.'

'Oh no.' Tory gave her arm a sympathetic squeeze. 'That's awful.'

'How about you?'

'I've just been talking to Mum.' Tory took Gwenna's raised eyebrows as permission to tell her story, so she did, beginning with the surprise of seeing her at the war memorial. By the time she had finished Gwenna was completely absorbed, and kept letting out little murmurs of surprise and understanding, punctuated with tiny snorts as Tory told her about Rebecca keeping the letter from Nancy.

'And she had the gall to be all sweetness and light at the festival? I think your mother's being too kind to her there.'

'Rebecca didn't know who I was at first, when she was being so friendly. She hadn't connected the *Victoria* on the letter to *Tory*, and after that she was definitely a bit more sniffy. I can tell you one thing for sure though,' Tory went on, 'Nancy is *not* having an affair with your father. She's really not the same person she was before she left.'

'I knew it.' Gwenna shook her head. 'He's not seeing anyone, I'm positive. I just wish Mum realised it too, it makes me so angry. She should know him better than that.' She looked back at the cliff path. 'Shall we go now? It'll be just about teatime when we get back.'

'In a minute.' Tory had been looking idly across the width of the cove, and her gaze lit on something that gave her a surge of mingled nostalgia and fear; at the foot of the cliff there was a mass of rocks, and a few feet up from them was the adit by which she and the other children had regularly entered the mine workings at Wheal Furzy . . . It felt as if today was a day for putting childish things away for good.

'Come and look at this.' She started across the grainy sand again, glad she'd worn sturdy boots for her afternoon walk, and soon she was clambering over the rocks towards the cliff face.

'Watch the tide, Tory!' Gwenna followed her, but was still wearing her Sunday chapel clothes, and stopped where the sand ended and the rocks began. 'What are you looking for?'

Tory pointed to the irregularly shaped hole, well concealed and around ten feet up the cliff face. The rocks around it were discoloured where the mine's runoff had carried mineral deposits with it, but they were dry at the moment, and Tory pulled herself easily up the cliff, her previously buried memories placing her hands and feet on the same jutting rocks she had leaped up so nimbly as a child.

After only a few minutes she was parallel with the adit, and able to lean across and peer inside. The sunlight didn't reach far in at this time of the day, and the upward slope inside disappeared into gloom very quickly. It should have been the work of seconds for Tory to step across and boost herself up into the hole, but a sudden, sweeping heat stopped her and forced her to draw a slow, calming breath.

Her fingers were shaking, although they were no longer supporting her weight, and her knees didn't feel strong enough to carry her up. The tunnel was dry, and the mine shut down; there would be no sudden rush of water that might have carried her back out of the adit and dash her onto the rocks – the great thrill they had faced as children. But the thought of stepping into that suffocating blackness and letting the world disappear behind her was terrifying.

'What's in there?'

'The tunnels that lead to the mine, and then the folly,' she called back, grateful for the connection to reality again. She tore her gaze away from the hole, and the labyrinth beyond, and climbed back down. 'We used to play in there when we were kids. Wheal Furzy blasted through to the back of that cave, which was pretty deep already, and used it to run off flood water into the sea.' She jumped the last few feet and brushed her hands to rid them of sand.

Gwenna was looking tense, as if she'd worried Tory would fall. 'Did you say it also leads to the folly?'

'Apparently it does now.' Tory picked her way back across the rocks, which were by now awash with regular surges of the incoming tide. 'It was just a cave back until then though. It would have been useful for smuggling stuff past the excisemen who patrolled the coast. This cove is hard enough to get to by sea, and there's only one way out by land, but a storage place like this meant the small boats could get in under cover of dark, stash the contraband in the cliff, and get back out to the merchantmen anchored out there,' Tory pointed out to sea, 'before anyone noticed them. Then someone else, probably Penworthy and his men, would come and get them once the ship – and the attention – had moved on. They'd have taken them overland in those days, and stored them in the room beneath Tyndall's Folly. Hard work, up that cliff path.'

'So the folly wasn't built as a sop to Tyndall after all then?'

'More likely as a way of doing business with him.' Tory started back up the beach. 'Coming?'

'What else do you know about it?' Gwenna asked, hurrying to catch up.

'Not much, just that someone clearly saw an opportunity when they started sinking shafts and tunnelling out from Wheal Furzy, because now the tunnel extends out there, and there's proper steps instead of just a hole in the ground. Why do you ask?'

'No reason.'

'Anything to do with Bobby Gale, or Irene?'

'What?' Gwenna stopped dead. Her face was red from the exertion of climbing the path, but there were patches of white beneath her eyes. 'Why would you ask that?'

Tory stepped off the rough path and sat on a clump of marram grass. She patted the ground next to her, and when Gwenna sat down she told her about the conversation she and Bertie had had, just last night. It felt like weeks ago. She explained their suspicions about Irene's interest in the folly, and about Bobby Gale's likely involvement, discerned from their two separate sightings of the van and its illicit outings. Finally she broached the subject of Irene receiving preferential treatment in her training. As expected, this last seemed to inflame Gwenna more than the rest of it.

'Why didn't you say anything before?' she demanded. 'That was the day I told you I passed my test, and you didn't say a word!'

'Well, that was *why* we didn't,' Tory defended herself in a low voice, and waited for a chattering family group to pass them on the path. 'After all the trouble you'd had,' she went on, 'we couldn't really turn around and say we thought Irene was getting the opposite, could we? It would have spoiled your day completely. Besides, we were only speculating about that, we have no idea why it might be the case.'

'You left me out,' Gwenna said. She sounded angry and miserable now, and Tory looked at her in surprise.

'Don't be like that, Gwen!' When the usual correction of the shortened name didn't come, she sighed and tried again. 'We weren't trying to exclude you from anything, honest. We both thought these things at separate times, and we just happened to talk about them when you weren't there. To be honest you've been busy a lot lately.' It came out sounding more accusatory than she'd intended, and she could see Gwenna had heard it the same way. 'I didn't mean—'

'Just go on,' Gwenna said, and turned her face away to stare out over the sea. 'I'll come up in a bit.'

'Well, what do you think about Irene?' Tory pressed. 'Getting a leg up the ladder like that? And why do you think she lied about where she comes from?'

'How should I know? Maybe she was right, and Birmingham *is* close to Wolverhampton.'

Tory pulled a face. 'Would you tell someone you lived in Truro?'

'If it would help them understand better, then yes!'

'I'd say I lived near there, then. Not *actually* there. I also think she rides better than she says she does.' Tory told her how she'd glanced back and noticed Irene's light touch on Bonnie's mouth, not yanking on the reins, as an inexperienced rider might at that speed, and the way she rode low over the horse's neck, steady as a rock in the saddle. After witnessing the girl's struggle getting into that saddle to begin with, it smacked of someone forgetting she was supposed to be putting on an act, and throwing herself into the moment.

'Ridiculous to think someone would bother to lie about that!' Gwenna stood up. 'I think you just don't like her, and are looking for things to be suspicious about.'

'What about Bobby Gale then?'

'What about him? If he's up to his tricks again, let him get on with it. I'm sure Peter will be keeping an eye on him. And by the way, while we're busy throwing accusations at Irene, why don't you ask yourself why Tommy Ash is suddenly so chummy with Bobby?'

Gwenna started up the path once more, overtaking the straggling family and putting more distance between herself and Tory's questions. Tory followed slowly, unconvinced by any of Gwenna's deflections; she hadn't said what she thought about Irene getting extra help, and her usual scathing response to anything regarding Bobby Gale had definitely been watered down. That final comment about Tommy was faintly disturbing, too. Tory made no attempt to catch up with Gwenna when she reached the road; her mind was once again full of questions without answers, and it was becoming exhausting.

FILTON, BRISTOL

Jenny sat beneath the window in the Twenties' barn, keeping her head well below the rough sill, and her back jammed up against the wall, as if she could melt into it if she wished it hard enough. What would happen now?

One hand gripped the rough material of her coat and wrapped it across her exhausted body, and with her other she pressed at the bandage she'd wrapped around her thigh, and hissed in pain and frustration. Alain Devereux, Ronnie's second-in-command, had made the right decision getting out of the Docklands Mob when he had; he'd vanished yesterday, like a wraith at daybreak, and now Jenny had to do the same thing while she still could. But she needed help. She heard the door open, and looked up to see her own second, Colette; a thin-faced woman who'd made a name for herself as one of the deeds, not words mob, alongside Emmeline Pankhurst.

'Well?' she asked, trying to sound cross rather than desperate.

Colette pursed her lips, and didn't reply for so long that Jenny started to grow worried, then she nodded. 'Leave it with me, you'll be on the next collection van.'

'Where?'

'Cornwall. The same place as Alain. If they can't fly you out, they'll get you out by boat, but it'll cost, mind.'

Jenny nodded. 'You know how to get what you need. Take the rest for yourself, just get me on that van. And it'd better not be a Dockers' collection that's going down, or I'll be dead before we get out of Somerset.'

'Don't worry, it's not them.' Colette checked the window, and Jenny reflexively stretched up to do the same, but nothing moved outside. The woman dropped to a crouch beside her. 'I'll take you back to the flat. Get some things together, and then lie low, I'll be back when I've arranged it. And here.' She dipped into her pocket and brought out a small but serviceable knife. 'Just in case. Come on.'

She dropped Jenny at her flat in Broad Street, then disappeared to make her arrangements while Jenny limped upstairs and pulled an old army kit bag from the top of the wardrobe. She pushed a change of clothes into it, and then picked up a framed photograph of herself and Victor; after a moment staring at the grainy photograph, focusing on the two solemn-looking children as if they were strangers, she used the knife to lever open the photograph frame, and removed the picture. She slipped it into the kit bag and pulled the string tight.

Then she sat on her bed and waited.

CHAPTER FOURTEEN

At lunchtime on Monday the four girls met for what had lately become a rare lunch together. Bertie was looking forward to catching up with everything that was going on in her friends' lives, even if she couldn't share much about her own; it seemed they all had something going on, and it had been some time since they'd managed to eat at the same time. Jude had taken advantage of the need to get her plane serviced, and taken the train to visit her family in Leeds, so there would be no flying until the weekend at the earliest. Bertie would miss their illicit trips out to Lynher Mill, but it would be nice not to have to lie to the others about where she was going. She made her way towards the canteen, pulling off her gloves as she went, and feeling a pleasant, anticipatory growl of hunger as the smell of spiced beef wafted across the grass.

'Fox!'

She turned to see Tommy waving at her from the doorway of the hangar where he was working. She waved back and he gestured her over. 'What time are you finishing tonight? Only I thought we might take a ride out to the folly.'

Bertie could feel the flush stealing up her neck, and he must have seen it because he gave a soft laugh. 'Much as that idea appeals,' he said in a lower voice, leaning in and nuzzling her temple, 'I was thinking we could explore the other exciting find of the day.'

'You mean you want me to stand guard while *you* go exploring,' Bertie said, knowing she sounded a little sulky. But at least she'd be out doing something, and better still, with Tommy. She sighed. 'Alright. You bring the torch though, if the others see me with one they'll want to know why.'

'How's the extra tuition going?' he asked casually, and she gave him a reluctant smile, recognising the subtle reminder that she had plenty of excitement of her own going on.

'Very well, thanks, and point taken.' Shaking her head at the laugh that followed her across the yard, she went to join the others for lunch, and Tory raised an eyebrow at the smile on her face.

'Someone's looking like the cat that got the cream.'

Bertie saw that the others were still fetching their meal from the counter, so she told Tory what Tommy had said about the folly. 'He wants to go digging around in there this time,' she said. 'Not literally of course.'

Tory frowned slightly. 'Be careful, both of you.'

'Careful about what?' The others had returned to the table, and Gwenna had evidently caught those last few words.

Tory shifted over so Irene could sit next to her. 'Bertie was just telling me about her motorcycle racing days,' she said smoothly. 'She's taken to riding on the back of Tommy's lately. Have you ever ridden on one, Irene?'

Irene looked horrified at the thought. 'I can barely stay on a horse, let alone a motorbike.'

'You did very well yesterday,' Tory reminded her. 'Did rather more than "stay on", I'd have said.'

Bertie followed Tory's lead. 'You enjoyed it, then, Irene? How long has it been since you rode out?'

'Oh, years.' Irene busied herself arranging her cutlery. 'I think Tory's being kind. She and Mack went off into a canter, and Bonnie just wanted to follow; there wasn't much I could do about it so I just clung on at first, then I sort of remembered how it felt, and relaxed a bit more.'

Tory smiled. 'You looked very comfortable when I looked back.'

Bertie saw through that smile in an instant, but it was unlikely anyone who didn't know her as well would have noticed anything strained about it. Gwenna, however, was frowning.

'Tory, why don't you tell the others what you told me, about your mother?' she asked, rather pointedly. 'I'd like to hear it again, too, there was a lot to take in.'

Bertie couldn't help wondering at her ability to deflect questions on Irene's behalf and why she, of all people, had felt the need to do so. But Tory's recounting of her mother's wartime experiences was enough to keep the conversation going throughout lunch and it was clear they would find out nothing more about Irene, during this meal, at least.

She was by turns astonished and sympathetic, to Nancy's predicament as well as Tory's. It was such a difficult thing to understand; she herself had only shadowy memories of the war years, when her own father had been gone for such long stretches of time, returning almost a stranger. Nancy had become a real stranger, even to herself; it was hard to condemn her for the choices she'd made once her memory, and the shame that came with it, had returned.

Tory told the story in a fairly matter-of-fact way, almost as if recounting the plot of a play or a film, but it was easy to see she was struggling to forgive the initial feeling of abandonment her mother's departure had left. Nancy's story was tragic, frustrating, and at times desperately sad, but her twelve-year-old daughter's experience would have been one of bewildered betrayal. The inevitable wounding of that young heart was going to be hard to overcome, no matter what the head told her, and Tory was going to need her friends more than ever while she navigated these unknown and potentially turbulent waters.

When classes were over for the day, Bertie met Tommy by the gate and they rode out to the folly again, where they were obliged to wander around pointing out the more interesting and attractive features of the little building to each other, until the few people who were there had left. Thankfully they didn't have to wait long until they were alone again, and memories of the last time were warm in Bertie's mind, and evidently in Tommy's too; before they set to work moving the wooden cover, he took Bertie's face in his hands and kissed every inch of it, while she tried not to laugh.

'That tickles,' she protested, but his only reply was to nip gently at her lower lip, and the humour turned to a sweep of pleasure as her hands found his hips and pulled him closer. 'We haven't got time for this.'

'Oh yes we have.' His nibbling turned to gentle pressure with his lips, and she returned it, feeling his hands drop lower and meet in the small of her back. He pressed her against him and she let herself fall into the kiss, dismissing the thought that anyone might come upon them at any moment. It didn't matter.

At length they broke apart, and Tommy's eyes were dancing as they met hers. 'I've never met anyone like you, Fox.'

'Good.' She gave him a smile but pushed him gently away. 'We'd better get on with things.'

'This will always be our place,' Tommy said, looking up at the unkempt, mossy walls that rose behind them. 'No matter what it means to everyone else, there's nothing sordid or trivial about what happened here between us.'

'How many other women have you brought here?' Bertie couldn't believe she'd risked this moment by asking, but Tommy had worked at the base since it had re-opened, and he was young and healthy, not to mention good looking. But he looked genuinely surprised at the question.

'Here? None. Honestly, not one,' he assured her, as she gave him a sceptical look. 'I've not had a girlfriend from town before, mind, just ones I grew up with in Lynher Mill. Our version of Tyndall's Folly is the stone circle on the moor, so that's where we went.'

'You'll have to point that out to me sometime,' Bertie said, comforted to know this place had become special to them both at the same time. 'In the meantime,' she went on, looking around nervously, 'I repeat my earlier comment about getting on with it.'

'Come on then.' Tommy began feeling around with his foot, and when he found the edge of the trapdoor he bent to the task of levering it up and sliding it away to reveal the stairway.

'I'm not going into the tunnel,' he said, to Bertie's relief, 'just to the door.'

Bertie stood by the corner of the folly and kept checking in all directions for anyone taking an evening walk that looked as if it might bring them close enough to see what was going on.

Behind her, and below, she heard Tommy rattling at the door of the underground room.

'It's definitely locked tight, not just stuck,' he called back up. 'Now I've got the torch I can see the padlock. Quite a new one too.' She heard a thump; presumably he'd kicked at the door, out of frustration or an attempt to force it open, she didn't know. She opened her mouth to tell him to stop, but a distant movement made her change her words.

'Someone's coming!'

'Damn! Walking or driving?'

'Walking.'

Tommy's quick footsteps sounded on the wooden steps, and as she strained to see the approaching figure more clearly Bertie heard him grunting behind her as he heaved the trapdoor back into place.

'It's Irene! Hurry!'

'How far away?'

'She's halfway down the path from the road. She hasn't seen me yet.'

'Well, if your suspicions are right, she's not going to want to be seen any more than we are.' Tommy appeared by her side, breathing hard with exertion. 'Come here. Don't look at her.'

Before Bertie could speak he had pushed her against the folly wall, and covered her body with his own. His mouth came down on hers and she felt the rapid beat of his heart through both their shirts, as he gave an enthusiastic performance of someone in the throes of desire and oblivious to all. She heard movement in the grass near the front of the folly, and then nothing.

'She's gone,' Tommy said at length, pulling back and peering down the path. 'She doesn't know we know she was here. What *was* she doing here, do you think?'

'It has to be something to do with that room.' Bertie frowned. 'Tory was right, she's definitely up to something, and it's obvious she couldn't care less about flying.'

'Shouldn't we report her?'

'For what?' Bertie shook her head. 'Imagine if it was completely innocent after all? She might just be meeting some married bloke, like we thought at first. They could have a cosy little love-nest under there.' The more Bertie thought about it, the more likely it was that it was Bobby Gale that Irene was seeing, but she didn't want to say that in front of Tommy.

Tommy tightened the chin strap on his helmet. 'Next time I come I'll bring a crowbar of some kind, or a hammer.'

'Do you think that's a good idea?' Bertie climbed onto the bike behind him. 'I think it might be better to follow Irene next time she comes up, instead. We don't want to go smashing down doors if we don't have to.'

Tommy shrugged. 'You could be right. Either way,' he brought his foot down hard on the kick-starter, and raised his voice to shout over the engine, 'that girl's been lying to you, and she's got free rein to go wandering around a military training base. I'd have thought the sooner we find out what she's up to, the better.'

Bertie was surprised and distracted to find Tory and Gwenna waiting by the gate when they returned. She climbed off and let Tommy go and park the bike, allowing herself to be guided rather bemusedly towards Tory's car instead of back onto the base.

'We're having supper at the hotel tonight,' Tory said.

'What about Tommy?'

'Don't mind me,' he said cheerfully, as he came back over. 'I'm checking over Singleton's kite while she's away, and it has to be done outside my regular hours.'

'Why?' Tory asked. 'She's using it for instruction, so surely it should come within the flying school's budget.'

Tommy shrugged and avoided Bertie's warning look. 'No idea, I'm afraid, I'm just the engineer. I'll see you tomorrow.' He dropped a kiss on Bertie's head, smiled at the others, and strolled back up towards the dormitory block.

'Why are we eating out tonight?' Bertie asked, as Tory guided the car down the road into town. 'Don't tell me I've missed a birthday?'

'No, nothing like that,' Gwenna said. After an odd kind of frostiness between her and Tory this morning, she'd seemed more back to her old self by lunchtime; never exactly the life and soul of the party, but at least she seemed comfortable in their company again. Bertie was about to take advantage of Irene's absence, to bring up what she and Tommy had seen at the folly, but they were already drawing into the car park of the Cliffside Fort Hotel, and Tory and Gwenna were both clearly eager to get inside. Perhaps it would be nice to talk about other things for a change, anyway.

Bertie's leg was paining her a little tonight, and she hadn't needed to take her stick with her out to the folly so she didn't have it now. She followed more slowly, and when she passed through the door into the dining room she saw Tory already scanning the room, looking for someone. Her mother, perhaps? She was bound to be wary, coming here again.

'There she is!' Gwenna pointed, and Tory turned to Bertie with a delighted grin.

'Someone's here to see you, she turned up while you were out.'

Bertie followed the direction of Gwenna's finger, and felt a leap of happiness as a stylish-looking blonde woman jumped up from her table and hurried over. 'Leah!'

'Let me look at you!' The woman held Bertie at arms' length for only a moment before drawing her into a hug. 'Oh, Bertie, it's *so* good to see you! You look absolutely wonderful.'

Her accent was her own today; a proud Welsh, often buried beneath any one of a remarkable selection of different voices, and her face was alight with the pleasure of her surprise, and its success. She was a few years younger than Bertie's mother, which would put her at around forty-five now, but she could pass for any age between thirty and a well-preserved sixty when she wished, simply by the affectation of certain mannerisms. Today she was definitely at the younger end of her range, but this time it was all natural.

'How's Uncle Adam?' Bertie asked, following her back to the table set for four. 'Still proud as Punch to have you on his arm, I hope?'

'I never neglect to remind him how proud he is,' Leah said with a grin. 'Now, sit down and tell me absolutely everything.'

After the meal, which passed in an hour's happy combination of news and reminiscences, Gwenna made her apologies, saying she had some last-minute study to do before her first flight tomorrow. She didn't look as excited as she might have though, and Bertie sighed.

'Her nerves must have got to her again, having to wait all this time,' she said to Tory as they waved her off. 'It's a rotten shame. I could throttle that Barry Hocking.'

'She'll be fine,' Tory said. 'She's as keen as you are. No doubt she'll be catching up with you in no time, too.'

'No doubt,' Bertie agreed. But she couldn't help feeling guilty as she imagined how Gwenna would react when she found out Bertie had already been augmenting her lessons with combat training. She'd feel horribly betrayed.

Leah took Bertie and Tory into the bar, where she gave her room number and settled them into a seat by the huge window that overlooked the headland and the cove below. Tory kept peering down at the little beach beneath them, and Bertie remembered her saying that was how she and the other local children had found their way into the tunnels that led to Tyndall's Folly. Her sea-mad sister, Fiona, would absolutely love it down at that rough-looking little beach, she thought with a twinge of mild envy; she'd never be able get down there herself. But—she looked across the bay, and the envy was replaced by a swell of satisfaction and a deep sense of accomplishment—the sky was all hers.

She felt a sudden desire to tell Leah everything about Jude, and her extra lessons, and part of her wished Tory would leave them alone for a little while so she was free to do so. But she was such wonderful company, and since the three of them had much to talk about, they chatted long into the evening anyway. It wasn't until their conversation had reached a natural pause, that Bertie and Tory exchanged a wordless question and assent, and Bertie cleared her throat and shifted in her seat. Her earlier qualms about intruding on Irene's life had faded, and now that Leah was here in front of her, there would be no harm in at least broaching the concerns she and Tory shared.

'Since you're here, Leah,' she began, and when the sentence remained hanging Leah raised an eyebrow.

'Go on,' she invited. 'Should I have my notebook out?'

'Good idea,' Bertie said, and waited until Leah had fished the book and her pen from her bag. 'It's about this new girl who's joined the flying school. We think she might be up to something crooked.'

Leah looked as if she wanted to laugh but just stopped herself. 'Crooked. I see. You'd better tell me everything then.'

Bertie and Tory did so, between them, and Bertie finished with the news that Irene had approached the folly alone tonight, but left when she'd seen that Bertie and Tommy had got there first.

'So . . . you saw her, but she doesn't know that?' Leah clarified, scribbling in her book with a speed that Bertie found astonishing until she peered over and saw she was using shorthand.

'She'd have turned tail as soon as she saw Tommy's bike. As far as I know she might not have recognised it, or even known I was there too.'

'Good. So she's got no reason to be wary around the three of you?'

'None.' Bertie looked at Tory, who was looking a bit troubled. 'What's the matter?'

'Gwenna's very defensive of Irene, and doesn't seem suspicious at all anymore.'

'Are you worried she might say something to warn her?' Leah asked.

'She might.' Tory glanced at Bertie, and her voice turned hesitant. 'She said something else that bothered me. She told me to ask myself why Tommy was suddenly such good pals with Bobby Gale.'

Bertie bristled. 'Nothing sudden about it, they've been friends for months. He told me how it started, something to do with Bobby lifting his watch, and Tommy catching him trying to sell it at Caernoweth Market. They had a bit of a scrap, but sorted it all out over a drink in the Tinners.' She scowled. 'Why is Gwenna trying to push suspicion onto Tommy, of all people?'

'I've no idea. I know she doesn't like Bobby though. Perhaps she thinks he's dragging Tommy into something and that we should pay attention?'

Leah was watching this exchange with an expression of keen interest. 'Did you say Gwenna and her fiancé have broken things off? Perhaps she's envious of your new relationship with Tommy.'

'That doesn't sound like her,' Tory said. 'But to be honest I didn't know her before she and Peter became an item, so I don't know. It's possible.'

Leah tapped her lips with her pen. 'Why don't you just report your suspicions to the authorities? You needn't leave a name.'

'Tommy suggested that, but it could just be that she's seeing someone she shouldn't be.'

'Which is none of your business,' Leah agreed. 'But you don't really believe that's what she's doing?'

Bertie and Tory exchanged a glance, and Tory shook her head. '*I* think it has something to do with smuggling. Storing something in that room under the folly. But if we go steaming in and get it all wrong, we'll only alert whoever's behind it, and then they'll get away with it.'

'Besides,' Bertie added, 'if Tommy's name's getting dragged into it, just because he's a friend of Bobby's, he could get into enormous trouble. I'd like to find out what's going on first.'

'I assume you want to engage Douglas and Coleridge's investigative services officially then, to look into what Irene Lewis is up to?'

Bertie looked hesitantly at Tory. 'Will it cost a lot?'

'I'll tell you what.' Leah put her pad away. 'Seeing as I sneaked off and got married without telling you, I'll give you the next few days that I'd planned to stay in Caernoweth anyway. After that we can talk about how much it'll cost in the time it takes me away from my other jobs, and if I've had to pay for any information. Does that sound fair?'

'If it helps to preserve Tommy's good name, Bertie, I'm sure your mother would be happy to help with any costs,' Tory said, and Bertie smiled.

'She's never met him. But once she knows how much he means to me, I'm sure she will.'

'And how much *does* he mean to you, exactly?' Leah asked. 'It wasn't that long ago that you were engaged to Jowan Nancarrow.'

Bertie could read the question beneath the question: was she quite sure that the reason she and Jowan had broken it off would not be an issue with Tommy? Children could be a thorny issue in the closest of couples, as Bertie and Jowan had discovered, but Bertie hadn't changed her mind; she simply didn't want them.

'Tommy and I haven't planned to marry,' she said, going straight to the point. 'If we do, then we'll have something to discuss, but until then . . .' She could feel the slow smile spreading across her face. 'Let's just say he makes me every bit as happy as Joey does.'

Leah blinked and looked to Tory for help. 'Joey?'

Tory nodded wisely. 'Oh, yes. You're going to *love* Joey.'

*

Gwenna approached Barry Hocking's house with no small degree of nervousness. Irene had returned earlier from her second visit to the folly, agitated, and bringing bad news. She had insisted it had to be Gwenna who told him; everyone knew he was Gwenna's flight instructor, whereas Irene supposedly had no connection to him at all. She had given Gwenna the address, and wished her luck, and Gwenna had trudged all the way out to Hocking's house in the dark, and with her heart in her boots.

Hazelmere lay on the far outskirts of Pencarrack; one of the large, older houses, still remote enough to stand alone in its own extensive grounds, though from out here Gwenna could see the gradually encroaching china clay pit. She'd heard Hocking complaining to his fellow instructors about that, and how it devalued his property, but the house was still probably one of the most expensive in the area, and Gwenna passed through the gate a good few minutes before she actually reached the front door. Hazelmere was almost as impressive as Pencarrack House, and now that Gwenna knew where the money came from to maintain it, she couldn't suppress a shudder of distaste.

She knocked on the polished oak door and waited, silently rehearsing her excuse if Hocking's wife answered: *my first flight is tomorrow, and Mr Hocking promised to take me through a few things.* But Hocking himself came to the door, holding a cigarette and a cut-glass tumbler of what looked like whisky, and with an irritable look on his face that dissolved into outright annoyance when he saw Gwenna.

'Do you have any idea of the time?'

She only knew it must be nearing eleven. 'I'm sorry. It's important, though.'

'Just a pupil,' he called back into the house, and caught at Gwenna's elbow to spin her around before pushing her in the direction of the side-garden.

He locked the wooden gate behind them, and faced her in the low light from the nearby kitchen. 'What is it?'

'Irene went up to give Devereux his food earlier this evening, and she found ... well, a courting couple there. So she had to leave, of course.'

'Naturally. And?' He was sounding even more snappish now, and Gwenna hurried on.

'She had to go back quite a bit later instead, while I was at dinner, and it seems that whoever it was had already found the entrance.' She flinched at the look on his face. 'Devereux told her that someone had actually been down there, trying to break down the door.'

'Break down the *door*?'

'Apparently the man had rattled it, quite hard, and then he kicked it. Devereux doesn't think whoever it was knew there was someone in there, just that he'd thought it was odd that it was locked at all. Then it went quiet until Irene came back later on with his food.'

Hocking was pacing the short distance between the gate and the side of the house, swilling the remains of his drink around in the glass and peering at it as if he thought it held the solution to this problem.

'Did she recognise this man? More importantly, was *she* seen?'

'She wasn't seen,' Gwenna said quickly. 'And she didn't know who it was either. Then again, she's new, so she probably wouldn't be able to name many people anyway.'

Of course, Irene had known exactly who it was, and in her heart Gwenna cursed Tommy Ash for getting Bertie mixed up in it all.

Hocking drew deeply on his cigarette, and as he exhaled smoke he gave her a penetrating look, made even harsher by the shifting shadows. 'And you? Do *you* know who went canoodling up at the folly last night?'

She shook her head. 'Lots of people go up there, but they stay out of sight inside the building itself. That's the whole point of going there. I know there was no-one around when we took Devereux his food yesterday, so how do you suppose they found the trapdoor?'

'I have no idea. But we can't risk leaving him there while we wait for his new papers. We've got to get him out.'

'To where?'

'I usually fly them out to St Agnes, in the Scillies, and they lie low until they can get offshore to pick up the boat from Cobh to Roscoff. After that I neither know nor care.'

'You sound as if this happens all the time! How often do you fly people out?' Gwenna realised she had spoken out of turn as Barry turned a baleful expression on her.

'That is absolutely none of your concern, and if you're wise you'll stop asking.' He took a gulp of his drink. 'My plane's out of action so—'

'Out of action?' Gwenna stared in dismay. 'But I'm having my lesson tomorrow.'

'Oh, that.' He waved his cigarette irritably. 'That'll have to be Wednesday now, if the Avro's fixed. As for Devereux, we'll have to get him out by boat. Or rather, Irene will.'

Gwenna tried not to show the flash of angry frustration. 'Will she be alright alone with him?' she said instead, hearing the tightness in her own voice.

'She won't be alone, I'll make sure … *someone's* with her.' Hocking looked as if he wanted to smile. 'He'll behave, don't you worry. You can do another pick-up from Truro, instead.'

Gwenna's heart sank. 'Why me?'

'How many people do you think I have working for me?'

Hocking finished his drink. 'Your former fiancé has his job to do, don't forget, but it's an afternoon run anyway, so you can go alone. This time we have customers ready and waiting for word from us, so we won't have to worry about storing anything under the folly.'

'Alright.' Relieved that this ordeal was over, Gwenna started past him to unlock the gate, but gave a startled cry as he grabbed her arm. He dragged her around to face him, and leaned in close enough for her to feel the damp heat of his breath on her skin as he spoke directly into her ear.

'You *do* know who it was who found the room, I could see it in your face.'

'I don't,' she began, but her words were cut short as he shook her.

'You're lying.' He shook her again, and she tried to pull away but his fingers sank harder into her arms. 'Who are you protecting, Rosdew, hmm?'

'No-one! Let me go.'

'If you don't tell me, I'll make sure your father knows exactly—'

'Al*right*!' Gwenna knew her fury and her fear were showing. Would he never stop holding her father over her? 'I'm not absolutely certain, but . . .' She slumped, defeated. 'She thinks it was Tommy Ash.'

'Ash,' Hocking repeated, then frowned. 'The engineer?'

'Yes.'

'And who was he with?'

'I don't know!' Bertie would have to stay away from Tommy while they were on the base; it was a safe bet Hocking would be watching. 'What will you do?' she asked, more timidly. 'You won't hurt him?' She felt ill at the thought, but Hocking was shaking his head, she could see the movement even though she couldn't see his expression now.

'He's too well liked, it'd arouse too much suspicion. No, don't worry, he'll just be kept busy on the base until Devereux has gone, then by the time he's got enough free time to go messing about up at the folly again there'll be nothing there to get excited about. Except his lady friend, that is,' he added with a lascivious little smile.

Gwenna nodded, relieved she hadn't put Tommy in harm's way despite her earlier anger with him. The whole thing should be over in a couple of days, with no harm done.

'What do I tell Irene then?' she asked, her relief increasing as he released her and moved to unlock the gate.

'Tell her to bring a spare torch, those tunnels are longer and twistier than you'd think. And you'll need to be there too, to shut the trapdoor behind her, so both of you are to be at the folly at five o'clock tomorrow morning.'

'Five?'

'Before it gets light.' Hocking made a shooing gesture. 'Best get on then, don't you think? You've both got a very long day tomorrow.'

CHAPTER FIFTEEN

'You're sure you don't mind showing Leah around?' Bertie asked Tory, hunting around for her gloves.

Tory fished them out from under the bed and handed them to her. 'Of course not.' It would actually be quite nice, especially since it still might be something of a farewell. 'It's not as if I have anything more pressing to do now,' she added, 'unlike you busy lot. Where's Irene, anyway?'

'She went into the common room early to study,' Gwenna said, holding her long hair in a tail while she searched for a band. 'She's a light sleeper, and I woke her when I went down to help Dad with the early delivery, so she got up anyway. Didn't you hear us?'

'I heard something around half past four.' Bertie tucked the gloves into her overall pocket. 'I didn't look to see who it was though. My word, she's keen all of a sudden, isn't she? Rather her than me, at that time of day.'

Gwenna turned to Tory. 'So, you're going to be introducing Mrs Coleridge to a few people around the town, are you? What's that about?'

'Oh, I'd forgotten,' Bertie said, before Tory could respond, 'you were still out when we talked about it. Leah has agreed to look into the strange goings-on of Miss Irene Lewis.' She emphasised the last few words, clearly hoping the comic effect would make it sound less serious, but Gwenna scowled.

'Why can't you leave her alone? What's she ever done to you?'

Bertie's smile faded. 'You mean besides lie through her teeth from the day she arrived?'

Tory gave her a warning look, silently reminding her that Gwenna's mood was bound to be a bit down, having to wait another day for her flight. 'It's nothing sinister,' she assured Gwenna. 'Leah's just going to ask around a bit, that's all.'

Gwenna look unconvinced, and still annoyed. 'What's the point? No-one will know Irene down here anyway.'

'They know Bobby Gale *very* well though,' Bertie said. 'If he's up to something, and has involved Irene somehow, then someone will know about it.'

'Irene might need someone to look out for her,' Tory added, trying to inject her usual diplomatic slant into it. 'If Bobby's spotted a weakness, and is exploiting it, he needs reining in.'

'*If* he has.' Bertie yanked opened the door. 'And if I find either of them has dragged Tommy into it as well, I'll bloody well push them both off the highest cliff I can find. Right, I'm going to class. Tell Leah I'll come and find her at teatime.'

Tory drove down to the hotel, but she and Leah left the car there and walked into town. She'd met Bertie's honorary aunt before, while staying at Fox Bay, but this was the first time they'd really had the chance to talk, and she learned a great deal about Bertie Fox during the short walk from the Cliffside Fort into

Caernoweth. But her attention was soon turned towards who Leah would need to talk to.

'The police would be a good start,' Leah said, looking around her. 'Where will I find them?'

'Sergeant Couch should be on duty, but you're more likely to find Constable Bolitho.'

'Why's that?'

'Couch is never the earliest bird in the garden,' Tory said, 'he's probably still having his breakfast.' She led the way to the police house and peered through the window. 'Yes, Peter's on the desk.'

Leah laughed. 'Always useful to be on first-name terms with the local policeman. Did you know him before, then?'

'I knew his grandad, Ern, better. He was on the boats with my dad. Peter and I are quite close in age though, and more importantly, he was, until very recently, engaged to Gwenna.'

'Ah, *that* Peter. I remember her mentioning him when she came to Fox Bay.' Leah pushed open the door. 'Are you coming in, or do you have other things to do?'

'I'll introduce you, then while you're talking to him I'll go on down to Priddy Farm and see if Mack's working.' Tory grinned at Leah's suddenly interested expression. 'Sorry to say, Mack's a horse.'

'How disappointing!'

Leah led the way inside, still chuckling, and Peter Bolitho's eyes lit up when they fell on the attractive blonde stranger, but they narrowed when he saw Tory. He clearly didn't want to be bombarded with accusations and questions about the break-up with Gwenna.

But Tory just smiled at him. 'Peter, this is Mrs Coleridge. She carries out investigations for people, with her partner Mr

Douglas. I thought you might be able to help her out with a few things.'

'Oh, I wouldn't be allowed to divulge—'

'Of course not,' Leah broke in smoothly. 'I just wanted a little chat, a taste of the town, if you like. Who're the ones to watch out for, that kind of thing.'

'Bobby Gale, perhaps,' Tory added. She guessed, from the way Peter lifted his gaze briefly to the whitewashed ceiling, that he was likely to unburden himself quite comprehensively on that subject once Leah had loosened him up a little. 'How long do you want, before I come and find you?'

'Actually, you can give me a couple of hours,' Leah said, and smiled at Peter. 'I'll talk to the kind constable here, and then have a little wander around on my own, and I'll meet you back at the hotel at one, for lunch. Is that alright?'

'Of course.' Tory went back out into the early September sunshine, and with plenty of time on her hands she allowed her walk to the farm to become more of a leisurely stroll, and a chance to absorb the atmosphere of the town she'd once known so well.

Caernoweth was coming alive at this time of the morning; the steep hill that led down towards the soaring memorial that marked its edge was thrumming with activity, as children wandered down to Priddy Lane School, and shops began opening for business. More than once someone stopped Tory with an exclamation of pleasure, and asked if she remembered this person or that one, and said how lovely it was to see such a well-mannered child grown so strong and pretty, and back among her own. It was enough to make her think again about her intention to move on, and as she made her way to the farm, her thoughts turned once more to the possibility of training as a vet and then coming back to live in her home town after all.

A pleasant hour spent at Priddy Farm, helping Keir's farmhand muck out the stable while the horses were working, reinforced the feeling, and she came back up into town feeling boosted by it all. However, she had to stop thinking about it now; she wanted to find out how much the people of Caernoweth remembered about her mother's past, and particularly if anyone else knew about Charles Batten's part in it.

She pushed open the door to Penhaligon's Attic, glad to see there were no customers in the shop. Anna was frowning down at a ledger and making marks in the margin, but smiled when she saw Tory.

'Hello, love. You're just in time, will you have a spot of half-past elevenses with me?'

Tory was tempted, but shook her head. 'I'm meeting a friend for lunch and I don't want to spoil it.'

'Ah, that's nice.' Anna's smile faltered as she looked more closely at Tory. 'How've you been? You're looking very serious.'

Tory wished she'd rehearsed a good opening sentence on her way up the hill, but it was too late to worry about that now. She took a quick preparatory breath, and pushed on. 'What do you know, or think you know, about my mother?'

Anna's gaze flashed quickly towards the door, but it remained closed. 'Where did that come from?'

'You know she's back?'

'I'd heard.'

'And you told Rachel Rosdew too, I gather.'

Anna shrugged. 'I mentioned it. She's my best friend since Ellen died.'

'And so you thought you'd warn her that wicked Nancy Gilbert was back on the prowl?' Tory's voice had turned bitter despite her telling herself she wouldn't take this tack.

Anna flushed. 'Come on, love. I only told her that—'

'That Nancy liked to chase the more popular men in town? Like your husband?'

'That's true enough,' Anna said, and now she sounded annoyed too. 'I know it's not nice to hear, Tory, but she wasn't too shy about pushing herself on an attractive man.'

'Give a dog a bad name, is that it?'

Anna sighed. 'It's only that Rachel was concerned that Jonas was seeing someone else, and she couldn't think who it might be. I'd heard someone say they'd seen Nan ... your mother. If she's anywhere near as beautiful as she was when she lived here before, she'd catch any man's eye.'

The crooked compliment might have been calculated to derail Tory's grievance, but she didn't think it was. Anna sounded envious, if anything.

'Are you worried she'll come for Matthew again?' Tory asked, curious now.

'She can come for him all she likes,' Anna said, somewhat tartly. 'I trust him and that's what matters.'

'But Rachel doesn't trust Jonas.' Tory frowned. 'I don't know them, but Gwenna says her mother's quite pretty for her age.'

'For her age?' Anna laughed then, and the atmosphere warmed a little. 'She's ten years younger than me, thank you very much. Early forties, nothing more. And yes, she's still a lovely woman.'

'Do you think Jonas would go after anyone else?'

'I must admit I was surprised when Rachel told me what she suspected,' Anna said, 'but your—'

'My mother is happily married. Her name is Stuart now. *Doctor* Stuart,' Tory added, with an edge of pride despite her deeper misgivings.

'*Doctor?*' Anna looked gratifyingly astonished. 'My word, who'd have thought?'

'So she'd have no wish to go reviving a reputation she might have gained in her younger days.'

'She must be awful proud of you.' Anna looked at her steadily for a moment. 'You've grown into a remarkable young woman.'

Again, it might have been calculated to disarm, but Tory didn't believe it was. 'Thank you. And my mother has become one, too.'

'So you've forgiven her for leaving you and your brothers then?'

'No.' Tory was caught unawares by the swiftness of her own reply, but it had been instinctive, and so she had to accept it as the truth. She considered it for a moment. 'I've heard her story,' she explained, 'and I believe it. I want to trust her, and she's promised to try and make up for starting what sounded like a series of events she hadn't much control over in the end. But,' she shrugged, 'words are easy, it's actions that really prove it.'

'If we could see into the future, we'd all make different choices,' Anna said quietly. 'No-one truly thinks their brilliant plans will be blasted apart, we all think we've got tomorrow to fix what we've broken.'

'You sound as if you're about to tell me not to be too hard on her,' Tory said, prickling again. 'After what you've been saying about her around town, that makes you something of a hypocrite, don't you think?'

Anna surprised her by nodding. 'Perhaps you're right. I don't know everything I thought I did.'

'So what *do* you know about her? What did Ellen Garvey tell you?'

Anna wiped at some imaginary dust on the counter top. 'Ellen and I had been friends since I first came to town. She was one of the first people who gave me a chance, when almost everyone else mistrusted me.'

'That's very nice, but it doesn't explain—'

'When my cousin Keir arrived, and took a job at your old farm, he and Nancy began seeing a lot of one another.'

'They were both free to do that,' Tory said quickly. 'My father was long dead.'

'I know,' Anna soothed 'No-one's saying any different. Anyway, Keir and Ellen became good friends, after a bit of a fiery start, but that's all there was between them for years. Ellen had nothing to do with why Keir broke things off with Nancy, that happened because of what *he'd* found out.'

'And what was that?' It was entirely possible Nancy had misread the opinion of the public; Tory needed to hear it from someone who'd heard only the gossip, since that was what had forced her mother to leave.

'I thought she'd told you everything?' Anna said, her eyes narrowing.

'She did.'

Anna studied her expression, and nodded. 'Alright. We heard that your landlord, Charles Batten, was taking his rent in kind. Nancy would ... be there for him, on collection day, and he'd leave with no money, but a tick in the rent book. D'you see?'

'Of course I *see!*' Tory snapped. 'I just wondered how much you knew. Who else did Ellen spill her nasty little secret to?'

'Tory, love,' Anna said, very gently, 'she didn't even know.'

Tory blinked. 'What?'

'Ellen never knew about Charles Batten, she only knew about the reputation Nancy had built by flinging herself—I'm sorry, but it's the truth—at people like Matthew and Keir. *I* only knew because Keir was having second thoughts about having broken things off with her. He came to me after Mr Batten died, asking if he shouldn't put it behind him now.'

'And what did you tell him?'

'That only he could decide.'

Tory nodded, but her heart hurt at the flimsy way lives were constructed, and how they could be altered so drastically by the decisions made in a moment. If Keir had chosen a life with Nancy she'd never have left Cornwall, they'd have been a proper family and they might have persuaded Joseph not to join up. He might still be alive ... She shook that thought away; *if we could see into the future, we'd all make different choices.* Indeed.

'So you see,' Anna said, 'your mother's secret remains her own but for Keir and me. And I didn't tell anyone else about her making eyes at Matthew.'

'Except Rachel Rosdew.'

'Not at the time, I meant. Besides, it never came to anything, Nancy was just lonely. Even Charles Batten was a widower, so there was no marriage there to break up. But Big Alice was sure she was going to try and get her hooks ... ' She coloured. 'I mean, get back with Keir, and break him and Ellen up.'

'And what did Ellen think?'

'She was sure of Keir. And she was right to be.'

'But Rachel isn't sure of Jonas,' Tory said again. Just to be certain.

Anna sighed. 'No, she isn't.'

'What do you think? They're your friends, as you keep saying.'

'Jonas can be ... a difficult man sometimes. Do you know much about him?'

Tory shook her head. 'Only what Gwenna's said, that he was a fighter pilot in the war, and well respected for it.'

'Very. He was an officer, and badly wounded in 1918 when he had to eject after a raid, but the attack retrospectively won him the Distinguished Flying Cross, which I'm sure Gwenna's told you about.' She waited for Tory's nod, and went on, 'He and Rachel moved here when he was invalided out of the RAF, but he's found it difficult to adjust to the life of a shopkeeper. Which isn't really surprising I suppose.'

'What did he do before the war?'

'He was a carpenter. Highly talented and sought after, by all accounts. He still does the odd bit, but his back and neck pain him too badly for him to have gone back to earning a living from it.' Anna shook her head. 'He struggles, but he and Rachel have been very happy, on the whole. And Gwenna's the light of their lives since they couldn't have more children.'

Tory sighed. 'Gwenna loves her mother, of course, but she wants so much to be like her dad. That's why it's been so hard to watch her struggling with her training.'

'Still, I hear she's going to be back up soon?' Anna said, her expression lightening.

'As soon as her instructor's plane is ready, yes.'

'Good for her. Jonas will be glad she didn't get that woman as an instructor, at least.'

Tory, who'd been preparing to take her leave, stopped in surprise. 'Really? Gwenna would have given anything to have made Jude's list. I'd have thought any father would have been glad to have his daughter taught by such an accomplished flyer.'

'That's the problem, apparently. I've heard that during the war Miss Singleton was something of an enigma; no-one knew who was flying that plane, at the time, and those who knew the name didn't know she was a woman. It was all very hush-hush.'

'Which is why—'

'And,' Anna went on, 'when the air base eventually opened again, she got work as an instructor, and Jonas, a local man with a wonderful reputation, didn't. He feels pushed aside, I suppose.'

'But if he's not physically capable of doing the job, he can't blame them for giving the role to someone who is.'

'He doesn't blame them, he blames her. Thinks she's lording it over him, since she's never taken the time to ask about him. He's supposedly the hero in town, and yet she comes in from up north and steals what he felt should have been his role.'

'Maybe *that's* the real trouble.' Tory sighed. 'Perhaps he's under the impression she thinks she's too important. I've met her though, and I'm sure she's not given it a thought.'

'Perhaps she should,' Anna said pointedly. 'Anyway, I hope we've cleared the air a bit, my love. It's been too long since we've seen each other, I'd hate for there to be ill feeling between us.'

'Of course there isn't.' Tory drew the older woman into a hug. 'I'll never forget how you and Freya helped us after Mum left.'

'You were all such smashing kids. Freya thinks the world of you too. I'll pass along her address in Scotland sometime, she'd love to hear all about your adventures after you left town.'

'Adventures?' Tory laughed. 'I'd hardly call them that. I'll write to her though, thanks.'

Outside once more, she looked across the road to Rosdew's grocery shop. She felt immeasurably better after learning that Nancy's past wasn't common knowledge after all, but with the rumours still muttering in the background that she might now be entangled with a respected local family man instead, perhaps it was time to put the record straight.

She crossed the road and went into the shop; living on the base since she'd come home, she hadn't needed to cook or clean, and so had never been to this shop before, or seen Gwenna's parents beyond a brief glimpse or two at the festival. She was curious, having heard they were a good-looking pair, and she wondered which of them Gwenna favoured. Immediately she saw it must be Rachel; tall and slender, with her dark hair twisted up and tucked beneath a plain brow band that kept it all in place yet looked stylish at the same time.

Rachel nodded a distracted greeting, and continued serving the customer who was waiting to pay, and Tory wandered around the shop for a minute or two until everyone had left. She could feel tension creeping through her limbs and her chest, and forced herself to breathe out and remember she was only here to have a civilised conversation.

She began it well, complimenting Rachel on her hairdo. Rachel smiled and patted the band. 'Thank you. I copied it from one of my daughter's magazines.' She looked more closely at Tory. 'You're a friend of hers, aren't you? I saw you talking to her the other day at the festival.'

'Tory Gilbert. I was born here, and only recently came back.' Tory held out her hand to shake, watching Rachel's face for a reaction to the surname. To the woman's credit there was barely a flicker, but her brows pulled in slightly as she shook Tory's hand.

'What can I get for you, Tory?'

'Nothing, really. I just wanted to introduce myself, since I was passing. I hope you're feeling better now?'

Rachel looked puzzled. 'Better?'

276

'Gwenna said you'd not been well.' Tory realised now that it had been a lie, and that Rachel was about to make up something to cover it, and she went on quickly, 'I've just been to visit Anna.'

'Anna Penhaligon?'

'Yes, she and I are old friends; she helped out a lot when my mother left town before the war.'

'Ah yes, she told me.' Rachel straightened some boxes of matches on the counter. 'I understand your mother and Anna's cousin Keir were ... close, at one time.'

'That's right. You've heard she's back?'

'I have, yes.'

'Do you know why she left?'

Rachel's face tightened. 'I have no idea, and even less interest. I'm sorry to be blunt, but I'm very busy today.'

'She's married now,' Tory said pointedly. 'Happily so.'

Rachel was clearly neither fool nor shrinking violet. Her gaze came up and met Tory's. 'I suppose Gwenna's been talking.'

'Of course, we're her friends. She's upset.' Tory hesitated, then asked, 'Do you really think Mr Rosdew is seeing someone else?'

She heard the impertinence and bit her lip, expecting the stiff, face-saving denial of a woman acutely embarrassed to admit her husband might not be all he claimed to be. But, perhaps because of Tory's friendship with Gwenna, or because of her own obvious reaction, Rachel seemed to see no point in maintaining a pretence. Her eyes swam with sudden tears that she tried to blink back.

'I know my husband, Miss Gilbert, and I know when he's lying to me. Even if it's not your mother, and I'm not saying I believe that, it's someone.'

Tory noted the reversion to polite title rather than first name. 'I'm sorry to have asked.'

'As I said, I'm very busy today, so if you wouldn't mind?' Rachel gestured to the door.

'It's a pity Peter's on duty today,' Tory said, moving away deliberately slowly. 'Gwenna mentioned how he sometimes steps in when Mr Rosdew's ... away.'

Rachel's eyes narrowed at the hesitation. 'Yes, he is *away*,' she clarified. 'He's gone to Bodmin for supplies, like he does every Tuesday.'

'Of course. I didn't mean to suggest otherwise.' Tory looked at her watch. 'Look, I'm meeting a friend in an hour, but I don't mind staying behind to help out.'

For a moment she thought Rachel was going to accept, then the woman's expression shut down again. 'That's very kind, but it won't be necessary. Jonas will be back by midday.'

Tory said her rather awkward goodbyes, and made her way slowly back up towards the Cliffside Fort, thinking she would sit on the wall in the sun and think everything through before it was time to meet Leah for lunch. But Leah was there already, looking encouragingly eager.

'I've had a productive morning,' she said. 'Come on, I'm famished.'

They gave their order to the waiter, and Tory looked impatiently at Leah. 'Let's have it then,' she said, pouring water into their tumblers. 'What have you found out?'

'Tell me again what made you suspicious of Irene. First of all, I mean.'

Tory opened her mouth to speak, but a sudden flash of understanding swept her words aside, even as she considered Leah's question: Irene penning letters she didn't want seen; taking up training in an activity she clearly didn't enjoy, but which Jonas

278

had loved and excelled in; disappearing for hours at a time and not returning for meals ... And she was away today, too ...

'It's her,' she breathed. '*She's* the one Jonas has been having an affair with.'

'No, she isn't.'

Tory shook her head. 'Excuse me?'

'You're right in that she isn't who she says she is, but it's not Jonas she's linked to.' Leah lowered her voice. 'I telephoned my partner, Sam, who used to be a police officer.'

'Oh, yes. I've met Sam.'

'Well, he still has friends who are willing to help him out now and again, and he looked into your Miss Lewis and telephoned me back just before you came. She's Barry Hocking's niece.'

'His *niece*? No wonder she kept that quiet,' Tory mused, then indignation stepped in. 'And no wonder she's getting preferential treatment!'

Leah nodded. 'There's more to it than that though. According to what Sam's been able to find out, she witnessed some irregular goings-on at the stables near Birmingham, where she works.'

'I knew she was a better rider than she claimed!' Tory felt a flash of vindication before curiosity took over again. 'What happened?'

'She was a promising flat racing jockey as a youngster, evidently. But she grew too tall to compete, so she took the next best path and became a trainer at one of the top racing stables. She was sitting with a sick horse, late one night in a stable, and discovered that one of the Birmingham gangs was running some kind of doping scam.'

'That's awful,' Tory muttered, thinking of the horses more than Irene, at this point.

'They were part of an owners' syndicate,' Leah said, 'and making a lot of money out of doping their own top horses, and then betting against them to win. Irene passed on the intelligence to the authorities anonymously, but it's still dangerous for her up there, so her uncle offered sanctuary.'

'Sanctuary I can understand, but why go to the trouble of learning to fly? She clearly doesn't want to.'

Leah shrugged. 'Maybe it's just his passion, nothing more, and she feels obliged. Whatever the reason, her mother, Hocking's sister, agreed, and between them they arranged her tuition fees.'

Tory gave her a cynical look. 'Arranged?'

'Waived,' Leah confirmed. She looked up as the waiter arrived with their drinks, and Tory forced herself to remain silent until they were alone again.

'So she's hiding out down here? For how long?'

'Presumably until the doping ring is cracked. Sam says they're working at it, but they have to get their timing right or the big fish will wriggle off the hook.'

She paused as their food was served, and in that time, Tory considered everything she had said. The thought of gang activity made her stomach roll, and lessened her appetite considerably, but she made a good show of enjoying the meal, while Leah explained more fully everything Sam had found out about Irene. Most of it was just family background, but the knowledge that Irene's boyfriend had been a member of the very gang that had exploited the betting system made her put down her fork and stop eating. She remembered her very first chat with Irene, in the kitchen late at night, when she'd asked about boyfriends and Irene had put the conversation swiftly to bed. *I did, once, but he . . . But now I don't.*

'Poor Irene.' She cleared her throat and took up her cutlery again. 'Will you speak to her?'

'I think she ought to be on her guard, yes. Even if it's only so she can cover her tracks a bit better. Will you and the others do it with me? It might be nice for her to have some friendly faces around when I put this to her.'

'Friendly?' Tory felt the guilty flush creeping up her face. 'I don't think we've been that, to be quite truthful. Something was so off about her, every conversation must have felt like an interrogation. At least now we know why she seemed so shifty and evasive, but I think the only one of us she really trusts now is Gwenna.'

'Then we'll have to make sure Gwenna's there.' Leah rolled her shoulders and let out a contented sigh. 'At least my job's done now, and I can relax.' She raised her glass. 'Here's to a few days off.'

CHAPTER SIXTEEN

As Tuesday morning rolled on into lunchtime, Bertie realised she hadn't seen Tommy yet, and her uneasiness grew as she asked around his workmates and found no-one else had, either.

'He's supposed to be here,' his manager grumbled. 'No day off listed in the book. When you see him, tell him I'm waiting for an explanation, and it'd better be a good'n.'

Bertie left the maintenance hangar and returned to the dormitory block, but he wasn't in his room, or the common room either. She glanced into his pigeonhole and saw there were still two letters he hadn't collected this morning, so she went out to the perimeter fence to see if the BSA was there. It was. She initially took it as a good sign; at least he wasn't lying out on the moors somewhere between here and Lynher Mill, but it just meant he should be somewhere close by, and he wasn't. Filling her mind now was that nonsense about him getting in deep with Bobby Gale and, as charming as Tommy said Bobby could be, Gwenna had made no bones about the fact he was also a seasoned crook. Bertie retreated to the common room to think, but was only alone for a few minutes.

'Penny for them?' Gwenna, who'd set time aside that afternoon for the flight that Hocking had cancelled, sat down opposite her, making her jump. 'You look miles away.'

Bertie told her about Tommy. 'He's going to get his wages docked if he's not careful,' she said, 'and it's not like him to just disappear.'

'Why don't we go into town and ask around? I'm free until about four o'clock.'

'You wouldn't mind?'

'Of course not. To tell the truth, I'm that jittery I think the exercise will do me good. Go and get your stick if you like, we'll go now.'

Gwenna and Bertie made their way into town, and Bertie reflected that, of the three of them, she and Gwenna had spent the least time together. It was strange, given that they were the keenest students, and had the most in common, but there had almost always existed a kind of tension between them. Even in their most relaxed moments Bertie thought she detected a constant judgement in Gwenna's manner, but Tory had always been the buffer between the two prickly personalities. Her determination not to notice when Gwenna made some comment about Bertie being selected as Jude's trainee, or when Bertie gave a characteristically sharp retort to something only meant as an innocent observation, always smoothed things before they escalated. Bertie felt it was time she addressed this, and was about to speak up to that effect when Gwenna gave a shout and a wave.

'Peter!'

The policeman was talking to a group of youngsters outside the bakery, arms folded, face stern, shoulders square. He looked over at Gwenna's shout, and the boys he'd been telling off began nudging one another. Peter coloured, but Gwenna ignored his scowl.

'Have you seen Tommy Ash?' she asked him. The lads scampered away, and once safely out of the reach of the back of Peter's hand they began to make cooing noises and exaggerated kissing sounds. Bertie smothered a grin, but it was wiped from her face a moment later.

'Certainly have,' Peter said. 'He's been taken in.'

'Taken in?'

'Arrested. They've got him into Bodmin, now, awaiting the next assizes.'

Bertie barely felt Gwenna's hand snatching at her sleeve, but when it twisted into the material she shook herself free in a flash of irritable confusion. 'For what? Whatever it is, it's a mistake!'

'No mistake, miss, I'm sorry. There's a van gone missing from the air base. A military vehicle,' he emphasised, as if Bertie were unaware of the importance of that part. 'And a witness saw Mr Ash in the area at the time. Creeping around,' he added, with an undeniable air of satisfaction.

'Creeping . . .' Bertie shook her head. 'Well, that's just stupid! He works there, why would he need to creep anywhere?'

'Exactly my question, miss.' Peter focused on the toe of his boot as it scuffed back and forth on the ground. 'I gather you and he are close then?' He looked up, assessing her reaction, and this time Gwenna's fingers found Bertie's and squeezed. Bertie winced, but a glance at Gwenna told her there was a reason.

'He's a friend, and a colleague,' she said. 'And he's good friends with my instructor too. I was wondering what I would tell her when she gets back.'

'That'll be Miss Singleton?' Peter looked interested, and a little bit too shrewd for Bertie's liking.

'Yes.'

He nodded, then gave her an apologetic but dismissive shrug. 'I don't know that there's anything more I can tell you, miss. Mr Ash has no alibi for the time in question, and the van's still missing.'

'When was it taken?'

'Sunday, early evening.'

Gwenna's short nails dug in, and it was as much as Bertie could do to stop herself pulling away again. Instead she gave Peter a brief smile of thanks, and turned to walk away. 'What the *hell* was all that about?' she hissed, as soon as they were out of Peter's earshot. 'What do you know?'

'N-nothing,' Gwenna stammered, but her eyes found Bertie's and they were miserable. 'Let me sort this out.'

'How, if you *don't know anything?*' Bertie was aware she sounded cruel in her imitation, but her emotions were running riot. 'How can they say he stole a van? Why would he? I just don't . . . Where are you going?'

Gwenna had started up the hill towards the base. 'I'm going to sort it out, like I said.'

'But—'

'I'll see you later.' She stopped, looking suddenly uncertain. 'Will you be alright to get back on your own?'

'Of course I will.' There was a snappish note in Bertie's voice but she didn't try to apologise for that either. She watched Gwenna take off at a run, and stared after her for a bemused moment before turning her attention to what she could do. Tommy had evidently lied to the police about where he'd been on Sunday evening, and if he couldn't tell them he'd been working on Jude's Camel, he must have had his reasons; if she went breezing into the police station in Bodmin now, even assuming she could get there, and made him into a liar, it would cast doubt on anything else he'd told them.

The person she needed now was Leah. She would know what to do, and who to go to for help, but Bertie had no idea where to find her, and she couldn't just wander around town in the hope of meeting her; even with her stick for support, her leg was already protesting the walk down from the air base. Her heart shrank at the thought of cheerful, smiling Tommy being seized and marched away, probably in handcuffs, to face a barrage of questions he couldn't answer without getting Jude into trouble.

She started back up the road in Gwenna's wake, albeit a great deal more slowly, and thought about how her friend had reacted, and who she might be going to see, who could fix things. Then she wondered about the van itself, and she stopped dead in the street. Tory had seen Bobby Gale driving it, or one of them at least, off the base the night Irene had arrived. And Irene had been out too, they'd said. Irene had vanished today, and the van was still missing . . . It *had t*o be the two of them together and up to something. Who would know him best? She couldn't think of a particular person, but it seemed likely there would be friends at his local drinking place at lunchtime. Bertie faced back down the hill again, and set off to the Tin Streamer's Arms.

The pub, midway down the hill, was no bigger than a small house, with one tiny window looking out onto the street from a crooked but freshly painted frame. The sign that hung over the door proclaimed it as dating from long before the civil war, and

Bertie could well believe it, as she pushed open the door and stepped into another world.

The bar was just a few steps away, with several tables dotted across the stone floor, and although the furnishings looked highly polished and well kept, there was a heavy fug of cigarette and pipe smoke that made her blink. Two of the tables were occupied, as was one of the small wooden benches that sat under the eaves at the far side of the room, and it occurred to her that she wouldn't know Bobby Gale from any of the men who'd swivelled to look at her as she came in.

'Can I help you, love?' the woman at the bar asked. 'There's pasties or stew for dinner.'

'I'm not eating, thanks. I'm looking for someone.'

'Oh?' The woman, in her mid-thirties, Bertie guessed, and a little tired-looking, was clearly trying not to show her disappointment, so Bertie asked for a glass of lemonade. The woman shrugged and picked up a jug. 'Who is it you're lookin' for, then?' She pushed the drink across the bar and dropped Bertie's money into a box, where it made a sad little rattling sound. Judging from the look the woman gave the men at the tables she was still awaiting their payment.

'Someone called Bobby Gale. Do you know him?'

The woman frowned, but nodded. 'He's my little brother. What's he done now?'

'Oh!' Bertie smiled. 'Nothing at all, I promise. Do you know where I might find him?'

'No.' The word was out before Bertie had finished asking, and Bertie's smile fell away.

'It's important,' she pressed. 'Please, I only want to ask him something.'

'Sally!' one of the men bellowed across from the table. 'Another jug when you'm ready!'

'Hold your water, James Rowe!' Sally shouted back, making Bertie jump. 'There's other people than you in this world!' She turned back to Bertie. 'What did you want him for? Only I know how word gets about. He's not a bad one, you know, and if someone's saying—'

'No-one's saying anything.' Bertie tried another tack, attempting a less urgent tone. 'I'm a friend of Tommy Ash, he told me Bobby might be able to help with something.'

'Tommy, eh?' Sally's expression cleared. 'You'm likely find Bobby down t'Porthstennack then. He'll be hangin' around at the harbour this time of day, puttin' that boat of his to a decent use for once.'

'How far is that?'

Sally looked as if she'd asked her way to the next room, but explained patiently enough. 'Down to the bottom of town, past the memorial, past Priddy Farm, and it's about a quarter mile after that.' She noted Bertie's expression, but with the walking stick automatically placed behind Bertie's back, she naturally misinterpreted it. 'Yer, it's a bugger of a hill on a warm day,' she agreed. 'But he'll be up here before too long, if you want to wait. An hour at most.'

Bertie was torn; it felt wrong to be sitting down doing nothing while Tommy was going through such an awful time, but on the other hand there was nothing she could do, and if it meant having the chance to talk to Bobby Gale it would be worth it. She thanked Sally, and took her glass over to one of the unoccupied tables, glad to be by the window so she could at least push it open and breathe something fresher than stale smoke.

Before long she was further relieved to hear familiar voices out in the road, and she leaned out of the window to see Tory and Leah approaching the pub from the other side of the street. She called to them through the window, and gestured to them to wait outside while she limped to the door, cursing the inflamed skin that rubbed the cup of her prosthetic.

Once outside she told them about Tommy, and seeing their concerned looks she very nearly broke down.

Leah immediately drew her close. 'Don't worry, darling,' she said, rubbing Bertie's back as she had when Bertie had been a confused and angry thirteen-year-old, grieving her father. 'I'll go there right now and find out what's going on. Do you want to come with me? Silly question,' she admitted with a little smile as she released Bertie and saw the look on her face. 'You wait here, I'll fetch my car down and pick you up.'

'I can walk,' Bertie said immediately, but it was a reflexive comment and she regretted it the moment the words were out. Leah, however, knew her of old.

'I know you can, *cariad*. But why should you? Go back in and wait, I'll be ten minutes.'

Bertie nodded. 'I might catch Bobby too, while I'm waiting.'

Leah looked at Tory. 'How about you? Do you have any plans, or would you like to come too?'

'Actually, I think someone should talk to Gwenna,' Bertie said. 'I'd love your company, Tory, but I don't know how she thinks she's going to sort it out, as she put it. She went haring back up to the base, though.'

'I suspect she knows quite a bit more than she's letting on,' Tory said, a little grimly. 'I'd be happy to talk to her, but we all need to get together and pool what we know. And soon.'

'I'll tell you on the way to Bodmin what I've found out about Irene,' Leah said to Bertie. 'In you go and finish your drink, I won't be long.'

Bertie went back inside to wait for Leah, glad she wouldn't have to walk after all, and thinking ahead to what she might be able to say to help Tommy. She sat and sipped at her lemonade, only half-hoping Bobby might come in, so it was a surprise when the door opened and Sally nodded to Bertie.

'Here's your man.'

Bobby Gale was in his early thirties, or thereabouts, tall and broadly built, with the all-year tan of someone who worked outside. He was dressed plainly in working clothes, which surprised Bertie, as she had been given to believe he made his living from other people's work rather than his own. His boots were covered in sand, and his trousers damp to the thigh; he'd clearly been working today. He was also blessed with a charming smile which he flashed at Bertie when his dark eyes lit on her.

'Who do we have here?'

'You're in luck, Bobby,' Sally said, drawing his beer. 'She wants to talk to you.'

He brought his drink over. 'How can I help?' he asked, sitting down uninvited.

'What have you dragged Tommy Ash into?' Bertie spoke more bluntly than she'd intended, and saw the wary look come into his face, though he did his best to disguise it behind a look of puzzlement.

'Dragged him into? Nothing, Tommy's a mate. A decent bloke.'

Bertie lowered her voice, though she knew it was pointless; the room wasn't big enough to swallow the sounds of conversation. 'He's been arrested. For stealing a van.'

Bobby nodded slowly as he wiped foam from his upper lip. 'Right. I see. And what makes you so sure it's down to me?'

'Because Tory saw you driving one off the base the other night.'

'Tory? Little Tory Gilbert?' He smiled. 'Great kid.'

'Don't change the subject!' Bertie fixed her eyes on his. 'Have you been forcing Tommy to let you have the van for whatever smuggling thing you've got going at the moment?'

The smile vanished. 'Christ!' He slid his chair back and stood up, knocking the table with his knees and making Bertie's empty glass jump and rattle. Heads turned at the noise. Bobby lowered his voice to match hers. 'Come out here.' It took only a few of his long-legged strides before he was behind the bar. 'Excuse us, Sal, we'll just be a minute. Business.' He pulled open a door and revealed a long, narrow corridor beyond, then looked back irritably at Bertie. 'Well, come on!'

Fighting the nerves that were making her hands tremble, Bertie rose and joined him behind the bar, aware of the curious looks that followed them into the corridor. Bobby slammed the door shut behind them, and she blinked in the limited light that crept up from a door at the far end.

'What's down here?'

'Just a storeroom, and a way out through the garden. I suggest you take it.'

'What? Why?'

'Because there's stuff going on you'd be better staying out of. I know I'm trying to.'

'What stuff? And what about Tommy?'

'He'll be alright, eventually. He's just . . . in the way at present.'

'It's a military vehicle! If it gets as far as a trial . . .' She went cold at the thought. 'Who's behind all this?'

'I can't tell you, it'd be more than my life's worth. And I've got family to think about.'

'You haven't told me what you mean by "stuff", either.'

Bobby looked less angry now, more wretched. 'I can't, I'm sorry.'

'Who pointed the finger at him, can you at least tell me that? Even Gwenna seems to know that much.'

'Gwenna?' Bobby gripped her forearms. 'Has she confronted him?'

'Who, Tommy?' Bertie once more found herself having to pull free from a panicky grip as he shook his head. She stared at him, perplexed. 'Who then?'

Bobby raked an agitated hand back through his hair. 'I can't say,' he repeated.

'Fine.' Bertie turned back up the corridor towards the pub door. 'I'm going to Bodmin to set the record straight.'

'Hell, woman! You do that and you'll just make things worse for us all!'

'And who exactly are you *all?*' Bertie demanded. 'You've told me nothing, and I owe you nothing. I owe Tommy though, and I'm going to see he gets out.'

'Please, miss ... What was your name?'

'Fox.'

'Miss Fox, there are people in this up to their necks, and once you go spilling your half-baked ideas down t'Bodmin you're going to destroy innocent people, along with those who do deserve it.'

'What people?' Bertie's already stretched patience was close to snapping now. 'If you don't start giving me some names, I'm going straight to Peter Bolitho and telling him everything.'

'He's one of them, you idiot!' Bobby looked appalled at the way he'd blurted it out, but something else seemed to happen to him at the same time; a lightening of what was clearly a very heavy load. He sighed and slid down the wall to squat on his heels. 'Bolitho's been turning blind eyes all over the place, because once Sergeant Couch retires, he's in line for the top job.'

The revelation came as a shock, but it made Bertie wonder if that was what had driven Gwenna and Peter apart; Gwenna hadn't been as surprised by Tommy's arrest as she should have been, though she had definitely been horrified by it. It was possible she'd known Peter was up to something, even if she didn't know what it was.

'Turning blind eyes,' she repeated. 'Then he's not the one in charge?'

'No, he's not the one running it all. Barry Hocking is. He's smuggling stuff in via the docks at Falmouth, using the freight line to Truro.'

Bobby rose to his feet again and checked the storeroom was empty, and then, his voice low and his eyes flicking nervously between the two doors at either end of the long passageway, he told Bertie about Barry Hocking's scheme.

'He hides it in a secret room underneath Tyndall's Folly. We both thought it was alcohol and tobacco at first, just like ... Well, just like everyone else did. You know the kind of thing: Hocking buys it cheap on the continent, sells it on to hotels, shops, and the like, pockets the difference in cash. Seemed harmless enough, and I was all for getting one past the customs and excise. Then I found out ... it's guns.'

'Guns?' Bertie's voice came out very small, and she too leaned against the wall. Though the pain was forgotten, both her legs were having trouble holding her up.

'I couldn't have no part in that, Miss Fox. I told Peter what

I'd seen, and we tried to back out of it, but Hocking had us both over a barrel. Pete would lose his job, and I'd be sent down and my family left with no breadwinner apart from my sister.' He jerked his head towards the pub door, and the barmaid beyond it.

'Who's buying these guns off Hocking?'

'Gangs from up the line. Using the damned things against each other, just as if we hadn't done enough damage in the name of king and country.' Bobby's voice had grown bitter, and Bertie wasn't sure what to say.

'Who else is in it?' she asked at length. 'Please tell me Tommy isn't.'

'God, no.' Bobby managed a short laugh. 'He'd never be so stupid.'

'Then why's he been taken away?'

Bobby fidgeted. 'A week or so ago I was arrested too. Hocking wanted to get someone else in, and he needed them to do their first job so they couldn't get back out. So, I was pulled out and Hocking couldn't take the chance that I might warn ... this person, and stop them getting involved. I was taken in on some stupid charge, which got dropped the minute his new recruit took that one step too far.' He sighed. 'Hocking's just been building his army, that's all.'

'And you're part of it.'

'Yeah. I drive for him, but I also have a boat. Only a small one, and it looks barely seaworthy, but it's enough to get me up and down the coast when needs be. And it's nothing to look at, so no-one thinks twice about it. Useful for someone like Hocking.'

Bertie began to see it more clearly now. 'And making sure you all know about each other, once you're in, is his way of keeping you all in line.'

'Exactly that, Miss Fox.'

'And Tommy?'

'I don't know why they took him.' Bobby sounded sincere about that. 'Maybe he's on the verge of finding something out.'

Of course he was, but how did Hocking know that? Then Bertie frowned, and any sympathy she'd felt for Irene waned; she must have gone straight back to Hocking after seeing them at the folly. So much for being the innocent, acting against her will. Before she could ask Bobby how much he knew about her, the pub door opened and Sally poked her head briefly into the corridor.

'Miss ... Fox, is it? There's a lady here looking for you.'

'That's Leah.' Bertie looked down at Bobby, who was watching her anxiously. 'What do I tell her?'

He stood up. 'Tell her what you like, only don't go to the police. *Please.* Let me find out what's going on, and why Tommy's been taken in, and I'll come and find you. Alright?'

Bertie chewed at her lip, torn between trusting him, and desperation to get Tommy released before he was charged and his career ruined. Bobby took her arms again, this time more gently.

'There's someone else involved that you should know about, and it might help you decide.' He checked Sally had closed the door properly and looked down at Bertie again, his eyes troubled but his mouth set firm with resolution. 'I didn't want to tell you, but now I think I have to.'

Bertie remained motionless, and her heart sank as he talked. By the time he'd finished she understood why there was no possibility of going to the police after all. As for how they could possibly uncover Hocking's role, and help the innocents who'd been drawn into his nasty little web, she had no idea.

CHAPTER SEVENTEEN

Gwenna found Hocking in the canteen, at a table with Flight Lieutenant Bowden and two other instructors. As he noticed her heading towards his table, and no doubt correctly interpreted the look on her face, he looked ostentatiously at his watch and murmured something to his companions.

He scraped back his chair and walked past Gwenna towards the door, not bothering to lower his voice as he barked, 'Follow me.'

Gwenna did so, noting the speculative looks of those at his table before they dismissed her and turned back to their conversation; they probably assumed he was giving her last-minute preparation advice. She joined Hocking outside, and he led her into his empty classroom, where she let her rage boil over the moment the door was closed.

'Why did you have Tommy arrested? You said you—'

'Shut up and listen.' He leaned against the desk. 'You still have the pick-up today. Half the boxes will go off tonight, and you'll collect the payment.'

She ignored him. 'You said Tommy would just be kept out of the way until Devereux was gone, and now he has.'

'But, as I also *just* said,' Hocking pointed out with exaggerated patience, 'we're only offloading half of today's cargo. The rest of it's going to have to stay for another few days, so we still can't have Ash poking around in the folly, can we?'

'There was no reason to cause such trouble for him,' Gwenna insisted.

To add to her fury, Hocking actually looked amused. 'Who says I caused it? The lad's been known to hang around with some unsavoury characters of late, so it's hardly my fault if he's fallen into their ways.'

'He's done no such thing, as you well know! Why didn't you just give him some extra work, like you said?'

'This was a more certain way. Anyway, I'm not interested in Ash now.' Hocking unlocked his desk drawer and removed a set of keys. 'The van's had to be kept at my house, for obvious reasons. This key,' he caught one up out of the small bunch and waved it at her, 'is the one for the garage. You'll find the van there, and that's where you'll take it back to until it's time to meet our customers at the folly. This other key,' he showed her, 'is the spare to the folly.' He threw them to her, then fished in the drawer again. 'These labels need to replace the coded ones from the dock,' he said, handing her a roll. 'Before you start driving back, make sure every crate has one of them on it, in plain sight. There's a tin of paste in the van, and a brush.'

Gwenna glanced at the labels, which were addressed to Caernoweth Air Training Base and declared a crate's contents, rather vaguely, as "Mechanical Components and Replacement Aviation Equipment". She, and Hocking of course, could then be plausibly shocked by any revelations to the contrary, should she be stopped for any reason.

'What if someone sees me at your house?'

'The wife won't be back until gone six, and then we'll both be going out again by eight. You should be back from Truro by half past, and you can wait in the garage until around eleven, when you can finish the job.'

'And you're sure no-one will come into the garage for anything?'

He shook his head. 'It only gets used in winter, when I want to put my own car away. I rarely even go in there myself between March and November.

'Look, I know I'm doing the actual run alone,' Gwenna said, hearing the nervousness in her own voice, 'and I'm not complaining about that, but you can't expect me to go out to the folly after dark without anyone else.'

'Of course not. I'm due at a dinner tonight though, and Irene has earned her rest after her trip to St Agnes, so you'll have protection from your copper friend instead. But he'll have to keep out of sight if he doesn't want any trouble, they know who he is.'

'Who are "they" anyway, the same ones as before?'

'Never you mind.'

'What's in the boxes?' She kept her voice casual, hoping he might respond without thinking, but he just looked at her levelly.

'I've told you what's in them. Booze. Tobacco. Now stop asking pointless questions and just be there by eleven tonight.'

Gwenna risked one more question, which seemed anything but pointless. 'What happens when someone sees the van's been returned? They'll have to let Tommy go.'

'Not necessarily. I'll get it taken somewhere it'll be found by a respected member of the community. Quite likely a policeman.' He grinned at the disgusted look on her face. 'They might even find something belonging to young Mr Ash in it. Just to aid with their enquiries, you understand.'

The web was tightening and she could do nothing about it. 'You can't do that to him!'

'Well, let's see if you can be a good girl then, and do as you're told, shall we?'

'If I do, do you promise you'll say it wasn't Tommy who took the van?'

'I'll think about it.' Hocking returned to business. 'Right, you've got the keys. Get on the road no later than four.'

Gwenna left the classroom with her anger unassuaged, and her frustration almost bringing her to tears, but although part of her longed to see a friendly face, she was relieved none of her friends had appeared before it was time to pick up the van. She didn't relish the idea of lying again, should anyone ask what she was doing that evening, but the fact that she was ready to do it was further evidence that she had progressed too far down the path she was on now, and there was no way back.

The pick-up went without incident, and Gwenna pasted Hocking's labels onto the crates before driving back to Pencarrack, where she spent the intervening hours in Hocking's garage, dozing fitfully with her head on the steering wheel. Occasionally she tried to stretch out across the driver's and passenger's seats, but she eventually gave that up and wadded her jumper for a pillow.

She was awoken by a creaking sound that echoed through the dark garage, and she shook away a patchy but vividly stressful dream where she was flying the van over open water and watching the crates spill out of the back and into the sea. The thin light from a torch touched the corners of the dusty space, and Gwenna used it to look at her watch; yes, it was time.

The van's back door was already open when she climbed out, and Peter was consulting a piece of paper and shoving boxes to either side. He turned as Gwenna approached, and relaxed as he recognised her. 'These on this side,' he gestured, 'are for taking tonight. Those others go in the storage room.'

'Good evening to you too,' Gwenna said tightly. She looked at the arrangement in the back of the van, and nodded to show she understood. 'Let's get this over with then.'

She drove carefully out of Hocking's grounds, and turned onto the Pencarrack road. 'Are you going to tell me how it went today?'

'The crossing was alright, Irene handled it well. It wasn't too choppy, considering we're into September now, but hopefully the next one will go out by plane, as usual.'

'What happens when they get to the Scilly Isles, anyway?'

'Not for me to say, or for you to know.' Peter sighed. 'Now stop asking questions and let's just get this done. I'm exhausted.'

Gwenna slammed the engine down a gear, and turned off the road onto the moorland track. It was hard to believe she had ever thought she could make a life with Peter Bolitho, his pomposity had become so marked lately. She felt a grim little smile cross her face as she considered how lucky she was to have freed herself before it was too late; he had given her the perfect excuse. Nevertheless, once she'd turned the headlights off and they sat in darkness behind the folly, she was glad he was there with her.

'Here they come,' he murmured, and she turned to look past him out of his side window, where a pair of lights picked out the ground ahead of a boxy-looking van that came slowly towards them over the bumpy ground.

'Do you know who's buying this time?'

'Redcliffe Cavers, apparently. They're a Bristol gang, used to run the docks before Ronnie Jackson and his lot moved in.'

'You seem to know quite a lot. So do you know what's in the boxes?'

Something about her tone must have told him she knew more than the last time she'd asked him the same question, because he took his gaze from the approaching vehicle and shifted it to her. 'Do you?'

She kept her answer ambiguous. 'I'm told it's tobacco and alcohol.'

'There you are, then.'

'But—'

'Go on,' he said, putting his hand into his pocket. He withdrew the gun and rested it on his thigh, his hand loosely curled around the grip. 'I'll be keeping a close watch. Only the boxes on the right for them, remember, and then I'll help you shift the rest into the room after they've gone.'

She took the torch from the glove box and climbed from the van, holding herself as straight as she could, and hoping her height would be interpreted as authority. The two men from the Redcliffe Cavers didn't pass any comment, and made short work of shifting the boxes into their van, though Gwenna was aware of the dark outline of a third person watching closely and was doubly grateful for Peter's presence. And, although she shrank from the thought, for the fact he was armed. She wondered why the third man made no attempt to help his companions, and tried to suppress the idea that he was aiming a weapon of his own at them.

The Cavers had their own labels, and had soon replaced the

interim ones Gwenna had painstakingly applied when she'd left the freight depot; the paste must barely have been dry.

When he had handed over the money, the larger of the two Cavers gestured to the shadowy figure in their van, and Gwenna's heart thumped a little harder.

'A last-minute adjustment to our arrangement,' the Caver said. He pointed at Peter. 'Your boss there will know what to do.'

So, another tenant for the cold, damp underground room. The man who emerged, carrying a kit bag, certainly lacked the height and bulk of the recently transported Frenchman, but Gwenna knew better than to assume he'd be less of a threat.

She briefly wondered if this was the mysterious 'Smith', looking to follow Devereux across the channel to Roscoff, and she didn't want to think what might happen should he catch up; what these gangs might or might not do to one another was a step beyond her comprehension.

It wasn't until the figure came closer, and into the arc of the van's lights, that Gwenna realised it wasn't a man at all. The figure was limping, favouring the right leg, but still there was an unmistakeably feminine lightness to the steps. The woman raised the rim of the hat she had pulled down over her brow, and looked at Gwenna. She didn't seem surprised, or put out, to see she was dealing with a woman, and her gaze was appraising rather than questioning.

'How did someone like you get involved in this?'

'What do you mean, someone like me?'

'You look like Head Girl at Swots University.'

Gwenna almost laughed at that, but there was no smile on the striking, sharply-angled features of the woman, who turned to her companions and waved them back to their van. Peter came over and joined them the moment the Cavers had gone, and his gun was trained on the woman. She ignored it.

'Well, are you going to get me out of here?'

'Not yet.' Gwenna jerked her head towards the trapdoor, remembering how Barry had dealt with Devereux. After all, why should she put the hard work in, when this woman was the one who needed her help?

'Then when?'

'This is just a safe place to stay while we make arrangements and get documents drawn up. Did you expect to get straight onto a plane and be flown to Paradise?' Gwenna heard the mild disdain and was surprised at her own confidence, but Peter looked even more so as he flashed his torch between the two women.

'What's your name, anyway?' Gwenna asked. 'Are you Smith?'

'Smith?' The woman's calm aura of superiority disappeared and she flashed Gwenna an angry look. 'I'll tell you one thing, if I ever set eyes on that wretch again, I won't be responsible.'

Gwenna flinched as she saw the woman's hand dip to her pocket and come back up clutching a short-bladed knife. 'Put that away,' she said quickly, 'or we'll take it off you.'

'I'd like to see you try.'

'Who *are* you?'

'Jenny Lyons,' the woman said, lifting her chin. 'Leader of the North Twenty.'

'Ex-leader now, I should think,' Gwenna pointed out, although her heart still raced at the sight of the blade. She had no idea who the North Twenty were, but Jenny seemed proud of her association with them anyway. To her surprise Peter handed her the gun, and she tried to hold it as if it was an everyday occurrence as she gestured with it at the knife. Jenny reluctantly put it back in her pocket, and winced as she shifted her weight again.

'What did you do to your leg?' Gwenna asked. The last thing they needed was to be slowed down once the escape was under way.

'A bullet grazed it.' Jenny met her eyes squarely, and Gwenna felt renewed revulsion for the gun in her hand.

'Is someone after you now?' she asked, fighting the impulse to peer away through the darkness of the moor. Every moment and revelation was eroding her protective sense of unreality; once that was gone she thought she might actually go mad.

Jenny shook her head. 'No-one but those Caver boys and my own second-in-command know I'm here, and they're not going to be letting on to the Dockers, you can rely on that.'

'The Dockers?'

Jenny gave her a mildly disdainful look. 'Don't you know anything?' When Gwenna didn't reply she shifted her weight, with another little grimace. 'Where do I wait then? In there?' She looked at the folly.

'No.' Gwenna shone the flashlight onto where the trapdoor still lay flush with the ground. 'Down there.' She tried to feel gratified at the look of dismay on Jenny's face, but felt only an unexpected sympathy. 'Don't worry,' she said, 'it's not as bad as it sounds. There's a room down there.' She nodded at Peter. 'He'll help you with the trapdoor.' A thought struck her. 'We can't leave those boxes down there now, can we?'

Peter's expression turned sour. 'I suppose not.'

'I mean,' Gwenna went on, feeling the devil on her shoulder suddenly, 'this nice lady might use that knife to get them open and, oh I don't know, *get drunk*, or something.' She gave Peter a grim smile as she watched realisation settle on his features. 'I'll take them back to the garage, shall I?'

'Leave them on the van.' Peter squatted by the folly wall and began to feel around, and he looked up impatiently when Jenny didn't go over to help. Gwenna saw the woman pressing her hand to her thigh, and saw the bulge of a bandage beneath the flattened material of her trousers.

'She can't,' she said. 'And I won't. I'm sure you can manage alone though, you must have done it in the past.'

Peter scowled, but set to work and was soon struggling to push the wooden slab aside. He stood up and gestured Jenny forward. Gwenna tossed him the keys, and held the torch so the light fell on the steps. Jenny turned to look at her, and her face, already bathed white by the torchlight, was tight and suddenly much older looking.

'Are you coming down?'

'No.' Gwenna straightened her back, which had been hunched in a kind of sympathy with Peter's awkward movements, and felt her confidence return. 'I need to find out if we can even help you at all. Go on, we'll check on you in the morning, and bring you something to eat.'

'How long will I be down there?'

'As long as it takes to arrange your route out. Where's the payment?'

'I'm not likely to be carrying it with me, am I? Not in a van full of Cavers.' She shrugged. 'My second-in-command paid for my transport out of Bristol. She'll wire Twenties' money direct to me, so I can pay whoever finds me a way out of England. And *only* that person. It's the only way I can guarantee someone doesn't try playing with toys they don't understand,' she added, looking pointedly at Gwenna's clearly amateur grip on the pistol.

It would have to do, and Gwenna waited, shivering in the chilly air, while Peter secured the padlock on the underground door, and then helped him shift the trapdoor back. When they both climbed into the van he half-turned towards her, and she had the idea he wanted to talk about the contents of the crates. But she didn't look at him as she started the engine, so he turned away again, remaining silent as she drove him to the top of town before returning to Hocking's house.

The house was still in darkness, but she was glad to close the garage door behind her and leave the van and its awful contents behind. All she could think about was the suffocating sense that she was being pulled more deeply into this mess every day, and when she started the dark and lonely walk back to the base, it came to her that she actually envied Jenny Lyons her imminent boat ride to freedom.

To get away from this terrible situation she was embroiled in seemed the only way she would ever properly sleep again, the only way to live without fear. And not just for herself now; Hocking's threat to Bobby's family still rang loud in her ears. Continuing to work for him put her own future at risk, but breaking free could prove just as dangerous for those she loved. The oppressive weight of it all was suffocating, and with her warring parents on the verge of breaking their small family apart too, it seemed that everything she'd held dear was being eroded day by day, minute by minute. Soon there would be nothing left at all.

The envy for Jenny had become resolve, by the time she let herself into the dorm, and she realised with a jolt that the answer was ridiculously simple after all: her family would only be threatened if she was there to witness it; if she was gone, such a gesture would be pointless. So she'd volunteer to take Jenny out to the Isles of

Scilly herself, in Hocking's little speed craft, only this time the boat wouldn't return.

*

Tory lay wide awake, staring at the first fingers of sunlight crawling across the ceiling, and running through everything she had learned last night from Bertie and Leah. It seemed that Gwenna's determination and passion for flying had, rather than worked in her favour, instead marked her as Hocking's logical victim; she was ensnared so thoroughly that it was going to be next to impossible to extricate her without also exposing her. It would have been so much better, for a hundred different reasons, if Hocking had picked on Tory herself, but there was no sense in dwelling on that now; Gwenna was the one who'd been pulled in, and she was the one who needed help to bring her out.

She glanced around the room at her slumbering companions; two of them her best friends, the third someone perhaps to be pitied, but also, it transpired, of whom to be extremely wary. She gave up trying to put everything from her mind; sleep was clearly over for the night, and fresh air might help her clear her head and find a way through this mess. She dressed quickly in the bathroom, then walked without conscious intent, but once she'd passed the Penworthy Memorial she realised she wanted nothing more than to take Mack for a fast ride along the cliff. Keir would already have been up for a while and he might be working both horses today, but it would be worth the walk down here for the small chance she might be able to take that remarkable colt out onto the quarry path again.

Midway down the hill, her early childhood home, Hawthorn Cottage, sat in its pitted yard, untouched by the intervening years. The gate hung awkwardly, one of the hinges rusted and snapped;

the roof of the cottage still dipped in the centre; and the door to the outhouse, where her mother had spent so much time putting clothes through the mangle, was still propped open with a stone to stop it slamming in the wind that continually came off the sea no matter what the weather.

Tory leaned on the broken gate, swallowing a sudden surge of emotion. She pictured Joseph climbing on these bars and counting how many times he could swing the gate shut before their mother yelled at him to get down. He had always urged Tory to pull it open for him once more, knowing he could easily manage one final juddering slam into the gatepost before being dragged off and sent indoors. Tomorrow he should have been celebrating his birthday, but instead that adventurous, mischievous boy lay in a field somewhere overseas, his last resting place unmarked. Tory cleared her throat and moved away from the achingly familiar house, leaving its current tenants, Bobby Gale no doubt among them, still sleeping away the earliest hours as the day lightened around them.

The yard at Priddy Farm was bathed in the pink colours of the rising sun, and Tory felt her spirits lift a little at the sight of it, and at the sound of stamping hooves from the stable; something about the sound made her blood race, and always had.

'Keir's out,' the farmhand said, emerging from the stable with a bucket. 'You're wanting Mack, are you?'

'If he's free.'

'Keir won't mind you making the most of him while you can, I'm sure.'

'What do you mean?'

'Mack's going to auction in a few weeks.'

Tory stopped stroking Mack's nose and turned to the farmhand in dismay. 'Why?'

'Can't afford to keep him. Never could really, but he's been too soft to admit it. Mack's too high-strung for the work, so we're going to make a bit of money off him and get a proper working horse instead.'

'Poor lad. And poor Bonnie.' Tory returned to rubbing Mack's cheek. 'I'll have him back in an hour,' she promised, but her spirits had fallen at the knowledge that this would be the last time she'd ride him. She'd said goodbye to countless horses over the years, and for many different reasons, but this one made her particularly sad. She saddled up and rode out of the yard, looking forward to feeling the powerful muscles stretch beneath her, and the wind of speed pulling at her hair. There was no feeling like it.

As they ambled up the fields parallel with the town, she turned her thoughts once more to how they could expose Barry Hocking's dealings without implicating Gwenna. Knowing Peter was in it just as deeply put him out of reach as a possible ally, likewise Bobby Gale, which was a pity. It would be down to just herself, Bertie and Leah, to do whatever had to be done, but what was that? She turned Mack's head towards the Cliffside Fort Hotel, in preparation for giving him his head along the quarry path, but was surprised to see a single figure sitting on the old castle wall, staring out over the sloping fields towards the sea.

'Leah?' she called.

The figure twisted at the sound of Tory's voice, and raised a hand from which a cigarette sent lazy spirals of smoke into the clear morning air. 'Are you alone?' Leah leaned back to look past Tory at the empty track.

'Just me and Mack here.'

'Good.'

Tory patted the horse's neck and swung down from the saddle to join Leah on the wall. 'Why?'

'I don't want Bertie to hear what I have to say.' Leah's voice was uncharacteristically subdued. 'Not yet, anyway.'

'I don't much like the sound of that,' Tory said. 'You'd better go on.'

'It's to do with her instructor, Miss ... Singleton, is it?'

Tory nodded. 'What about her?'

'Well, after you went back to your base last night, I went back to the pub down the road, just to ask around and see if I could find out anything unsavoury about Barry Hocking. I found some of your mechanics down there, and we got chatting. They didn't have anything much to say about Hocking, just that he's generally well liked. Kind, you know. But one of them did mention that ...' She gave Tory a sharp look. 'You have to promise me you'll not say anything to Bertie until I've verified this.'

'You have my word.' Tory frowned as her uneasiness grew. 'What was it?'

'There's been talk about Miss Singleton's plane, and what it might be being used for.'

'What?'

Leah tapped her cigarette on the stone, dislodging a glowing chunk of ash, before taking another drag on it. 'It's possible she might be using it for something other than flight lessons.'

'Well, it's her plane,' Tory pointed out.

'That's as maybe, but the hours and the fuel don't measure up, apparently.' Seeing Tory's puzzled look, Leah went on, 'You must know yourself how it's all logged. The flights, the fuel usage, maintenance and so on.'

'Of course.'

310

'Well, the entries Miss Singleton's making in the records don't properly match the amount of fuel that's actually being used. It's close, apparently, but not quite right. And there are some replacement parts that shouldn't be needed yet if the plane's being used in the way it's recorded.' She gave Tory a quick look from under her fringe. 'Ordered by Tommy Ash.'

'Tommy's the one she trusts to work on Joey,' Tory said, but her heart sank. 'Who drew their attention to all this though? Why did they know to check in the first place?'

'An anonymous source. No-one knows.'

'And what does it mean?' But Tory had a horrible feeling she knew.

'It means it's possible Miss Singleton is using her own plane to carry out trips she doesn't want recorded.' Leah spoke carefully, but her meaning was clear. 'And the fact that it's Tommy who's ordered the spare parts, and, as you say, who does most of her maintenance, makes it all look a little bit bleak for both of them. I'm not too bothered about Singleton one way or the other; if she's smuggling goods in or out of the country, she should face justice just as Hocking should. But we're going to have to be very careful how we go about exposing Hocking if we don't want to drag Tommy into it as well.'

'You don't think he should face justice too?'

Leah took another puff of her cigarette, then stubbed it out. 'I don't know Tommy Ash, but I do know and trust Bertie. If she tells me the young man's being coerced into helping Singleton against his will, just as Gwenna's being forced to help Hocking, I'll believe her.'

'And if she says the same of Jude? Miss Singleton?'

Leah stood up and brushed grit off the seat of her trousers.

'That's going to be harder to prove, given that it's her plane.' She gave Tory a sober look. 'I don't know that we're going to be able to save everyone. If we want to help Gwenna we're going to have to pick our battles very carefully.'

'What will you do now?'

'I'm going to have a chat with a Flight Lieutenant Bowden. Do you know him?'

'He's my instructor,' Tory said, as she gathered up Mack's trailing rein. 'Why on earth do you want to talk to him? He's about to leave anyway.'

'Because,' Leah lowered her voice and dropped a slow, exaggerated wink, 'he's about to leave anyway.'

CHAPTER EIGHTEEN

Bertie and Tory waited until Irene had gone for breakfast, then when Gwenna began to follow her Tory caught gently at her arm, and Bertie closed the door so the three of them were left in the dorm.

'What's all this?' Gwenna looked from one to the other, and Bertie thought she was trying to look amused at what must seem like theatrical behaviour, but the attempt fell short. Instead, she looked as if she wanted to either cry or be sick. 'I don't want to miss breakfast, come on.'

'We ought to have a little chat,' Bertie said gently. 'Come on, Gwenna, sit down just for a minute.'

Gwenna did so, looking very small and lost as she stared up at them. 'I don't like this.'

Bertie sat next to her and took her hand, while Tory sat on her own bed opposite them. She'd been up early and gone for a ride, and her skin was flushed and healthy-looking, particularly in comparison to Gwenna's pallor, but she was more solemn-looking than Bertie had seen her in a good while. She'd sent Bertie a silent message, on her return to the dorm, indicating the three of them with a discreet finger which she then placed across to her lips, and Bertie had understood it was time to bring Gwenna back into the circle.

'We know all about it,' Tory began, looking at Bertie for support, and Bertie nodded.

'Leah found out some stuff about Irene, and then Bobby Gale helped us piece it all together.'

'What exactly do you think you know?' Gwenna asked, and now she sounded stronger, almost defiant.

'We know that you've been forced to drive down to Truro to pick up illegal weapons, and bring them back here for Hocking.'

'And that he stores them in a room under the folly,' Tory added. 'We know Peter is involved too, that Irene is Barry Hocking's niece, and that she's been coerced into doing it too. Neither of you two is doing it willingly,' she went on quickly, 'we *know* that. We don't know about Peter though. We want to try and help you, but we'll need you to help us too.'

Gwenna's lips parted as if she were about to deny everything, but her eyes abruptly filled with tears and she covered her face with her hands. Bertie slipped her arm around her shoulders and exchanged a helpless look with Tory. 'It's alright now,' she said quietly, pulling Gwenna close and feeling the tall girl's frame shaking as the sobs broke free. 'We're going to get you out of this somehow, we promise.'

When Gwenna had herself under control she sat upright again and took the handkerchief Bertie proffered. 'If you know Irene doesn't want to do it either, why did you wait until she'd gone?'

'Because she was the one who told Hocking that Tommy knew about the folly,' Bertie said, her voice hardening now. '*She's* the reason he's been arrested.'

Gwenna went even paler. 'No, she isn't,' she whispered. 'I am.'

'What?'

'Irene told me she'd had to go up later than planned to feed Devereux, because the first time she went up she'd seen Tommy there. Then Devereux said someone knew about the room, so I had to report back to Hocking. I pretended I didn't know who it was, but he ... he got it out of me.'

'You must have given in pretty quickly!' Bertie was about to say more on the subject, but stopped, and she and Tory looked at one another, both puzzled. 'Who's Devereux?'

'So you don't know everything, after all.' Gwenna moved away from Bertie, who was still trying to grasp that Gwenna had betrayed Tommy, albeit unwillingly. She told them about the criminals who were being smuggled out of the country, and paying highly for the opportunity of escape and a new life in Europe. Probably America, eventually. 'This was a Frenchman,' she said, 'he was taken out to the Isles of Scilly yesterday morning, to meet a bigger boat going to Roscoff. Irene took him, in Hocking's own little motor launch, and Peter went with them.'

'Who on earth was he?' Bertie asked, the other issue temporarily pushed aside by this new revelation.

'Just some gangster from Bristol. It doesn't matter now, anyway, he's gone.'

Tory's eyes met Bertie's and her earlier healthy flush had faded to a sickly grey. Bertie understood; dealing with weapons was bad enough, but at least they'd been one step removed from the people who used them. This was entirely different, and that this gangster was from Bertie's original home town made it feel even worse somehow. Thank goodness he'd been moved on now. But

315

Gwenna was still talking, and it took a moment for Bertie to realise it wasn't over after all.

'I did another pick-up run yesterday, after I left you, Bertie. I told the truth when I promised I was trying to find out why Tommy had been taken in. The thing was, Hocking had told me he was just going to keep him out of the way with more hours of work, and just until Devereux had gone.'

'But you still knew more than you let on!' Anger was coiling in Bertie's insides again. 'So did he say why he'd gone back on his word?'

Gwenna shook her head, her eyes bright with tears of remorse. 'He made me do the collection in the afternoon, and then the evening run out to the folly as well.' She cleared her throat and wiped her eyes. 'That was when *she* turned up.'

'Who?'

'The girl gangster, Jenny someone. Said she was the leader of some crowd with a number in their name. Twenty-something.'

'The North Twenty,' Bertie said, and Tory looked at her, startled.

'You've heard of them?'

'I'm from Bristol originally, remember? I was only thirteen when we moved away, but I can remember hearing about them on the news, and my parents talked about them sometimes. I expect Leah will know quite a lot about them though, we'll have to ask.'

'And this Jenny is *here*?' Tory asked Gwenna.

'In the room under the folly,' Gwenna confirmed. 'Hocking's going to make arrangements, and then she'll be gone, too.'

Bertie thought for a moment. 'What if we go over Peter's head to Sergeant Couch, and make sure he's standing by at the boat, so he can catch Hocking red-handed?'

'No!' Gwenna said quickly. 'I'll be with her when that happens, then my father will find out. I . . . I couldn't bear that.'

Bertie took her hand again, anger fading into concern. 'Your parents will understand that none of it is your fault.'

'Please, *don't* set a trap for us,' Gwenna begged. 'I have to be able to trust my friends, if no-one else.'

Her choice of words had its desired effect, and Bertie nodded reluctantly. 'Alright. We'll do everything we can to make sure your name is kept out of it.'

But Tory didn't share her confidence. 'How though?'

'I don't know,' Bertie confessed. 'We'll talk to Leah. She'll work something out I'm sure.'

She hoped her faith was justified, but she felt better just knowing her old friend was around and involved; it reminded her that people were willing to help, and that she sometimes had to let them. She'd never been very good at that, and when Leah had nursed her as she recovered from her accident, she had reminded Bertie gently, but forcibly, every single day. It was a lesson she had learned unwillingly at first, but now it was a comfort.

'Gwenna,' Tory said thoughtfully, 'how does it work if it happens by plane instead of boat? You said Hocking had done it before, and he'd have used his plane this time if it wasn't still in for repair.'

'I assume he just gets them out of the room first thing, and back here to the base, then hides them in his plane before anyone's up to see them.'

'That would work,' Bertie agreed. 'One more plane in the general day-to-day racket on the base wouldn't make any difference.'

'And will Hocking's Avro be ready in time to take Jenny?' Tory asked.

'He said we might fly today instead of yesterday, so I assume so. But I can make sure I'm there when they make the arrangements, and let you know what he says. The money's being wired to Jenny, so she hasn't paid him yet either and nothing will happen until she has.'

Tory nodded. 'Let's talk to Leah in the meantime, and see if she has any ideas.'

'I've got classes,' Bertie said, 'and so have you, Tory.'

'I'm not going,' Tory said. 'There's no point, is there? Why don't you skip it just for today as well? It's not as if you're behind . . .' She glanced at Gwenna and flushed. 'Sorry, I didn't mean—'

'It's alright.' Gwenna brushed at her still-teary eyes and shook her hair back. 'I can't go in to breakfast like this, I'll go out for a bit of fresh air. I'll see you both for lunch and you can tell me what Leah comes up with, if anything.' She gave them what looked as if it was trying to be a brave smile, but Bertie couldn't help feeling, as she and Tory left her, that she looked as close to the edge as anyone she'd ever met.

Bertie and Tory made their way down to Tory's car, in order to go and find Leah, and instead found her waiting just outside the perimeter fence, her expression solemn. She seemed relieved Gwenna wasn't with them, and fidgeted with the bag she carried over her shoulder.

'I was escorted off the base.'

'What happened?'

Leah glanced around them. 'Look, I need to talk to you both. Can we drive somewhere quiet?'

Tory drove them out to the old quarry pool at Polworra, and once they'd made themselves comfortable on the grass, Leah

318

began to fill them in on what she'd been up to since she and Tory had parted company before breakfast.

'I found that flight lieutenant we talked about, Tory. Graham Bowden. He was in early to clear out his office, and he agreed to have a little chat with me. Said it was highly irregular, since I'm not officially the law, but he didn't mind this once.'

'He's strangely not that bad,' Tory said, in response to Bertie's look of surprise. 'Since he decided to leave it's as if he's found a heart underneath all those charts and test papers.'

'Speaking of test papers.' Leah pulled a brown paper folder from her bag. 'I was asking him about his new job, and just generally chatting away, putting him at his ease, if you like, and all the time he was busy packing up his desk. He found this.'

She placed the folder on the grass between them. On the cover was stencilled, *Rosdew, Gwenna Marie. 1930/2.* 'The 2 means it's second intake, apparently. He said he didn't know where it had come from, but it was in amongst a pile of old files to be destroyed. He refused to let me see it of course, and began making noises about how I was not supposed to be there, and that I ought to leave.'

Bertie raised an eyebrow, and looked pointedly at the folder on the grass, and Leah smiled and shrugged. 'I remembered you saying how strange it was that Gwenna had failed two prior tests, against all expectations, and I mentioned this to Lieutenant Bowden. I said that I was investigating a possible case of victimisation, and I dropped Hocking's name into it to see how he'd react.'

'And?' Tory leaned forward.

'And he reacted very strangely,' Leah said. 'He put this file aside. Then said he had to leave the room for approximately five minutes, to fetch someone to escort me off the base, and that he was putting me on my honour not to touch anything.'

'I don't think he ever liked Hocking,' Bertie said, pleased. 'Did you look first, or just take it?'

'I looked first, of course. I wanted to be sure it was worth the risk. Sadly . . .' Leah reluctantly folded back the cover and Bertie saw a completed *Instruments 2: Advanced* test paper sitting on the top of the pile, with a 67% scribbled in the top corner. She moved that sheet aside, and saw another beneath it, marked 63%. Both were dated prior to 23rd August, when Gwenna had apparently taken the test for a third time and passed.

'She did fail, after all,' Tory murmured. 'Oh no.'

Bertie's heart sank. They'd been so sure. 'Poor Gwenna. At least she's passed now, but we can't blame Hocking for holding her back.'

'No.' Tory sighed. 'That's one less arrow in our quiver, but we're not down yet. Leah, we wanted to talk to you about something.'

'Fire away.' Leah started to gather up the test papers, but Bertie put out her hand.

'Just a moment.' She picked up the first paper and frowned at it. Some of the answers had their calculations in the margins, and she could tell the formulae were correct, but this particular answer had a line through it. She did the calculation again herself, then peered more closely at the answer and frowned. 'Look at this.' She passed it across to Tory, who glanced at it and shook her head.

'What?'

'Look at the eight in the answer to question four, and compare it to the one on the answer above.'

'It looks a bit more childish,' Tory observed.

'As if it used to be a three? Now look at the three that Gwenna's written in the calculation. Which is correct, I checked.'

Tory did so. 'And it's not just question four is it?' she said after a moment. She picked up the test with the lower mark. 'The same thing's happened here. And there's a seven that's magically become a two, look.'

Bertie did so. 'The absolute pig,' she breathed, wishing Hocking was there so she could let him know exactly what she thought.

'He's kept her so hungry to pass,' Tory said, her voice flat. 'She was *desperate* to prove to her father that she could do it.'

'She was so proud when she finally did it. Officially, I mean.'

'What can we do with this though, now?' Tory asked, pushing the papers back together before the wind could take them off into the huge green quarry pool nearby. 'You've stolen it from Bowden's office.'

'And *you're* going to put it in Hocking's,' Leah said. 'He won't be expecting it to be there, so he won't go looking for it. I want it to be turned up in a legitimate search when I'm able to get the police in there.'

'And how will you do that?'

'I haven't worked that part out yet,' Leah confessed. 'But if you could make sure the file's in there, and well hidden, that'd be a start.'

'We could give it to Irene to put in there,' Bertie suggested. At Tory's dark look, she shrugged. 'Look, she doesn't want to do this either, does she? And he's not going to suspect her for one minute. Now we know it wasn't her fault Tommy was arrested—'

'What's this?' Leah asked, and Bertie explained everything Gwenna had said to them that morning. When she reached the part where they'd been talking about Jenny meeting Hocking, in order to pay him, her grey eyes took on a gleam Bertie recognised very well, and welcomed.

'You've thought of something.'

'Let me think a bit more.' Leah pushed the file back into her bag. 'Leave this with me for now, I'll talk to Irene myself.' She drew her knees up to her chin and rested on them, frowning into the distance. 'Did I understand right, that Hocking's not met this gangster woman yet?'

'Not yet.'

'Hmm.' Leah chewed at her thumb knuckle for a moment. 'The accent's no problem,' she murmured, and Bertie wasn't sure if she was talking to herself, 'but I'd need to talk to her to get the nuances of the speech right. The, you know, the . . . ' She clicked her fingers.

'The lingo?' Tory suggested.

'Yes! The way a gang member would phrase things. It sounds as if Hocking's dealt with these people enough to be able to tell if someone were trying to pull the wool over his eyes.'

'He probably hasn't met many female gang members,' Tory said, 'so it shouldn't matter that much. Particularly since you'll be trying to give him the only thing he cares about.'

'Money,' Bertie agreed. 'Tory's right, I wouldn't worry too much.' She caught Leah's look, and smiled. 'Alright, saying that to you is like telling a concert pianist not to mind if they hit a single wrong note.'

'I wouldn't recommend going up there though, even so,' Tory said. 'From what Gwenna said, you're not likely to get much co-operation out of her.'

'I still need to think about it a bit more.' Leah climbed to her feet and held out a hand to pull Bertie up after her. 'Let's meet again this evening, shall we? All of us this time, including Irene. We need to pool everything we know, and make our plan together, otherwise it just won't work.'

'Everything?' Tory asked, and Bertie didn't miss the lightning quick glance that passed between her two companions.

'What was that for?' she asked.

'Nothing important,' Leah said, 'and perhaps by the time we meet up later it'll actually be nothing at all.'

'Can I drop you back at your hotel?' Tory asked Leah, before Bertie could pursue it, and Leah shook her head.

'No, you and Bertie get off and do what you have to do today. We'll meet there at five o'clock.'

*

Gwenna found her steps taking her naturally towards home as she left the others. The one thing she hadn't been able to tell her friends was that she still planned to leave alongside the gangster woman, but there was time for that later, should she choose to. Her parents, however, were another story; there was nothing she'd be able to say that would explain to them why she was going, and so all she could do was to see them today while she had the chance, and try not to break down in front of them.

They would have finished their breakfast a while ago and already begun their workday, so Gwenna went in at the shop door instead of into the house at the back. Her mother looked up with the usual bright, welcoming smile she wore for customers, but as soon as she saw Gwenna the smile faltered and she bit her lip hard. Gwenna went to her, alarmed.

'What is it? What's wrong?'

'Your father's gone again,' Rachel said. 'He was out all day

323

yesterday, though he said he'd be home by noon, and today he was gone before I even woke up.'

'Gone where? I know yesterday was—'

'Picking up supplies,' Rachel broke in. 'But he didn't come home with any.'

'What did he say about it?'

'Just that there was a problem with the paperwork.'

'Then that's what it'll be. He's probably gone back to fix it today.'

Rachel began to nod, then her eyes flooded. 'Oh, Gwenna, what if he's left me for her?'

'Nancy Gilb ... Stuart? He's not seeing her, I'm sure of it.' Gwenna hugged her, thinking with dismay how thin she had become.

'Whoever it is, then. What if he's been planning this new life, and now he's gone?'

'He wouldn't, Mum, I'm sure of it. He's not the kind of man to do that. He's not a coward.'

'You mean he's too *brave* to run away without an explanation?' Rachel gave a single, hiccupping laugh. 'Oh, your view of your father is something to behold, Gwenna Rosdew, it really is.'

Gwenna retreated a step, stung. 'What does that mean?'

'He's just a man! I know to you he's always been this glowing, god-like creature. A war hero, a tragic character who had to sacrifice his love of carpentry and creation to become a *boring shopkeeper*, and who never complains about it.' Rachel was agitatedly moving things around on the counter as she spoke, and Gwenna caught at her hands to stop her.

'I'm not an idiot,' she said quietly. 'I know he's got failings just like everyone, but I also know he loves us both too much to

324

just leave us without a word of explanation. And yes,' she went on, her voice rising slightly, 'he *did* have to give up the work he loved after the war, and I don't think you really understand how it's affected him deep down, because he's had to hide it from you *every single day!*'

Rachel blinked in surprise at this vehemence, but Gwenna had only just allowed herself to realise what she herself would be giving up, and it went some way towards helping her understand what her father had been through. Somewhere in Cornwall there was the last wooden train ever crafted by Jonas Rosdew, being trundled across the floor in an unknown house, by a child who had no notion of what he held in his hands. All that artistry, and the long, painstaking hours in the workshop that had produced it, seemed meaningless now, yet Jonas had somehow put aside his bitterness at losing the career he loved. So what if he did sometimes bring up his gallantry award a bit too much? What if he gave in to the pain that had ruled him ever since? Wasn't he entitled? Gwenna knew she would be the same, once she had cut all her ties with aviation training and accepted she would never fly after all.

Her mother was looking at her oddly, and Gwenna realised she had fallen silent as these thoughts, and the great swell of grief for her own career, took over. She shook her head.

'I'll come and see you this evening,' she said. 'Dad will be back by then, and we can spend an hour or so together before ... before I have to go back to the base.'

'You seem certain of him,' Rachel said, and since she seemed to be taking some heart from that certainty, Gwenna gave her a smile to reinforce it.

'I am, and you should be, too. See you this evening.'

*

She walked back up through the town, intending to return to her maintenance class just for the sake of passing the time until she was able to talk to the others again; it would take her mind off the awful thought of leaving everything behind, and perhaps they might even have come up with some kind of plan to help her by then. She passed a couple of well-dressed ladies by the civic offices, and one of them looked familiar; her heartbeat picked up as she recognised Hocking's wife.

It occurred to her that, with Hocking at the base, now might be a good time to search his garage, to which she still had the key, for anything incriminating. And even his house if she were able to get in. She wished she'd thought about leaving at least one of the boxes of guns somewhere in the garage, where it might have gone unnoticed when Hocking took the 'stolen' van out to leave it somewhere public. Still, there might be *something* she could do, and she didn't know how much time she had before Mrs Hocking returned home, so she picked up her pace, and almost ran full-tilt into Bobby Gale who was stepping out of the butcher's shop.

He laughed and steadied her. 'Whoa!' Then he recognised her, and his smiled faded. 'Gwenna, listen, I had to tell—'

'I know.' Gwenna only hesitated for a moment. 'Do you want to try and help?'

'Help how?'

'Come with me to Hocking's house. Help me search it for some kind of evidence of what he's been up to.'

'You can't do that!' He looked around them quickly, and lowered his voice. 'D'you suppose I haven't thought of it? I can't risk getting sent down, and leaving my family with nothing.'

'We've got someone else helping us now. A private investigator. She knows what she's about, so maybe if we can find just one little

326

thing that would help, it would be worth it. We'd do everything we could to keep your name clear, too.' She saw his resolve falter. 'Well, I'm going anyway, and it has to be now while they're both out. At least I hope they are. Come with me or not, it's up to you.' She began walking again, her stride long and determined, but was secretly relieved when he fell into step beside her, shoving a wax-wrapped packet of sausages into his coat pocket.

As they started on the road towards Pencarrack and Hocking's house, she told him that Devereux had gone, but that there was already another one waiting, only a matter of a few hundred yards away from where they now walked, and finally she told him that she intended to disappear this time too. He stopped in the middle of the road and stared at her.

'You can't,' he said, 'it'd destroy your ma and pa.'

'If they find out what I've been doing it'd be even worse. For all of us. I can't face them every day and see their disappointment if it comes out. Which it will,' she added. 'It's sure to.'

'I thought you were pinning all your hopes on this investigator,' Bobby said, resuming his former quick pace and checking over his shoulder for Mrs Hocking's return. 'I mean, you said your friends will do all they can to keep your name out. And mine too, I hope,' he added, but without much conviction.

'What if she can't though? I'm just preparing for the worst, that's all.'

They hurried on in silence, and Gwenna was reassured when she saw Hocking's car wasn't in the drive. A gardener loped along the bottom edge of the grounds with a rattly grass cutter, but he didn't look up as Gwenna used Hocking's key to unlock the garage, and they both slipped inside and pulled the door closed again. The window was dusty, but the mid-morning sun streamed in nevertheless, falling in a muted golden path through the middle of the roomy garage. The van was still there.

Gwenna gave a triumphant cry and opened the back of it, but her spirits sank again as she saw that, not only had the crates gone, but that the paste, and the torn-off labels, along with the unused ones, had been removed as well. In answer to Bobby's silent query she told him what she'd hoped to do.

'It still wouldn't prove he was involved in it,' he pointed out. 'He could say he had no idea who was using this place.'

'He did say he rarely comes out here,' Gwenna said reluctantly. 'Damn.'

'The only way he'd find it hard to wriggle off the hook is if we find something in the house itself. We don't have to take it away, just tell your friend where to look.'

Although that had been part of Gwenna's plan earlier, now they were here she felt a flicker of trepidation. 'We can't break in though, it'd be illegal. And what if they came back?'

'Let's at least try the doors,' he urged. 'You never know, place this size with a hundred doors.'

Gwenna smiled. 'Three, at most, I think.'

'That's two more than Mrs Hocking came out of this morning.' Bobby shrugged. 'She might not have checked the others. Come on, where's that Rosdew fighting spirit?'

Gwenna followed him cautiously out of the garage and around the building, where they found, to their disappointment, the side and rear ground-floor doors were locked. Bobby cupped his hands around his eyes and peered in at the nearest window.

'Kitchen,' he said. 'No staff that I can see.'

'I'll go around to the front.' Gwenna saw his worried look and shook her head. 'If the gardener sees me, I'd have an explanation for calling on Hocking. If he sees you, he'll have Sergeant Couch up here before you can blink.'

He chewed at his lip for a moment, then nodded. 'Go on then. But be careful.'

'Oh, I will, don't worry.'

Gwenna made her way around to the front, glad to see the gardener was still making his slow way along the border at the lower edge of the huge garden. She stepped into the porch and tried the door, almost crying out in surprise as it opened under her hand; luck was on their side after all. She hurried through the wide hallway towards the kitchen, planning to unlock the back door and admit Bobby, but her attention was caught by a voice drifting out of the open door to another room just ahead, and she stopped, her heart hammering in her ears. She'd promised to be wary, and here she was thundering through this large, echoey hall; another step and she'd have been caught with no reasonable explanation why she should be actually inside the house. For that matter, why was Hocking here instead of at the base? He had lessons scheduled today, she knew that, and his car hadn't been outside. It had to be something clandestine.

She could see into the kitchen from here, and out through the window. Bobby had seen her, and gave her a triumphant grin and a wave from outside, but she shook her head frantically at him and began to back away. The front door seemed to be miles behind her; her skin was clammy with sweat and her heartbeat still crashed after her close call. Someone replied to whatever Hocking had said, and she froze, unable to breathe for a moment. That voice . . .

'Who's there?' Hocking barked, and the door was jerked wide by a tall, roughly dressed man with startlingly blond hair.

'Just a girl,' he called back, but Gwenna's attention had already moved past him and to the room beyond, to Hocking who looked utterly furious, and to the third man, who was looking at her with a trapped, horrified look. He had one hand in a wooden crate that sat on Hocking's desk, and in the other he held one of the guns, broken open. A box of shells sat beside him.

'Gwenna, love . . .'

But Jonas must have known that no words he found now would change what she had seen, and what she now understood, because he fell silent, and only his eyes pleaded with her. Then, before anyone could speak again, the blond man grasped her wrist and yanked her into the room, and slammed the door shut behind her.

CHAPTER NINETEEN

'So, we're agreed?' Leah, pacing her hotel room, looked at each of the three in turn, and Tory tried not to be annoyed with Gwenna, who hadn't returned from her walk. Someone said they'd seen her go into her parents' shop earlier, so presumably she'd been roped in to help, but surely this was more important? She was the one they were trying to help, after all.

Bertie was looking strained and angry too, having now heard about Jude Singleton's supposed fuel discrepancies, but Tory thought she also looked as if she were bursting to add something that would explain it away. The silent *but . . .* had shown in the set of Bertie's lips, but she had subsided and remained frustratingly silent on the matter while Leah had outlined the next stage of the plan. Tory kept trying to catch her eye, but she avoided it with an unsettling determination.

Irene sat silent and dry-eyed but still looking bewildered at the speed with which everything had happened. 'This is just a fact-finding exercise, Irene, nothing more,' Leah assured her. 'You'll take me to your uncle and we'll tell him I'm Jenny Lyons. While we're talking, you're to plant this file,' she tapped the folder where it sat at on the dressing table, 'in his house, somewhere he won't find it right away. I'm going to use this chance to wheedle as much out of him as possible that I can take to the police.'

'How will you get them there?' Tory asked, but Leah shook her head.

'I really don't know yet,' she admitted. 'I'm hoping Hocking will give me something to work with. Irene, I'll meet you outside the base at seven, to give Hocking time to get home before we drive out there.'

Irene and Bertie rose to leave, but Tory hung back. 'You go on,' she said, I'll be out in just a minute, there's something I want to talk to Leah about.'

'More finger-pointing about Jude?' Bertie guessed, her expression clouding again. 'I'll wait outside then.'

'I think Tory and I can both see you have something to say about your instructor,' Leah said. 'We'll be out in a minute.'

Bertie looked as if she wanted to blurt it out right there and then, but shot a look at Irene and nodded. 'Alright.'

Tory understood that look; whatever was behind the questions that had arisen about Jude, it would likely have some impact on her career, and whatever else she was, Irene was still Barry Hocking's niece. She waited until the door closed behind the two of them, then turned to Leah.

'It's about something you said earlier today. I can help.'

It was around ten minutes before she and Leah joined Bertie, out in the hotel car park. As soon as they arrived, Bertie began to talk, and Tory and Leah listened in growing awe as they heard about the extra lessons. It was no wonder Singleton's fuel was being used up so fast; she must have known she'd be found out eventually, but the fact that she considered Bertie worth the risk was undeniably heart-warming.

'Tommy was working on her plane after hours on Sunday,' Bertie explained, 'which was why he had no alibi. I can't go bursting into the police station and telling them that though, even if Jude were here to give me her blessing.'

'It would show him up to be a liar,' Leah agreed. 'And it would follow that if he'd lied convincingly about that, what else might he be lying about.'

'Exactly.' Bertie looked at them helplessly. 'And Jude would lose her job too. So I can't do anything, except prove someone else was responsible for the theft of that van. We *have* to prove Hocking was behind it, but without incriminating Gwenna.'

Tory rubbed her face. 'What a mess . . . Who's that?'

Bertie twisted to look behind her, to where Tory was squinting against the sun at an approaching figure. 'It's Bobby. He looks pretty upset about something.'

'I haven't seen him for years,' Tory mused. 'He looks *hellish* upset.'

Bobby came closer, his face sweaty from running. 'I asked for you at the base,' he said to Bertie, 'but they said you weren't in your lesson.' He barely spared the others a glance. 'I need to talk to you.'

'This is Leah,' Bertie indicated. 'She's the—'

'Investigator, yeah. Listen, Gwenna Rosdew's up at Hocking's house, with Hocking and some other bloke.' He took a deep breath. 'They've got her locked away.'

'What?' Tory stared at him, suspecting some poorly timed prank, but the famous Gale mischief was nowhere to be seen today. 'What other bloke?' she demanded. 'And why?'

He finally acknowledged her with a little start. 'Little Tory Gilbert? Blimey.' He shook his head briskly and gave a brief account of their trip to Hocking's house, which ended when he'd seen, through the kitchen window, a well-built blond man pulling Gwenna into a room and the door slamming shut. When she hadn't emerged a few minutes later, with her tail between her legs after a telling-off, he'd begun to fear the worst and left to find help.

'Why didn't you go to the police?' Bertie demanded.

'Because she told me she's planning to leave town if things go wrong, so I didn't want to put the wind up anyone. I don't think they'll hurt her, even Hocking doesn't have the stomach for that, and anyway he's spent a long while training her up. He needs her. But they'll keep her out of sight until they can fly her out, and I know she'll not give them any trouble, because that's what she wants too.'

'Did you say the man was blond?' Tory asked, feeling a helpless crawling down her spine. 'Describe him.'

'Nothing much to say. Not a posh bloke like Hocking. His hair's more white than blond though.'

Tory exchanged a glance with Leah, who nodded gravely, and Tory backed away from the little group.

'Bobby, can I have a word? And, Bertie, I'll have something to ask of you later, and something to tell you. You might hate me for both, but I have no choice. Meet me at the dorm in two hours.'

Tory drew closer to the folly, her eyes darting about the landscape every time a movement caught her eye, but always it was the swoop of a bird or a gorse bush dipping in the wind; she was alone out here, except for the woman sitting in the damp dark beneath the old stone building.

Part one of the plan was now in place, with Bobby Gale more than eager to play his part. Part two, the more worrying part, was looming, and Leah and Irene would take care of part three later this afternoon, as they made their attempt to release Gwenna. As for part four ... Well. That remained to be seen, and might turn out to be absolute lunacy, but Tory couldn't deny the way her blood was thrumming in her veins. This was living again, for sure.

The drone of an aircraft made her look up; it was an Avro trainer, which made her think of Gwenna and what she was prepared to give up, and her heart hardened further against Barry Hocking. At the folly she mentally went over Bertie's description of where she and Tommy had made their discovery, and she was soon crouching, and patting her way around the edges of the wooden trapdoor. When she found the handholds and was able to push it away she was surprised at how well it all fitted together; there was a well-crafted frame for it to sit in, and the stairs that led away into the darkness looked, in the bright sunlight that fell on the first few at least, to have been made with great skill and were finished with an eye on preservation against damp.

Now came the hard bit. Tory hoisted the satchel over her shoulder, felt in her pocket, and withdrew the keychain she had taken from Irene in the hotel. She wrapped it around her fist, partly to have the key close to hand, and partly because it hurt just enough, when she clenched her fist, to distract her from the way her chest closed up as she descended the steps into the earth. She turned and knelt down, so she could manhandle the heavy wooden cover over the hole, leaving only a small gap through which she looked up at the sky and the wisps of cloud one last time.

She told herself she was being ridiculous, but the stern thought lacked conviction as she reluctantly resumed her descent and felt the cool air stirring at her ankles. Not good, clean air, but stale, blowing up from waterlogged holes and centuries-old shafts connecting to the various derelict engine houses that peppered the moors. The more she thought about the maze of tunnels stretching out beneath her, and all around, the tighter her chest became. She and Harry Batten had escaped with their lives that day, but there would be others down the years, kids and adults alike, who hadn't been so lucky. She couldn't dispel the thought that, if she listened hard enough, she'd hear them moaning in the everlasting darkness of this subterranean landscape. She shook her head briskly, squeezed the key chain harder, and somehow reached the bottom of the steps. Only then did she switch on the torch, take a deep breath, and fit the key into the padlock, calling in a low voice, 'I've got food.'

From the other side of the door she heard footsteps coming closer, then backing away to make way for the opening door. The key turned easily and released the padlock, but Tory's hand was shaking as she wriggled the lock out of the loops that held it, and she almost dropped it before she was able to slip it into her pocket. This was it ... She slipped the satchel off her shoulder and pushed the door open very slowly, keeping hold of it just in case, and lowered the food onto the hard floor.

The woman in the room blinked in the torchlight, then looked at her more closely, and as her eyes adjusted she took a couple of quick steps back. '*Smith?*'

Tory could see her fumbling at her coat pocket and knew there would be a weapon of some kind in there, and she felt her entire body tense, waiting for a possible gunshot. But Jenny pulled a short-bladed knife from the pocket, and Tory hissed and let go of the door seconds before the blade sliced the wood where her fingers had been. Before Jenny had managed to recover from the mis-timed swipe, Tory brought the edge of her hand down and knocked the knife from Jenny's hand. It went spinning away into the darkness, and Tory dropped her torch, and grabbed at Jenny's shoulders, pinning her against the rough stone wall.

'Stop it and listen!'

'Traitor! I'm going to—'

'This is important.' Tory gave Jenny a little shake. 'Never mind what's happened between us in the past, I'm all you've got right here and now. So *listen!*'

'I swore I'd do for you if we ever met again,' Jenny hissed at her, and in the strange light thrown upwards by the fallen torch Tory could see tears—of rage, no doubt—glistening in her former friend's eyes.

'I'm not that fond of you either,' she said grimly. 'But Ronnie Jackson's up there, and *he's* the danger now.'

Jenny's shoulders slumped as the words hit home. 'Ronnie? How?'

'I'm guessing someone betrayed you to the Dockers,' Tory said. 'Could it have been someone in the Twenties? Whoever set this escape up for you?'

'The only person who knew was Colette.'

'Colette Newman? For goodness' sake!'

Jenny threw Tory a filthy look. 'I needed a new second once you'd run off. She wouldn't betray me though, she hates Ronnie as much as I do.' She wriggled against Tory's grip. 'You can let me go now.'

'Can I trust you?'

Jenny's eyes narrowed. 'I need to hear about Ronnie. You can trust me that long at least.'

Tory studied her for a moment longer, then spared a glance back to where the knife had come to rest against a kit bag. She released Jenny and bent swiftly to pick it up.

'Tell me what happened on the docks that night,' she said, reaching behind her to move the bag she'd dropped and push the door closed, 'then I'll tell you about Ronnie.' She blinked away unexpected and unwelcome tears of her own as she remembered the stand-off: sister against brother, and neither one prepared to back down. 'Did ... did you kill Victor?'

'No.' Jenny evidently saw the beginning of a relieved look on Tory's face, because she shook her head quickly. 'He's dead, but I didn't kill him. Ronnie did.'

'But you shot him.'

Jenny sat down on the rough blanket that was heaped in the corner, and drew her knees up to her chest. As she did so she flinched and gripped at her thigh, but when she began to talk, any concern Tory might have had for her vanished.

'Yes, I shot him. I had to. But he didn't die, and he was just screaming ...' Jenny's voice caught and she cleared her throat. 'I didn't realise at first what had happened, hardly even heard Ronnie's gun, but then Victor went quiet and I knew Ronnie had done the only thing he could.'

'He *could* have taken him to hospital!' Tory felt her fingers tighten around the handle of the knife, and saw that Jenny had seen it too.

'It was too late,' Jenny said quietly. 'Vic couldn't have lived more than a few minutes.'

'So you *did* kill him, no matter how you try to deny it. Your own brother.'

'It was him or me, you saw that!' Jenny shook her head. 'He betrayed me and Ronnie. And so did you. Between you, you ruined everything.'

Tory shook her head. 'What ruined it was you and Ronnie getting involved in guns to start with.'

'What did you care? You were getting ready to move on anyway, I could tell that old wanderlust had set in! You could have just gone. But you *had* to tell Victor we knew about the guns, didn't you? You should have known he'd tell Ronnie, and he'd guess I was planning to take them for the Twenties.'

'I had no idea what you were planning,' Tory protested. 'Victor and I were just talking, he asked what I was doing that evening, and we were supposed to be on the same side!'

'Victor's loyalty was always to Ronnie, not me. And vice versa.' Jenny pressed her hand harder to her thigh. 'You have to understand how it was for Victor and me, how we got started in it all.'

'Tell me then.' Tory sat opposite and fixed her with a level stare. 'Go on.'

'Didn't he tell you?'

Tory shook her head. 'We talked about a lot of stuff, but neither of us was in any hurry to dredge up our past.'

For a moment it seemed Jenny wasn't going to tell her after all, but she must have simply been searching for the best place to start. 'Our dad and older brother joined up in 1915,' she began at last. 'I was fifteen, Vic was only thirteen, so we went to live with our gran on Dad's side. Dad and Neil never came home, and after that Granny Lyons was never the same.' She dug into her kit bag and pulled out a bent and dog-eared photograph. Tory took it and studied it, recognising the ghost of the adult Victor in the solemn little boy who stared back at her.

'We were more or less left to our own devices,' Jenny went on, 'and when she died, about a year later, we didn't have anywhere to live. Being that bit older I used to go into town and nick stuff, and I found the North Twenty by accident. I liked them. I convinced them I could be one of them and they took me in. Vic wanted the same, but, well you know.'

Tory nodded. 'Only females allowed in the Twenties.' She felt the pain behind Jenny's casual words about her father's and brother's fates; she knew only too well how it hurt to express it in any other way. 'So Vic found the Docklands Mob instead, I take it?'

'By way of the Redcliffe Cavers, yeah. That's who he joined first. The Cavers ran the docks, but then Ronnie and his lot moved in, banished the Cavers, and took over.' She took the photograph back. 'Vic decided he wanted to be on the winning side, but I'd already made some friends in the Cavers. Useful ones.'

'Good thing for you two that the Dockers and North Twenty worked so well together.'

'Good thing?' Jenny snorted. 'It was *because* of us. Vic pulled Ronnie's strings, though Ronnie would never admit it.' She straightened her position against the wall, and fixed Tory with a bright, bitter smile. 'And then *you* came along. Fingersmith extraordinaire ... We couldn't *not* take you on, could we? How lucky we were to have found you. Traitor.'

'We were friends once,' Tory said quietly. 'Good friends. The four of us, in that house ... those are the memories that I want to keep. And I was loyal to the Twenties,' she added, growing indignant again. 'We worked *with* the Dockers, as far as I knew, it's not my fault you were keeping things from Ronnie.'

'You destroyed us, and ran away.' Jenny shifted again, and this time didn't manage to stifle the hiss of pain.

'What happened?' Tory nodded at Jenny's leg.

'I tried to kill Ronnie. It went wrong.'

'That would explain why he's come down here after you then,' Tory observed wryly.

'It was the other way around, actually.' Jenny prodded at the bandage. 'He was already on the warpath, I went after him in order to protect us.' She sighed. 'Things changed after Vic died, the Twenties turned into a mob no better than the Dockers, or even the Cavers.'

'How did it happen?'

'He'd had a couple of my newer girls attacked, after they tried to rip off his second, a bloke called Devereux.'

'I've heard of him. What did you do?'

'I went to his place, waited in his bed – with my clothes on under the covers mind – and made like I wanted to put things right between us. I was going to plug him through the eiderdown.' She gave a bitter little laugh. 'He guessed what I was up to, and he hit my arm just as I was trying to bring the barrel up. The gun went off.'

Tory winced. 'Bad?'

'Just a graze, but it bled a lot. He went to a cupboard for his own gun, and that's when I managed to get out and back to our barn.'

'Will you be able to make it out?' Tory tried not to sound impatient, but this might severely impact their plan.

'I don't have a lot of choice, do I? I might need a clean dressing though.'

'I only have this.' Tory dug into her pocket and withdrew the large handkerchief she could never bring herself to throw away; knowing who was waiting for her, she had taken it from her

341

bedside drawer in the dorm when she'd changed for this task, but she hadn't known she would need it for this. The handkerchief had *fides omnia* embroidered in the corner, and Jenny gave her a wry smile as she took it.

'Not much *fides* from you, was there?'

'I'm trying to put that right,' Tory said quietly. 'I'm here to get you out, but we can't go above ground, not with Ronnie on the prowl.'

'Not even when it's dark?'

'No, because if it wasn't Colette who double-crossed you—'

'This time.' Jenny waved the handkerchief with its hollow promise of loyalty stitched into the cotton.

Tory sighed. 'This time,' she conceded, 'then it must have been Barry Hocking. He's not going to give away this hiding place, it's too useful to him, but you can lay your last quid he'll tell Ronnie exactly where you'll be getting on his plane. You won't stand a chance then, you'll be a sitting target.'

Jenny's bravado faltered. 'Why doesn't this Hocking bloke come and get me now?'

'Why should he risk it? You're nothing but merchandise, and he's already sold you on to Ronnie.' Tory knew she sounded blunt, but she kept remembering Jenny holding the gun on Victor, the only family member she had left, and then picturing Ronnie putting his own gun to Victor's head and finishing the sickening job.

'I can't believe you chose to come back here,' Jenny said, turning her fear into scathing venom. 'This ridiculous little place has nothing! It's all hills and farmland, cow muck and washerwomen. After the excitement of Bristol, and London, and with your skills and knowledge, how can you bear to be stuck somewhere so ... *provincial?*'

Tory opened her mouth to reply, but she knew it would be pointless to try and explain it to someone like Jenny. 'You're stuck here too, without me,' she said instead, 'so I'm going to tell you what happens next, and you're going to listen and not interrupt.'

To her surprise Jenny didn't argue. 'Go on.'

'I can't stay here now, since there's no-one to slide the cover back over the hole.' And she wouldn't anyway, she could already feel the walls closing in, but there was no way she was going to reveal this weakness, especially to Jenny Lyons. 'I'll leave you with the food now, and be back tomorrow morning first thing to get you out. To make absolutely sure Ronnie doesn't see you, we're going through the tunnels under the moor.' She saw Jenny's eyes widen, but the former gang leader remained obediently silent.

'A friend of mine will have a boat ready,' Tory went on, 'but it's only a small one, and Hocking's is faster and sturdier, it'd have no trouble catching us up if we're seen. So instead of risking it out to the Scillies, you'll be taken up the coast a bit, to a place called Trethkellis. I'll wait there to drive you somewhere you can get a plane out safely.' Tory stopped, in order to send a silent but fervent prayer that Bertie would be willing, and able, to get Jude's Camel fixed and up to Lynher Mill.

'Why would you do all this?' Jenny asked, sounding genuinely curious.

'Don't go thinking I've forgiven you,' Tory said. 'My friend is involved in all this, against her will, and she's the one I'm trying to help.'

'Your friend is the head girl?'

'The what?' Then Tory smiled a little, surprising herself. 'I suppose so.'

'She seemed nice. Nervous, but nice.'

'She's nervous because she's in over her head,' Tory said. 'She's currently being held captive by your new friend Hocking, until everything's sorted with the paperwork and she can get you out. But I don't want her involved in any more of it, so I'm going to get you out myself. We just have to delay things and hope no-one comes looking for you.'

'I see. Can I trust whoever is driving the boat?'

Tory stood up, and looked down on her former friend with a thin little smile. 'As much as anyone can be trusted.' She picked up the torch and flashed it onto the satchel she'd dropped by the door. 'There's enough food in there to keep you going. Don't make any noise, people walk out here in the evenings but they won't find a way in unless you make it easy for them.'

'I won't. Oh, Smith?'

She turned back. 'My name's Tory.'

'Tory then.' Jenny hesitated, and for the first time she really seemed vulnerable. 'Do you swear you're not going to betray me again? Tell Ronnie about me?'

'Why would I? I never meant to do it last time.'

Jenny studied her for a moment, assessing her. 'Alright.' She rose to her feet, clutching her leg. 'Can you bring a fresh dressing?'

Tory nodded and left her, making doubly sure the padlock was secure. The last thing she wanted was for all their hard work to come undone, and for Jenny Lyons to be running free around town with vengeance burning in her heart.

CHAPTER TWENTY

'You want me to *what?*' Bertie sat down on her bed with a thump. 'I don't believe it!'

'Can you do it?' Tory insisted. 'We need to think about it now, we don't have long to come up with an alternative if you can't.'

'You're actually asking me to break the law. It's *stealing*, Tory!'

Tory sat forward on her own bed, where she'd flopped down the moment she'd come in. 'If you think about it, you're already stealing.'

'Don't talk rot!'

'No? What about all that fuel that Jude has been claiming for, and not using for legitimate lessons? Who pays for that?'

Bertie floundered. 'I don't know. I assumed the pilot trainers paid for their own.'

'Now who's talking rot?'

'Well then, *we* pay for it in with our tuition fees.'

'And you pay extra do you?' Tory shook her head. 'You've been getting at least twice the flying time of any other trainee, Roberta Fox, so don't come the "we pay for it" nonsense. Look, the important thing is protecting Gwenna, don't you agree?'

'Of course.'

'And the best way to do that is to get Jenny Lyons out of the country before Hocking makes Gwenna do it, and Gwenna is either caught and arrested, or leaves forever.'

'And this is the only way?' Bertie looked miserably at her. 'I don't like the thought of stealing from Jude, not when she's done so much for me.'

'Call it borrowing then. Do you suppose she'd begrudge you the chance to help someone else?'

Bertie was running out of excuses now, but the thought of what Tory had suggested terrified her. To break into the hangar overnight, finish whatever job Tommy had started on Jude's plane, and then fly it out to Lynher Mill ... And that wasn't the end of it.

'I don't even know how to get to the Scillies,' she muttered, and didn't miss the flash of triumph on Tory's face.

'I'll fix that part for you. So you'll do it?'

Bertie opened her mouth, hoping some reasonable denial would find its way out, and instead, bizarrely, she heard herself laugh. 'Yes, you lunatic! I'd have expected an idea like this from Leah, not from you!'

'Leah's playing her own part.' Tory looked at her watch. 'Won't be long now, I hope she remembers everything I told her.'

'What *did* you tell her?' Bertie asked. The news about Gwenna's capture had temporarily taken over her attention, but Tory hanging back to talk to Leah alone had been such an odd thing to do. She was looking particularly shifty now too, and wearing the expression of someone who knows it's time to come clean, but what she said was astonishing, enlightening, and possibly the most fascinating thing Bertie had ever heard.

'You're a *gangster?*'

'Was,' Tory corrected her quickly. 'Not for a few years.' She told the rest of her story, and as Bertie pictured the rainy dockside in Bristol that she herself knew well, and the brother and sister facing each other, each prepared to kill, she began to piece things together; little comments Tory had made about travelling, the way she'd been so vague about where she'd been since leaving the farm – apart from when she talked about her years in Europe with the distressed war horses she had given no details at all, but it made sense now; sunny, calm, easy-going Tory Gilbert, with her way of throwing oil on the troubled waters of Gwenna and Bertie's rivalry ... She must have learned to be extremely diplomatic if she'd been involved in two different gangs, each with a volatile leader. A skill like that would literally have saved lives, Bertie had no doubt about that, and the thought made her shiver.

'So you think you owe Jenny Lyons a safe passage out, do you? After what she's done?'

'She was a friend,' Tory said quietly. 'It was one of those awful situations where there could be no winners. I don't suppose for one minute she intended to kill her own brother.'

'But this Ronnie Jackson's out for her blood.'

'I'm certain of that, if nothing else. She put him in a terrible position, and on top of that she tried to kill him herself. It's a war, Bertie, don't imagine it's anything less.'

'And you've picked your side.'

'She's not so bad, and I do owe her. I can't let Ronnie find out where she is. Hocking's betrayed her once so he's likely to do it again, but not at the expense of giving away his hiding place, so there's time yet I think.'

'So then,' Bertie stood up, rubbing at her leg where the skin

347

had become inflamed again. 'Bobby Gale is prepared to punt Irene and Jenny up to Trethkellis, is he? He must be fond of you.'

'He's a good one, deep down, no matter what they say.'

Bertie nodded. 'Alright then, I'll do my part too. I need to ask you a favour first, though.'

'Name it.'

'Take me to see Tommy?'

Tory blinked. 'Today? Look, we'll get him out of there soon—'

'Not soon enough for him to fix Jude's plane,' Bertie pointed out. 'Which is why I have to do it, and I have no idea what's wrong with it.' She looked at her watch. 'There's nothing we can do until tonight, and it's only dinner time. Come on, I have a maintenance lesson to attend in Bodmin police station.'

*

Gwenna sat in the small study off the main library, listening to the arguments going on next door. Just last night she had wondered how she would cope when that thin film of comforting unreality was torn away, and now she knew: she would sit in numbed silence and wait for the next blow to fall. It was a miserable discovery; she had assumed she would be strong and decisive, finding a vein of strength when she needed it, but there was nothing there. Seeing her father with his hands on those guns had sent any thoughts of emulating his courage clattering into a big black hole.

The one good thing that had come from it, was realising that Hocking no longer had any leverage over her. The threat of telling her father what she'd been doing had been empty all along; he had known what she was getting into longer than she had. Bobby Gale's words floated into her mind, back when they had talked at the base, and she had said the girl at the depot might have been anyone: *Most likely to be you, considering who else is involved.*

348

And she had thought he'd been talking about Peter, who in turn had been so relieved when he'd realised that Gwenna's probing questions, on the way to the beach, had only been about whether Jonas was having an affair with Nancy bloody Gilbert.

'I've been so stupid,' she muttered, a little frightened by the sound of her own voice. 'No wonder Dad was so keen for me to keep going with my training. No wonder he encouraged it from the very start.'

She'd hoped to find out he'd been coerced, as she'd been. As Irene had been, and even Peter, to a degree, but the fact that he'd been in there, freely handling the weapons, told her he was a trusted and loyal part of the operation. There were so many questions she wanted to ask: how had it all started? Where did the connection with the gangs originate? Who else was involved? She recalled Hocking's hateful little almost-laugh when he'd told her that 'someone' would accompany Irene out to the Scillies with Devereux, and her mother's distressed announcement that he'd been gone all day yesterday. Peter's vague little assurance that the crossing had been calm . . . He hadn't even been there!

'Who's that now?' Hocking's irritated voice cut through Gwenna's thoughts and she shifted her focus back to the next room. She had evidently missed the sound of the doorbell, or knocker, because now she heard her father mumbling something about 'getting rid' of whoever it was who'd come calling. She had heard the blond man leaving, not long after he'd pushed her into this room and locked the door, so perhaps it was him returning.

But it was a woman; Irene. Gwenna stood up, her heart beating a little faster, and moved to the door where she could listen properly.

'She says she'll pay you, Uncle, but only you,' Irene was saying. 'Face to face.'

'I'm not going up there,' Hocking grunted, 'I'll have that Jackson bloke on my tail, and I can't have him finding out about that room.'

'She understands that,' Irene said. 'So she said she'd come here, but only if you'll let her stay here until it's time to leave. She can't bear being in that little room.'

'Preposterous!' Hocking laughed, and it was so much like his falsely friendly one, that Gwenna actually found herself missing that man she'd thought she'd known. 'Your aunt would raise the roof!'

'You've got plenty of rooms you can use,' Irene said, and Gwenna jumped back as the voice came closer and rattled the doorknob of the study.

'Leave that,' Hocking said sharply.

'Why's it locked? It's not usually—'

'I said leave it.' Hocking paused, then went on, 'Alright. Tell her she can stay here until I've arranged her papers. Make sure you bring her by five, your aunt gets back from her WI meeting at twenty minutes past.'

'Are you sure that's a good idea?' Gwenna's father put in.

'It's not as if she's going to be trying to escape, is it?' Hocking pointed out. 'She needs us. Go on then, and make sure no-one sees the two of you at the folly. If you see a tallish blond man anywhere, come away. You hear me?'

'Is he that Jackson person you mentioned? Who is he, anyway?'

'Never mind, just remember what I say. Get going then.'

Gwenna subsided into the chair again, and tried to imagine Jenny Lyons begging to be let out of the room. She couldn't do it.

Not long afterwards she saw the handle of the door shift slightly again; not the inquisitive rattle that Irene had given it, but the touch of someone who knows it's locked and is simply resting a hand on it. A voice came through, low and broken-sounding.

'Gwenna, listen. It's not how you think. I didn't have a choice ... No, that's wrong. I did have a choice, but it was ... I chose badly.'

Gwenna assumed Hocking must have left the room, and she moved closer, hardly daring to hope she might find some way to understand after all. 'I need to know why,' she said, resting her head against the door. 'Did you know about the guns?'

'No, not at first.' His voice faded, as if he'd moved away to check he was still alone, then came back. 'I'll tell you all of it when I can, and it's not something I'm proud of, but for now just know I'd never have hurt you, or your mother, for anything. You'll be alright, he won't hurt you. I'll try to get him to release you soon, but it's better if he isn't unsettled by anything just now. Better for all of us.'

'Mum thinks you're leaving her,' Gwenna blurted. 'Go and tell *her* the truth, at least. She'll stand by you if she knows you need her.'

'I will. There's something else I have to apologise for,' he said, and now he sounded truly wretched. 'You have to tell Jude Singleton I'm sorry.'

'For what?'

'For getting them to check her plane's records. The fuel use, the spare parts. All of it.'

'What?' Gwenna was aghast. 'But ... why would you do that?'

'I'm sorry,' he said again, his voice receding.

'You going or what, Rosdew? Those papers need arranging before tonight or we'll be stuck with her another day.'

'I'm going.' Footsteps, a door closing, and then the front door clicking shut as well. Gwenna retreated to her chair and rested her head on her arms. She wanted to believe him, but then he wasn't claiming to be a victim, so perhaps there was nothing good about him to believe in anymore. And he had pointed the finger of blame at an innocent, so how could she ever trust him again?

Hocking left the library, and the house fell quiet once more. She dozed.

Some time later she came awake with a jerk as voices sounded in the hall. Hocking, of course, and Irene, but the third voice, though female, wasn't one she recognised. It wasn't Jenny Lyons, she knew that much. This one was broad Bristolian, like Jenny's, but whereas Jenny's voice had a bored undertone to it, a kind of tired cynicism, there was a barely contained energy about this one. It sounded tense, as if the woman were constantly looking over her shoulder mentally, if not physically.

'I'm having the money wired over,' she said. 'I'll give Irene here the password, and she can collect it from the telegraph office tomorrow. We goin' out by plane then?'

'We are. Early. Let's hope your friend Ronnie likes to sleep in of a morning, eh?'

The voice turned sour. 'Was it you tipped him off then? Sly bastard, in't you?'

Gwenna frowned as she listened to the difference in the voice, then it clicked. This was Leah! The temptation to rattle the door handle again was almost too much to resist, but she remembered her father's advice to keep Hocking calm for now, and she folded her arms instead. Bobby must had found them and told them she was here, and now Irene's testing of the door made sense, too.

'Who else you got workin' for you?' Leah demanded.

'None of your business,' Hocking said shortly.

'Tetchy.' Leah laughed, and even that sound was tense. 'Where'm I sleepin' then? In here?' She grabbed at the door handle, as Irene had done, and received the same snappish order to leave it alone.

It was now clear that Leah was ostensibly making herself a prisoner here in order to help Gwenna escape, and Gwenna was deeply touched by the way old friends and new acquaintances were prepared to go to such lengths for her. She'd never experienced anything like it before.

Leah continued her chatter, sounding hard and uncompromising one moment, almost flirtatiously friendly the next, and it was clear Hocking didn't know what to make of her. By the way her voice faded and came back, Gwenna imagined she was now wandering around the room with a casual, perhaps impudent curiosity, that would no doubt be masking a much sharper search.

She turned to look at her own temporary prison properly, for the first time, and her gaze lit on a box shoved against the wall. Something about it looked familiar ... She went over to it and pulled open the top to see several rolls of labels; some blank, others printed with: *Mechanical Components and Replacement Aviation Equipment*. She stifled a small hiss of triumph, and closed the box again; this might be just what they needed. They had to find a way to get a policeman – anyone but Peter Bolitho – in here. She felt certain that if anyone could, it would be Leah Coleridge.

*

It was around five o'clock the next morning when Tory slid the key into the padlock for what she fervently hoped would be the last time, and shone her torch into the tiny room under Tyndall's Folly. She expected to see Jenny ready, with her kit bag on her shoulder and her old sense of urgency about her, but instead the torchlight picked out a huddled shape in the corner.

'Jenny?' She stepped in, trying to force down the panic that climbed into the back of her throat. The form was motionless and didn't respond, and Tory knelt beside it and pulled back the heavy coat that covered the girl's face. Jenny's eyes closed tightly against the light, and Tory gave a brief sigh of relief before realising her old friend was gritting her teeth against a moan. Jenny's hands were gripping her thigh and they were coated in a slick film of fresh blood.

'Come on, love,' Tory said gently. 'We've got everything waiting for you.'

'I can't,' Jenny whispered. 'I can't walk.'

'Let me look,' Tory said, fighting the rising frustration. Part four of the plan was collapsing in front of her. 'Come on, at least let me see it.'

'No!' Jenny spoke through gritted teeth. 'Just ... Give me a minute. I'll be alright, I just need to prepare myself.'

But after five minutes, which felt more like an hour, Tory accepted that Jenny wasn't going to be able to make it out of the room, let alone down the tunnels.

'Can't we *please* go overland?' Jenny managed, as if she could hear Tory's thoughts.

'No, I told you. Besides, it's three times as far by road as it is by tunnel, and Bobby's boat's going to be waiting in a cove that only has one way in and out.' Tory could hear herself chattering and realised she could have stopped after the first word for all the attention Jenny was paying her. She lowered her head and groaned. 'What the hell are we going to do now? Leah's keeping Hocking distracted, but she won't be able to hold him for long, and Bertie's going to be waiting for you with the plane.' *I hope* ...

But she didn't voice that part. She knew Bertie had worked long into the night, and that she was fairly sure she'd adequately installed the replacement rocker arm, and done the other minor repairs Tommy had been planning to do. Getting Joey out to Lynher Mill was going to be terrifying enough, but if it turned out to be for nothing, Bertie would never forgive her.

'I need it looking at properly,' Jenny muttered. 'Get a doctor.'

'Down here? Are you mad? Besides, that's a bullet wound, it's going to raise questions neither of us can answer.' She couldn't go calling on her mother with this, it was too risky.

'Please,' Jenny whispered. She sounded as if she were drifting in and out of awareness now, and Tory hoped the wound wasn't infected. Without looking at it there was no way of knowing, and Jenny had already vetoed that.

There was no help for it. Tory lifted the torch and checked her watch, but the surgery wouldn't open for another four hours. 'I can't get a doctor yet, it's ...' The protest tailed away. 'It's his birthday,' she finished quietly.

'What?'

'Joseph, my brother. It's ... *would* have been, his birthday today.'

Jenny made a small sound that might have been an attempt at a condolence mingled with a grunt of exasperation. 'What's that got to—'

'Hush.' Tory pulled the coat back up to Jenny's chin. 'Try and sleep, if you can. In another two hours I'll get you a doctor.'

An hour and a half later Tory was sitting on the ground, leaning against the side of the war memorial, and watching the sky turning pale in the east. The grass was wet and her trousers were drenched through, and a short distance away a troubled and troublesome young woman was doubtless cursing her in her usual fierce language, but as the morning crept on, Tory felt a strange kind of peace fall over her. It was the first real calm she could remember in days, and this village, newly sprung, but with a sense of the land's unknowable ages of history, seemed to close around her with a protective warmth. She closed her eyes and waited.

Presently a scuffling in the grass signalled the end of that wait, and Tory stood up. Nancy gave a small cry and stopped, her hand to her throat.

'Tory!'

'I need your help,' Tory said. 'It's urgent.'

'Medical help? What's wrong?' Nancy stepped closer, worried, but Tory shook her head.

'Not me. Go and get your bag. *Please*. And don't tell anyone. Meet me at the folly.'

Nancy studied her for a moment, and Tory could see the questions building, but at length her mother just nodded and turned back, hurrying away across the grass without any argument. Tory went back to the folly and waited again, trying not to think about Bertie, even now going about her frightening task of getting Jude Singleton's Camel out of the hangar, with Irene's decidedly inexpert help. Or Gwenna, still imprisoned at Hocking's huge country house and praying he wouldn't suspect Leah was a decoy.

When Nancy arrived, with her bag and a large bottle of water, Tory led her wordlessly down the wooden stairway and into the room beneath the old folly. Jenny had pulled herself upright, no doubt listening to their approach with a renewed hope, and as soon as Nancy saw the bloodied trousers she dropped to her knees and unbuckled her bag. She didn't ask any questions when she identified the bullet wound, but turned to look at Tory, who simply held the torch steady and didn't offer any explanation.

Nancy worked quickly and efficiently, cleaning and disinfecting the wound with the swiftness and lack of concern for her surroundings that she had doubtless perfected helping Frank during the war. She wrapped a clean bandage around Jenny's leg, and as she eased the filthy trouser leg back down over it the gratitude and relief on Jenny's face affected Tory more strongly than she had expected.

Nancy stood up and emptied the remainder of the water over her own hands, washing as much of the blood off them as she could. 'I'm only going to ask one thing,' she said in a low voice to Tory. 'Was it you?'

'No.'

Nancy nodded, and laid a hand gently on Tory's shoulder. She moved past her towards the stairs again, and Tory gave Jenny a look that said, *stay there and don't move.* She followed her mother out into the morning air, where she gave the briefest explanation she could, about what was happening.

'Thank you,' she said quietly, when she'd finished. 'We wouldn't have been able to even consider it without your help.'

Nancy nodded, unsmiling. 'How did you know where to find me?' She shook her head. 'It doesn't matter, I know how. I had to come today, but I think of him every day. Just as I think of all of you.' She looked as if she felt she'd said too much already, and the hand she'd lifted to touch Tory's face fell to her side again. 'I'm glad you felt you could ask me, when you needed help,' she said quietly.

A wholly unexpected tide of emotion surged, and Tory struggled to keep her voice steady. 'Who would I ask, except my mum?'

Nancy's eyes brimmed and such a look of hope lifted her face that Tory couldn't bear to think she'd been the cause of its loss. She stepped into Nancy's embrace and clung to her like a little girl, although she was the same height. Only a noise from the road made her break away and look around worriedly, remembering what she still had to do.

'I'll come and find you later,' she promised. 'I'd like to talk more, if you're happy to?'

'I'd love that,' Nancy said, and now she did lay her hand on Tory's cheek. 'I love you so much, Tory. Now go and do what you're supposed to be doing.' She smiled at last, and it lit her face with the brilliance Tory remembered from her childhood.

'Not a word to anyone,' Tory reminded her.

'Are you really going to take her out through those tunnels? Why don't you use your car?'

'They'll be watching the roads,' Tory said, wiping her eyes on her coat sleeve and turning her mind back to practical matters. 'The only place we can leave from safely is the cove under the hotel, and the only way in and out of there is by the cliff road—'

'Which is in full view of the Cliffside Fort,' Nancy finished for her. 'I see. Well, you'd better get down there then, and let me help pull this trapdoor closed. Keep you safe a while longer, at least.' She sounded almost blithe about it, but she had been gone from Tory's life long before Tory and Harry Batten had become lost underground, so she had no idea of the effect closed-in spaces had on Tory now.

Tory gripped the key chain tightly again, and nodded. 'Time to go, then.'

CHAPTER TWENTY-ONE

The Camel felt, strangely, like an entirely different beast without Jude in the back. Bertie remembered the first time she'd ridden her motorcycle alone, and the sense of freedom mingled with panic it had given her, but she hadn't expected to feel the same with Joey. She'd taxied, taken off, flown and landed this bird countless times, often not giving a thought to the woman who sat behind her. But Jude had always been there. Now Bertie was going to be flying with a total stranger all the way to the Isles of Scilly, and before that she had to find her way solo to the exact spot on the moor at Lynher Mill where there was enough space to land safely.

What if she got the wrong place? The only landmark to guide her was the ring of standing stones near the village, but the moor spread out in every direction from those, so what if she got Jude's co-ordinates wrong and went north instead of west of the stones? There was a massive natural lake up that way, she knew that; Dozmary Pool ... it wasn't properly light yet, what if she misjudged, and mistook it ... Bertie shook the thought off, with an annoyed grunt. Between those notions, and the gnawing worry for Tommy, she was sure she'd never feel normal again.

'Are you ready?' Irene called. She sounded even more nervous than Bertie, but she had no need; her part in all this was done. It was Tory, Gwenna, Leah, and Bertie herself who carried the weight of the success or failure of this venture now. She thought she saw the same realisation on Irene's face, and even detected a glimmer of something like disappointment; despite the fear it was undoubtedly an exciting time, and Irene had played a huge role in both sides of it, just as Gwenna had. Now she had to stand aside and wait, and hope that role wouldn't land her in deep, deep trouble.

Bertie gave the controls one last glance over, then climbed onto the wing and slid down onto the hangar floor. She knew she should have enlisted some more help for this part; Robert Penhaligon would have given it without a moment's thought, especially since he was giving up training, but it wouldn't have been fair to involve him. Jude would have been invaluable of course, but she was still in Leeds, and blissfully unaware of the trouble she was in. The mechanics and engineers wouldn't be here for another hour at least, but they were unlikely to help her anyway, not without Jude around to tell them it was all above board. It was all down to her now. Bertie adjusted one of the buckles on her thigh so it no longer pinched her skin, and nodded to Irene.

'Come on, then. The sooner we get her out, the sooner we can see how well you've learned to swing these propellers.'

Together they pushed the Camel out into the pre-dawn chill, with Irene visibly putting everything she had into it, to spare the risk of Bertie injuring herself. The two of them lifted the tail around so the plane was facing into the wind, and Bertie found herself embracing Irene before she climbed into the cockpit.

'You've done us, and yourself, proud,' she said. 'Now go back and tell people what you need to tell them so they don't come looking.'

'There's one more thing I'll have to do first.' Irene had the beginnings of a smile on her face, and Bertie would have sworn that smile had a devilish edge to it. But there was no time to find out what the girl was up to now; it was time to go.

Five minutes later she was calling 'Contact!' and watching Irene take the propeller in her hands. Irene was tall, and reasonably strong, but it still took a few tries before Joey rattled into life. Bertie pushed the stick fully forward to begin taxiing, and worked the throttle lever and the fine fuel adjustment. A moment later she felt the tail lift and then she was up, alone in the dawn sky, feeling the vastness of it pulling her up until she levelled out and turned Joey's nose towards Lynher Mill.

The exhilaration never lessened, but today it was different, she was doing something real; helping Tory repay a debt, and protecting Gwenna from the need to throw her entire career and family away. She only hoped Jude would understand, when it was all over and the full story came out. As she flew east towards the familiar moorland that was also Tommy's home, she remembered how worried he'd looked yesterday when she'd spoken to him, and how he'd tried to hide that worry. But the danger to his career and liberty was real, he had no way of proving he hadn't stolen that military vehicle, and Bertie couldn't bear to think what penalty that might carry. They'd parted with both of them struggling not to let the other see how they were feeling, but it had been a futile exercise on both sides.

Bertie determinedly put Tommy and his predicament to the back of her mind, and after a while she began to scan the ground for familiar landmarks. She saw the waking village of Lynher Mill off to the west, with its circle of standing stones and its burned-out mill on the horizon. She checked her co-ordinates and looked down at the ground, expecting to see Tory's car waiting nearby, but there was nothing. Still, it was early yet; Bobby's boat was supposedly a nippy little thing and would make quick work of a trip up the coast, but they still had to get here from Trethkellis by car.

Bertie guided Joey down without hesitation, hearing Jude's wry northern tones in her ear as clearly as if she were sitting behind her, and once the plane was safely on the ground, she took her helmet off and a great sense of well-being stole over her; it was all going to be alright after all. But for now it had been a long, long night, after a stressful day yesterday, and she'd need to be alert and ready soon, for what might well be a terrifying flight over open water, so, with a little sigh, she rested her head back and closed her eyes.

When she woke, the sun was already climbing, she had lost almost two hours, and there was still no sign of Tory.

*

'Keep your voice down, your aunt's still asleep.'

Gwenna sat up from where she had been dozing with her head on her folded arms, and pulled her confused, half-sleeping thoughts together. It was still early; the light coming through the curtains was bright but still low, and when her bleary eyes found the clock, she saw it was a little after half past six. Her throat was dry and her lips felt puffy, and there was an insistent pressure in her bladder, but a cautious hope made it all unimportant; the awful, long night was over. If anything had gone wrong with her friends' plan in the early hours there would have been some commotion, she was sure of it.

She rubbed her face and went to the door to listen to the voices in the library. Irene had evidently picked up Jenny's new documents herself, from whichever print shop did Hocking's illegal work for him. Much as Gwenna was disappointed that it wasn't her father who'd brought them, this showed that Irene was still in her uncle's favour and that he had no idea she'd turned against him.

'Are they what we need?' Irene was asking now.

'They're a bit bloody late,' Hocking grunted, 'but they're fine. Better go and fetch her down. *Quietly,*' he added again. 'She's in the yellow room.'

A moment later the key turned in the lock of Gwenna's prison room, and Hocking jerked his head for her to join him in the library. 'Irene's gone to fetch the moll.'

'She's not a moll,' Gwenna pointed out 'she's a gang member in her own right. Just like your blond friend, and every bit as dangerous. You should make absolutely sure of her before you—'

'Don't tell me my business. Now.' He put down the documents and checked the time. 'You can drive me and Lyons down to the air base, and Irene will collect the payment from the telegraph office and meet us there.'

Irene led Leah into the room, and Gwenna was struck anew how different Leah managed to look, with just a change of clothes and attitude. Her hair hung limply around a face scrubbed clean of make-up and tense-looking; her jaw was tight, and her eyes flicked around the room, taking in every detail as if she expected someone to be standing in the corner with gun.

'We ready?' she asked in her flawless Bristolian accent. 'I in't waiting around all bloody day, I'm payin' good money for this.'

'You'd better give Irene here the password for the telegraph office then, and as soon as she brings the money we're off.'

'Trust her, do you?' Leah gave a faint sneer as her gaze passed between them. 'Big Uncle Barry and his little niece, eh? Sweet.'

'How do you know—'

'I hear things.' Leah sat down. 'Like about you gettin' all mixed up with the Dockers and Ronnie Jackson. You want to be careful, *Uncle Barry*.' She sent him a suddenly sunny grin. 'Ronnie's no pussycat, if you cross him, he's not going to give you no second chances.'

'Cross him?'

'By gettin' me out, when you've told him I'm here for the takin'.' Hocking frowned. '*I've* told him?'

'Don't play games. I know he's here, so you must have been the one to tell him. Why'd you do it? You must have known you'd get no money from me, and no thanks from him. Storin' up favours, is that it?'

Gwenna had been enjoying Leah's performance, but as she turned her attention more fully to Hocking she began to wonder. He seemed genuinely confused. His frown had deepened as Leah had continued talking, and now he cast a look towards the window and his expression had become one of unease.

'I don't know what you're talking about, Miss Lyons, but if you're saying I've double-crossed Ronnie Jackson—'

'Well, you've double-crossed *one* of us, Mr Hocking.' Leah's eyes slitted. 'Which one is it? Because I'm not paying you one red cent until I know you can get me out without him seeing me.'

'I can.' Hocking licked his lips. 'But you've got it wrong. Ronnie turned up here yesterday, I had no idea he knew you were here until then. I've not double-crossed either one of you!'

Leah appeared to echo Gwenna's own doubt now, but she

shrugged. 'It don't exactly matter now anyway. Just get me out, alive, and you'll get your money.'

'But what about Ronnie?'

'He's your problem, not mine.'

'He's someone else's problem entirely now.' The voice from the doorway cut through the taut atmosphere, and four faces swivelled to see Peter Bolitho, in full uniform, with his arms folded and a smile on his face. Gwenna blinked in astonishment; of all the people to come to their rescue ...

Irene, in particular, seemed delighted to see him. 'Thank God! I knew you'd sort everything out!'

'Thank you for speaking to me.' Peter came further into the room. 'You did the right thing, Irene.' He turned to Leah, and gave her a reluctant nod of approval. 'Yes, you'd fool someone who didn't know, I suppose. Quite convincing, really. You mustn't feel bad for not realising,' he added to Hocking. 'If I hadn't met Mrs Coleridge here myself, earlier, I'd have doubted Irene's story.' A sudden, sharklike grin at Gwenna replaced the easy smile. 'Luckily, I've salvaged the problem.'

Gwenna's heart leaped in horror and she turned on Irene, whose face had gone pasty white and shocked. 'What have you done, you *stupid*—'

'I thought he'd had enough of it all,' Irene stammered. She flung Peter an accusing, but helpless look of betrayal. 'You said you wanted to get out, just as we did!' She sat down heavily and pressed the heels of her hands to her eyes. 'What *have* I done?' she whispered.

'You've made it possible for me to despatch Mr Jackson to the cove, to intercept Miss Gilbert and her little fugitive friend,' Peter said cheerfully. 'So thank you for that. Ronnie sends his regards,

Mr Hocking, and says he'll be back to see you as soon as he's taken care of things at the beach.'

'But I didn't tell him Lyons was here,' Hocking protested again, staring at Leah as if he still believed she was Jenny.

Peter shrugged. 'That's probably what he wants to talk about.'

'But then how did he know?'

'Because *I* told him.' Peter closed the door and snapped down the latch. 'He's been good to me over the years, and he's proved himself more worthy than your sainted father,' he added to Gwenna. '*He's* gone trotting off to the police in Bodmin to tell them it was him who took the van, not Tommy Ash.' He shook his head. 'And I believed Jonas Rosdew was someone to look up to. Heroic? Maybe once, but not anymore.'

'I'm glad,' Gwenna said, her voice hard and angry, without a trace of the trembling she was feeling inside. 'He's worth a hundred of you, especially now.'

'You can still say that, after finding out what he's been doing all this time?' Peter shook his head. 'Well, he's shown his true colours now, and he'll do time for what he's done.'

'You've done things just as bad!'

'I've proved myself loyal where it matters though,' Peter said patiently. 'I'll be taken care of.'

'Very clever of you.' Leah spoke up, in her own voice. 'Now what happens?' She shook her lank hair back, and the hard-bitten, narrow-eyed look disappeared as the expression softened and the real Leah re-emerged. 'Let me guess: your knight in shining armour comes galloping up to deny you've had any part in it, and save you from arrest?' She gave a short laugh, sounding genuinely amused. 'Oh, you poor idiot.'

Peter glared. 'What does that mean?'

'It means your precious Ronnie's hardly going to hang around in town after he puts a bullet in his ex-girlfriend, is he? He'll be off before Jenny hits the ground. So let's sit and wait.' Leah's grin was as savage now as Peter's had been. 'We'll see who turns up first, shall we?'

*

The tunnels were darker and more twisting than Tory had remembered, even in her most claustrophobic, memory-drenched dreams. Water dripped from the low stone ceilings, and the torchlight seemed to only pick up a few feet ahead, thanks to the bends and turns the miners had created as they'd followed the mineral lodes through the rocks. More than once she, in the lead, had cracked her head on a protruding lump of rock and called back a warning to Jenny; her own hair was soaked and she couldn't be sure how much of it was water and how much was blood, but she suspected it was a fairly even mixture of both.

She could hear Jenny cursing as she stumbled along behind her, and could tell it was partly in pain, but there were no more complaints about not going by road. Tory was trying not to think about the tightness of the space around them, and to remind herself that the outside was still there, waiting for them, but it was becoming harder and harder.

The further we go, the closer the adit, she chanted silently.

The further we go, the deeper we go, her treacherous mind chanted back. She shook the thought away but it kept coming back. And what if she'd mis-remembered the way after all? She'd have been able to draw a picture of the route if someone had asked her to; she remembered exactly where Tyndall's Folly tunnel met the Wheal Furzy shaft they were heading for, and which one it was, and she could have easily traced the way on an archaeologist's diagram . . .

She had traversed it regularly, but now she was bigger, and the tunnels seemed to shrink around her, pressing inward, granite fingers brushing her shoulders and rapping her skull.

She rounded another bend, and with a small sigh of relief she saw the sheer walls of the main shaft coming down from Wheal Furzy. Just a little way along was the tunnel where an explosion had nearly killed Matthew Penhaligon and a couple of his fellow miners, back in 1911, which meant she was only a few feet from the adit that would take them out to the cove, and Bobby's boat.

She turned back to pass on the good news to Jenny, but the words locked in her throat as a loud crack echoed up through the tunnel. A gunshot. The sound screamed towards them in waves, sounding like half a dozen more shots as it reached them, and she heard Jenny give a small cry. She sank to her heels, her hand reaching for Jenny to do the same.

'Don't move,' she breathed. She shut the torch off, and to her added dismay she heard the light pattering of falling rock up ahead. Not great chunks, but enough to be a worry.

'Who is it?' Jenny whispered.

'How the hell should I know?' Tory shot back, fearful and irritable.

She pushed away the picture of Ronnie Jackson running up the wider tunnel towards them; there were no tramlines down there to hinder passage as there were here, since no ore carts were needed in that tunnel, and anyone hurrying up towards the working part of the mine would need only a flashlight to prevent them knocking their head on the low parts of the tunnel roof. She strained to hear movement, and grew hopeful when none came at first, but then she heard distant footsteps and her chest tightened.

'He's coming,' Jenny whispered unnecessarily, and her fingers closed tight around Tory's arm. 'Hocking must have found out, and told him! Have you got a gun?'

'Don't be stupid! You heard how that shot ricocheted down there! Even if I had one, I wouldn't use it in here. You've got your knife, keep it handy.'

'Should we go back?'

'No, we'd never make it in time to get right out, and we'd end up trapped.' Tory thought about the layout as she remembered it. 'If we can get to the main shaft before Ronnie, and *if* the ladders there are iron ones, we might be able to climb up far enough to get into one of the side tunnels. Then we can wait for him to go past, climb down again, and run like hell for the adit. He won't be stupid enough to shoot again.'

'Can't we just climb all the way out, instead?'

The innocent question almost made Tory laugh aloud. 'It's hundreds of feet to grass,' she said with strained patience, 'and if the wooden sections of ladders are rotted through it's hundreds more to the bottom of the shaft, and screaming all the way down. So no, we can't just *climb all the way out*. Now follow me, and don't hang around.'

'Aren't you putting your torch on?'

This time Tory didn't even dignify the question with a response. She'd thought Jenny had something about her, but once out of the city, and her crowds of eager acolytes pulling at her coat-tails, she was no cleverer than half the dazzled fools she had swindled over the years. Tory felt ahead with her feet, wincing every time her shoe knocked a tramline or a lump of ore, and listening hard to try and gauge Ronnie's progress, but it was impossible; he might be twenty feet away or two hundred. Every sound behaved like a live thing down here.

The darkness was total, there was no question of simply allowing their eyesight to adjust; as she'd told Jenny they were hundreds of feet below the surface and no light reached them from the main shaft. Moving so slowly, for fear of finding her foot stepping into nothing at any moment, she realised with a sinking heart that they weren't going to make it. She felt the walls becoming wider apart, and followed the left-hand tramline as the corridor widened near the entrance to the shaft, but ahead of them the footsteps were coming closer.

She had to risk a quick flash of the torch, however, and the bright imprint of the image told her all she needed to know: the platform that led around the perimeter of the shaft, enabling miners to reach the adit without having to swing across the centre of it, was intact, but the ladders leading to the next level up were wood, not iron. The risk was too great.

She turned to Jenny and murmured, 'We have to go around, not up.'

But she hadn't been quiet enough, and a voice drifted down from the adit. 'Little Tory Gilbert? Is that you?'

Tory sagged against the tunnel wall, the strength running out of her legs. '*Bobby?*'

'At your service.'

Tory heard the grin in his voice now; he was evidently even closer than she'd realised. She switched her torch back on and shone it across the centre of the shaft to where he stood.

'Why didn't you say it was you?'

'I couldn't be sure it wasn't just that gangster girl, and I haven't got a torch like you have.'

'Who is it?' Jenny wanted to know, but Tory ignored her. She rose to her feet, although still hunched over to avoid another painful crack on the head, and began to lead the way around the narrow platform.

'Why are you here?' she asked Bobby, as she reached safety on the far side and was drawn into an unthinking but warm hug.

'You never turned up when you were supposed to,' he said, releasing her, 'and just when I was starting to think you'd changed your plans, some white-haired bugger showed up at the cove.'

'Is that who fired the gun?'

Bobby's face, in the light of the torch, lost its relieved look. 'He must have been watching to see where I went, and when you didn't turn up, he followed me into the tunnel.' He spoke quietly now. 'Idiot fired a shot, missed me, and ended up with a bullet in his own head. Probably never even knew it'd happened.'

Tory heard Jenny snatch a horrified breath, and tried to feel sorry for her, the woman had loved Ronnie once, after all. But she couldn't.

'Are you still going to be able to take her up to Trethkellis?' she asked. 'It's not safe to go by road, he'll have others out there.'

Bobby looked past her, with evident distaste, at Jenny who was standing with her head lowered. 'You still want her to get away, do you?'

'I owe her. It's a long story.' She touched his arm and handed him her torch. 'Can you do it?'

He hesitated, then nodded. 'I reckon I'm alright with that. We've got to stick together, in the end, haven't we?' He squeezed Tory's arm and turned to lead the way back.

Before she followed him, Tory looked over her shoulder at Jenny. 'Yesterday you asked me how I could bear to be stuck somewhere like Pencarrack? Well.' She looked after Bobby's torchlight as he moved away. 'One of my friends is prepared to fly a stolen plane across the sea just because I've asked her to. Others have put themselves in just as much danger, and Bobby there has just risked his life and his property, and quite likely his liberty. Does that answer your question?'

She shook her head at Jenny's uncomprehending look; it would sink in, when the woman was alone in a foreign land, with no friends around her. A stranger in her own life, as Tory had been for so long but wasn't anymore. 'Come on,' she said wearily, 'you've got a boat to catch, and, as long as Bertie hasn't given up on us, there's a plane waiting at Lynher Mill. It's time to leave this horrible, *provincial* little place, and see what glories lie waiting for you across the channel. I'm sure you'll be drowning in friendship and riches within a day.'

CHAPTER TWENTY-TWO

In Barry Hocking's house, the time had passed with agonising slowness. Each clunk from the second hand of the huge grandfather clock in the corner had driven Gwenna's nerves higher, and she kept looking out of the window expecting to see Ronnie approaching, the news she dreaded on his lips.

Mrs Hocking had poked her head around the door and greeted everyone with a cheery 'good morning!' and, absurdly, they had all chimed 'good morning!' back at her. She'd not have seen anything out of the ordinary after all, just her own niece, the local policeman – with whom her husband had a perfectly healthy acquaintanceship – and one or two others. No cause for alarm, and she'd gone off for her morning walk blissfully unaware of what was happening in her house. Gwenna and the others had sat looking at one another in a sort of bemused silence since she'd gone.

The telephone blared and Hocking picked up. After listening for a moment, he passed the receiver to Peter. 'Sergeant Couch,' he said. 'Evidently you told him you'd be here.'

Peter took the telephone. 'Yes?' He listened a moment longer.

'I'll be right there.' He replaced the receiver with a trembling hand, and turned to Hocking. 'Apparently Ronnie Jackson has been found on the rocks beneath the old mine adit. He's dead.'

Gwenna's initial reaction was shock, then she exchanged a suddenly hopeful look with Leah. 'Has anyone else been hurt?' she asked Peter.

'Not that they've found.' His voice was shaking as much as his fingers had. 'What are you doing?' he asked Hocking, who'd crossed the room to a tall cupboard.

Hocking pulled out a flying coat and helmet. 'I don't want anyone to connect Jackson with me, or with the base, so you'd better come up with a good theory to clean this case up.'

'But—'

'You're a copper, Bolitho! It's in your gift to keep this away from my door.'

'But ... the guns! You can't leave them here!'

'I'm sure you'll find somewhere to hide them before the proper police turn up.'

Peter visibly bristled at that. 'You ought to hope I do,' he said, his voice suddenly cunning.

Hocking stopped shoving his arm into his coat, and fixed him with a glare. 'You're implicated every bit as much as I am,' he said. 'And as much as these two.' He pointed at Gwenna and Irene. 'So between you perhaps a trip to Tyndall's Folly might be a good idea?'

He left them, and a moment later they heard the front door slam and then his car start up. Peter stared around him, still in shock at the news of Ronnie's death, and now clearly panicking about the task Hocking had left him with; Sergeant Couch would be waiting a good while for his junior officer to attend this particular crime down at the cove. Peter looked at Gwenna, who let out a short, sharp laugh.

'If you think *I'm* helping you hide those guns, you can think again.'

'You will,' Peter said, 'if you want to stay out of prison.'

Gwenna looked across at Irene, who was staring at her feet. 'See what you've done, you idiot? Why on earth did you have to go blabbing to him?'

'I told you, I thought he was on our side now!'

'Well, now you know.'

'Yes! *Now* I know.' Irene blew out a heavy breath. 'And Uncle Barry's probably going to get clean away now. They'll never catch him.'

'But they'll catch me,' Gwenna said, 'and they'll catch you. And once your name's in the papers, that horse-doping ring will be onto you before you can blink.'

Irene looked horrified, and Gwenna was sorry she'd brought it up. 'Maybe we'll be able to keep that part quiet.'

'I can try to help there,' Peter said, '*if* you help me now. Check the other rooms for anything that might tie him in with the business. Anything at all.'

With an apologetic look at Gwenna, Irene got to her feet and went out to search the rest of the house; Gwenna knew she wouldn't make any attempt to run, not with Peter's promise ringing in her ears. She tried not to look at the door to the little study, where she'd seen the labels, but knew it would only be a matter of time before Peter or Irene looked in there.

After around half an hour, during which time Gwenna had made grateful use of the bathroom, and Peter had manhandled two of the four crates of guns, unaided, into his own car, Irene returned with a few papers. Peter locked the library door and looked through them, clearly unimpressed, but threw them into the grate, and applied a match. Gwenna had no idea what they were, but he seemed proud of himself as he watched the flames curl across the paper and take hold. Transfixed, even. He stared into the flames as if he were picturing Hocking's expression of gratitude, and hearing his thanks; he'd never get them, just as he'd now never be rewarded for betraying Jenny to Ronnie Jackson.

A brief knock at the front door was followed by a crash, and Peter jumped and turned, white-faced, towards the library door. He glanced back once at the scraps burning in the grate, and then crossed to unlock the door and pull it open. He adopted a brisk, official tone.

'Sergeant! I was just going to call you. I found her,' he gestured to Gwenna, 'setting fire to something. I was too late to put it out, I'm afraid. No idea what it might be, but she seemed terribly guilty about something.'

'You needn't bother, son,' Sergeant Couch said, looking more animated and lively than Gwenna had ever seen him; he was locally renowned for having the most apt surname of anyone in town. 'We've got him.'

'Got who?'

'Barry Hocking. We intercepted him at the air base. We'd never have caught him, but something went wrong with his aircraft and delayed him. He was carrying an illegal weapon, so we've come here to search the premises for any more.'

'I'll get to work,' Peter said at once.

'No you won't, you'll stay in this room.' Couch turned to the front door and gestured in two constables who'd been waiting outside. 'These gentlemen have kindly come up from Truro to help. Seems the train yard down here has been ... misused, shall we say? And we've reason to believe the goods that came through there are being stored in the Pencarrack area. This seems as good a place to start as any, given what we found on Mr Hocking.'

'Where did all this information come from?'

'Not at liberty to say, sir.'

Peter turned a fierce look on Gwenna, and she didn't bother to try and hide a smile of gratitude for her father's attempts to right his wrongs, even if he paid a heavy price for doing so.

'If you'd just like to sit there then, sir?' Couch said, indicating the chair behind Hocking's desk. 'We won't take up much of your time.'

'But I'm a police officer! I can help.'

'Your kind of help, Bolitho, we can do without.' Couch's polite tone had vanished, and now he looked on his officer with extreme dislike. 'Mr Hocking's told us all about you.'

'He's lying, whatever he's said! I only came here today, to—'

'I'd save that, if I were you,' Couch said. 'You'll need to explain it all to a solicitor I should think. Now, I'll be getting on if you don't mind. Pengelly?'

One of the Turo officers turned, eyebrows raised. 'Sir?'

'I'd start with that car in the driveway, if I were you.'

'Oh, Sergeant?' Gwenna said, as the officer left, and Peter dropped his pale face into his hands. 'Perhaps you ought to check in there, too.' She pointed to the study. 'There's a box of labels in the corner that you might find quite informative.'

'And in the yellow room upstairs,' Leah added, 'you'll find a brown paper folder in the dresser drawer.' She looked at Gwenna.

'It proves that Mr Hocking has been deliberately failing students by lying about the marks they've achieved on their tests.'

Gwenna swallowed hard. 'He told me he'd burned those,' she said, feeling her eyes prickle.

'He probably meant to. But, like most over-confident idiots, it slipped his mind because it just didn't seem important enough.' She smiled. 'You can thank Flight Lieutenant Bowden for me finding them.'

'Bowden?' Couch turned back. 'Funny that, he was extremely helpful in identifying what was wrong with Hocking's plane, too. Something to do with the block tube, where it joins the carburettor. Jammed or something? Anyway, he knew exactly where to look for the fault.'

'Well I never,' Irene said, and something about her voice made both Gwenna and Leah look at her more closely. She wore no expression except wide-eyed surprise when Couch turned to her, but when he looked away again, to instruct his remaining officer in the search, a thin, satisfied smile touched her lips. 'Poor Uncle Barry. What rotten luck.'

EPILOGUE

Saturday 20 September 1930

The grounds at Caernoweth Air Training Base were a-buzz with the families and friends of those students who had, today, completed their six-month training course. Gwenna had been worried she might feel jealous of her friends, as she had yet to catch up on all the flying hours required and so wasn't yet ready to pass out. But instead she felt nothing but pride as she watched them both collect their certificates, and saw the same expression on the faces of Bertie's family who'd come down from Fox Bay for the celebrations.

Tory's mother, and the rest of the Stuart family, were also in attendance, and Nancy was drawing many an admiring gaze as she jumped up and down, clutching her hat and waving madly, tears on her cheeks and an enormous smile on her face. The other Doctor Stuart, and Aaron and Rebecca, looked pleased enough but mildly embarrassed – Nancy clearly cared not one bit, and that made Gwenna smile too.

Gwenna's own parents were working things out, slowly.

Jonas was awaiting trial, but Rachel visited him whenever she could, and had learned how he had originally become involved with Hocking.

'They flew together in the war,' she'd told Gwenna, after her first visit to the prison. 'So after the raid where Jonas was shot down, Hocking felt he'd been awarded the medal unfairly, just because he'd been injured. He felt he should have had one too, so he's been wanting for a long time to muddy Jonas's reputation, and when he started up his awful business he found a way. He deliberately got Jonas involved by commissioning him to build those steps you told me about, into the room under the folly, and Jonas badly needed the money. Besides, he thought – like you did – that it was contraband of another kind. From that moment on though, he was implicated. Just like you were. He even thought he might be able to fly again, and he sometimes persuaded Hocking to let him up, but his neck movement was restricted and he couldn't manage well enough.'

Gwenna remembered the appalling landing she'd witnessed in Hocking's plane, and how she and Tory had even discussed how poor it was. To think that might have been her father filled her with shame. 'So do you think the two of you will be alright again?'

Rachel had smiled, and that was all the answer Gwenna needed. She looked up now, as Tory approached. 'Congratulations again,' she said, nodding at the certificate in Tory's hand.

Tory glanced at it. 'I'm ridiculously proud of myself for getting it,' she said, 'but I haven't changed my mind, I'm not carrying on. Nor is Irene.'

She and Gwenna each took a seat at the little table nearby, and Gwenna looked around her at the milling groups of families.

'They've closed that horse-doping ring, so Leah says. So does that mean Irene's free now?'

Tory nodded. 'But of course she now knows her boyfriend was a major player in that racket, so I don't think she's likely to move back to Birmingham just yet. I was wondering ... Do you think she'd be interested in starting up a little business with me?'

'What kind of business?'

'Riding stables. A school, perhaps.'

'With what?' Gwenna stared, astonished. 'That kind of thing costs a huge amount!'

'I've never claimed to be poor.'

'Well, no, but—'

'I'm not rich either, but I've got a bit put away. My time with the Twenties wasn't entirely wasted, how else do you suppose I paid for my tuition here? Might as well see some good come from it.' Tory raised a hand to catch Irene's attention. 'Let's test the water, shall we?' she murmured. 'A pound says she bites my hand off for the chance to stay, and to work with horses.'

'No bet.' Gwenna laughed. 'She'll say yes before you've even finished asking.'

Irene came over, looking a little wary. 'Congratulations.'

'Thank you. Won't you sit down?'

'No, thanks.' Irene's expression didn't change. 'What did you want?'

'I'm just after your opinion really. I was thinking about setting up a little riding stables on the outskirts of the village. What do you think?'

'It's a good idea. Sounds lovely, in fact.'

Gwenna noted the slightly wistful tone in her voice, and smiled to herself but said nothing.

'Hmm, yes,' Tory mused. 'Pencarrack Riding School. It has a nice ring to it, wouldn't you say?'

'Absolutely.'

'So, I was wondering, how would you like to make it a joint—'

'Yes!' Irene dropped into the seat beside Tory's, her face alight with excitement. 'I have enough money to help out. There's bound to be some land we can buy! How many stalls, do you think? Should we take absolute beginners? Oh, we could buy Mack before he goes to auction! Couldn't we? What do you think?'

'I think that's a yes,' Gwenna said, amused. 'Congratulations, ladies.'

Tory held out her hand to shake Irene's, and Gwenna looked around delightedly for Bertie, so she could pass on the news, but instead she saw Bobby Gale, a speculative little smile on his face as his eyes followed Tory's every move. He caught Gwenna watching him, and his smile became wider as unabashed roguishness replaced the almost tender expression on his face. Gwenna watched Tory as she excitedly planned her future with her new partner, completely unaware of the little exchange that had gone on over her head ... Her friend had no idea how much more interesting her life was going to become.

*

Bertie watched her friends laughing together in their little group. Gwenna had blossomed, and so had Irene, and Tory was back to her old self, albeit with clumps of hair still much shorter in places where she'd had her awful scratches and cuts treated. She and Irene were shaking hands, so Bertie guessed Tory had broached the subject of that riding school she'd mentioned, and that Irene had been just as enthusiastic as they'd hoped.

She listened to her own family around her, chattering away

383

amongst themselves, and with Leah. They had forgotten her for the moment, even though the celebration was hers, but she didn't mind, it was nice to just listen to them, she missed them. Jude Singleton waved for her to come over to where she stood next to her beloved Camel, and Bertie quailed inside; she hadn't had a chance to speak to her since she had borrowed Joey and flown her to St Agnes and back, there had been too much going on. The investigation into Jude's additional fuel usage was still ongoing, and that little jaunt hadn't helped things – it was the only black cloud on Bertie's horizon, and she still felt queasy every time she'd thought about how to explain it. Now that time had come, and there was only one thing to do: get it over with.

'Congratulations,' Jude said. But she didn't sound as if she meant it. 'I've been hearing a lot about the goings on here while I was away, and I've got one or two things to say.'

'Of course.'

Tommy appeared at Bertie's side. 'Hello, Fox. Singleton.' He slipped an arm around Bertie's waist, and she knew that outwardly the gesture would appear simply flirty, or friendly, but that he also meant it as a sign of support. She leaned gratefully into him, feeling her legs tremble. She hated the feeling of having let Jude down.

'This lad told the judge about the extra lessons I've been giving,' Jude said, and Bertie jerked around to stare at Tommy in shock; he must have known it would mean the end of her training. She moved away from him, her heart plummeting.

'Why would you do that?' she managed.

'It was the only way to explain the fuel business,' Jude said. 'Otherwise I'd have been a suspect in all that other nonsense with Barry Hocking. Tommy had no choice but to come clean.'

'But ...' Bertie tried to tell herself she understood, but she still felt the weight of betrayal. She swallowed and nodded. 'I understand. I don't know what I'll do now, but I do understand. And, Jude, I'm so sorry about borrowing Joey to fly Jenny out.'

'Aye, he told me about that, too. I gather you made a pretty good fist of it though.'

Bertie felt a flush of pride, despite everything. 'I think I did, yes. But I would never have done it if it hadn't been—'

'I know.' Jude held up a hand. 'No harm done. I'd have done the same thing in your situation.'

Bertie blinked away the tears that started to her eyes at the thought of leaving all this behind. 'When will they call me in, do you think?'

'They won't.' Tommy took her hand. 'They've already sacked me instead.'

'And me,' Jude said, and Bertie was astonished to see a little smile lift the corners of her mouth.

'What?'

'I told them *I* was having the lessons,' Tommy said. 'That Jude was teaching me, not you. So they gave me the push. I didn't mind, I was ready for a change.'

'And I were going to retire anyway,' Jude said, shrugging. 'That's one of the reasons I'd gone back home, to sort things out for when I pack all this in.' She smiled and patted Bertie's arm. 'I've done my bit, lass. I've had enough now, and I've found the perfect person to take Joey on. You'll have her, won't you?'

Bertie shook her head, still bemused. 'You're *giving* her to me?'

'Who else?' Jude gestured at Tommy. 'This lummox wouldn't be any good, would he? And I don't trust anyone else like I trust you.'

Bertie felt Tommy's arm go around her again, and she was grateful for the support once more, but now for a very different reason. Jude was laughing, her voice travelling across to where the others were standing, and several faces turned in their direction, smiling in response to the sound.

'Just make sure you keep the old bird well maintained.' Jude nodded at Joey. 'Between the two of you, you should be able to manage that. And don't forget, Bertie, if you go into a stall, just give her—'

'More right rudder,' Bertie said, and she felt the smile spreading across her face as she said it. 'Always more right rudder.'

She looked up at the sky, arching over the air base, clear right to the horizon, with the sun setting it alight as it sank into the sea. Behind her, laughter and chatter swelled and ebbed, echoing the tide below them, and beside her Tommy and Jude murmured practicalities and future arrangements. But in this moment there was only Bertie, Joey, and a fiery, molten gold sky.

Her sky.

ACKNOWLEDGEMENTS

During Nancy's telling of the Zeppelin raid on Great Yarmouth in January of 1915, she mentions a neighbour, Samuel, who was killed in that raid. While Nancy is, of course, fictional, Samuel Smith is not; he was one of the first civilians fatally injured by aerial bombardment who, at aged 53, was reportedly standing in the road as the Zeppelins passed over St Peter's Plain. Nancy's mention of a young boy, killed in King's Lynn on the same night, is also based on fact; tragically, 14-year-old Percy Goate was killed in his bed when a bomb landed on his family's home.

And now on to complete fakery . . .

Readers of any of my previous series will no doubt recognise several places, characters and incidents they encounter in and around Pencarrack. The village sprung, as mentioned in the book, from a run-down row of miners' houses at the top of Caernoweth, a town first encountered in the Penhaligon Saga. Twenty years on from the setting of that series, the town is still inhabited by many of the same people, so we will be catching up on these characters even as we explore new ones. Bertie, Tory, and Gwenna will also be familiar to anyone who has read the Fox Bay Saga, and I hope you have enjoyed following them through this latest adventure.

The dark history of the Caernoweth and Pencarrack area – largely that of the town's founder, Malcolm Penworthy – was gradually uncovered in a series of diaries discovered in the Penhaligon Saga. More fully explored in a series that features Tommy Ash's home village, Lynher Mill, it is a tale of greed, mystery, piracy and heroism; a history that forms the bedrock of Caernoweth, Lynher Mill, and Pencarrack. To me, it all feels as real as the desk where I sit to write this, so naturally all my Cornish books share this history and geography.

I hope you enjoy discovering more of it with me!

I would like to thank everyone who has supported and encouraged me through the writing of this book. Huge thanks as always to my wonderful editor at Piatkus, **Eleanor Russell**, and to my brilliant but long-suffering copy editor, **Robin Seavill**, who probably wishes I'd stop mentioning dates altogether. Thanks, as ever, to my writing friends and groups, to my wonderful family, and to my non-writing friends, who never fail me when I need a night of chat and nonsense. Turns out that's quite often, these days.